**Christopher Boon** spent his formative years in a small village in rural Hertfordshire. He studied English at Manchester University and, upon graduating, worked for three years as an English teacher in Ogaki City, Japan. He now works as a teacher in southern France.

*The Passing of the Forms That We Have Loved* is Christopher's debut novel. He started working on it after his father died of oesophageal cancer in 2008 and whilst writing it his mother also succumbed to cancer. These experiences helped shape the novel.

Christopher has also written a trilogy of screenplays based on loss and is currently working on his next novel.

*To Mike,*
*From a fellow teacher!*

# THE PASSING OF THE FORMS THAT WE HAVE LOVED

16/09/21

époque press

Published by **époque press** in 2021
www.epoquepress.com

Typeset in Caecilia 45 Light/Italic, Caecilia 55 Roman/
Italic, Dunbar Tall Light, Dunbar Low Light.
Cover design by **Ten Storeys®**

Printed and bound in Great Britain by Clays Ltd, Elcograf S.p.A.

British Library Cataloguing-in-Publication Data.
A catalogue record for this book is available from the
British Library.

ISBN 978-1-8380592-6-2 (Paperback edition)

*"The world, as we know it, as we have seen it, yields but one ending: death, disintegration, dismemberment, and the crucifixion of our heart with the passing of the forms that we have loved."*

Joseph Campbell

# THE PASSING
# OF THE FORMS
# THAT WE
# HAVE LOVED

# PART I
## DEATH

Long before this there were those interminable afternoons with her. Afternoons spent in the sitting room of her terraced house with the view out over the garden bathed in sunshine or given to a grey and restless gloom. Afternoons of simmering tensions with sandwiches and scones served on tiered cake stands and tea in delicate porcelain cups near translucent in the light.

Why does it seem to start with my grandmother? With that sombre room from whose scalloped lampshades tassels hung and from whose walls were interspersed upon the picture rail her drab watercolours of austere fenland vistas and nameless rivers throwing off the sapped lustre of autumn afternoons? Perhaps because she was the first of them to die. Perhaps because in some distant way she seemed the genesis of things.

An image comes to me of my father in one of the armchairs with his hands resting upon its lace antimacassars and slatted light from the window blinds falling across him. My mother beside me or on the patio with the grey of the sky cast about her. How I would sit with one of the piecrust tables drawn to me and my comic books or sketches spread upon it and the hatching of the pencil tip oftentimes the only sound in the room beyond the hands of the tambour clock on the mantel. Or further back in the long ago how they would bathe me in the kitchen sink and blow soapsuds into the late summer's light where they would pitch and dip and pop upon the plinth of the sill.

The arguments in the hallway at day's end. Embittered name calling. Accusations. Slammed doors. The time she called my mother a whore. Another time a slut. My father a failure. Driving away through those mournful streets my mother would shred a tissue on her lap and there would be nothing to say. Nowhere to look. In the falling dusk we would slip from the suburbs into barren flatlands with the silhouettes of stunted trees along the verges. Sometimes we'd stop in a pub for dinner halfway home and my mother would offer to drive the rest of the way so that my father could have a beer. After the meal they'd talk quietly while I drew in my sketchpad. I'd glance up at them now and then and my father would make faces at me from across the table. That look in his eyes when he stared at the light dying beyond the window.

Eventually she suffered a stroke then later dementia. She went down to the riverside one afternoon to meet a long dead friend and was pulled near dead from its reedy shallows by a fisherman who had seen her fall. Preparations were made to have her admitted to a nursing home and afterwards I went with my parents to clean out the house and it was the first and only time I ever spent the night there. We bought fish and chips from the place up the road and ate it from the paper with wooden forks at the heavy antique table in the dining room. The dining room a shrine to some forgotten past or past imagined. Chinaware in the dustless cabinets. Her polished ornaments along the window casing head that years later would be sold off for a pittance as with all the relics of that house. The table at which we sat and upon which we never ate of yore for fear of scuffs or marks so out of vogue that it was taken to a charity shop. The same with the other furnishings. With her ivory handled butter knives and mothballed linen and old crocheted doilies. With the pictures upon the mantelpiece. Her watercolours hanging in the sitting room. All kept as totems of remembrance before succumbing to obsolescence. My mother asking me if I wished to have anything from the house to remember her by but there was nothing that conjured or kindled any fondness for her.

At the service in the forlorn crematorium building I am staring down at the lectern and drizzle is falling in spits against the windowpanes. I look at the psalm and I look at the scattered mourners in their brogues and tweed and my father in front in his old varsity tie with my mother beside him in her funeral hat. Staff from the nursing home are at the back and everyone is looking at me or at the coffin beside me with its varnished lid reflecting the small floral tribute arranged upon it. Reading a psalm I've never seen before to an assembly of people I don't know seems of little consequence and yet this being at the lectern will dog me for years to come and I will look back upon it and think back upon my grandmother with a kind of sad foreboding. I will think back to the funeral parlour where the undertakers had laid her out for us to see. Her mouth glued shut. Her lips set in a sneer. Pinned to her coiffed hair one of the old luncheon hats she wore into town when she would sit in the windows of tearooms with her friends watching the riffraff go by. My father beside me. The way he stared down at her without speaking. Without moving. The motes of dust in the air as if suspended.

Afterwards in the drizzle we make small talk with the other mourners and then file into cars to the wake. My parents and I are taken in the cavalcade and the town through which we drive is fractured by the spears of rain breaking up upon the glass. But really there is little to see beyond characterless shopfronts and the oily reflections of tired redbrick buildings

3

in the river and the domes of umbrellas passing lachrymosely along the vaulted stone bridge. We pull up outside a hotel on the corner of town where platters of sandwiches and cubes of cheese on cocktail sticks and bowls of nuts and crisps have been laid out on a folding table by the window overlooking the river. On a neighbouring table plastic cups of bucks fizz and the hotel's house wines and a few cartons of orange juice. A waiter and waitress stand at the door to welcome us in and there they stay without occupation for the remainder of the afternoon. I talk to a few people but no one seems to know who anyone else is so eventually I retreat to the window and look out over the town at the dull sheets of cloud above the rooftops and the steeple of the church outlined against the sky. From time to time I will look back in at the other mourners and at my father in their midst. They are such as he in their tweed and neckties and yet there is something in my father's bearing that stands him apart. Perhaps it is that he is finally free from her yoke. Perhaps simply a quiet grief. He holds a plate of sandwiches but these remain untouched as does the cup of wine he pours himself. My mother is now beside him. Now with a woman I dimly recognise. Now alone.

When all is done we go for a walk along the river and the drizzle has eased but the sky is still bruised with impending rain and the osiers of willows trace wakes in the water. There are fishermen along the riverbank with the tips of their floats twitching against the river's current as it courses away eddying and deadpooling around knots of reeds and bulrushes. We go along to the next bridge and double back on ourselves and on the journey home as of old we stop for dinner in an inn along a country road and at the table we are the three of us silent. My father looks tired and thin. He orders sole with new potatoes and my mother a steak and ale pie from which gravy seeps in runnels down the sides of the pie dish. Vegetables are brought for us to share and I watch the faint tremor in my father's hands as he spoons them onto his plate. He picks at his food and my mother looks across at him.

Okay chooch?

I don't seem to have much of an appetite.

You've barely touched your fish.

I know. Perhaps I shouldn't have ordered it.

Well. You've been through a lot today.

He crosses his knife and fork on his plate and pushes it to one side. My mother puts her hand on his arm and glances at me. Asks me if I'd like a dessert. I tell her I'm fine and that I'll just have a coffee. The waitress brings this out and I watch her as she places it in front of me and then as she cuts her way back across the room.

In the carpark after the meal my father doubles up coughing and my mother goes to him and puts her hand on his back. It's dark and a cool wind has started up in the trees and there are still a few spits of rain in the air. Light from the mullioned pub windows falls in jaundiced squares across the gravel. The coughing goes on for a while and afterwards he draws up phlegm and spits it into the undergrowth and apologises. I drive us home with my mother in the passenger seat and my father in the back and along the pitch lanes I will sometimes look at him in the rearview mirror when the lights of passing cars illuminate his pale features from the cocoon of darkness around us. So too at my mother's profile as it flares.

And this is how it begins.

\*           \*           \*

I'm the first to arrive that morning. I'm out in the covered parking area loading cases of wine into the van when suddenly she's standing there. Light's filtering in through the entranceway as she steps forward to introduce herself.

Hi. I'm Bea.

It takes me a moment to bring her into focus. It's her eyes I notice first. An intense yet enigmatic blue lightly accented with eyeliner. A quality to them I can't quite place. Neither then nor a long time after. Something unknowable in them. But at the same time an odd familiarity.

Bea?

From Beatrice.

That's an unusual name.

It's French.

I know her name already. Have listened these past couple of weeks to all the talk and speculation about her ever since it was announced that she would be taking over as assistant manager. Ben and Jon eulogising. How Jon met her once at the Christmas party. Ben on a stock run someplace. The both of them completely smitten. Standing with her now it all begins to cohere. She brushes a strand of hair behind her ear and smiles. I try to marshal my thoughts. To seem casual. To remember the French I studied at school.

Um. Enchante.

It's not meant as a joke but she laughs.

Tu parles francais?

Un peu de franglais.

She gives another little laugh.

Tres bien.

Merci.

I feel myself blush as she continues to hold my gaze. I take in the rest of her. Her rounded lips and lightly freckled nose. Her mismatched earrings. The curve of her shoulders. She's dressed in faded jeans and a company shirt with a frayed canvas bag slung over her shoulder. About my height and slim. A quantity of half dreadlocked hair mussed chestnut and blonde knotted atop her head and loose tresses of it across her brow. From somewhere amongst it a length of green paisley fabric holding it roughly in place. Again I marshal my thoughts. Ask her if she found the place okay. If she came by bus or walked. Other such sundry. Of her replies I make little sense. Listen instead to her accent. Watch her lips. The delicate lines that form at the corners of her eyes when she smiles. Details glanced upon and ruminated over later. In the store that day. In my room that evening when I'm trying to sleep. To the questions she asks my responses are vague and stilted. Asks me how long I've worked here and where I was before and whether I know so and so. I tell her I'm not long moved here myself and am still finding my way around. She asks what Rachel's like. Jon and Ben. I give the briefest of replies and we fall to silence. A bus goes by. Pigeons take flight from their roost in the roof girders and disappear through the entranceway. We look at each other a moment before she makes a little motion towards the store and asks me if there's somewhere to make coffee. I tell her yes. Of course. Sorry. I should've offered. I dust off my jeans and take her through. She places her bag on the counter and sits on one of the stools while I go through to the kitchen. I dig around in the cupboard for the cleanest mug we have and when I come out again Jon's there. She's laughing at one of his jokes. I put her coffee down on the counter and Jon looks across at me.

Are you going to make me one as well mate?

You can make your own.

He shakes his head and smiles at her.

Dickhead.

She laughs.

Through the morning I'm at the back of the store putting stock away. It's hot and my clothes are dusty and the palms of my hands raw from the corners of wineboxes. Jon is in the aisle across from me and the only sound is of the angling of

7

wineboxes upon the splintered pallets and the puncturing of their tape seals with key fobs and the periodic resounding of bottles lined along the lips of the finished stacks. The store's warm and the whitewashed brickwork throws back damp. I keep glancing towards the counter. I watch her with Rachel. They're there an age going over stock runs and store codes and delivery schedules and only when they finish and she's alone do I head to the kitchen to fill my water bottle. She looks up at me as I go by.

Hey.

Hey.

I'll help you put the stuff away in a minute.

It's okay. I'm into my stride now.

No really. I will.

It's up to you.

Can you just go through this with me first?

What's that?

Your annotations in the orderbook.

I go over and stand beside her and look at her leant over the counter. She points to some of my pencilled handwriting and asks me of my abbreviations and of the customer base and the local area. As I respond she stares at me and I find it difficult to look at her and difficult to look away. Echoes there of some half forgotten half remembered past. Of a copse beneath a night sky with the serpentine writhing of moonlit grasses and light auroral about a marquee below. In a meadow on a picnic blanket as the wind starts up in the trees and the first leaves of autumn fall. A bedroom with books spread upon the desk. Yet these echoes merging with an imagined future born of this new association. Proleptic images of lying with her on the mezzanine with starlings acry in the eaves of the villa opposite and the scuff of children's feet on the gravel beyond the terrace. Of her walking along the path by the river with the tassels of her sarong hem trailing against

8

the grasses grown along its bank. Of the sere breeze along the dunes behind us and parasols arrayed along the beach. Later by the lagoon watching the setting of the sun as whitecaps gently lather the shoreline whilst she gathers the volute shells of fossilised molluscs and carapaces in her shawl and back at the villa we sit out on the terrace watching tigermoths amongst the honeysuckle and at night the tramontane blows in and rattles the shutters. Images inhabiting that moment and the repercussions of that moment for time to come until the reverie is broken by the peeling of the door chimes and a customer walking in.

Late afternoon she is amongst the stock at the rear of the store and I am watching her as she reaches up to place a case upon the top of a stack she has built. The day's heat has grown more suffocating and the girders and roof panels groan as they warp in the sun. From time to time she or I will pause to drink and when she does so I glance up at the patina of sweat upon her brow with all else as parentheses but for impressions of her here and hence. See her amongst her house boxes in an imagined room of an imagined house share with her eyes towards the window or at some nebula beside her or of a morning in the flat we come to share with last night's clothing scattered across the floor and her soft breaths beside me.

And so it continues. On into evening. Rachel and Ben leave early and by seven the stock is away and the empty pallets are stacked in the corner of the carpark. Jon and Bea and I congregate at the counter. Jon brings beers from the fridge and opens them with the fob of his keyring and passes them around. He sits on the swivel chair by the computer and Bea up on the counter and I lean against the wall by the kitchen disinclined to enjoin their conversation.

So. Good first day?

Yes. Not bad.

Where are you from originally Bea?
North of France. Brittany.
And what brings you across the channel?
Originally an exchange programme.
University?
No. School.
Oh. For how long?
A year.
Wow. How old were you?
Sixteen.
That was brave.
I wanted to improve my English.
It seems to have worked.
Thanks.
And then?
I came here for university.
What made you stay on? The food and rain?
Bea chuckles.
Something like that.
And why a wine shop?
I've always liked wine.
What was your old store like?

She tells of its quietude. Of the regulars. Of the champagne they opened at Christmastime. Of the town and the studio she rented in the suburbs. He asks where she's living now. At the bottom of the hill next to the park is her reply. Jon gestures at me with his beer bottle and tells her that we're virtually neighbours. She looks across at me and asks me which street I live on and I name mine and she hers. A flicker of something passes across her eyes. Is this so or do I imagine it? Reconstruct it later that evening and on subsequent evocations? I ask her whether she's climbed to the top of the park and seen the views from its slopes and she tells me no. Not yet. And so I range there with her as with those pastiches of the river path with her sarong hem trailing against the grasses. See us on the brow of the hill at summer's end or in the wintertime when the skyline lies lit against the black trough of night below.

Day's end Jon takes the van and offers to drive both of us home but I tell him I'd prefer to walk and I'm surprised that Bea declines also and says she'll walk with me. It's still warm out and contrails coppered by the sun slowly fade in the sky. We walk in silence past boutiques and cafes long since closed with coloured ribbons of bunting strung in the windows and clothless tabletops throwing back the subdued light. Her bag strap creaks and her jeans hiss in walking but aside from this there's little sound along the street. Though I've angled for time alone with her all day I'm unable to muster conversation and it is she who speaks first. Asks where I'm from originally and what brought me here. I sketch out details. Tell her vaguely of my time out east after graduating. The journey to school by the cherry trees. The harvesting of the rice fields. The fireworks in the summertime on the banks of the river. Past the nursing home at the crossroads we pause at the kerb for the lights and I look across at her. A breeze starts up along the street and soughs in the canopies of the planes and plays through her hair. Away from the store her eyes are more lucent yet and the more I look at them the more I feel like I recognise her in some way. Like I've known her for a long time. The lights change and we cross and fall once more into step. We take a shortcut past the broadway and at its end come to the brow of the hill with the city splayed beneath us. Evening traffic at the roundabout. Pavement tables outside cafes and bars. A sense of beginning and ending. She comments on how peaceful the city looks from up here. I nod and we go on and down the hill the pavement narrows and we come abreast of each other and I feel her shoulder grazing against mine. On her doorstep we talk awhile and then she waves and is

11

gone and I am a long time on her pathway before finally turning as a car's headlights illuminate the street and pitch my elongated shadow across the porch of her house.

*    *    *

Another evening my parents call. Rick picks up and comes to get me.

 Call for you.

 Thanks.

 I follow him along the landing. It's my mother on the line. I lean over the banisters and stare down into the stairwell where particles of dust silvered by the bare lamp bulb hang in the gloom.

 Hi sunshine.

 Hi mum.

 How are things?

 Okay. You?

 We're decorating at the moment.

 Yeah. You said.

 We've almost finished the study.

 Good.

 You'll have to admire it next time you're back.

 I will.

 How's work?

 It's okay. The same.

 Have you been out yet? Seen the sights?

 A little.

 And the new place? Is it nice?

 It's fine. Small but okay.

 And your housemates?

 They're nice.

 We went for a lovely walk today.

 Yeah?

The weather's beautiful here.
Good.
Is it nice where you are?
It's okay. The store's baking.
I bet. Is the store nice though?
Not really.
You mean the customers or the place itself?
Both.
Maybe it just takes a bit of getting used to.
Maybe. I doubt it.
Have you had your dinner yet?
I had a sandwich earlier.
But you are having dinner?
I'll see how I feel.
Make sure you eat properly.
I will.
I'm cooking a casserole tonight.
Nice.
The one you like. With the kidney beans.
Okay.
Hopefully dad will be able to have some.
What do you mean?
He's still got that thing with his tummy.
What thing?
You know he was sick a couple of times.
Is that still going on?
The doctor said it's nothing to worry about.
Okay.
He thinks it's probably stress after nana died.
That's what they always say.
He gave him some tablets to help his digestion.
Indigestion?
Said to check in again in a couple of weeks.
The receiver is cradled against my ear. A near dead plant

on the dresser in the corner hangs down into the gloom and laundered sheets long since dried are folded on the banisters. The smell from the kitchen is of stale milk and burnt toast.

Was it Doctor Wilson?

No. He's away at the moment.

Right.

But the locum seems nice.

A locum?

Yes. I forget his name.

And he's sure about the stress?

He seemed to know what he was doing.

Afterwards I go back to my room and sit on the edge of the bed. A knot in my stomach. About Bea. About the way I spoke to my mother. The lack of engagement. Everything a monosyllable. A sigh. Always the same feeling of guilt afterwards. The idea that I should phone back to apologise. But of course I never do.

\*       \*       \*

This is all happening a month ago. Maybe more. Another present sees me driving homeward with the late sun falling through the trees and rippled tracts of its light upon the trunkroad that leads out into the suburbs past retail outlets and drivethrus and hinterland parks upon whose wrought railings dying and dead flowers for dead drivers are hung and upon whose stretches of grassland drifts of litter play. The city peters out along this road's spine of anonymous streets and intersections and its dismal rows of shops and takeaways. Stopped at the lights of its intersections I will stare unseeing at the road ahead until cars from behind sound their horns and I notice that my knuckles are white from gripping the steering wheel too hard. Before the orbital I pull into a side street and shut off the engine and sit in the silence watching the empty avenue of houses before me. Trees line the street and cars the roadside and the houses' darkened bay windows throw off grainy reflections of the dusk sky. I drink some water and take a painkiller from my bag and close my eyes. The silence distils into soft layers of sound. Evening traffic on the trunkroad. The sometime lament of wind in the trees. The engine ticking as it cools and my thoughts drifting to John's party.

That evening it's just Bea and me in the store. Rachel has gone home early to change and the others are off and in the half hour before closing Bea and I are sitting across from each other on the counter by the tills with each a beer and our talk gravitating to the past. To hometowns and family. To university and travels abroad. The conversation turning to the party I ask her what time she's aiming to get there.

I'll have a bite to eat then head out. You?

I guess about ten.

Do you know where it is?

Yeah. Roughly.

I look across at her and then down at the floor. For some reason nervous about finally asking her. I try to sound casual.

We could go together. If you fancy it.

Okay.

She says it without hesitation.

Great. Shall I come and find you at yours?

Sounds good.

She jumps down off the counter.

I'll make enough dinner for two.

It's not a question or a suggestion.

Do you want to get the boards in or cash up?

The illusion of my having known her a long time has deepened in the weeks since we met. Most nights we walk home together. Sometimes partway with Ben and Jon.

15

Sometimes stopping with them for a drink. And as on that first day I will see her home and linger on her doorstep or on the pathway with the light faded in the sky. Now and then we'll go down through the park and some evenings people will be out on the grass on blankets with bottles of wine and picnics and couples will be walking hand in hand along the palace's terrace or leaning over its railings. Another evening it starts to rain as we're descending. Clouds lour overhead and the rain comes on suddenly and moves in waves across the city below. I'm about to hurry on when she puts her hand on my arm to stop me. Stands there with her face angled skyward and her eyes closed and the rain crawling through her hair and bringing to her skin an oleaginous glow. The rain soaking into her shirt and tracing out the shape of her body beneath. I watch her then without respite. Mesmerised by her stillness. By the otherworldliness of her skin. Her rent reflection upon the pathway. She goes on and after a pause I follow. On her doorstep that night she stands in the light of her hallway and her shadow is cast upon me and long after she has closed the door I feel myself in its thrall.

I'm soon beyond the city and into the outlying croplands over which buildings of rooks wheel darkly in the darkening sky. I have the windows open and there is in the air a residual scent of petrichor from the day's earlier rainfall. The evening is cloudless and as I come to the viaduct the glasslike marshland below runs amber through anthracite in its passing. I pass over the railway line and the river and upon the latter a houseboat is moored. Children are at play on the riverbank nearby and along from them at a bend amongst the rushes are the suggested forms of fishermen. I come off at the slip road beyond the viaduct and a time later I'm on the narrow lanes that lead homeward. The banks are grown high with grasses and wildflowers and the moon is newly risen on the horizon. Nearing the village the valley sides slope gently away and barley darkly illumined in the flattened afterdusk light sifts in the breeze. The houses at the edge of the village come into view. First the house on the corner. Light from the living room falling across the garden mutedly defines the apple trees and picket fence and picnic table and as I pass I glance at the lighted windows of the house but of movement there is none. The light from the porch falls across the yard and this too is empty and so are the neighbouring houses. As I go on by I glimpse the darkened meadow sloping away to the windblown treeline of the old quarry at the rear before it is swallowed by the briary undergrowth along the stream known locally as the Bourne. And so on into the village. Past the stark windowless edifices of farmhouses. Past the tumbledown bus stop fallen into disuse these many years and given now to bindweed and rotted timbers and a collapsed roof. Past the old playing field and allotments. Finally to a driveway pooled in shadows from the great sycamore at its brow.

Bea comes to the door in an old white camisole and striped pyjama bottoms and her hair roughly bundled up and tied at the crown with sticks from which it falls about her shoulders. She's wearing a pair of novelty animal slippers and she's holding a spatula. She leans forward and I kiss her on each cheek and then she motions for me to follow her inside. The hall is communal with unclaimed mail on the shelf mounted along the left wall and shoes in a rack beneath it and overhead an old pendant lightshade with cobwebs around the cable from which it hangs. We go through a doorway off to the right that yields to a stairwell and as she sashays up it I watch the shape of her body beneath the tight camisole she's wearing. Her pyjama bottoms are loose around her waist and the outline of her underwear is visible through the fabric near diaphanous with age. The camisole is ribbed with thin straps at the shoulders and the pyjama cuffs frayed at the hem where they drag on the floor.

We come out onto the landing. Her room and her housemate's are at the rear. She leads me to the kitchen living room area at the front. It's open plan with large bay windows overlooking the street below. Music is playing and bowls and spoons and torn packets and peelings of onionskin are scattered across the worktop and a colander and griddle pan are hanging from a curtain rod over the sink. There are pans steaming on the hob and in the middle of the living room is a table laid for the two of us with kitchen roll for napkins folded in wineglasses and mismatched cutlery arranged around corkboard place settings and sliced bread in a tattered breadbasket with a dish of butter melting beside it. At the centre of the table is a candle in a wicker hackled bottle striated with multicoloured tallow and tealights not yet lighted in glass jam jars beside it.

Bea goes into the kitchen and tells me to take a seat. The chairs around the table are rickety and dotted with old spots of paint. I sit at the farthest so I can see her across the worktop. She tells me to pour myself some wine.

Is your housemate in? What's her name.

Becca. No. It's just us.

I watch as she stirs a pan on the hob and tastes the back of the spoon. Sprinkles in some herbs. A pinch of salt. Pepper from a peppermill. Tastes it again. Finally takes up her wineglass and comes over to the worktop and leans across it on propped elbows.

Won't be a minute.

What's on the menu?

You'll see. Nothing fancy.

French?

No. It was all a bit last minute.

18

You didn't have to cook for me.
It's fine. I wanted to.
I should've mentioned it sooner.
It's okay.
Perhaps I can return the favour.
What do you mean?
I could cook for you sometime.
She swirls her wine around her wineglass.
Can you cook?
A little.
What's your speciality?
You'll see. Nothing fancy.
Bea laughs.
What's the expression? You're a dark horse.
I don't know about that.
Her smile fades and she looks across at me still swirling the wine in her wineglass.
Okay.
Okay what?
Next time you can cook for me.


I pull up on the yard. Light from the kitchen and living room windows filters across the lawn. The moon is up and it's quiet and there are pipistrelles around the eaves of the house. I take my bag from the passenger seat and climb out and stand on the yard listening to the insects in the undergrowth and the strains of laughter from one of the neighbouring houses. I look towards the kitchen. Condensation is upon the window and through its brume I see my mother at the hob with steam rising around her. Watching her I wonder how this homecoming will be. Wonder how things will be with my father. I step onto the lawn and walk across the grass to the patio windows hoping I might be able to see him in his chair doing his crossword but the curtains are drawn. I look up at the house. At the darkened upper floor windows and the twines of dead wisteria wound around the trellis. At the nesting boxes mounted on the brickwork up near the soffit and the facade's faded paintwork. I shudder involuntarily before doubling back across the yard and entering the garage via the side door and picking my way through the mess to the back door. I push it open. My mother doesn't see me at first. The radio's on and she's busy at the hob.

Mum?

She doesn't hear me. She opens the oven door and pushes a skewer into a cut of meat roasting in a roasting tin and then slides it back in and closes the oven door and busies herself with a pan on the hob.

Mum?

Louder this time. She turns and looks at me. For a moment doesn't seem to recognise me. This hollowness in her eyes. Something dead there. Then comes over. Hugs me. Cries on my shoulder. Keeps saying my name. I don't know what to do. I kind of hug her back. Not really. I tell her it's okay. Everything is going to be okay. But the words are empty and without conviction. I look past her at the condensation sliding down the windowpane and our fragmented reflections there.

At meal's end Bea leaves me in the living room while she goes off to shower and change. I pour myself some more wine and sit picking strips of tallow from the bottle's wicker hackle and melting them anew into the molten wax around the wick. The dinner plates are still on the table. She told me I wasn't to touch them but after some moments staring at the candleflame I take them over to the sink and leave them to rinse. I can hear her showering and I peer through the kitchen window and see along the sidewall of the house the frosted glass of the bathroom. Steam issues from the open upper awning and I watch it disappear into the darkness saddling the alley below. The tap drips. The boiler purrs. I drain the wine from my glass and go back over to the table and pour some more. I make some kind of attempt to clear the worktops but this is short lived and I'm soon wandering around the living area with the exposed floorboards sounding beneath my feet. Along one wall there's a shapeless sofa thrown with drapes and along the wall opposite a defunct fireplace with a vase of dried teasels and twisted bamboo canes where once the grate would have been and along its mantelpiece burnt out joss sticks and little ornaments and trinkets of the type found in markets abroad and at the farthest edge a near dead spider plant. Above the mantelpiece is hung a monochrome view of a city in a cheap frame and beside it a calendar of prints open at the wrong month. There is a television in the corner on an old tea chest and behind this a bookcase part filled with a miscellany of unordered books. The room is dominated by the large bay window and I go over to this and look out at the street below and at the reflection of the landing behind me in the darkened glass.

I'm there until I hear the shower shutting off and after a time the snap of the pull switch and then I see her transparency briefly illuminated by the layered landing light as she walks beneath it with a towel wrapped around her and her bare shoulders catching in the lamp bulb's nude hue. She goes to her room and closes the door after her and I turn and look along the length of the landing at the prints on the floorboards of her wet feet fading in the halflight and a couple of minutes later find myself drunk in the bathroom. It's heavily scented and the mirror shows faintly where she's cleared a section of it with her hand but this too has nearly misted over again. Water slides down the shower screen and with the awning still open steam swells around its aperture. Suds are lathered on a loofah in the shower caddy. I look at the perfumes and lotions lined along the plinth of the bath and I wonder which is Bea's and which Becca's and I pick a few of them up and read the labels before carefully replacing them.

When Bea emerges from her room a short while later I'm again at the bay window. Her hair is pushed back beneath a headband and it's the first time I've seen her in makeup. She's wearing an off the shoulder sweater from which her red bra strap is visible and ripped jean shorts with laddered tights and heels.

You look nice.

Thanks. You ready?

Yeah.

She takes her keys from the table and from the newel of the banisters a cropped leather jacket and then I follow her down the stairs and out into the hallway.

A faintness of light from beneath the living room door falls across the lacquered parquet floor but otherwise the hallway is mantled in darkness. I pass along it and in this passing my steps become slower and more deliberate. I near the newel of the stairs and from the transom above the front door a little more light penetrates and in its argent wake motes of dust hang unmoving in the still air. The stairs rise stark and soundless beyond. At their foot before the threshold of the living room I pause and the house falls eerily silent with even the noise from the kitchen as if suddenly stifled. A vivid intimation begins to form in my mind that my mother and father have both passed on long ago and the house has fallen empty these many years and is haunted by some distant reverberation of their being. I look up at the transom and see the moon through the prisms of its bevelled glass and I look along the hallway wall at the light it casts upon the rows of hanging plates and picture frames and at the farthest end my grandfather's old barometer that until his death hung in his own hallway. Echoes of him wreathed in pipe smoke or by the fireside those Christmases of old with sweat darkening his paper crown. Along the hallway echoes of other half buried pasts. An old clay pot I made at school on the chest beneath the banisters. A photograph beside it of my university graduation with my mother and father either side of me. The utility room at the end where the dog used to sleep before cancer ate away her eyes and mouth and she started to shit blood. Echoes of schooldays. Of study dates and a burgeoning optimism. Of its yin of foreign odyssey. And the house silent and dark and ageless throughout.

I push open the door to the living room and go in. The television is on with the sound down low. My father is in his armchair with a folded newspaper on his lap. On the table beside him is his dictionary and upon it a pen and his spectacles. He's asleep. I walk over to him. His hair has thinned and greyed. He's lost weight. Through the open collar of his shirt I can see his raised collarbone and sternum. I can see the shapes of the bones in his face. His skin is waxen. His lips are cracked and there's spittle at the corners of his mouth. I look at his hands. These too are waxen. Papery. The veins showing. He's dressed as he's always dressed in a polo shirt and cotton twill trousers but his clothing seems ill fitting. His slippers are on the floor by his chair and one of his socks has a hole in the toe. I look across at the hearth. The dark grey flue. The tiered brickwork unadorned but for the occasional matchbook or postcard. The fire already laid for winter with a wickerwork of kindling and pinecones and coal glistening blackly in the scuttle. Wonder then and after whether these observations of his apparent disintegration are real or given to reshaping and embellishment in the dark hours when I'm lying awake in my room staring at the ceiling. Ruminating on the interplay of his appearance with that of my grandmother in the mortuary. I look back across at him and he wakes and slowly focuses on me.

Hi.

Hey.

I didn't hear you come in.

It's gone nine thirty by the time we leave Bea's but we decide to go for a drink at the pub down the road before heading to the party. It's a soulless place and largely empty with slot machines and a pool table and branded whiskey mirrors on the walls but the windows concertina out and open onto the street and this is where we take a table. I ask her what she wants and head over to the bar. While I wait for the drinks to arrive I look across at her. She's in profile by the window with her legs crossed and her hand on the tabletop. Across the street I watch a bus pull in and passengers alight and disappear home along the leafy backstreets. Disappear home and to what end. To those rows of darkened houses. To quiet domesticity. I look back at Bea as she stares fixedly at some indistinct point in the near distance. I wonder at us. How it came to be that I'm with her now and what will come to pass. In looking at her she seems to transcend her surroundings. I barely notice the landlady placing the drinks in front of me. She clears her throat and I turn to her and smile apologetically.

Sorry. I was miles away.

Pretty girl.

Pardon?

She gestures at Bea.

She's pretty.

Yeah. She is.

Can't take your eyes off her can you?

I feel myself blush. The landlady smiles.

It's all right. I was young once as well.

I pay her for the drinks and take them over to our table.

Bea looks up at me and smiles as I sit across from her.

Thanks.

It's the least I could do.

What do you mean?

After making you cook for me.

You didn't exactly make me.

She takes a sip of her drink.

You certainly took your time asking though.

About what?

Going together.

I know. I wasn't sure you'd want to.

Why not?

I don't know.

Of course I wanted to.

The wind picks up in the trees and tousles her hair as she looks out along the street.

We eat dinner in the dining room and my father takes his usual seat at the table but for him no place has been laid. A bottle of wine has been opened but for him no glass has been set out. My mother quietly dishes cuts of lamb and potatoes and vegetables onto her plate and we set to eating and my father looks on and for a long time we are silent. Now and then I glance at my mother and it pains me to watch her eat. The quiet earnestness of it. The continuation of a ritual now pantomime. When I look at my father he smiles.

How's the lamb?

Lovely.

Yet I have no appetite. I push the food around my plate and manage to clear about a third of it before crossing my knife and fork and laying them to rest in a marbled pool of gravy. My mother looks concerned and I feel guilty because she has gone to so much effort and the lamb is from the butcher's and expensive but I just can't bring myself to eat any more of it with my father's gaunt and sunken eyes looking on. My mother frowns.

Not hungry?

Not right now. Sorry.

It's okay.

I'll have some tomorrow for breakfast.

We can put some clingfilm on it.

Okay. Sorry.

She smiles at me. Selfless. Compassionate. Benevolent. I try to reciprocate but find myself blinking back tears. We wait for her to finish and my head is bowed the whole time. I stare down at the table at the saltpetre and the pattern in the lace cloth and I notice that the best chinaware has been brought out and that the knives and forks are from the special box used for special guests and special occasions. The sound now is of the cooling of the waterpipes and the soft scraping of my mother's cutlery as she methodically scoops mounds of food onto her fork and this too fills me with an almost unbearable sadness. I look away at the cabinet opposite. At its carefully arranged knickknacks collected over the years in antiques fairs and markets and from trips abroad. See myself a few years from now placing them into boxes. Wheeling them out into a waiting van. There's a photograph of me as a little boy in a curtain cloak on a grassy summer bank beyond the village and the dog by my side and I look at this for a long time remembering how she came to die. The melanomas in her mouth. On her eyes. The tarblack strings of mucus she coughed up in her final days. The blanket we wrapped her in. The pit we dug.

After dinner I offer to help clear the plates away but my mother won't hear of it and tells me to go through to the living room instead to be with my father. I pour myself a large brandy from the cabinet and sit on the settee. My father takes his spot on the armchair. From here through a gap in

the curtains I can see the rotted strips of wood at the base
of the patio windows and I remember how in the springtime
the billywitches would come. I look across at my father in his
faded polo shirt and the creases my mother has ironed in his
trousers. He's engrossed in his paper.

Crossword?

Yes.

How long will it take to finish?

Oh a day or two.

We sit in silence as he leafs through his dictionary. I go
back to the settee and drink some more brandy and then I'm
staring at one of his oils on the wall. A row of plane trees
along a rural road with vineyards sloping away on either side
to a ridge of mountains veiled in haze. The piece is framed
in plain wood and my father's signature is in the corner with
the date beneath in numerals. When he retired I bought him
a set of horsehair brushes and palette knives and my mother
bought him a box of oils and some canvases and a grease
paper palette.

Still painting?

Still painting.

Good.

Still using those lovely brushes you got me.

The way in which he says this troubles me then and
long after. This pedestal they place me on. His life of
selfless drudgery and for what. He picks up his pen and fills
something in on his crossword. I drain my glass and pour
myself another and go over to the patio windows to look out
across the darkened garden.

We don't speak much on the way there. We're on the top
deck at the front and Bea is beside me. I look at our reflections
warping over the rows of shops and cafes and restaurants
lining the street to the station. It's getting late and there are

small knots of smokers outside pubs but otherwise it's quiet and the bus itself near empty and so too the underground platform we wait at later with her hand sometimes brushing against mine. With the coming of the train warm static wind courses through the tunnel and a sheet of newspaper is carried along the tracks where blackened mice scurry through the gaps beneath the rails. As the train pulls in nobody alights and the carriage we take is empty with tags scratched into the glass and wrappers along the sills and a drinks can ricocheting across the ridged floor at the far end. We're both drunk and she puts her arm through mine and rests her head on my shoulder and I look down at the laddering in her tights and the frayed ends of the shorts she wears.

It comes to our stop and we disembark and head through the station and once outside I lead her through the darkened streets. Much of the strength is gone from me now and though I'm experiencing an almost overwhelming yearning for her I'm held back by a familiar fear. We go in silence and the details of the street take on a chimerical quality as I imagine our union. Here on the street corner. In the hot melee of the club. On the return trip when the night is deserted and the sky inflected with the coming dawn. I imagine the moonlight upon the bedsheets in her room. Imagine waking beside her awash with morning light. I'm so caught up in these thoughts that when at length we reach the club I've little sense of how we've arrived there. Little sense of how long the journey has taken. On the threshold I'm plucking up the courage to make some lofty proclamation of my feelings when she sees the hunched figures of Jon and Ben smoking cigarettes by the wall and rushes over to them. I watch their shared embrace from afar and then we are the four of us entering the club past the doorman.

Later I'm at the bar and I look across the pother of dry ice and disassembled limbs on the dancefloor and see her with Jon. Her arms are on his shoulders and his hands are around her waist and their lips are close to touching and as I look away again into the cancerous shadows everything this evening seems suddenly for nothing. The way she looked at me on her doorstep. The dinner at hers. All those conversations. All that I assumed to have been of import easily explained away by the fact that she didn't know how to get here and I said I'd show her. The dinner offered out of politeness. Suggestions of further dinners the mere continuance of a fledgling friendship. I see quite clearly that had it been Ben or Jon working with her this evening it would have been them in my stead. I do a couple of shots one after another. I'm supposed to be getting a round in but everything feels pointless now and there is a sad inevitability about my being here alone at this bar. Obliquely I see that night many years ago with the marquee in the moonlight and the cars parked in the driveway. I watch as Jon leans in and whispers into her ear and she leans back laughing. Another whisper and she is pressed against him and his hands come farther around her waist. I turn away. I buy a beer and take it to a vacant table in an alcove and sit with my back to everybody. Music thuds against the backrest and all the adrenaline of the evening starts to filter away until there is only fatigue.

I'm unable to sleep. I lie in bed looking up at the stippled ceiling. Looking up at the old screw holes where once model aeroplanes hung. I would build them with my father. We would sit at the kitchen table with newspaper spread across it and carefully snip the moulded pieces of plastic from their sprues and with a file sand away the nodules and assemble them piece by piece wiping away the glue with a roll of tissue and camouflage them using coded tins of paint and clip the transfers into squares and float them in a cup of lukewarm water before sliding them onto the wings and tailfins. Finally we'd knot thread from the fuselages and hang them from the ceiling to collect dust. The propellers when blown upon would rotate. Years later I took them down and stacked them in a box in the loft snapping the propellers and wingprops and the little wheels on the underside of the tails. Later still I lined them along the fence in the back garden and shot them with an airgun splintering the cockpits and the little pilots and the shells of camouflaged plastic. I took a hammer to my father's galleon one Sunday and cracked through the hull and snapped away the bowsprit and crowsnest with pliers. I don't know why. I remember going with him to buy it from the model shop one Saturday in town. The mast was webbed with thread rigging and it stood on the bookshelf in my room for years. I don't know if my father ever noticed it was gone. I hear him in the night from next door. When he rolls over he pules and my mother will sometimes wake and try to comfort him and this makes the night draw on so much longer until finally dawn is beginning to break and there is birdsong in the trees.

I leave the club before the others without saying goodbye. The trains have stopped running and I don't really know where I am so I just start walking. I'm drunk and tired and all I can really focus on is my footsteps. It's starting to get light and I begin to recognise very vaguely some of the shops and pubs. I look inconclusively at the route map in one of the bus stops but it's all jumbled together and difficult to distinguish the names of any of the destinations. And so with the neuralgic dawn spreading across the sky I decide to walk on.

\*           \*           \*

A summer evening's storm. Sheets of lightning. Rain against

the window. The air oppressive. I'm with Rick in his room drinking a bottle of wine I brought back from work. He's sitting on his bed and I'm on the floor leant against its frame. A film is playing. It's a Saturday and our other housemate Jas is out with friends and the landing and adjoining rooms are quiet. I shift position and the bedframe creaks. Rick asks me if I'm okay.

Yeah. Fine.

Do you want a cushion or anything?

No. I'm okay.

I drink some more wine. The film reaches its climax and then the credits start to roll. At their conclusion Rick flicks through the channels. There's nothing on. He turns down the volume and we sit there staring at the screen. Some advertisements. A gameshow.

Doesn't seem to be much on.

No.

How are we doing for wine?

I hold up the bottle.

Another glass each.

Maybe we should go out for some more?

I've got another in my room.

Okay. I'll buy next time.

He starts to flick through the channels again before settling on some kind of horror film.

This okay?

Fine.

Not seeing your lady friend tonight?

What?

The girl from work.

Bea?

Yeah.

She's not my lady friend.

You spend a lot of time together.

That doesn't mean anything.
You like her though.
I don't answer.
Don't you?
Yeah.
I drink back the rest of my wine. We watch the film.
Did something happen with her?
No. Why do you ask?
You were getting on really well before.
Nothing happened.
So what's changed?
Nothing. I just...
Just what?
I don't know. I like her and everything but...
But?
I don't know if she feels the same.
You won't know if you don't ask.
I know.
So what's stopping you?
My track record isn't great.
It can't be that bad.
It is.
Doesn't mean it won't happen this time.
She was all over Jon the other night.
At the club?
Yeah.
You mean they got off with each other.
No. They were just dancing.
But they didn't kiss or anything?
I don't know. I got in a mood and left.
Jesus.
What?
You're terrible.
What do you mean?

Didn't you at least say goodbye?
I was drunk.
No wonder things are awkward.
Maybe.
You should just talk to her.
Yeah. I know.
What have you got to lose?
My self respect.
You don't have any.

A while later Jas comes home. We're on our second bottle by then and another film has come on and the rain continues against the window. Jas has friends with her and a bagful of wine and they come to join us in Rick's room. After introductions Rick and Jas light cigarettes and the room is soon filled with smoke and the smoke is a dense pall we're all staring through with yellowed veils of it hanging lifeless about the lampshades. They talk and I look at them one and another and say nothing. Sometime later after the wine is gone Rick and I go to the convenience store down the road for some more. The rain has eased and clings now in mizzled clouds around streetlamps in whose pale radiance shadows of the trees are dispersed across the wet pavements. We come to the main street at the end of our road. It's quiet and the traffic signals at the intersection shift in the empty night and clouds move bruised above the rooftops. We cross to the convenience store. I look along the street at the pub I visited with Bea and see a simulacrum of us there by the cantilevered windows shut flat with the wicklike reflections of streetlamps upon their darkened panes and mosaicked light across the pavements from the empty storefronts. Briefly alone there I remember the darkened hallway before I went through to see my father. The dark parquet. The moon through the bevelled glass. The dust in its afterglow. How stark and ageless the house had seemed and how everything I'd known

33

had seemed to erode as I prepared to cross the threshold. Perhaps it's the breeze or some other entity that causes me to shudder. The darkened forms along the street take on a strange impermanence as if converging across different eras. Converging memories of the past and some unknown future. I look then through the stickered window of the store and see Rick peering along the shelves of wine and here too there is an impermanence as if my being here on this street looking in on him is somehow tangential to a more fated reality. He is immobile and the man behind the counter is immobile and no one passes on the street and no cars go by. I look down at the wet pavement. Discs of gum dried black glisten on the dank flagstones. The rain travels in waves. Static. Languid. I glance back up. Rick at the store's wine shelves. He lifts a bottle and studies the label and replaces it and takes another. Replaces it. Strays to the magazines. At the end of the street a car comes to a stop at the traffic signals and idles there and fumes from its exhaust drift into the night. It moves off again and finally I go through to Rick and stand beside him and he shows me the label of one of the wines.

I was thinking maybe this one.

Fine.

Or maybe this.

Whichever.

Do you think we should get two?

Sure.

It's not like we won't get through it.

Let's get one each.

You bought the last two.

It's fine.

Which do you want to get?

I don't mind. Either.

He hands me one and we go to the counter.

Should we get some snacks? Some crisps or something.

Okay.

What flavour do you want?

Whichever.

He picks out a tube of crisps and replaces it and picks out another and reads the label and places this with his wine and a couple of bars of chocolate on the counter and the clerk looks up from his paper and nods a greeting and rings everything through.

Jas and her friends are still in Rick's room when we get back and the air is stale with cigarette smoke and mouldering damp and somebody is asleep on the bed. We set to drinking again and after the next bottle is finished I tell the others I need some air and then I'm sitting on the stairs. Through the open sash window a cool breeze blows in off the waning storm. I replay conversations in my mind. The one with my mother about the locum whose misdiagnosis caused upwards of a month's delay in treatment. Later updates. That the surgeons are optimistic. That they've caught it early enough and should be able to operate. Appointments and consultations that sometimes happen and sometimes get pushed back while the next course of action is mulled over by oncologists. That perhaps chemo or radio would be a better option. My mother singing the praises of the medical professionals in spite of everything. One of them is such a nice man. So thorough. Really wonderful. Rick comes out onto the landing. Doesn't see me at first. Almost goes on by then stops and looks down at me over the banisters.

You okay?

Yeah.

What are you doing out here?

Just getting some air.

Do you want some more wine?

Maybe in a minute.

Are you sure you're okay?

Yeah. I'll come back through in a sec.

Do you want some toast?

Are you making some?

Yeah.

I'll come through with you.

I follow him to the kitchen. He turns on the grill and takes the bread from the cupboard. I ask him if he wants a glass of whiskey.

Have you got some?

Yeah. In my room.

Since when did you have whiskey?

Since my father told me that as he couldn't drink anymore I should help myself to whatever I wanted from the drinks cabinet. I go to my room and pour us both a measure and we stand in the kitchen drinking it while Rick drunkenly makes toast.

That girl likes you.

Which girl?

Sara.

Which one is she?

The one with the striped top.

What makes you think that?

Jas told me.

Told you when?

Just now.

Huh.

Didn't you notice her looking at you?

No.

She's quite fit.

Toast pops up from the toaster. He spreads margarine onto it and hands it to me.

Here.

Actually I don't really fancy any right now.

You sure?

Yeah.

He takes it back.

You should ask her out.

I should ask everybody out according to you.

You should ask somebody out.

Somebody. Anybody.

He bites into the toast.

So what's stopping you?

Sometime just before dawn I go to bed. By then the rain has stopped and the penumbral landscape lays wet and eerily still. For a while I sit on the edge of my bed. The window is open a gap at the bottom and the net curtains gently rise and fall and birdsong starts up in the black ligature of trees beyond the garden. I think distantly of my father. I think of Jas' friend and the continuance of those glances long into the night and the pointlessness of it all. Mostly I think of Bea. Clouds move across the sky and with the slow coming of the light my reflection in the glass starts to die away.

\*          \*          \*

It comes to the end of some period and we are about the stacks with clipboards and countsheets and there is the sound through the store of the tips of pens tapping against bottlenecks and the sometime sound of trolley wheels over the pitted floor or the peal of the telephone through the airless heat. Behests for deliveries. Parties for the coming throes of summertime. For christenings. Wakes. One or other of us in the stockroom out back going through the picked stock on the shelves or through the stock picked in wire trolleys by the entranceway or peering down the gaps of stacks where carpenter spiders enmeshed in disjointed webs hang from the splintered stringerboards of the pallet pedestals.

I mark off the stack I'm at and move on to the next. It's a

promotional wine and the cases are piled eight high in a base of rotated layers and there are bottles precariously arranged at eyelevel along the lip. I have to step up onto the corner of the pallet to see to the back and as I'm tallying off the wines my foot slips and I send one of the bottles ricocheting down the gap between the stacks. There's a hollow crack as it hits the concrete. Red wine spatters the boxes and shards of glass scatter out into the aisle. Jon looks over and slow hand claps. I kneel and peer beneath the pallet's deckboards. Wine funnelled along veins in the concrete thickens and slows as it mats through the dust and mangled rags of old web and splintered glass glinting in the dark. I swear and head to the carpark to fetch the mop and bucket and dustpan. On the way by Bea looks up from the spirits shelves. She's crouched there with a pencil poised over her countsheet and another stuck through the knot of hair tied upon her crown.

Ca va?

I just broke a bottle.

Do you need a hand?

No. I'm okay.

You sure?

Yeah.

I go on by. It's been like this for a while. Strained conversation. Fleeting eye contact. A monosyllable here or there in passing. Quirks of the rota in the days that followed the party meant we didn't see each other for a time and afterwards fell out of the habit of walking home together. Sometimes Rachel would let one or other of us leave early. Other times I'd pretend I had an errand to run on the broadway or would go off to the pub with Ben. Some nights Jon would take her home in the van. Watching them I'd see mirages of that afternoon in the meadowlands with the first leaves of autumn falling or those study dates of old or the aftermath of the party in the dark of the field with the stars revolving in the sky and moonlight illuminating our footprints in the dark grasses.

Remember in the evenings other passages. Other replications. How the cooling breeze through the window would summon those late days of summer out east when the winds would blow through the town from winter mountain. Or how the turning of the leaves fringing the park would recall those bistered stretches of woodland fallen to autumn nearing home with the view below of some great river stirring and writhing in the twilight with eddies about the buttresses of the great bridges traversing it and a faint mist upon its walled banks and across the skyline the domes and spires of the city beneath a coral sky. On my bed in the dark I would see too a homecoming. Back in my old room with my bag at my feet and my jumper threadbare and holes in the toes of my shoes. Seeing distantly that final day at the school. The speech I gave on stage before returning home to pack the last of my belongings. The ferry terminal the next day and from the deck of the ferry at dusk the city gradually fading into nothing before days and nights spent at sea with the curvature of the earth upon the ocean and flying fish at the hull or from the stern the restless wake of its passage lapsing into oblivion. Months later watching a thunderstorm at night along the beach with the rain tattooing the sand around me and forks of lightning blistering the distant mountains. Days by the sea with diggers shoring up the embankment at the farthest breakwaters and at dusk the palms along the promenade jagged against the dusk sky and the snowcapped ridges at the edge of the plain rising into the crepuscular blue haze. At night through the skylight of the mezzanine or from the terrace the waxing moon and myriad constellations over the rooftops and the sidereal curvations of satellites. Seeing out those final days before the last passage home revealed fleeting glimpses of passing suburbs and arrondissements and homeward landscapes eroding through a flat and windswept drizzle. Finally standing down by a river with a postcard skyline and upon its bridges flashbulbs flaring in the gloom. The sky hung with cloud over the flint grey surface of the water. Finding myself in a pub staring through the window at the rush hour traffic going by and within at the fruit machines and the optics of the bottles arrayed along the bar and the faded tables and wainscoting and mantel. Everything a facsimile of some forgotten time. Onto the rush hour train homebound. A route I'd once known. The names of stations. Standing in my frayed clothes with my bag between my feet amongst the office workers reading papers with briefcases and overcoats slung here and there and retail parks and intersections and flyovers splintering across the glass. My father waiting at the wicket in the lobby. Twill trousers. Old coat and scarf. A strangeness born of familiarity after so long an absence. Walking with him wordlessly to the car through the raw December air and wordless for much of that journey home. Nearing the village broken cloud over the darkly furrowed fields and the headlights of the car searching out the tatterdemalion grass grown high along the banks flanking the lane. The village in the dark miniaturised and surreal. The car tracing out the pitted road with mud spattered rags of teasel dead and broken through the railings lining the Bourne and spatters of mud from pits in the road thrown up against the windowless walls of the barn on the corner. Unable to stare much at the passing houses. Stare instead at the banks of leylandii along the opposite bank of the Bourne. Finally the sign I painted one summer at the foot of our drive. My father reversing up with his arm over the back of my seat and in the wing mirror the house coming into view. The apple trees cold and bare. The fence around the garden old and worn and the borders dead. On the yard in the cold my breath misting. My mother through the window of the kitchen. The old picnic table in the garden. Remembering how things had been in the summertime before I left. Days with little occupation. Reading. Long and aimless walks. Watching television in my room. Finding in an atlas after I was notified of its location the town where I would be living. Correspondences with future colleagues. Going with my mother to town one Saturday to buy a suit and some shirts and a pair of shoes. Sending these ahead to the address I'd been given. My father writing it out in kanji. Remembering then how things had been after. After the day down by the water meadow with the horses in the streambed. Smoke from izakaya drifting through the night. The rice fields on the way to work. Cicadas in the cherry trees. Fireworks on the riverbank at summer's end with pitchers of beer and cartons of fried octopus balls and stalls hung with fans and woodcrafts and bird whistles on coloured lanyards. Later the cold. Hatsuyuki on winter mountain. The snow falling at night along the two five eight or in town walking the strip after we'd all come back from Christmas. The darkness unyielding. Remember going through to my mother. Christmas music over the radio. Pastry across the floured worktop. A bowl of mincemeat. The way she'd hugged me. Going then to my room and dropping my bag on the floor and sitting a long time on the edge of the bed with all around me familiar but unfamiliar. The unit where I used to do my homework. The pictures pinned there of old friends from school long forgotten. Of her. Of us. My old red pen pot fanned with desiccated pen nibs and brushes stiff and discoloured and a palette knife still contoured with paint. Dead cacti. The after days and after months. Reunions in town. Old friends displaced to new locales. Finding myself alone among crowds. Something in them I recognised from long ago and something irredeemable also. A disconnect. In socialising a mania. A frantic need to be reborn there yet finding little association. Staring out of the windows of the flats they shared. Most evenings at home during that time I'd go walking and I'd be out in the woods in the dark without a torch and I'd stop amongst the dead bracken or in the meadow just beyond and lie on the hard gelid earth and stare up at the sky and wish that I was back there in my old flat or walking along the river to work with cicadas in the cherry trees and cormorants fanning their wings on sluice gates. On these walks at night when it was clear stars would blanket the sky and in the woods I'd feel the frost biting and clawing through the undergrowth and cracking away at the hoary bracken. I would track in the moonlight the pathways crisscrossing the woods and overhead the cold dead trees would finger at the sky. Over the months that followed a gradual withdrawal until unanswered messages and invitations from old friends eventually stopped coming altogether. Months in this way out in the village until finally it was time to move on.

The bucket is still filled with feculent water from the previous spillage. I take it to the storm drain outside and pour it in and watch the sludge settle on the catchbasin grate. I watch a bus travel along the street until it disappears from view. Stare after it and toe through the sludge on the catchbasin grate. Push it through the gaps. Trickle of it. Drip of it. I head back inside and go by Bea. She's still at the spirits shelves and I glance at her and then I am at the stack from beneath which streaked arteries of wine are cankered with dust from the floor. I look up at the wineboxes. Dismantling them to get to the bulk of the breakage would be too laborious a task and without much real merit. Better to pick away at the shards of glass visible and leave the rest to fester at the back unreachable. The mop and bucket and dustpan really just for the illusion of intent. I use the handle of the broom to flick out from beneath the pallet the larger shards of glass. These I place in the dustpan and then after screwing the mop in the bucket's wringer I map the mophead through the spattered wine with the dust and blackened cobwebs ulcerating beneath the pallet.

Late afternoon I'm at the gatepost taking a break when I hear footsteps approaching. At first I don't turn around but am soon aware of somebody beside me. I glance over my shoulder to find Bea standing there with two cups of tea. She hands one to me and I thank her and we are silent. It's clouded over and the air is warm and close. Pigeons murmur in the rafters. I take a sip of tea and look across at Bea. She smiles uncertainly before speaking.

Are you okay?

Just taking a breather.

Mind if I join you?

No. Not at all.

There's a pause. I look up and down the street. Spray from the neighbouring carwash hazes the air. The sun breaks through the cloud and the spray is briefly aglow with prismatic light and then it's gone. At length Bea speaks again.

So what's been up?

I glance at her and look away.

What do you mean?

We haven't spoken in a while.

No. I know.

Was it my cooking?

I laugh in spite of myself.

No. Your cooking was great.

Then what is it?

I'm silent a while. Mulling over the question.

My dad has cancer.

As I speak I stare down at the ground and push around a piece of grit from the pavement with the toe of my shoe. My eyes start to well up. I turn away and wonder at the motivation for telling her then and there. The need for release? Because she's my assistant manager and should probably know in case I suddenly get called away in the night to witness my father's necrosis and death? Or simply for affectation? To create an aura of quiet stoicism?

I'm so sorry. I had no idea.

It's okay.

When did you find out?

A while back. A few weeks.

Why didn't you say anything before?

I don't know.

I've been worried about you.

Sorry.

I thought you were angry with me.

No. It's just difficult to talk about.

We don't have to if you don't want to.

My hands are shaking and my throat feels dry. I take a sip of tea.

No. It's fine. It helps.

What type is it?

Oesophageal.

I touch my neck.

Will he be okay? I mean what's the...

Prognosis?

Yes. Prognosis.

My mother is positive. Tells me down the phone that they will get through it because they are strong and have too much to look forward to to let a silly little thing like cancer get in the way. Tells me that the oncologist used the word cure. Cure. They don't use that unless they mean it. Yet for me those inchoate ideas of disbelief will sometimes yield to blind optimism and other times to tired fatalism. Disbelief that he could ever die. Not so soon after his retirement. Not when its precedent years of work in the city are taken into account. Yet concurrent with this is the acceptance of its inevitability. My father's broken voice when he comes on the line to ask of me my news or to report upon a walk he went on with my mother or to express his hope of being able to eat a piece of dover sole with new potatoes and butter once he's better.

I don't know.

She puts her hand on my shoulder.

I really am so sorry.

Thanks.

If there's anything I can do. Really.

Okay.

I know people say that but I mean it.

I touch her elbow and she takes my tea and places it on the floor beside hers and hugs me and I can feel through her polo shirt the contours of her body and against my cheek and neck her neck and cheek and I wonder again at my revelation to her regarding my father. When she withdraws I look upon her and my eyes feel heavy. Drugged.

Thanks Bea.

You don't need to thank me.

Okay.

Anything I can do.

Yeah.

Even if it's just a drink sometime.

That might be nice.

Just let me know.

Okay. And sorry.

About what?

If it seemed like I was avoiding you.

Don't be silly.

She smiles and kisses me on the cheek and then picks the cups of tea back up and hands me mine. She starts back across the carpark and says over her shoulder

I haven't forgotten by the way.

What?

That you still owe me a dinner.

\*          \*          \*

My mother comes to meet me at the station. I don't know why I didn't drive that time. After a while these details start to blur. She's down by the ticket barriers in pleated cotton slacks and flats and a pastel cardigan with a mauve kerchief around her neck and has clearly dressed up for the occasion but my father's illness is much in evidence. Her hair has greyed and the lines around her eyes are more pronounced and her shoulders are stooped. We hug for a long time and at first she holds onto me tightly but then I feel the strength go from her and she starts to cry on my shoulder. Afterwards we walk wordlessly to the car. It's parked up in the rise where my father used to leave it when he commuted to work each day. The trees along the roadway are near bare and fallen leaves mottle the kerbstones. My mother draws her cardigan about her shoulders and unlocks the car.

Do you want to drive or shall I?

I had a beer on the train.

Are you allowed to drink on the trains?

I don't know. I just fancied one.

I go to open the passenger side door.

You might want to sit in the back.

Why?

Your dad has some of his stuff in the front.

What stuff?

His pills and shakes and things.

Okay.

You might be able to squeeze in.

I open the door. Cartons of protein shakes and blister packs of pills litter the footwell. Cardboard bowls and cotton tip swabs are piled on the seat. It smells acrid. Sweet. I take up one of the bowls.

What are these?

Your dad's pulp bowls.

Pulp bowls?

From the cancer people.

What are they for?

He needs them to spit in.

And these? The cotton buds?

You moisten them and dab his lips.

Why does he need his lips dabbed?

His mouth gets dry.

Right. Of course.

Is there room to sit in the front?

No. I'll go in the back.

Sorry. I meant to clear it away.

It's okay.

I was in a bit of a rush.

It's fine.

I'll be your chauffeur.

She smiles and wipes her eyes again. I try to smile back. Journey home she asks me about work but I've little to say that seems in any way meaningful and we fall to silence. I watch the scenery go by. The fields are ploughed now and angular hacks of mud scythed smooth and glasslike by the ploughblade rise from the banks along the lane upon which wild grasses gone to seed grow amongst the desiccated skeletons of sedge and hedgeparsley. At the top of the coombes along the upper banks the trees are gnarled and leafless and briary undergrowth chokes the old chalkpit. We pass the old footbridge with the footpath rising up through the bare field and I remember being there that summer's night with the wheat stirring darkly about me and seeing in the distance the marquee lights and hearing in the stillness a dull percussiveness and pitching into the dark a spent bottle and hearing it shatter someplace below. Remember too those fields in another time another era when at summer's end hayricks rolled in coils or stacked in bales would punctuate the burnished sweeps of wheatstubble. We would range the landscape with about us the dogs at play and the low sun burning darkly or on autumn weekends I would go walking in the woods with my father with the smell of damp bracken and fungal bark upon the air. He would tell me the names of the trees or the flora or of the elderly sprite who came with the morning mists and left traveller's joy in the hedgerows before the first frosts of winter bit into the earth and homeward we would collect logs and kindling for fires to be lit late October when the nights drew in and the wind would moan through the flue. Remember the old coat my father wore with the pockets gaping from the seams. An image of him in the back garden in the musty reek of raked leaf bonfires with the smoke rolling tumescent in the sky. Schooldays with the view from the classroom of the mist hung baulk or of raincloud creeping over the rooftops of the village below. The afternoon we were taken to the churchyard to frottage headstones. How she and I had used a stick to scrape out the name of an epitaph long given to lichenous anonymity with its scrolled and fluted edges weathered indistinct and its softened grooves inscribed long ago all but eroded in the grey stone. The snarled muzzles of the gargoyles along the church spire faded also with crows about the crenels and in the tops of the yews cawing softly. In another corner in the freshly raked soil of a recent grave a wreath of dying flowers lying in the grey damp beneath a simple wooden cross and a boy who will later be buried nearby picking at its petals and crumbling through his fingers the mud.

We thought we'd go to the secret place tomorrow.

What secret place?

The meadow we used to go to when you were little.

I'm not sure where you mean.
We used to tell you no one else knew about it.
Oh. The one with the stream at the bottom?
Yes. If you fancy it.
Okay.
If the weather's nice. If your dad's up to it.
Might he not be?
We'll have to see.
She seems to be framing her words.
You might find he looks a bit different.
What do you mean?
He's very ill.
I know he is.
He's lost a lot of weight.
You said on the phone.
I don't really notice because I'm always with him.
There's a pause.
Sorry I haven't been back for a while.
I didn't mean that.
I know. Still. I've been meaning to.
Well. You haven't been in your new place long.
Yeah.
He and I know you've got your own life to lead.

She looks at me in the rearview mirror and smiles. When we arrive home I'm sent through to the living room where my father is standing by the patio windows with his trousers gathered in at the waist and his polo shirt once a tight fit hanging slackly from his emaciated body. He looks up from some task at the window and comes over and we hug. He's all bones. Almost without substance. We draw back and he looks at me and I at him. He's smiling and his teeth are yellowed and there's spittle in the corners of his chapped lips. His skin has a waxy quality and there's a gauntness about his eyes and cheeks. He tells me I look well and asks about the journey and work and I say everything's okay. Work's work. He takes up from the back of the chair where he left it a metallic device with handles and a toothed cog.

What are they?

Leather eyelet pliers.

Eyelet pliers?

From the little ironmonger's in town.

What are they for?

Punching a new hole in my belt.

He positions the pliers around his belt and tries to compress the handles. Tries with both hands.

Damn thing won't seem to go through.

Do you want me to try?

You can if you like.

Here.

I take up the pliers and belt and look along the leather to where he's already made a series of indentations.

About here?

Yes. That'll do fine.

I punch one of the teeth into the belt. It goes through easily. A little disc of leather pops out and falls onto the floor.

You must've started it off.

Yes. Must've.

I hand back the pliers and belt. He asks me if I want tea.

Mum's making some.

I thought she might be.

Are you not up to having any?

Not yet. Shall we sit down?

Sure.

My father goes to his armchair. Amongst the pillows there's an inflatable cushion and beside the chair a little table set out with a stack of pulp bowls and a dish of water with swabs in and around it and a half drunk protein shake. There are various packs of pills and from a box a scattering of fossilised and blackened tissues. He pulls on a cardigan and sits rather awkwardly on the cushion and it takes him some time to adjust his body position so that he's comfortable.

Need a hand?

No no. Just give me a sec.

He manoeuvres himself into position. The inflatable cushion creaks beneath him and he disturbs his newspaper from the armrest. I retrieve it and place it back alongside him but he doesn't seem to notice. He shifts again and his eyes cloud briefly and he grimaces.

You okay?

Yes. I'm okay.

You sure?

Yes.

My eyes drift to the window. To the flue. Back to him.

I like your cardigan.

Your mother bought it for me.

It's nice.

Said it was about time I had some new clothes.

Probably true.

She got me some trousers as well.

Not those ones?

No. They're upstairs.

I can't remember the last time you got new clothes.

The waists are too big on most of my others now.

Right.

I've lost quite a bit of weight.

Yeah. I can see.

Not quite the diet I had in mind.

No.

Excuse me a minute.

He takes up one of his pulp bowls and spits into it. Stringy black mucus spools from his lips. He coughs and hacks up phlegm and this beads down unbroken into the pulp bowl. He reaches for one of the swabs and uses it to break the chain. He coughs and spits again and this time the mucus is laced through with blood and some of it runs down his chin and he uses one of the tissues to wipe it away and I notice some of it dribbling down onto his new cardigan and this more than anything brings tears to my eyes.

I look away. Across the garden. I wonder when we got a birdbath. It's old and covered in moss. There's no water in it. Then I remember it was my grandmother's. Remember how she would call them the dicks and watch them from the sitting room window beneath the pelmet of the curtains with those porcelain ornaments of dancing girls in summer hats arranged along the windowsill. The same scene later from the window of her room in the nursing home. Out across the birdless garden. The girls in dancing hats fewer in number. Just one or two we'd salvaged. The rest lost. Look from the window to the chest. Upon it the lacquer box and plate they bought when they came to see me out east. Remember that day up on the mountain with the view out over the plain and cherry blossoms blowing across the pathways on the slopes below and the raked bands of clouds feeding westwards. Remember afterwards beneath a tissue of darkening stormcloud going to the park in the castle grounds and sitting on a bench by an ornamental water garden with dank cusps of fungus frilling the mossy arbour and moisture hanging in beads from maple lobes. The packed lunch my mother had prepared. Little omiyage candies and beanpaste cakes they'd found in torn awning boutiques and ramshackle grocery stores on the Friday when I was at school. The parcels of sushi wrapped in vine leaves with noodles of julienned daikon and pickled ginger. How in the evenings when I got back from work they would tell me of their daytrips to corners of the city I never knew existed. How my mother would make dinner and we would have bottles of chilled lager or wine but I would find it difficult to connect. Remember that night we'd had an argument and I'd gone to bed without saying goodnight. My father at the airport in his spring jacket and my mother in a shirt she'd bought in one of the department stores. This yearning to be alone again but then returning home to find the dinner my mother had left me in the fridge and the note on the kotatsu thanking me for everything and telling me how much they missed me. How I'd gone out onto the balcony to compose myself and sat out there long into the night staring up at the dark sky and sometimes crying. How you never realise until it's too late.

I look back at my father. He smiles and presently my mother comes in with a tray of tea and biscuits and the next morning she and I are in the kitchen while my father sleeps upstairs. It's bright out and sunlight through the net curtains casts muslin shadows across the walls. My mother offers to make me a cooked breakfast but I tell her I'm not that hungry and that I'll just have cereal and coffee. We set out the breakfast things together and I brew some coffee in the cafetiere and after we've eaten she tells me the latest news. The initial proposal to remove the cancer has been abandoned. My father is too weak to withstand the procedure. Instead the doctors are going to put something called a stent into the lower part of his oesophagus. My mother tells me that this will bypass the cancer so that he will be able to eat again and after this he should be able to cope with the rigours of chemotherapy or radiotherapy or a combination of both. She speaks with admiration of the doctors and oncologists.

They're so professional.

You'd hope they would be.

What do you mean?

It is their job.

Yes. I know. But still.

What about the operation?

They can't operate at the moment.

But is it off the table completely?

For now.

So yes?

No. For now.

It just seems...

What?

That they keep changing their minds.

I think that's all part of it.

Part of what?

What they do.

It's just difficult to trust what they say.

Why do you say that?

After that fucking idiot got it wrong.

What idiot?

The locum.

He's not an idiot.

He didn't even do any fucking checks.

Well. Your nana had just died.

So what?

He thought it was linked to stress.

That's such a cop out.

It's just one those things.

He should have at least done a blood test.

She refuses to condemn him. I get up to make some more coffee and while the kettle's boiling look out of the window. The grass needs cutting and there's still windfall from the apple trees here and there rotting on the lawn. The fence collapsed in one corner. Leaves in the pond. I ask my mother if she'd like another cup of coffee but she tells me she's fine and after I've poured some for myself I take it back to the table and sit across from her.

Sorry I swore.

That's okay.

I didn't mean to get like that.

I know. I know you're upset.

Yeah.

It's a difficult time for all of us.

Think dad'll be well enough for a drive today?

We'll see when he comes down.

Okay.

He didn't sleep too well.

No?

No. Did he wake you up at all?

No. I slept through.

We sit in silence. I drink my coffee. My father comes down after half an hour or so. If anything he looks worse than last night. He's pale and somehow more gaunt and through his part open dressing gown the raised frame of his sternum shows more prominently. He kisses my mother and puts his hand on my shoulder and sits down. The sleeves of his gown ride up and there are large livid bruises on his arms and I notice once more that cadaverous and waxen quality to his skin. His fingernails are pitted and there's stubble in a line along his neck where he's tried to shave himself. His hair's combed but thin and dry and there's a brittleness to his posture.

Late morning we head out in the car. My mother has packed a picnic lunch with a flask of tea. Has packed the old plastic plates and cups we used to take on breakfast hikes or camping holidays and the tartan picnic blanket and cool box. Has packed too my father's various medications and fluid receptacles. Pulp bowls and boxes of tissues and cotton swabs. He sits in front and my mother drives and from the back I look silently out of the window. I don't really remember the route to the secret place and much of the landscape looks unfamiliar now after so long an absence. We go through villages with thatched cottages overlooking

55

carefully tended greens and church spires through the trees and by smallholdings and farmsteads with eggs or vegetables and honesty boxes roadside and country pubs upon whose signs are painted scenes of rural life long since forgotten. Pass along wooded lanes with the tree limbs interlocking overhead such that the sunlight falls stippled with our passage before coming finally to more open country with views out over rolling fields tilled or left fallow or sown with winter seed with their borders demarcated by footpaths or hedgerows or coppices.

My father starts to cough. At first softly but then with more persistence. Racking and guttural. He fumbles for one of his pulp bowls and spits into it and then my mother asks him if he wants us to stop and he nods as the coughing continues. We pull over on one of the verges. My father opens the door and climbs out clutching his pulp bowl. We follow out after him. He hunches over and my mother goes and places her hand on his back. She holds a tissue and uses it to wipe his mouth. At first he spits into his pulp bowl but then drops it into the grass. He brings up some bloodied phlegm. My mother goes to her bag for some more tissue and a long unbroken runnel of bloodied mucus drips to the ground. My father by now has his hands on his knees and along his arched back the raised nodes of his spine are visible even through the shirt he's wearing. His face reddens with the continuation of the coughing and the veins in his temples show. He retches. It sounds as though he might be sick but nothing comes. He retches some more and then my mother is wiping from his mouth another runnel of blackish green mucus shot through with blood. The tissues fall sculpted about her feet. He starts to dry heave. I'm struck by my mother's composure. The way in which she continues to caress his back very gently. I'm struck too by my own feelings of inadequacy. As if the man before me is no longer my father but some aberration of his being. My mother glances back at me and there's something like apology in her eyes but a distant part of me reads it as resentment. Of my detachment. My confusion. My mounting horror and revulsion. Perhaps I imagine that she gestures for me to come over but I do so regardless and place my hand on my father's back and rest it there feeling the tortured heaving of his breaths and seeing in the long grasses at his feet the amniotic miasma of bloody phlegm. He heaves again. Spits. My mother wipes it away. A fit of retching shudders through his whole body. I can feel him trembling. Can feel his bones moving reptilian beneath the papered translucency of his skin. My mother is making noises. It's okay. It's okay dear. Get it all up. It's okay. You're okay. From his diaphragm he brings up a mucosal cocoon of blood laced phlegm and spits into the grass. He stays there with these short wheezing breaths coursing through his body. I look out across the landscape. A skein of geese travels noiselessly across the sky. A gasgun goes off somewhere distant. Slowly the retching and coughing begins to subside. He is there a long time hunched over the viscera in the grass before finally managing to right himself. His face is contused and there's blood at the corners of his mouth. My mother wipes it away with a moistened tissue and brushes the hair from his eyes. We stand on the verge in the sunshine as his breaths begin to steady. He looks first at my mother and then away. Looks at the ground. Looks across at me and smiles. There's nothing to say. No words. For this is how it becomes.

My mother gathers up the bloodied tissues and presses them into the wetly spent pulp bowl. She goes to the car and pours some water into another pulp bowl and with a swab cleans his lips and moistens his mouth. She caresses his back. I look at her. Her face resolute. I realise now that it's hardened by the continuation of this ritual. The swabbing of fluids and the repetition of reassurances. I look then at my father. Moisture encrusts the corners of his eyes and I wonder whether it's from tears or the relics of exertion. Remember hiking with him through lakelands and on mountainsides and across fells. Photographs of us on peaks overlooking vales with tarns and meres in the noonday sun. Of monochrome landscapes nearer to home when drifts of snow would blow across the lanes. Of yuletides seated around the table with gold chargers and decanted claret.

He turns to us each and makes some apology. To me that he's sorry I had to see it. I reassure him. It's okay. Don't be silly. We can go back if you're not feeling up to it. But he tells me that he wants to go on. He wants to see the meadow.

And thus we go on. We stop twice more before the meadow and on the latter occasion we are again on a grass verge and the coughing is as before but this time in retching he manages to bring up some liquid almost luminous in its yellowness that I take to be pure bile. Births it from his pursed lips in a greasy chrysalis of phlegm and blood that gestates in the grass at his feet. Takes longer than before to right himself and afterwards as before my mother wipes from his lips the remnant spools of blood and from his shirt with another tissue a thread of the yellow bile webbed there luminously in the sunlight and that final stretch of road before the meadow I watch how my father stares from the window at the scenery going by with the encrustations of tears at the corners of his eyes and his hands lightly clasped in his lap and his breaths short but even.

Okay now dear?

Yes. Okay now.

How are you feeling?

Still a bit icky sicky.

It registers with me for not the first time this trip how with the progression of his illness his speech has become more infantile. How he feels funny in his tummy or headachy before bedtime or icky sicky after the evisceration of so much blood and bile and mucus on the roadside. My mother strokes his shoulder and glances at me in the rearview and smiles a smile shorn of much substance and presently we are parking up in a layby just beyond a stretch of woodland.

My mother and I climb out and my father stays in the car while we get the picnic from the boot. I roll the blanket beneath my arm and in one hand take the cool box and in the other the bag containing the plates and cups and flask so that my mother will be able to help my father down with his spit bowls and medications and blood swabs.

I go on ahead through a gap in the hedge and over a rickety stile that leads to a narrow pathway through a short stretch of woodland. The day is warm and I pause to remove my jacket and sling it over my shoulder and then I go on. Little seems familiar. Yet presently the wooded trail opens out onto a grassy meadow grown wild at its borders with a pathway down to a brook below shaded by a copse of hazel and ash. A willow touches its scintillant water and it is a scene I recognise so intimately from my childhood.

Disturbing craneflies from the grass I go down a way then stop to look back. My mother and father are just emerging from the woodland. He's wearing a sunhat and making halting progress on her arm. I watch the unerring patience with which my mother tends to him and the frailty of his footfalls and the way they pause now and then for him to draw breath. My father looks up and raises his arm in salutation. I drop the picnic gear in the grass and go back to them. Take my father's other arm and help to guide him down. He comments on the craneflies and the weather and asks me if I remember the last time I was here. I tell him no. Not really. In fact remember just these fleeting images of being down by the brook and seeing fry in the wreaths of algae and watching the cows grazing in the field and playing

French cricket atop the cool box after a picnic was done.

We go on down to the shores of the brook in whose dappled shade gnats hover and in whose peaty shallows little eddies of water vacillate. I unroll the blanket and set out the plates and I bring from the cool box the triangles of sandwiches and sticks of carrot and celery my mother prepared and from another bag packets of crisps and a funpack of half melted chocolate biscuits. I lay these out with serviettes and pour into plastic cups hot tea from the flask. We stand silently on the riverbank watching in the adjoining field a herd of grazing cattle flicking at the clouds of flies with their tails. My father sits on the blanket and my mother asks him whether he wouldn't like his shoes and socks off so that he can enjoy the grass beneath his feet. He nods and she sets about undoing the laces of his old brown brogues and once done removes his socks. He smiles and the impression of his sitting there with his bare feet outturned as he wiggles his toes calls me once again to the coming of his second childhood. We sit for some time on the blanket not really speaking and then my mother prepares a nutrition shake. He drinks it in small sips and I watch the slow convulsions of his body and then look away.

Sometime later after we've eaten and the empty crisp and biscuit packets are weighted down by stacks of dirty plates my mother goes down to the brook and paddles in its shallows by the osiers of the willow with cloudshadow now and then moving across the meadow behind us. My father is sleeping and I am by his side and presently he wakes and I ask him if he's okay and it takes him a while to come to and remember where he is. He says he's okay. Looks at me and smiles. Asks in turn if I'm okay. We both of us watch my mother a while and then my father asks me if I'm seeing anyone. I glance across at him. It's not something we often discuss. Not since that summer a few years back. He's still looking down at my mother and there's a quiet intensity to his expression. A yearning perhaps. Tells me I've grown up into such a kind and gentle person and that I would make somebody very happy. I look away and blink back tears. Tells me that not being alone makes life so much more fulfilling. That without my mother he'd be dead by now. Of that he's certain. We're silent. I play out a few scenarios in my head. Eventually decide to tell him.

There is this girl I like.

Oh yes?

Bea.

Bea?

From Beatrice. She's French.

How do you know her?

We work together.

Yes?

She started a few weeks after me.

And she's nice?

Yeah.

Pretty?

Very.

Have you been out with her yet?

Kind of.

What do you mean kind of?

We go out with the others from work sometimes.

But never alone?

No. Well. I mean she cooked for me once.

Sounds as though she likes you.

She's friendly with everybody.

But has she cooked dinner for everybody?

No.

Maybe you should reciprocate.

What do you mean?

Cook dinner for her.

Maybe.

You're a good cook.
Actually we had talked about it.
Yes?
I kind of invited her.
What does kind of mean?
Nothing's in the diary yet.
So what are you waiting for?
I don't know.
You'll never know if you don't ask.
So people keep telling me.
What will you cook?
I haven't really thought about it yet.
You can take one of my wines if you like.
Which wines?
One of the expensive ones.
That's okay. I'll drink them with you.
I look across at him.
You know. When you're better.

My mother calls out to us. Gives a little beck. Asks me whether I'd like a paddle. I look down at her and a cloud moves across the sun.

\*             \*             \*

I cut across the grasslands at the end of my road and head up past the spinney onto the lower slopes. The palace's cloistered archways and rose window and radio mast rise into a cloudless sky. I follow the walkway that bisects the park through a broader stretch of woodland and leads to the upper slopes where I pause and look out over the city. The skyline's straddled in a thin haze with chalk white traces of the downs upon the distant horizon and in the beyond the cockle shacks and candy stalls we'd visit with my grandfather. Remember the steep cobbled streets lined with giftshops hawking windmills and kites and rubber rings with children crabbing on darkened breakwaters in the afternoon sun. Along the coast a funfair old and faded with a ghost train and swaying gondolas on a ferris wheel and a helter skelter worn bare by the coarse bristles of mats.

It's a Sunday and there are others abroad. I make my way across the grass and find a space for the blanket and unroll it just beyond one of the great oaks with an uninterrupted view out over the city. I watch a child's kite angling against the sky before unpacking from my bag and arranging upon the blanket the plastic bowls and borrowed flutes and the punnet of strawberries from the broadway and in the wine cooler the wine my father gave me during my last visit. After all is done and finding myself still early I lie back watching a vapour trail as it slowly fades and remembering an afternoon one summer's end long ago as we walked in file through a field of barley with the wind astir in the tillers and in the sky another such vapour trail reddened by the sinking sun. The scaled and fissured mud was baked hard along the pathway for there had been a drought that year and in the fields left fallow the wind would blow the topsoil to dust. Remember the pitch chip notes of swifts and martins skimming the barleyheads as up ahead at the field's edge she climbed the stile to the baulk and turned to wave in the tempered light. Remember the umbra of night afterwards. Returning home beneath a harvest moon with the moonswept landscape before us and the world silently uterine. Moths at the porchlight on her doorstep and something of a beckoning in the way she looked down upon me. The fleeting contact of our hands and a momentary though engulfing hesitation before the silent walk alone along the lane after I left her. Its accompanying sense of loss unprecedented then as of opportunity missed. A shadow moves across the sun and I sit up to find Bea outlined against the sky with the light of the afternoon upon her as

63

she leans to me and kisses me on each cheek.

Found you.

Hey.

In her hair a familiar length of fabric falls across her shoulders. There's a hint of mascara on her eyes. On her lips a hint of colour. She's still wearing her work jeans but as she takes off her leather jacket I see that she's changed from her company shirt into a red argyle sweater. She sits down beside me and I watch as she unlaces her trainers and slips them off. Removes her socks and balls them up inside. Finally I ask her how her day was. She smiles distractedly and looks down across the parkland.

Comme toujours.

Same old same old.

How's that?

Same old same old.

Like same shit?

Yeah.

She motions to the items I've laid out on the blanket.

Look at all this.

Impressed?

Looks great.

I got strawberries.

I can see.

And this.

I take the wine from the cooler. She studies the label.

My dad gave it to me.

Is he doing okay?

Not great. Here.

I hand her the glasses and she holds them while I pour.

He has all this wine stored away.

Yeah?

Years' worth.

I replace the wine in the cooler. She holds her glass to the light and studies it.

He can't drink it anymore.

Because of his...?

She looks at my neck. Faintly touches her own.

Yeah.

She takes a sip of wine. Lowers the glass. Seems to meditate on this for a while. Chews on a hangnail. I sense the mood slipping so change the subject.

How is it? The wine I mean.

Lovely. Tell your dad.

I will.

Later she's lying prone with her head resting in the crook of her elbow and her dreadlocked hair swept to one side such that her neck is exposed. Her eyes are closed and the breeze will now and then trace over her but she remains motionless. The empty strawberry bowls wiped clean with serviettes are lying in the grass. I drain the wine from my glass and hold the bottle up to the light. It's nearly finished. I pour the remnants into each of our flutes and sit there holding mine by the stem and turning it so that the wine forms legs at the sides. I look out across the city. The sun goes in. Wind pushes through the woodland below. A discarded wrapper drifts across the park. Beneath the broken sky scattered lights start to emerge in the office buildings and on the cars and buses moving up and down the steep inclines of the terraced streets. I look back at Bea. She stirs and turns her head and edges a little closer and opening her eyes and looking up at me motions that she's cold. I take her jacket and lay it across her shoulders. She clasps its collar and draws it to her then closes her eyes once more.

When it comes to dusk we are walking along the palace esplanade with flapping sacks of scaffold along the eastern wing and pigeons circling the girders of the old radio mast and the slotscopes along the railings stooped in disinclination. Cloud has moved in across the city with only a thin strip of sunshine now visible on the distant downs. The end of the esplanade opens out onto a terrace bedecked with picnic benches and here we pause. Bea steps up to the iron balusters and folds her arms over the cap rail and I stand by her and watch as she sways gently to and fro and the newly lit streetlamps along the road below illuminate her eyes against the gathering grey. I ask her if she'd like a drink from the palace bar and she looks down at me and asks in reply if I'm trying to get her drunk. I blush and after holding my gaze for a while she nudges me and tells me she's just teasing me. Tells me to take a seat while she goes in for the drinks. I'm about to protest but she's already walking away and I watch her until she is gone from view.

I sit at one of the benches and as I place the picnic bag on the ground the empty wine bottle is dislodged from it and rolls across the concrete. I retrieve it and take it back and look at the label. Old. Gnarled at the edges. Dust from its long storage still on the curvature of the glass. Bought one holiday when we'd been driving through the Pyrenean mountains and had happened across a winery. One of those days that seemed to define not only an era but also the threshold of an era. Of being with my parents but not yet suffering the embarrassment of their company. Of enjoying the trip for what it was. Of sitting out with them in the evenings and in the daytime visiting chateaux or forested hillsides or crowded beaches or market towns. Too young to drink back then but the patron of the winery had given me some to try regardless. Wonder at its intended end as I trace my fingers over the label. How an end such as this could never have been envisaged.

I replace it in the bag as the last of the sun fades. Down across the greying parkland crows can be heard in the treetops. See them take flight and scatter across the sky. So too the pigeons in the palace archways. Scattering through the greying gloom. A bus goes by on the road below and the passengers look out through the misted glass of the upper deck and at the stop the bus pulls in but nobody alights and nobody disembarks and then it is gone. A bank of stormcloud rolls in over the palace's portico darkening the dusk yet further. I watch it lingering over the conservatory domes and when I look down again Bea is approaching with her replicated shadow enfolding itself around her. She places down the drinks and sits across from me and with the accession of the cloud a few spits of rain start to fall. I watch her as she stirs her drink with a swizzle stick and then takes a sip of it through a thin black straw. I ask her what it is and she tells me a gimlet and I look at it briefly and then back at her and then the rain starts to fall. Seems to reach us in slow motion. Nascent across the park. Eroding first the horizon. Then the treeline just below. Finally across the esplanade. At first she makes no attempt to move as around her the rain as static blurs all. Blurs the baluster brickwork and sentry slotscopes. Blurs the palace portico and down below the roadway wending through the woodland. Blurs the tabletop slats' split veins of varnish and splintered parasol hole and planed grains of wood. Only Bea remains defined. The rain runs through her hair and begins in fine rivulets to streak from her eyes her mascara. Begins to form in beads that glissade upon the leather of her jacket. A distant rumble of thunder sounds followed by flashes in the clouded dusk of sheet lightning. Flashes in her eyes of the lightning sheets as the sound of its thunderhead recedes across the sky. Motionless for a time until she draws close the lapels of her jacket and turns up its collar and the beaded damp thereon slides away in thin veins. She pushes back her matted hair and the streaks of mascara show darker now against the flush of her skin given lustre by the fallen rain. Water pools and ripples on the tabletop and the air is soon impregnated with the damp must of parkland foliage and dampened concrete. Impregnated too with the musk of wetted wood and leather. I continue to stare at her as she starts once more to stir with the swizzle stick her gimlet and then bring to her lips its tip as another rumble of thunder sounds and rolls across the flattened landscape. She looks back across at me and something of a smile plays at the corners of her lips. Rain soaks my hair and runs down the nape of my neck but I pay it little heed as for a long time she watches me and I her until by some unspoken communion I am following her at a run across the rippling flagstones of the esplanade to the palace bar where we take a table by a window and Bea peels off her jacket and hangs it on the backrest of the chair beside her and pushes from her brow the damp strands of her hair and water from its tips trickles down her neck and the wet of her sweater presses upon her chest its cockled fabric. She wipes from beneath her eyes the lustred rain and streaks across her cheeks the run mascara. To her lips she brings the tip of the straw and as she drinks looks back across at me. Lightning splits the sky. A gust of wind harries rain against the windowpane. The thunder comes long and low. I look away. At the diffracted light in the rain streaked glass. At the duplications of her form there. At the water sliding in thin flutings upon its surface. We neither of us speak. I think of the meadow where we took my father and of my mother in the streambed with the sun stippled through the trees. A timelessness in the way she looked back at us but in her expression a finality also. A sense of ending. How we had headed back to the car and on the way home my father had been sick again. Black spatters of it on the upholstery drying in the dying sun. On the shirt my mother bought him. Darkening in a patch upon his slacks. Its acrid reek. The meek lament of his bated apologies. My father yet and yet not he. During dinner that night the scraping in the silence of my mother's fork upon her plate. I cast my eyes down to the table and align my glass on its coaster.

What are you thinking about?

Nothing.

It must be something.

Why do you ask?

Your mood changed.

I'm okay.

You sure?

I get like this sometimes.

Because of your dad?

Him and mum.

How's she doing?

She puts on a brave face and everything but...

Bea looks across at me levelly. Waits for me to continue. I feel suddenly choked up.

But you can just see it in her eyes.

I look to the window. Wipe away a tear. Only half hope she hasn't noticed. She reaches across the tabletop and presses my hand.

Sorry Bea.

Don't be silly.

I didn't mean to...

It's okay.

She gives my hand another squeeze.

I didn't mean for you to see me like this.

It's good to let it out.

I know.

You always seem so calm.

I guess only on the outside.

You can talk to me about it any time.

Thanks.

On the way back to mine for dinner the fallen rain upon the pavements ripples in the lamplight yet none falls now.

Water drips from the overhanging foliage and here and there the streetlamps rise into the folds of the wet black tree boughs and illuminate the half leaf limbs from which dead leaves will now and then fall and lay splayed upon the wet roadways weaving down by the park's perimeter. Broken tracts of cloud move across the sky revealing glimpses of a harvest moon reminiscent of a moon at harvest long ago in a sky without cloud orbed above a field broken by sheaves of gathered hay. See in the darkness the house at the perimeter of the field and moonlit figures repairing towards it. See upon its lighted lawn the dark forms of apple trees bare against the sky and scattered around their shaded boles the coronae of fallen leaves.

A flurry of wind. The boughs stir. Rainwater strews the street. In crossing I feel her hand brushing mine and notice the coldness of her skin. I look at her sidelong and see a paleness I'd not discerned before.

Are you okay?

Yes. Fine. Why?

You look cold.

I'm okay.

Are you sure?

Yes. I'm sure.

We go by the crossroads at the bottom of the hill. She hugs her jacket around herself as another gust of wind blows along the street. Faces gaze out through the windows of the pub on the corner. A few cars go by. A bus. But with the rawness of the weather there's a quietness to the streets that seems to herald the coming of winter. We come to my road.

Do you want to stop by yours?

What for?

So you can change.

You don't like what I'm wearing?

No. I didn't mean...

What's wrong with it?

I just meant because of…

I picked this out especially.

Because of the cold.

She nudges into me. A playful smile on her lips. She shakes her head.

Trop facile.

What's that?

Too easy.

Trop facile.

Trop facile.

I knew you were joking.

Sure you did.

I'm not that dumb.

No?

No. Well. Maybe.

Definitely.

Okay. I am.

We walk on in silence for a time.

You do look cold though.

Maybe a little.

That was why I suggested it.

Perhaps I could borrow something of yours.

Sure.

A sweater or something.

I'm sure I can manage that.

Back at mine I give her a towel and the cleanest sweater I can find and she goes into my room to change. I busy myself in the kitchen. Put a pan of water on the stovetop to boil. Season two seabass fillets. Chop some garlic and shallots. I pour myself a measure of vodka and drink it back and swill out the glass. Presently Bea comes through. The sweater's oversized and the weight of it defines the shape of her breasts and the loose knit neck shows the curve of her shoulder. Her

71

hair's towelled dry and there's a becoming glow to her skin. She leans back against the worktop by the sink and I ask her if she'd like a drink.

What do you have?

Wine or beer.

Maybe wine.

Red or white?

What white have you got?

There's a Riesling in the fridge.

Shall we have that?

Okay.

I take two glasses down from the cupboard and set about opening the wine.

Are your housemates in?

No. Jas is out with friends. Rick's working.

So it's just us.

I pull the cork from the wine.

Yeah. Just us.

After dinner we are on the settee in the living room. The wine is gone and it's late and the night now still. Beneath the part open window curls of paper warped by the sun ripple softly in the breeze and from the floor the fronds of an areca palm are cast elongated across the walls from the glow of the table lamp on the side. I don't know what time it is. Gone midnight. Maybe two or three. On the side by the table lamp are stacked our empty plates and by these Bea's tumbler of untouched whiskey through the flamenco glass of which the glow from the lamp casts lattices across the tabletop. I've moved little in the past half hour or so for her head is resting upon my shoulder and she's breathing evenly as of sleep. Sometimes she'll stir and I will remain motionless as I stare at the dark areca patterns on the opposite wall. Remain motionless but for the slow turning of my own tumbler on the armrest of the settee. Remember my parents giving them to me as a housewarming gift when I moved into my old place. Remember how they'd presented them to me in a little box with a bow and a card they'd both signed wishing me every happiness in my new home. New home in some forgotten backwater. Coital moans through the thin walls. How they'd come to see me once I'd settled and I'd been so very cold with them. Always coldly indifferent until news of my father's cancer engendered in me a belated sense of filial care. I raise the tumbler and watch the liquor run viscously down the sides.

\*             \*             \*

They've fixed a tube in his penis. A catheter. The tube protrudes from his puckered urethra and snakes down to a pouch filled with dark yellow piss hooked to the side of his bed. I don't know the ins and outs of how he got here but when I arrive he's fucked on painkillers yet still has the strength to keep clawing at the thing. What is this fucking thing? I told them not to put this fucking thing in. I told them I didn't want this fucking thing in my dick. A little more piss drips into the pouch. A couple of clots of blood in it. He squirms in the bed. He's wearing a hospital gown tied loosely at the back and his dick keeps popping out. His legs are thin and his balls shrivelled. Get this fucking thing out of my dick. I told them not to put this fucking thing in my dick. Get this fucking thing out. My mother is by his side doing her best to keep him restrained. It's okay dear. It's okay chooch. Don't keep pulling at it. It needs to stay in. It's there for your own good. His feet thresh against the bedframe footboard and he grips one of the safety rails. He has a cannula plastered to his hand connected to a drip which flays hither and thither. Another little spherule of bloody piss drips into the bag. I note all this from the doorway upon arrival and relive it a long time after.

My mother sees me as I step into the room. She rises still clutching my father's arm and gives me a cursory hug. I move to the other side of the bed and help pin him down. He's weak. The touch of him all paper skin and bone. There's spittle at the corners of his mouth and his lips are graven. At first his eyes are rolled back in his head but then he looks across at me and asks in his delirium what I'm doing there.

I came to see you.

They've put...

It's okay.

This thing...

I know.

I didn't want them to...

It's okay dad.

My dick...

It's all right.

I didn't...

It's okay.

I didn't want...

He grips my hand. His cannula hand. I look down at it. The cannula's up a grotesquely engorged vein. There are bruises around it. Bruises up his arm. He starts to thresh again. His gown rides up. His little mushroomed dick pops out. The drip tube flays. The catheter slinks on the bed. I can feel his hand digging into mine as he tries to get at it. He swears some more but his voice is grown weaker now. Told them I. This fucking thing. Told them. Told them I. Until his hand slackens and he starts to drift into some tortured netherworld. I glance across at my mother. She's looking at the wall above my father's head. Her face is pale and there are dark circles beneath her eyes. I ask her if she's okay.

I'm okay.

And dad?

They don't know yet.

Have they run tests?
Bloodwork and whatnot.
But nothing back?
No. They've gone to the lab.
My mother wipes her nose with a tissue from her sleeve.
What happened?
He took a turn.
This morning?
In the night.
She continues to stare at the wall above my father's head.
I thought that he…
That he what?
That he was gone.
She strokes his hair. It's difficult to know what to say. Really there's nothing to say. I look down at the heap of him on the bed. His breaths come in reedy gasps. Spit bubbles at the corners of his mouth. There are stains on the sheets. Piss or blood or shit. Blood in the cannula. A yellow stain on the hem of his gown. My mother wipes at the spit with the corner of a licked tissue. His breaths falter and there's a moment and then they come again. Gasping. Reedy. I look away. Out across the garden. It's small with crisscrossed pathways. A water feature. A sculpture. A birdbox on a tree for the patients to look at while they die. We are a time in silence. This is how it is. Panic and silence. Nothing to say. I look around the room. My father's cardigan is hanging from a hook on the door. His shoes are aligned neatly by the basin. I wonder vaguely how many people have come through here. Aligned their shoes. Hung up their cardigans. Died writhing on the bed with their wives or sons or mothers or daughters staring out across the lawn at the sculpture. At the water feature.
Piss.
Drip of it.
Drip of the drip.

People passing along the ward.

My father starts to writhe again. He cries out. Moans. My mother rises and presses her hand to his brow. The catheter slinks. Slithers. The tubes flay. The swearing recommences. His arm slips from my grip and then he has his hand on the catheter. He starts to pull at it. I see it slide out some. There's blood in it. Blood around it. My mother glances across at me imploringly. I manage to wrestle the tube away and pin his arm back down. His eyes are open and he's staring about him wildly but without recognition. A stain spreads across the sheets. My mother pushes the emergency button on the wall. A nurse comes. She glances over the bed end clipboard before going to my father. She checks his drip and the cannula and the bag filled with piss and then leans over him.

Now then.

Fuck.

What's all the fuss?

This fucking thing.

Let's just leave that in shall we?

I want it out.

How will you get better if it's out?

It's in my...

I know where it is.

In my dick.

Yes. That's where it's supposed to be.

Fuck.

This goes on for a while. She seems unconcerned. I suppose she's seen it all before. Heard it all before. My mother apologises. Says how unusual it is for my father to swear like that. The nurse says that's okay dear. They often do. She suggests we step out into the corridor so that my father's sheets can be changed. My mother wipes her nose and nods okay. The nurse calls for another nurse. We exit the room.

The floors of the corridor are polished clean but it still

smells of piss and shit beneath the antiseptic. Orderlies and nurses walk this way and that and sometimes pause at a desk to look at a computer screen. My mother and I go to the waiting room just down the way. She takes a seat in the corner while I stare out of the window at the carpark. Time passes. A woman cries as she puts coins into the pay and display machine. An orderly pushes a man someplace in a wheelchair. Visitors and patients smoke near the entranceway. A bus goes by on the street beyond. I ask my mother if she'd like a coffee from the vending machine.

I'm okay.

Are you sure?

Yes.

Or tea?

No. You have one though.

Heading down the corridor I pass one of the wards. There are beds on either side occupied by the ruins of men. A little girl and her mother sit by an elderly husk breathing through a tube. Another man sucks water through a straw from a plastic cup on his overbed table. Another man with a bandaged head reads a newspaper. I go on by. Out in the small carpeted lobby near the lifts dispensers of hand sanitiser are mounted on the wall surrounded by posters for diseases I might have caught during my visit and other posters list symptoms for things like bowel cancer and flu and chlamydia. The vending machine is in the corner and while waiting for my coffee to pour I stare at the floor and then I take the coffee to the window and stare out at the carpark. The view is much the same but from a slightly different angle. This is how it is. Panic and silence. Silence and panic. Looking at carparks. I drink my coffee and take a couple of painkillers.

The afternoon passes strangely. My father is unconscious from another hit of morphine and without the dual entertainments of swearing and catheter tugging there's not actually that much to do before visiting hours are over. Our vigil is thus defined by occasional trips to the vending machines and by the reading of magazines found on waiting room tables and by periods of quiet watchfulness with the drip of the drip and the drip of the pisstube bridging the silence. A few times my father stirs and there's some brief activity to break the tedium. Fluffing his pillows. Stroking his hair. Moistening his bloodcracked lips. Afterwards when the cotton bud swabs are dropped into a beaker of water the water will turn faintly yellow and there will be gristles of his bloodcracked lipskin afloat upon its surface. Periodically I will take his hand and look across at him and as before his gaunt pallor will call to mind my grandmother's dead face after they'd laid her out for us to see. After they'd embalmed her. Fixed her hair. Glued her together. Sometimes I will watch him to check he's still breathing and his breaths will now and then take too long to come and I will be on the verge of announcing to my mother that he's dead when he will breathe again and I will go back to reading articles about the best cufflinks to wear with striped shirts or why double vent suit jackets are not to be tolerated. I become intimately acquainted with the small room. Its sterile furnishings. The overbed table. The table by the basin. The drip bag. The four leg two hook drip stand. The catheter tube. The handwash laminate on the wall. The hand sanitiser by the entranceway. The commode in the corner with its plastic seat and pail into which my father is supposed to shit after pulling on the emergency cord above the bed. After the nurses have come. After they've disconnected his drip. Hoisted off his gown. Lifted him onto it. After they've arrived too late to find him crying in a pool of his own watery shit. Also in the room are the items my mother asked me to bring from home on my way here. The holdall containing spare underpants and toiletries for my father. His reading spectacles and fountain pen. My mother's unread book. Remember being in that empty house en route and foreseeing in its emptiness his coming death. Remember pulling up on the drive and seeing on the washing line the bedsheets from the night before still ringed with a halo of excrement.

Towards the end of visiting hours the nurse comes in to fix the drip and change the pissbag and then we are hugging him and saying our goodbyes. I turn to look at him as we leave wondering if it's the last time I'll see him. He raises his hand to wave and the drip tube sways and then we are moving down the corridor. I am impressed by my mother's fortitude but then as we are exiting the building she breaks down on one of the smokers' benches. I place my hand on her shoulder and there's nothing to say. She pulls a tissue from her sleeve but it's so shredded that I take one from my own pocket and give it to her and she cries for a long time while I look out across the carpark at the rows of cars and drifted leaves across the roadways from the half bare trees. After the crying is done my mother says fucking fucking cancer and then we head to the car.

I drive us home and my mother sits silently in the passenger seat watching the ploughed fields sloping away in neatly tilled lines and the skeletons of windswept hedgerows and as we approach the village an image comes into my mind of that last day down by the water meadow before I went away with the horses grazing and whickering down by the streambed. Then my mother asks me what I'd like for dinner. For this is how it is. Silence and panic. Chicken kievs from the freezer.

When we get home I go up to my room to phone Bea. I tell her that I may need to stay for a few days. She says not to worry about work. That they can cover for me and I should take as long as I need. I thank her and there's a silence in which I want to say something else but eventually just tell her

I'll be in touch with updates on his progress. After I've hung up I take up my sweater from the bed. The one she borrowed and returned to me laundered and folded. I sit with it on my lap feeling its fabric and staring down at the carpet. When I close my eyes that night I see the hospital room. I see my father with the tube in his penis. I see the raw sores scabbing around his arsehole when he rolls over. I see the ridges along his spine beneath the gown. I see the stains spreading across the sheets. And I replay in my mind the conversation I had with Bea in which she'd asked about my father. About what kind of a man he is. This was in the small hours after the meal was done and we were in the living room. At first I hadn't known how to answer her. Instead I'd stayed silent watching the night's rain on the windowpane. She'd shifted and looked up at me. Perhaps to see if I'd fallen asleep. Perhaps to gauge the impact the question had made on me. Eventually I told her that I'd never known him to raise his voice nor to speak ill of anyone. That his life was marked out in those small rituals that seem to define an existence. His long commute. Which necktie with which shirt. The Sunday crossword. Repainting the study. Going to garden centres with my mother. I told her also of the period many years back when he was out of work and had spent the afternoons with me watching cartoons and taking me on walks when we'd crouch beneath the cornheads and he'd tell me to close my eyes and imagine that we were by the sea. How sometimes I would do this and other times keep my eyes open so that I could watch him. That old vision of him with his hair golden in the summer light and the collar of his polo shirt rippling in the breeze. There was a long silence. I poured some more whiskey. Told her finally how such a life is rewarded. With degradation and misery. With suffering. How it seems the embodiment of a futile and godless world. When it came to dawn I roused her. Made her coffee and toast. Walked her back to her place with a light mist above the gardens and dew in the cobwebs hanging from the privet hedges along the way. On her doorstep I apologised. She was still in my sweater and had her damp clothes bundled up in her hand. She asked me what for. I told her the turn of conversation last night. She leant forwards and kissed me and then was gone. In the halflight I look at the sweater hung from the back of the chair. Look at the deep shadows about the room. Panic and silence.

The next day continues in much the same way though my father seems more sedate now and in the afternoon the consultant takes my mother and me into his office and tells us the good news. My father has a urinary infection that they should be able to clear up relatively quickly with antibiotics. It's only tangentially related to his cancer. He will need to be kept in for observation over the next couple of days but then he will be able to come home again. My mother cries. The morning of the fourth day the catheter and drip is removed and that afternoon we help him to the car for the journey home. He sits in the passenger seat and my mother in the rear and no one speaks.

In the evening I'm sitting with him on the settee stroking his back in slow circles the way my mother showed me a few weeks back. His head is slumped forward and his eyes are closed. My mother is in the kitchen making tea. Through his shirt I can feel his raised spine and shoulder blades. I look across at him. His hair thinned by chemotherapy. The deep cannula bruises on his hand. I look at the photographs on the mantelpiece. One of him from another time at a birthday party. Dressed up in a shirt and tie. Remember them sending me a copy of it when I was away. My mother's writing on the back. Happy memories of a happy day. I didn't even know when it was taken. Whose birthday it was. Had put it in a box and left it in a wardrobe with other such oddments. My mother's letters. Postcards from their holidays. Photographs of the garden. The village. Barely looked upon all those years. Rarely finding the time to call home. Sundays listening to the phone while I watched films in the living room and choosing to ignore it. Its echo in the flat long after it had rung off. On the journey home also. Bazaars and hutongs and half sunk luggers hauling coals upriver. Lunar landscapes of the steppe or tundra. Infecund wildernesses awaiting the coming snows of winter. Never pausing to write or to call. Never a thought. Presently my mother comes through with the tea tray. The pot in its cosy. A little jug of milk. The sugar bowl. Some biscuits on a plate. When she sees me she makes this face and shakes her head and I ask her what's wrong. She sets down the tray on the nest of tables by the settee and calls me into the hallway.

What is it?

The doctors said not to do that.

Do what?

Stroke his back like that.

I thought they said to.

They said not to now.

Why not?

They said it spreads the cancer.

Spreads it?

Like margarine.

I look at my mother in the hallway's gloom. At her grave face in the grave heavy shadow. Again that sense of abandonment. Of being here many years hence with all about me a deepening silence as of some final reckoning. Of closing the door one last time and going on to what end. To anniversary visits. To cleaning with a sponge their faded headstones. To a slow neglect as of those lichenous epitaphs in the churchyard rendered illegible by the years until all has passed out of existence and memory. We go back through and sit either side of my father. Put our arms around him. He leans back and we are like that a long time. Staring out into the silence.

I stay the next day. I call Bea in the morning to tell her I'm needed in the house to help out but will be back tomorrow or the day after. She tells that she won't see me for a while because she's going back home for a short break.

Home?

Yes. France.

When are you leaving?

Tomorrow. In the morning.

So I won't see you?

No.

I fall silent and she asks me if I'm still there.

Yes. Still here.

Are you okay?

Yes. I'm okay.

What's wrong?

Nothing.

You sound distant.

Really I'm fine. I'm just…

Quoi?

Sorry I won't get to see you before you leave.

She chuckles.

It's only a week.

I know. But still.

We'll go out again when I'm back.

Yeah?

If you like.

Sure. Let's do that.

Say hi to your dad for me.

After I've hung up I wander downstairs. My mother is in the kitchen. She asks me if I'd like breakfast but I tell her I'm not hungry.

Tea or coffee?

No. I'm fine. How's dad?

Still asleep.

I thought I might go for a walk.

Okay.

Just to clear my head a bit.

Where will you go?

Just up round the fields.

Before heading out I go upstairs to check on my father. The curtains are still closed and the bedroom is enshrouded in shadow. He's lying on his side and all I can see of him is the back of his head beneath the duvet. I listen for his breaths which come shallow and uneven. Outside there is birdsong but within only the uneven shallowness of his breaths and his form beneath the duvet rising and falling softly. I go to the curtains and lift them to one side and peer down at the garden. Fallen apples and leaves litter the lawn. The grass is unmown and flowers dead or dying wither in the borders of which my mother was hitherto so proud. Vineweeds grow through the fucked fence slats. I look down at the windowsill. My father's notebook. An old glasses case. A pot of pens. A dish of foreign coins. He stirs and I turn to look at him. See him rise half up and then crumple back down again. Half breathing half coughing. Then silence. I wait. Wait for his breaths to come.

I go by the Bryce house at the edge of the village. Past the garden and up into the meadow a path has been cut through the long grasses that grow there with wildflowers going or gone to seed. The bordering trees shed leaves that flutter through the shaded knots of the woods to the bosky floor. The day is unseasonably warm and the sky given to drifted cloud that casts across the valley sides tracts of light and shadow moving slowly east. A light breeze moves through the wildflowers and old seed heads sift amongst the grasses and the grasses at the sides of the cut path are still and then astir.

The meadow rises to a copse before which is an old rusted cow trough and beyond the copse the meadow rises once more to the upper treeline. I come to the cow trough and look into its rusted bowels. Plaits of algae cling to the sides beneath the green slag of duckweed upon its surface. Spidermites crawl along the leaves of the creeping thistles grown around the hull. I kick against the trough side lightly and a few peelings of rust are shaken loose but the choked pellicle of water remains rippleless. I continue on up to the copse and sit in the shade there against the trunk of a hazel with the husks and kernels of hazelnuts scattered in the dirt around it. Rooks are in the nearby woodland and I listen to their plaintive cries as I look back down across the meadowlands to her garden. All as it was and has ever been. The apple trees upon the lawn. The little gravel pathway to the pond. The white fence palings. Words from long ago in the shade of the copse and footprints in the meadow grasses leading by the trough down to the lawn from which light issues upon the flats of the meadow as it tapers away. See further back. Out in the fields after the hay had been harvested and set into ricks. Down below through the window of her room looking back to the copse. I look down at the ground and wonder vaguely why here. Why now.

When I get home the district nurse is there. She's in the bathroom with my father and has him sitting in a bath while she sponges down his back and the sores around his dick and arsehole. The water faintly pink. Sometimes my father will moan mournfully but generally the sound is of water rilling softly across his sallow skin. My mother is at the door leaning against the doorjamb neither watching them nor looking elsewhere. I go and stand by her as the nurse lifts my father's limp arm and sponges beneath his armpit and then squeezes water from the sponge gently over his head as of some monstrous baptism caricatured by the bulbous protuberances of his head neck spine jaw joints. All angular bone. Fibreless skin. We none of us seem conscious of one another. In a voice barely audible my mother asks of my walk but the question seems addressed to nobody and my barely inaudible reply is lost. I don't know the nurse. She's wearing a pinafore and mobcap and her tights are white and her shoes pointed brown oxfords. My mother tells me later that her name is Gladys and she lives at the top of the village and helps provide care for cancer patients. Her bicycle is propped up against the wall outside. Having never seen her previously I will see her many times hereafter and I will see her always as with my father that first time gently lifting his arm and sponging down his sores and squeezing baptismal water over his head. After a while I tell my mother I'm going to my room. She asks me if I'd like a cup of tea but I tell her no. I go on by.

Panic and silence.

\*　　　　　\*　　　　　\*

On the way to the club we start to lag behind the others until eventually they are gone from view. She asks me to wait for her while she goes into an off licence to buy some water. We are in an area of town I little know. I lean against a junction box and look up and down the street at the rows of restaurants along the pavement with their terraces demarcated by branded windbreak barriers and their branded awnings sloping from three storey redbrick buildings with baroque cornices and pediments angled against the sky. Cars and buses pass endlessly and people are disgorged in waves from the underground station along the way. The pavements are crowded with deeper pockets outside the pubs. Presently she materialises and we continue up the street before reaching a bench where she suggests we stop a while. I sit beside her and she pulls from her bag a half bottle of vodka.

I thought you went in for water.

This too.

I look across at her as she drinks from it. She's wearing an old leather jacket and against the turned up fur trimmed collar her skin is coldly pale. The delicate shape of her profile is traced out by the soft lamplight and as she lowers the bottle a residue of vodka glistens on her lips.

Here. Have some.

I take it from her and swallow a sip and go to hand it back. She gestures for me to have some more and I take another swig. She follows suit and afterwards rests the bottle in her lap and looks across at me with her mascara darkened eyes shining in the cold night.

We arrive at the club sometime later and the others are already lost in knots of vapour as it turns through a darkness wall to wall with the apparitions of revellers illuminated by the rigs of parabolic lamps pivoting and gyring overhead. Bea leans in and says something into my ear but I can't hear her over the concussive layers of noise pitching through the laser lit gloom so in lieu of a response she takes my hand and leads me to the cloakroom. Stood behind her I watch as she slips off her leather jacket to reveal a fitted white vest top that glows in the ultraviolet light with the curve of her shoulders showing preternaturally dark against it. After we've checked our coats she takes my hand again and leads me through the throngs of people to the bar and pressed against her as we wait to get served I experience a sensation of cocoonlike dislocation from the crowd. I look at the strip of bluish light across her shoulder. The strap of her bra beneath her vest top. The finer strands of hair along the nape of her neck. Behind the bar there's a mirror with our dual reflections sharply defined and those around us cut through with disparate light. The barman siphons through the gauze of a cocktail shaker an opaque liquid into two martini glasses and into the liquid zests the rind of a lime. He slides them across the counter on black napkins to a girl and then scanning the ranks of waiting customers gravitates naturally to Bea even though she is latterly arrived. I continue to watch as on tiptoes she leans across the counter to him and places her order. Now the nape of her neck. Now the verdigrised light of the bar upon her shoulder. She takes from her bag her purse and passes two banknotes to the barman for which return she receives two bottled beers and two shots. She pulls me to her side and we drink back the shots and afterwards the air is suffuse with aniseed.

Before finding the others she leads me to a corner behind one of the speakers and has me pen her in such that my back is to the dancefloor. She hands me her bag and looks furtively over each of my shoulders before reaching down inside her vest top. I watch her closely. Part shaded light plays in her eyes and searches out then casts in shade the lineaments of her face. Red through yellow through green through blue. Illuminates and shades the contours of her chest and fine tone of her skin. The feeling of dislocation from before intensifies with even the music seeming to fade. Her own eyes this time are upon mine and in their gaze the environs become consumed. I continue to watch her as she extracts from her bra a small wrap of clingfilm which she unpeels to reveal a single white pill. Into my ear she asks for the water from her bag and I hand it to her. She bites the pill in two and swallows half with a sip of water. The other half she places onto my tongue and transfers from her own mouth into mine another draft of water. I swallow back the pill and find that my hands are upon her waist and hers upon mine and our lips are in close proximity. She's smiling and I begin to feel her hips moving to the music.

Okay?

Yeah.

Enjoying your birthday?
Yeah.
Let's go have a dance.
Okay.
Stepping past me and starting across the dancefloor she places my hands on her hips and I watch from behind the movement of her body through the disintegrating crowd. Watch the turning licks of vapour from the fogger curl around her and the turning rigs of lamps strafe light glancing off her shoulders. Apparitions of people. Of revellers. Glances of their jet black eyes. Watch those eyes upon us as we cut through and jostle and steer and negotiate before coming suddenly upon them. Jon and Ben and Rachel and Rick. Rick with his arms aloft and his eyes dilated. Rachel in knee boots drinking cider through a straw. Bea finds her way to Ben and Jon. Tall Jon in a pressed white polo with his hair slicked back. Stocky Ben in an old band shirt and jeans. They greet her excitedly as she dances in between them and pushes against each in turn. For a while I stand there looking on. Yet gone is the jealousy I felt previously for even in the midst of them her eyes never leave me and there is besides a great ardour coursing through my system in which nothing much seems to exist beyond her and the easy fluidity of her movements. I watch how her body in the sometime bursts of stroboscopic light seems to leave teeming traces of its motion in the afterdarkness. How the laser light fanning out through the crowd seems to search her out and crest her figure. How in the rising crescendos of music she seems to rise also and inhabit the space in the flitters of broken haze rolling across the ceiling. I watch the spiked and matted outline of her hair take silhouette against further flashes of light. Watch how even amongst the tapestry of dancing shape around her she is separate. Solitary. Unalike. And soon she is beckoning to me and as I go to her I am engulfed by that selfsame solitariness

89

so that she and I and none besides exist. She kisses me and the taste of aniseed is still upon her lips and then in continuation of a dance flickerbooked by another burst of strobe she closes her eyes and starts to rake her hands through her hair in seeming solicitation of my gaze. Propagated snapshots of her body nickelled against the darkness. Her lustred arms. Lustred shoulders. Lustred phosphor of her skin. In the sequential aura of spotlights the transcendent interplay of colour across her neck and chest. Her softly shaded breasts. The curve of her torso. The strip of midriff between vest hem and waistband. Her eyes still closed and her arms still moving sensually through her hair the solicitation to gaze seems also to invite contact. She remains solitary in the darkness. The music little more than white noise. The backdrop little more than atomised wisps. Within me the fervour continues to build and as I step closer to her the air is filled with electrostatic pulses. Time decelerates. I feel something of her essence begin to encompass me even before I've touched her. And then almost without consciousness my hands are about her waist and she opens her eyes.

Sometime in the small hours she and I leave together. We take a bus partway home and with our coats on our laps and our arms pressed against each other the clamminess of the club sticks together our skin. Her head is resting on my shoulder and her hand upon my leg and I watch the almost imperceptible movements of her fingers on the fabric of my jeans. There's tinnitus in my ears but this only adds to the impression of encompassment. Of our being alone here on this crowded night bus. The dreadlocked tips of her hair bristle against my cheek and she smells of the club. Of dry ice and alcohol and the sweet musk of her sweat. Something else there also. Hints of the perfume she wears. The incense she burns at home. Vanilla. Cedar. Sandalwood. With her other hand she toys with the silver chain around her neck and I will sometimes glance down at it. I lose any sense of where we are for the outer world is obscured by the heavy reflections shuddering across the bus windows. In these reflections I look at her and me and see a natural togetherness. An intimacy. As if this is and has been since the beginning the way of things. She reaches across me and presses the stop button. I look from the window to see where we are but it's all still unfamiliar.

Where are we?

We can walk from here.

You're sure?

On se casse.

The bus comes to a stop and I follow her down the stairs and out onto the pavement. It's eerily quiet with neither traffic nor footfall and foxes slinking moonlit along the adjoining roadways. She takes my hand and we start along the deserted residential backstreets. Her pace is neither hurried nor ambling. I ask where we're going.

You know the old railway line?

I don't think so.

We can walk along it to get back.

Yeah?

She seems to sense the uncertainty in my voice and presses my hand.

It'll be fun.

Okay.

There was a mugging last week.

I look across at her to find her smiling. I try to read the expression in her eyes but can't quite make it out. Maybe she's joking. Maybe it's the thrill of impending violence. Farther along we come to a pathway that leads through a tangle of undergrowth. Not wanting to seem diffident I offer to go first and she steps aside to let me by. After climbing a steep slope we come out onto a broad track lined with trees.

You know it now?
No. I don't think so.
I came along here for a walk last week.
Okay. Which way?
She points left.
Towards the spriggan.
What's the spriggan?
I'll show you when we get to it.

In single file beneath the darkened mesh of near bare trees we continue on our way. Though approaching dawn there is yet no trace of light in the cloudless black sky. Sometimes I glance over my shoulder at her. She's using her phone screen to illuminate the pathway and with her body plunged in shadow she seems almost to float above its thin wake. Our footsteps on the gravelly track sound loudly in the empty night and though we go largely in silence a feeling of disembodied union lingers. Images from the club play out in the cold night. The continued disintegration of everything around us. Fleeting impressions of the others now and then penetrating. Somebody dropping a bottle of beer. Ben falling over. Rachel crying. But for the most part our shared isolation. And now as I listen to her rhythmic breaths overlaying mine it seems to grow in intensity.

We come to an old bridge above an empty street flanked by rows of dark shops. The bridge is covered in graffiti and in the trees there are torn shreds of plastic bags and about the ground discarded cans of beer and cider in the scrubby undergrowth. We lean over the wall and I look across at her. She draws her jacket around herself. A car goes by below and its headlights play across her features. She shudders and I move closer to her so that our shoulders are touching. She leans into me and I'm about to put my arm around her when she suddenly gasps and slips her bag from her back.

I almost forgot.

What?

She unbuckles it and brings out the bottle of vodka from before. She drinks back a mouthful and I watch the faint contractions in her neck when she swallows. Watch her eyes water. Glass over. Watch as she purses her lips. She glances at me. Faint smile. Proffers the bottle. I take it and drink. Slowly. Trying to taste a hint of her on its rim. Aniseed maybe. Maybe mint. The gum she chewed on the bus. We pass it between us until it's gone and the whole time she looks out below neither meeting my gaze nor shrinking from it.

We set off again and come to a series of darkened archways set in the wall where in the uppermost haunches of one she points out the spriggan with its one hand upon the pier and the other pushing forth beneath the keystone and through the kinks and knots of ivy a garland of leaves about its leering visage. She uses the light of her phone to illuminate these details such that the figure's shadow pitches darkly into the arch's crumbled haunches and shifts beneath the slewing veins of ivy. She moves the light down to the old brick of the arch and to the tags and throwups in the lower span with the layers of paint palimpsests faded and resprayed and to the adjoining arches with their spans' throwups and tags so too resprayed and to their bare haunches bedraped about the keystones with ivy and finally back to the spriggan to rest upon its garlanded head and cocked leg below. I glance only fleetingly at these details for my attention is upon her still. The way the light from the phone moves around her. Her upcast eyes. The tilt of her head. She switches out the light and we stand in the dark.

Later we reach an old disused platform and sit there with our legs hanging down from its lip into the dead stingers below and looking to the dereliction of the platform opposite with its sloping verges gnarled with old tree roots and wiry foliage. For a long time we are silent. The darkness draws around us until there is no platform. No pathway. No foliage below. I feel against mine her shoulder and thigh and feel rather than see or hear the cadence of her breaths. Our hands come to touch too. Still we stay silent. The tinnitus in my ears amplifies the womblike quiet of the night. I feel her fingers gently interlacing mine. The touch of them warm in the cool night. She says hey. I look at her. The light from the moon tracing out the shape of her lips. Her eyes. I say hey back. Sotto voce. She asks me what I'm thinking. I give my head a little shake and she smiles. Leans in.

We find our way out onto a deserted street ovalled with lamplight and lined with leafshed plane trees rising lamplit into the predawn sky. The road forks and forms in the interstices a small benched lawn cornered with the low boughed limbs of horse chestnuts. We cross the grass and scuff through the conker husks carpeted around the hummocks of the trunks with the shed leaves rotted and piebald from the summer hatchings of minermoths. Somewhere in crossing her hand finds the back pocket of my jeans and mine her waist and coming onto the pavement our shadow beneath the streetlamps lopes upon the flagstones. The road slopes down and along its flanks gabled townhouses graze the sky with their dormers reflecting pane to pane the silvered moon and in the privet hedges bordering their lawns the webs of orbweavers are hung with dewfall in whose silvered droplets the moon shines dimly. We skirt bins left lined for collection along the mosscracked walls and here my hand will clasp more tightly her waist and her hand in my pocket will press more firmly against me. Of this union we have not spoken and since leaving the pathway after the platform upon which we kissed we have walked in silence. Birdsong rises someplace distant. Eventually Bea speaks.

Do you think the others minded?

About what?

That we left without them.

No. They'll be fine.

Your housemate too?

Him too.

She draws closer to me. Rests her head upon my shoulder. Her hair against my neck. It's not until we come to the main street that she speaks again.

Are you happy?

About tonight?

Oui. Ce soir.

Really happy.

I watch our reflection morphing in an unshuttered shopfront.

And you?

Pareil.

When we get to our street we come to mine first and sensing my hesitation at the gate she guides me on by. Tells me we can go to hers as Becca's away for the weekend. I feel some of the strength go from my knees. Knowing what's foretold.

Okay?

Okay.

Dawn's beginning to break across the sky and a bus can be heard on the road below.

\*         \*         \*

I'm on my way to work when the call comes. My mother's voice. Cracked. Distant. I'm going to need you to come home. I'm so sorry. You need to come home. I ask how long. She simply repeats. You need to come home.

I'm at the foot of the hill. Traffic's queued halfway to the top. The trees scratched bare. The pavements wet from the night's rain. I tell her okay and hang up. There on the corner all is as it should be. A bus at the lights. My work keys in my pocket. The pub Bea and I went to last night. Everything sanitised. Ordinary. Neat. But the life drained from it. Rain debris grits the windows of the pub and its panes reflect dimly the grey morning. Debris from the night's rain clots the hill's storm drains and the headlamps of the waiting bus ripple sodden yellow in the murky film of the puddle before which it idles.

Surreal also. As if happening from afar. I look down at my phone. Check my recent calls to ensure it actually came through. Yes. Home. Nine seventeen. I replace it in my back pocket. Stare across the street at a wall. The prevailing emotion is one of numbness. The lights change and the hill's traffic goes on by before once more coming to a standstill. The wall wet. Grey. Cracked. Grown over with weeds. It's difficult to know how long I've been staring at it. And then for some reason I'm walking up the hill. Not back for home but towards work.

On the broadway I stop in a cafe as usual to buy a pain au chocolat and coffee and as I order it I can hear my own voice very distantly and as I speak I have only a vague notion that I'm forming words. I look at the barista and cannot decide if I've ever seen her before and the cafe itself is as if a facsimile of reality. The same decor and the same issuing of steam from the nozzles of the coffee machine and on the countertop the same arrangements of pastries with little handwritten price tags affixed to the hindmost of each tray. But something is off. Something not right.

I go back out onto the broadway. Spectres along the wet pavements. Everything washed out. Colourless. Everything in slow motion. All along the street there are Christmas star lights as yet unlit on the lampposts and in the snow sprayed windows of the stores lightless tinselled trees with empty gift wrapped boxes strewn about their bases. I look up at the church on the corner. Its gothic spire and finials jut against the sky and seem with the looking to lean. Something about Jesus on the yellow signboard below. Dark hints of the morning beneath the dull wet tracery of the gothic windows. I continue on my way.

Even today I'm the first to arrive. I unlock the gate and go through the carpark and open up the store. After I've shut off the alarm I stand in the punctured gloom. Christmas deliveries are picked on sack barrows and flatbeds by the entranceway. The winestacks show signs of yesterday's frenzied commerce. Some pared down to bare pallet. Crenulated. Cases dug into. Rags of old tape. Rags of old cardboard.

I turn on the lights. I rearrange the wines coffined in one of the trolleys. I wipe storage dust from a vintage port. I check a couple of orders. Check yesterday evening's scheduling for the day ahead. Finally I go into the office and unzip my coat and go to throw it over the back of the chair but it misses and falls to the floor and I leave it there while I smooth my hair in the dim reflection of the glass windowing the store. Looking out across the empty aisles the silence starts to intensify. I replay in my mind the conversation I had with my mother and hear in that silence the quiet resignation in her voice. You need to come home. I'm so sorry. You need to come home. Picture her with my father perhaps already dead. Leant over him. Her stifled sobs in the empty living room. In the dim glass the shifting focus between store and reflection starts to disintegrate. I look down at my hands on the desk with the numbness having rendered me inert and I think how much I want my father to die. I think what it will mean to be fatherless. How my mother will be in that house. Each room haunted with some grotesquery of his illness.

When I emerge Rachel is behind the counter going through the orderbook. I greet her and go into the kitchen to make coffee. My hands start to shake as I mound coffee into the cafetiere and while it draws watch the convection of the grounds in the liquid before plunging down the mesh. I pour milk and sugar into two cups and take it all out on a tray and stand by Rachel. She starts talking about the delivery schedule and I stare down at the counter and nod without listening. She extracts a sheaf of orders from the book and asks me if I'll pick them but as she goes to hand them over she pauses. Perhaps sees that I'm shaking. Drawn. Pale. She asks if I'm okay. It takes me a long time to answer and my voice seems not my own.

My dad's going to die.

She says what and I repeat it.

My dad's going to die.

She asks me why the hell I'm still there then and I tell her I don't know. I wanted to check in I guess. She tells me not to be bloody silly and starts herding me towards the door with her hand on my arm. Don't worry. Just go. We'll get cover. I tell her I don't know how long it will take and she says to take as long as I need and then I am outside with my coat on and my bag over my shoulder not really sure how I got there.

The surrealism returns. Is perhaps even more pronounced now. Most of the stores along the broadway are open and the lights in the windows are flickering and on one of the corners charity workers with a bucket are dressed as elves singing carols and their voices seem to follow me long after I've passed them. Down the hill I go by mine and head straight back to Bea's. It takes her a while to answer and because she's off for the day she's still dressed in the pyjama bottoms and faded shirt she was wearing when I left her and her hair is unkempt and matted about her shoulders. She knows almost immediately that something is wrong and asks me in for a cup of tea and as we sit there drinking it at her table I stare down at the mug cradled between my palms and feel completely blank and emotionless as I tell her that my father is on the slide and will imminently die. Even when she embraces me I feel nothing. She asks me if there's anything she can do and I tell her no. That I'll call her when I know more. On her doorstep we kiss and she embraces me one more time before I head off down the street once looking back to find her still there leaning against the doorframe watching me and giving a little wave and I wave back and continue on back to mine and it's not until I've gone up my garden path and am searching for my keys that I almost pass out.

The rest is a blur. Hurriedly throwing clothes into a duffle bag. Not knowing how much to take. Not knowing how long it will be. His death distilled into ruminations on the number of pairs of pants I'll need. The number of pairs of socks. Jas is at work and Rick's asleep after a night shift so I end up pinning a note to the kitchen corkboard next to Jas's cautionary missive about the necessity of our reaching some kind of agreement with regard to the washing up. Gone back home. Dad's ill. Not sure how long I'll be. Something like that. And although I hit ninety on the trunkroad home my journey is delayed by a layover in a layby because I think I'm going to be sick but it eventually abates and afterwards I sit on the bonnet looking down the carriageway at the traffic going by and later coming into the village the fields are all black and frostbitten and the lane broken with waterfilled potholes. After reversing up the drive I sit in my car with the house sombrely overlooking the lawn and its rainblack apple trees bare against the sky and the borders matted tangles of dead foliage. Unfamiliar bedclothes hang on the line.

I take up my bags and go straight through to the living room surveying it initially from the doorway. The furniture has been rearranged to accommodate a large hospital bed in the corner upon which my father will shortly die. There's a mattress flung with bedsheets next to it and a metal frame commode by the window. Around the commode are various lotions and wipes and a towel and around the room various medicines. By the bed a drip. My father is seated in his armchair with my mother on a kitchen chair beside him. She's leant over him clutching his hand. They don't see me at first. My father is in a hospital gown and slippers with tubes extending from his nose to an oxygen tank. Beneath the gown there seems very little of him. His arms and legs are cadaverously thin and the skin of his forearms contused on the undersides all along the veins and his hand near black from a cannula. His head is bony and angular. His skin grey green. Faint baby hair is starting to show through after the chemo. In sunken sockets his eyes appear bulbous and reptilian. I wonder if he's dead. If he died a while back and my mother is yet to move. She sits there staring at him herself near immobile. I think about knocking. I think about retiring to the kitchen to collect my thoughts. But then I hear his breathing. Gasping. Broken. Glottal. Part of me feels relieved by this and yet a larger part disheartened. That his suffering will continue. That I shall bear witness to it. I wonder which I fear more. My mother sees me as I place down my bags. I go over and hug her and it's not until I draw up another chair by my father that he slowly opens his eyes and sees me also.

What are you doing here?

I came to see you.

What a...

He seems to drift momentarily then come back to consciousness.

What was it?

How are you doing?

I'm okay. Just on the...

There's a long pause. He licks his chapped lips.

Just on the what dad?

On the what?

You were saying something.

Was I? I don't...

You said you were just on the...

I don't remember.

It's okay.

Is it the...

He looks about him. Seems to see me as if for the first time.

When did you get here?

Just now.

We weren't...

Weren't what?

What dear?

You said you weren't...

His head slumps. I look at my mother. She's facing the wall. Crying softly. We sit there a while in silence. My father breathes shallowly. Some way between sleep and semiconsciousness. His hand is in mine. I look down at it. The swollen veins. The blackened skin. The pitted nails. My mother asks me if I'd like a cup of tea. I tell her I'll make it but she looks across at me and gives her head a little shake and I understand by this that she'd like my father and me to be alone a while.

After she's gone I draw my chair closer to him. His eyes are closed. His lower lip sags and through the gap his teeth are yellow with plaque against his winedark gums. The skin sags around his neck and his collarbone juts out. Wires of hair scrub his sunken chest. Sometimes his fingers will twitch or a shudder will run through his body. His breathing will stop. Start.

I've started seeing someone.

The words seem to come from outside of me. Somebody else speaking them. I see that first dawn after the moonlit walk with the morning's light falling across the bedclothes. Her arm across me. I am awake lying prone with tinnitus still ringing in my ears and through the open window there is birdsong.

She's the girl from work I mentioned.

At the meadow. Down by the stream. You remember when mum was paddling and we were on the blanket? Bea from Beatrice. I wonder can he hear me. His head still slumped. Rattle of his shallow breaths as I describe her. How pretty she is. Her blue eyes and brown hair. The bridge of light freckles across her nose. Should I say how much I'd like him to meet her? That I'd like to hear them converse in French together? It rings too hollow. Thought about bringing her. Just so he could at least see her. See that finally I'd...

He briefly wakes. Looks at me through heavy eyes. Some kind of recognition there. Mumbles incoherently. Drifts off again. I sent him a letter recently. An expression in writing of everything I failed to say in life. Thank you for all the. I know it wasn't easy sending me to. I will always cherish the memories of. Sorry I never got to. Do you remember when we? I think it was because of this that. I've always felt so. Even though I might not have said so I. A way to ease my own conscience for my role as son. For the scant return for their love. Wonder if this is how all sons are. All children. Seeing with clarity too late and even then.

Presently my mother comes back with the tea. We take it to the settee pulled to the far corner of the room to accommodate the bed. With my father unconscious she tells me quietly how things are. The cancer has spread to his brain. He will die soon. Difficult to say how long. Maybe tonight. Maybe next week. All we can do is keep him as comfortable as possible. Speak to him. Be there by his side. Gladys will come in the mornings and evenings to help provide palliative care for him.

And thus do we pass the afternoon. With his periodic waking. With his coughing and the production from his mouth of gouts of various substances that my mother will wipe away with a tissue and toss into one of the many pulp bowls around the room. I will watch her stroke his hair here and there grown back blond. I become acquainted with each of the stains on his gown. Down his chest. Around his groin. I become acquainted with the medicinal smell of disinfected excretions. With the various swabs and fluids and lotions. One time he wakes coughing up bubbles of algal green phlegm that my mother wipes from his mouth and afterwards he stares at her with this look of almost primal fear in his eyes.

On towards early evening my mother informs me that Gladys will soon be here and perhaps beforehand I might like to go for a walk to clear my head. I offer some mild protestation but quickly acquiesce. I dump my bags up in my room. The smaller of the two is my workbag from this morning. I unzip it and take with some reverence the lunch Bea prepared for me. A tuna and cress roll wrapped in clingfilm. Carrot sticks and hummus. All neatly packed in a plastic box with a serviette. Remember watching her at the worktop. Her old pyjama bottoms. The faded shirt torn at the shoulder.

Half an hour later I'm on a verge along the lanes eating the roll with the view out over the fields below and a building of rooks wheeling in the sky and half an hour after this I return to find Gladys with my mother in the living room. The both of them crowded around my father who is awake though barely cognizant. Murmuring in pain. Eyes half open. Spittle. Stains. After a cursory greeting Gladys asks me if I'll help lift my father so we can take him over to the commode. I go over and position myself to my father's side and next to his wasted kernel I feel strong. Healthy. Young. We brace ourselves and Gladys gives the nod. My arm is beneath my father's and as we go to lift him he cries out in pain. A hollow kind of wail. Pitiful. Worse than anything I've yet heard. We set him back down. Gladys comes over to my side and I look at my father's gown and see a bloodstain spreading next to where I was holding him. Gladys says didn't you know and I reply about what and my mother says she's sorry she didn't tell me. Gladys leans my father forward and undoes his gown at the back and pulls it free so that he's naked. All shrivelled and thin and grey. She lifts up his armpit to reveal a lump of gristly black matter clinging limpetlike to his skin. The size of a pingpong ball. Purulent. Suppurating. Blood across its cratered surface and smeared about the skin to which it's attached. I say I'm sorry. My mother says it's okay. Says it's her fault for not telling me. Gladys uses a swab to wipe it down. My father winces. There are tears in his eyes. Gladys shows me another on his navel. Some kind of oily residue around it. Weeping from it. Green brown black. Pus. The residue staining down to his groin. Groin shrivelled and bald. Penis pink and raw. Sores. Sores actually all over him. Testicles. Thighs. All down his legs. Maybe bedsores. My father continues to grimace and moan as Gladys gently sponges the tumour beneath his arm. Telling her please stop. Please. I can't stand it. Please. My mother gently soothing him. Stroking his wisps of blond hair. It's okay dear. You remember Gladys don't you? She's here to help you. And Gladys saying nearly done now dear. It's nearly over. And my father saying please stop and what are you doing and please I can't take it and...

After he is semi pacified we set about lifting him once more. I take him with greater care beneath the arm and we guide him naked to the commode with the stained and yellowed gown a crumpled heap on the floor by his chair. He stands astride the commode on the buckled struts of his legs and supports himself on our arms as he waits for us to guide him down and after we have done so he farts loudly but does not shit and then a thin trickle of piss can be heard splashing plaintively into the plastic bucket beneath him. He is crying and my mother is still stroking his hair and I keep looking at his hands all knotted and thin and bony and patched with black bruises. After he has urinated Gladys wipes off his dick with a tissue and with another swab squirted with baby lotion wipes down his raw scabbed arsehole then tosses these along with her vinyl gloves into the plastic bucket. She asks me to run a bowl of warm soapy water and when I return with it she very gently gives him a sponge bath. He is leant forward on the commode over the bowl and water trickles across the back of his head and down beneath his ears and then she is lifting his arms and very delicately sponging his armpits and sides and chest down to his legs and in between his toes. My mother brings him a fresh gown which we pull over his head and afterwards it is put to me by Gladys that I might like to shave him.

Shave him?

Yes dear.

She lays her hand on my arm.

It'll be nice for you.

Okay.

For you and your dad.

I take the bowl to the bathroom. After rinsing it out I refill it with warm water and take from the plinth his soap stick and shave brush and razor and strop and from the drawer a clean washcloth. I lay these items out on an old tea tray and carry them with the water bowl back downstairs and when I come into the living room my mother and Gladys retire so that I can be alone with my father. They've seated him on one of the kitchen chairs by the patio windows and draped a towel around his shoulders. I draw up a chair next to him and with the warm wetted washcloth start to moisten his skin.

How's that feel?

Hm?

Is it okay?

Hm.

I work the washcloth over the growth of stubble across his cheeks and neck and jaw now and then rewetting it in the bowl with the dripped water blotting into his gown. His eyes are closed and his breaths come evenly and we are both of us silent with the only sound in the room the softly wrung water from the washcloth. After his skin is moistened I lather suds from the soap stick with the shave brush and apply this in circular strokes to his stubble.

Good?

Good.

Not too cold?

Hm.

I lather beneath his nose and over his mouth and with the tip of a pinched towel clear the line of his lip remembering the while his teaching me the same one afternoon long ago and sometimes in the studying of his face trying to recognise in some way the person he was but finding only the marks of his suffering. I take up his old straight razor and briefly work the blade on the strop before tautening his skin between my thumb and forefinger and shaving him on the downward bed of his stubble. Remember how we stood before the bathroom mirror with the cartridge razor and gel he'd given me that morning. Remember his showing me how to load the blade and lather the gel. How to manipulate the skin and cut with the bed. How to tap against the basin the blade to loosen the bristles. The silence now is punctuated by the cropped scrape of the razor. By its periodic swilling in the water. Sometimes my father seems to smile almost imperceptibly. His eyes remain closed throughout and whether sleeping or conscious it's difficult to tell. Remember my mother telling me how his sensitivity to touch had been heightened by the cancer. How she'd stroke his hair in the evenings. Stroke his back. Spread the cancer like margarine.

After I've finished I towel the razored lather from his face and massage balm into his skin while in the bowl the marbled suds of soap start to scum and bristles crust the opaque cysts of bubbles at its sides. I look at him in the light. Some ghost there of who he was. Some ghost of my father. Gladys and my mother come back in and my mother in looking at him starts to cry and Gladys places her hand on my shoulder and I smile up at her. In the bathroom I turn the shave brush beneath the tap to rinse off the lather and I remember him in the mornings at the bathroom mirror before work with the long mesmeric strokes of the razor. How sometimes his reflected glance would find me as I went by.

In the evening after Gladys has gone my mother and I eat a light supper in front of the television and share a bottle of wine and then later I go up to my room to phone Bea. The conversation is brief. She asks of my father and I tell her the headlines. I ask of the store and she tells me not to even think about it. After I've hung up I sit for a long while numbed and unable to move. Later still I take my mattress and bedclothes down into the living room and set them out on the floor. Night time the three of us are lying in the darkness with the December wind in the trees outside and my father asleep.

Are you still awake mum?

Yes sunshine.

Are you okay?

I'm okay. You?

Yeah.

There's a pause.

There's something I wanted to tell you.

What's that?

I told dad earlier.

Yes?

I'm seeing someone.

My mother doesn't answer for a long time. I hear her

crying. Eventually she speaks in a broken voice I will come to know so well over the next few hours days months years.

Who is she?

A girl from work.

From the store?

The new assistant manager.

What's her name?

Bea. She started just after me.

Did you say Bea?

Yeah. From Beatrice. She's French.

I hear her start to cry again.

I'm so happy for you.

Thanks.

What did your dad say?

He was happy too.

That's such wonderful news.

It's still early days but...

But you think it might...

I hope so.

Another pause.

I wanted her to...

To what?

You know.

In the small hours it starts to drizzle. My mother is sleeping fitfully and I'm standing over my father in the darkness. He's on his back with green spittle crusted around his mouth and his skin ashen. I'm not sure what woke me. Maybe the rain. Maybe something else. Looking down at him I don't know if he's dead. I listen and watch for his breaths but everything is still. Suspended. My heart is racing and I can feel my legs begin to give as I wait for some kind of sign. A murmur. A twitch. His death throes. Thinking how profound it would be for me to have woken because by some filial kinship I had sensed his passing. That perhaps his fetch was still there with me. But then he starts to splutter with bile gargling in his mouth and his chest wheezing. My mother wakes and hurries over. Asking what happened. What happened? Is he okay? Did something happen? I tell her it's fine. Go back to bed. He's fine. Rain crawls down the dark windowpane as we stand there looking down at him.

Gladys comes by in the morning to swab and disinfect the scabs putrefying around his arsehole and the blackened limpets of cancer in his navel and armpit. He lies there first on his side whimpering and then on his back whimpering with his eyes staring blankly at the ceiling and I wonder what's left of him. What really. She feeds him through his enteral tube and my mother uses a cotton bud swab to wipe away the bile from the corners of his mouth and to rehydrate his shrivelled tongue. He's given morphine and his whimpers start to die away.

Late morning there's a knock on the door and I answer it to find the vicar on the doorstep. I vaguely know him. Have seen him around the village on occasion. He's dressed in his surplice and tippet. Grey combed hair. Wire rim glasses. Holding a bible. I ask what he wants.

Your father has asked for me.

What?

Your father has asked for me.

What for?

He wishes to take communion.

I fight back an urge to laugh.

Communion?

Yes.

I don't...

May I see him?

Um...

But then my mother comes to the door and invites him in. Asks him if he'd like a cup of tea or a sandwich. He seriously thinks about this but then politely declines and she leads him through to the living room whereupon he goes to my father's bedside. I watch from the doorway as he takes my father's hand and opens up his bible and starts to recite a prayer. My mother is by the window looking on also. Biting a thumbnail. Tears in her eyes. I hear very little of what is said. Simply stand there watching the grotesque pantomime. My father continuing to writhe in a skeletal heap on the bed. Sometimes hacking up bile my mother tries to wipe away with a tissue. The hem of his gown riding up and his penis flopping around. His spindly legs kicking at the footboard. The vicar carrying on regardless. One hand on my father's hand and the other on the bible. Crossing himself. Crossing my father. The recitation of further prayers. The kissing of the tippet. The looking to heaven. His soft intonation lost in the tortured murmuring from my father's mouth. By the end I'm staring down at the floor wanting all of this to be over. Not just this laughable charade but the continuation of my father's agony. Take a pillow and hold it over his face. Something to silence those tortured invocations. As the vicar leaves he places his hand on my shoulder and tells me to be strong. I laugh openly. After my mother has seen him out there's a brief lull before Gladys gives my father the once over and tells us that it won't be long now.

She goes back to hers and an hour or so later my father starts in his delirium to writhe and claw weakly at the tubes in his nose and chest weakly clawing at the bedsheet covering his lower half weakly clawing at something in the air just beyond his reach his bottom jaw fallen back and when this agitation passes he starts to talk in words slurred and gurgling with all the mucus on his chest and my mother stroking his hair and me clutching one of his hands and with the other stroking his shoulder and he says I'm sorry he says I'm so sorry I'm sorry I'm sorry I'm sorry sorry sorry my dear

I'm so sorry oh I'm sorry writhing around and with tears in the corners of his eyes and my mother continues to smooth his hair from his brow and calm him saying you have nothing to feel sorry about why are you saying sorry it's okay dear you of all people don't need to say sorry but he continues in the same way I'm I'm sorry I'm so sorry I didn't mean I'm sorry so sorry please I'm sorry I'm sorry and my mother is sobbing and stroking his hair gently and his fingers in mine writhe and wring but there's no fight in him nothing left he keeps saying I'm sorry so sorry I'm so sorry sorry sorry sorry growing fainter into a whisper until his words are largely indistinguishable from the sound of his laboured breathing gurgling wheezing and after far too long maybe five minutes maybe ten he finally falls silent and I think he's dead and I put my hand on my mother's shoulder and her weeping is silent now the emotion almost spent in her but actually he has merely fallen into a light sleep a fleeting coma breathing softly and intermittently and sensing that the end is near my mother suggests that perhaps I'd like to have a few minutes with him on my own whilst he is still vaguely conscious and silently I nod my head.

She exits and then we are alone. My father and me. The crumpled raw scabbed heap of him beneath me. With each breath his sunken chest weakly expanding and falling. Bones outlined against his thin skin bones dimly lustrous in the dim light bones marrowed with cancer fingers still twitching wringing in my hand his head motionless but for the occasional tick spasm jerk. I lean in close to him so that my head is on the sheets beside his face and I can smell faeces urine disinfectant but also something more familiar my father's remnants his skin the fine strands of his hair and I put my lips close to his ear and hold his hand tighter and tell him in a whisper that I love him that he was always there for me that he made so many sacrifices for me that I never

111

expressed that much gratitude was just morose and irritable but loved him of course loved him never stopped always respected his intelligence his gentleness and as I am speaking his fingers sometimes squeeze against mine I don't know if by some tortured reflex or whether he can perhaps distantly hear me hear my cracked voice and as with him my words start gradually to become indistinguishable. I am close to him studying the lines of his brow his hair the bruises clustered around his veins on his chest by his tube a black spidered contusion his skin pinched clawed from within eaten by tumours of cancer clinging in clusters to organs bones cells clinging here here here here in balls from his navel here in balls beneath his arms remember my mother saying cancer attacks the thing you are started on his oesophagus to curtail love of eating worked to lungs the love of walking the woods and nature worked finally to his mind the love of crosswords languages grammar worked relentlessly through him a tide a mire somewhere beneath his lightly twitching eyes ravaging and strangling weeks months this gradual deterioration the hope and the setbacks and the slow realisation and the inevitable and inexorable succumbing to it clawing you down sucking the last vestiges of your humanity from you until you are shitting into a plastic bowl having your genitals sponged down having the scabs swabbed from your arsehole having tubes up inside you taking everything that you were devouring it slowly from within devouring everything that made you you lying now in swaddling stained yellow brown green hearing distant whispers hearing those light flaccid waves of drizzle that have started to fall against the windowpane before finally my mother comes back in creeps back in softly softly lays her arm across my shoulders and I hug her watching the drizzle the patterns it makes watching the trees beyond obscured by the rain watching the grey sky the foliage and then peeling away to the cold beyond to the back doorstep the garage cold and black and...

I stare into its dark recesses. A faint tremor in my hands. For a while I wonder if I might collapse but the feeling gradually subsides. I try to go over the past few minutes in my mind. What was said. What I might have said. The way the words were just there. Came tumbling out. A stream of fomenting ideas. I love you respect you you made so many sacrifices I'll always cherish the memories of. Yet there was a kind of empty ring to them. A lack of depth and emotion. Perhaps because my father wasn't really there. Was little more than a husk. More talking to the dead. And in talking to the dead or near dead with no belief in any hereafter how null it seemed. Wonder also whether I said enough. Whether years from now I will look back and wish I'd told him x. Told him y. Some lingering guilt also. Have I done enough? Been up to see him enough? I hear the sound of my mother crying in the living room and wonder if finally he's dead. I wonder if she might call me in when he's on his way out. Do I want to be there? Might it prove cathartic? Give some sense of closure? Will the moment of his death be clear? Differentiated from his slow succumbing? It makes little difference now. I've said my piece and his pain is almost at its end.

At length my mother emerges from the living room. I wait for the final announcement. The wearied proclamation that he's dead. But it's not forthcoming. She merely shakes her head. Mouths not yet. I ask her if she wants tea but she doesn't answer. Rather sits at the kitchen table and stares down at her hands. I boil the kettle. Make tea in the pot. Place the cosied pot with milk and sugar and biscuits on the old tray my father at one time would use to bring us tea in the mornings but has latterly been employed for the transportation of medical supplies around the house. We sit in silence waiting for it to draw and in silence after it's poured. Really there's very little to say. Suppose the real summation will come later. A precis of all that was said. All that could have been said. Could have been done. The locum who misdiagnosed him. The promises of the oncologist. People who came to visit and those who stayed away. Finally my mother tells me how proud both she and my father are of me and what a dutiful son I am. My mother who's barely left my father's side since his diagnosis. Has been intimately involved in his excretory urinary habits. Has fed him. Spoon fed him. Fed him through a tube. Dressed him. Changed his dressings. Witnessed in graphic detail his downward spiral into halfdead man rotting from within. And yet I am the one of whom they're proud. I look down at my teacup. I'm yearning for my father's death now. I want the relics of his passing to be distant and forgotten. Replaced by promised memories of how he was. How he used to be. I want him to be the photographs on the wall consummated by time. A part of me wants to go back through and witness his death. Witness each strangled second of it. Exorcising and purging with his last breaths the lingering memories of his cancerous suffering. And yet another part of me wishes simply to go to my room. Sit there and leaf through a magazine. Stare up at the ceiling. The underdusk fades as we are sitting there and his fetch seems almost with us. At the vacant space at the table. Or from without staring in at us through the darkpaned glass. His fetch seems sometimes to fill the vacant recesses of the house. The landing in the morning. His space by the fireside at night. On the doorstep gouging dried mud from the welts of his boots.

After the dusk has gone to darkness Gladys returns. She seems surprised to find him still breathing though by now he has slipped into a state of unconsciousness. We are again at our vigil by his bedside. Clutching his hand. Smoothing his hair. Fretfully glancing at one another each time his breaths grow faint. Gladys takes his pulse and checks his drip. It takes a while to find the former and the latter is perhaps of little importance now. After she's finished and after the dressings have been checked and the tubes inspected she tells us that she'll be back in the morning.

While my mother sees her to the door I stay with my father holding his hand and staring at him dispassionately. Searching for signs of life. For a flicker of recognition. A chance for a last goodbye. But there is little and I wonder again how we will know that he is dead. What that moment will look like. And I'm conscious as I stare intently down at him that I'm searching myself also. For signs of emotion. For sadness. And yet there is none.

We eat dinner off our laps that evening. Microwaved pasta and cheap red wine. Ineffably we stare at my father and listen to the intensifying rain on the windowpane overlaying his frail breaths. Occasionally I will feel my mother's eyes on me but I will intentionally avoid any kind of contact. After dinner we sit for a long time in the halflit gloom waiting for him to die. The dinnerplates on the side. The wine gone. Eventually my mother exhales and suggests that we try to get some sleep. I get straight into bed. The mattress and rumpled sheets are in a heap on the floor. Lying there I realise how utterly exhausted I am. I feel my eyes grow heavy and then suddenly it's three in the morning and rain is still streaking the windowpane and my mother is by the bed crying and frantically calling my name wake up wake up didn't you hear me calling you didn't you hear me calling your name wake up dad's dead dad's dead.

Wake up.

Dad's dead.

# PART II
## DISINTEGRATION

The window is open and the vernal breeze tousles the pot plant on the sill. The bed is a tangle of darkly creviced bedsheets with the duvet corner hanging off the edge of the mattress and her hair across the pillow. Strewn across the floor amongst the hair tufts and dust are trails of last night's clothing and on the bedside table wine dries mottled in the troughs of two fingerprinted wineglasses.

Out in the kitchen the matt ghosts of footprints fade on the floor. By the window a warmed square of light frames the pooled tallow of candles and the scattered ash of incense sticks. The window here is open too and the tunnelled breeze from the bedroom fans the nub of the blinds against the glass. It is nearing the end of March and we are not long moved here. Boxes as yet unpacked are still in piles against the walls. The kettle comes to a boil. I open the cupboard door above the worktop. Arranged within are our conjoined items of crockery from the move and the miscellanea we've bought together over preceding weekends. A pair of matching mugs from a trip to the country. Matching eggcups. A ying yang pair of salt and pepper cruets locked in embrace. I find Bea's favourite mug and mine and make us both tea and on taking it back through to the bedroom I brush by Bea's freshly dry cleaned trousersuit and laundered blouses hanging from the doorjamb and at the head of the stairs her new shoes are already set out. I place the tea on the bedside table and climb back into bed beside her. I lie on my back with my head propped on a pillow against the headboard and she lays her arm across my chest. For a long time we are like this with the softly wind slapped blind slats sounding against the windowpane.

Later she's fixing her hair in front of the full length mirror while I'm by the window overlooking the back garden. Her overnight clothes are laid out on the bed along with the presents she bought when she went back home just after Christmas. Pralines and calvados. Sucres de pommes. I look between her and the garden below where garden birds are upon the roofed bird table at garden's end and pools of rainwater sopping upon the tarpaulin furniture covers catch in the morning light. She makes a few final adjustments to her hair then turns sidelong to the mirror and smooths the hem of her fitted plaid shirt.

Are you sure about this?

I told you. You look great.

It's definitely not too casual?

You're not meeting the queen.

I know. But still.

Really. Stop worrying.

I go over to her. Stand behind her and put my arms around her waist and look at us in the mirror.

She'll like you whatever you wear.

You think so?

Of course. Look at you.

I slip my hands down the front of her jeans. She manoeuvres them back out again and takes up her makeup box from the chest of drawers beside her. I move my hands from her hips to her midriff. She moves them away again.

Can you just...

What?

117

Go over there.

Why?

You're in my way.

She shepherds me to the bed. I sit back against the headboard and watch her as she returns to her station by the mirror. She starts to apply her mascara before glancing back at me.

You don't have anything to pack?

No. I'm all ready.

Do you have to keep watching me like that?

Like what?

Like that. You're making me nervous.

I've nothing else to do.

Take your stuff to the car.

How long will you be?

I'll be quick.

You always say that.

I will this time.

You always say that too.

She makes a shooing gesture. I grab my bag and kiss her on the cheek and head outside. Though it's still cold and the night's rain clings yet to the woven strands of foliage by the pathway the wetted flagstones up and down the street are patched with sunlight through the broken layers of cloud. I lean back against my car and close my eyes and after ten minutes or so Bea is beside me with her bag over her shoulder and a cableknit jumper over her shirt.

Ready?

Ready.

She climbs into the passenger seat and as I drive us out of town she applies lipstick in the sun visor mirror and fixes her hair. En route we buy flowers from a petrol station and these she keeps in the footwell between her feet the rest of the journey now and then rearranging the bracts and corollas.

We go over the viaduct and I name to her the towns splayed below and above the mirrored marshlands at the foot of the piers waders stalk or fly and along the towpath of the canal walkers pass glazed plashes in the track mirroring the sky. Soon we are upon the lanes and I name to Bea the hamlet through which we pass and tell her of the walks and of the pathways across the fields. Approaching the village she places her hand on my neck and starts to stroke my hair and any misgivings I might have had about my being back again are soon allayed. We go by the Bryce house on the corner and I glance up at it and at the sloping meadow through the broken undergrowth but little stirs in me. Little stirs at the sight of those broken meadow grasses sloping to the copse or of the windowpanes of the house glazed by the flattened light of day. Throwing off road spray to the tangled verges along the Bourne we go by the old farmhouses and bus stop and the meadow on the corner yet these too are without undercurrent and soon we are pulling up on the yard. At the window of the kitchen my mother looks out and even before we've gathered our bags from the back seat she is there to greet us. She's clearly dressed for the occasion in a mauve cardigan and pressed grey slacks with her hair set and a brooch pinned to her lapel. And yet.

I make the introductions. Mum this is Bea. Bea this is mum. My mother beams. Hugs Bea and tells her how nice it is to finally meet her. That she's heard a great deal about her. That she's been looking forward to this so much. Bea reciprocates and then my mother comes to me and hugs me also and tells me Bea's even prettier than she'd imagined and that it's so wonderful to have us here. I tell her okay. Shall we go inside.

A frangipane on a cake stand cools upon the kitchen worktop and the table has been set for tea with the special occasion teacups and saucers and the matching milk jug arranged on a tea tray. With a look in her eye my mother suggests I might like to take our bags upstairs while she and Bea put the finishing touches on the frangipane. Bea nods her approval so I go on through to the hallway and at its end before mounting the stairs stand on the threshold of the living room looking in. Of its morbid history there's little sign now. The bed was taken out with the body and the settee now occupies its old position in the corner. Only simulacra remain. My father's reading glasses on the nest of tables by the armchair. His dictionary down by its side. On the old tea chest his crossword pen and tissue box. From the kitchen my mother and Bea talk softly and there's a measure of unreality in the quietude. I try to picture my father as he was in the photographs on the units and I try to picture the wreck of him on the bed but no images come to mind. As if nothing of him remains. I slowly withdraw and stand in the hallway watching impressions of my mother and Bea in the kitchen. Bea with a sieve sieving icing sugar. My mother with an old wire whisk whisking cream. The smell in the hallway of floor polish. Of home indefinable. Ascending the stairs the treads of the steps sound beneath my feet and dust given body by the windowlight above slowly turns in the cold air of the landing. At the stairhead I look down through the window to the street corner below upon whose grassed verges a willow grows and of this willow and its history I see only dim suggestions from long ago.

I go on along the landing and then to my room where I sit on the corner of the bed smoothing the neatly folded towels my mother has placed there. The fish tank filter purrs purling spume from the elbow of the uplift but aside from this my room as the house is quiet and still. I tap on the tank glass in whose algal waters a ghostkoi librates over a length of furred bogwood but it remains motionless. I listen for the sound of their voices downstairs. For some trace of my father along the landing. Yet nothing remains. I survey my room and its relics of old. The withered plants. The dust furred bottles along the lip of the wardrobe. The unit upon whose shelves old folders from school are lined and upon whose sides are tacked snapshots from school or home or holidays or nights out of old. The one of us on the bench by the pond. On a hayrick with the molten sun yonder. The tank filter purls spume. Fine plumes of bubbles in a flurry rise to the surface. I listen again for my father. For their voices downstairs. For any trace of being. I close my eyes and listen to the deepening silence through the house and try to conjure some emotion at my father's death. Sadness or remorse. Anger. But all that comes is a kind of weightlessness. These past months no real attachment to reality. Rather days without recall. Some nights finding myself sleepless at the window staring at the night sky or at some transmuted reflection on the glass. Finding myself unable to reconfigure in my mind any fragment of his being.

When I go down again they are the two of them seated at the table. Spread before them are the cosied teapot and cups upon the tea tray and upon the place settings porcelain plates with pastry forks on napkins and in the centre on the cake stand the dusted frangipane garnished with blackberries. My mother asks me if I'm okay. I tell her I'm fine. That I was just going through my things. I take my place beside Bea and she touches my arm. My mother asks whether Bea might like to cut the frangipane while she pours the tea and there follows some ceremony to both. Questions are asked regarding the consumption of tea in Bea's family and whether they take it with milk and whether the milk or tea goes in first and the conversation is met on both sides with unwavering fascination. Another conversation follows regarding frangipane and its preparation and how best to blind bake pastry and I enjoin the conversation little for I'm pleased by its meaninglessness. Pleased that for the first time in many months a meeting with my mother does not revolve around my father's mortification or funeral or the wording of his headstone's epitaph. Pleased that the focus is not on me or my suffering in the midst of his coming death or its aftermath. The only signs of it now are my mother's occasional glances at me across the table and though these are infused with melancholy there is something else evident that I take to be pride. Pride in my being with Bea and melancholy that my father never got to meet her. When she talks with Bea I take occasion to look across at her. See much of the life gone from her eyes. Her hair greyed and her face lined. I will look at Bea besides and see in her the contrast of youth. Will look then at the kitchen's fossils. My grandfather's old scales on the worktop. His old dented pan on the stovetop. On the tabletop one of my grandmother's ivory handled knives tarnished and misshapen from repeated sharpenings. An old sand timer. An old egg timer. In the corner some old shrivelled conkers collected one autumn and bored with awls for strings but left unused these many years.

When I first take Bea up to my room she slowly inspects it. Studies the posters on the wall. The books on the shelf. Studies some of my old drawings. The photographs on my old workstation. Sometimes reaching out to touch them or to smooth their edges. One of me with school friends after we'd finished our exams. Flares and turtlenecks and safari suits. Another of me with a wayfarer met en route during my gap year. The tops of our heads balanced with beer bottles. A palm beach background. She gravitates towards one at the centre.

Who's this?

I know the shot she's referring to even before I see it properly. Overexposed and faded. Two figures seated on top of a haystack.

Just an old friend.

She moves on. Handles the old stiff paintbrushes in the plastic cup teasing the tips of their bristles. Flicks the shutter of a camera I won at a fete. Rattles plastic bullets in an old whiskey tin. I watch her the whole time. Watch her fingertips travel over the surfaces and come to rest and thumb the spines of books on the shelves. Watch her sit on the edge of the bed and tap the glass of the fish tank. The fish unmoved spits sucked grit. Watch as she leans back and with her fingertips touches upon the wall the brush marks of paint and the skinned discs of paint from the tack of old posters. I go to her. Kneel by her and stroke her hair as she stares up at the ceiling and then across at me. I lie beside her. Start to caress her. The cloud breaks and the sun comes cold and rimy through the windowpane.

Late in the afternoon we go for a walk. Heading out of the village the lanes are quiet and we are soon on the path down by a stretch of the Bourne used as a drainage channel for the sloping coombes. The field to one side has been left fallow and the weedy soil is cobbled with flint and here and there whitened by chalk and the field to the other side grown to grass with sheep ranging its uppermost slopes. Clouds crested by the sun are at the southern periphery of the landscape. The Bourne is near to full with its ferric bed lain thick with writhing plaits of reed and the teaselled undergrowth of its banks weeded with dead sprays of cowparsley and sedge. Gasguns discharge at intervals and from the woodland woodpigeons and carrion birds will scatter to the patchwork sky before coming to land amongst its shaded depths.

At a crook in the Bourne we come to a bridge and we lean for a while on its rusted rail and look down into the passage of the water below and I remember something of my being here of old when in the summertime we would make camps beneath the bridges when the Bourne ran dry and the air would be dank and cool and the concrete hung darkly along its joins with stalactites and how on primary school trips we would come down this way for picnic hikes or to sketch the fields for art projects or to meet the farmers who worked the land. We cross into the woods with its bosky undergrowth all overgrown with dead briars and the slopes clouded with dead ferns and the fallen boughs of trees furred with mosses and the path we take cuts up across its hillocks and down amongst its troughs and in the less densely wooded sections the ground is furrowed by rabbit warrens and where there are birch trees the bark has here and there been stripped on its lowermost trunks and in the woodland floor are the cloven tracks of deer and I remember being here with my father collecting wood for the fire or in later years following the deer tracks and seeing the herd in the hoary tracts of woodland with at its head a great stag whose breath clouded the air.

On the far side the woods open out to meadowland and as we come upon it wind sweeps in waves across its undulant slopes. We find a bench on the pathway that skirts the woods and sit the three of us on its dampened slats and watch the low sun over the meadow. Dew is already starting to form and hang in a spectral mist above the landscape and on the cold wrought arms of the bench. The woods darken to a limpid black behind us and the duskwept sky slowly subsumes the distances. Subsumes the cottage at the edge of the next field and the faint animal tracks crossing the dewy meadow and the treeline beyond. We are there neither moving nor speaking until the sun is descended.

Back home I light a fire and Bea in her jogging bottoms and sweater sits at the hearthside and stares into its slowly collapsing lattices of kindling as it begins to take and hiss into the sooty flue. I leave her there and go to seek out my mother in the kitchen where she's busy at the worktop. I ask her if she needs a hand but she tells me she's fine. I watch her work the tip of a knife blade into a leg of lamb and into the slits push rosemary and garlic and then across the skin rub oil and seasoning. She glances up at me and asks me how I'm feeling.

I'm fine.

It's not too difficult being back?

No. It's okay.

Bea seems lovely.

Yeah.

Really nice.

I'm glad you like her.

I'm so pleased for you.

Thanks.

You deserve it.

And then after a moment's hesitation

Would you like to see your dad?

What do you mean?

His ashes.

She gestures to a cardboard box standing on the dining room table.

In the box?

Yes. You don't have to.

No. I want to.

She seems on the brink of saying something more but I go on through before she's able to and close the doors behind me. The room is lit by a single lamp and the curtains are not yet drawn. The tabletop is bare but for the box. I look at it for a long while. Look then at the photographs along the unit where the lamp stands. Family portraits through different eras. Me with my parents. Holidays we went on. My graduation. I step at length to the table and take up the box and pull from inside it the cardboard scattertube containing the ashes. I'm surprised at how heavy it is. I hold it to the light and turn it in my hands. It has a woodland scene printed on it. Birch trees surrounded by bluebells. On the lid there's a bow and a small loop of string for opening it. I'm not sure of the protocol. Whether I'm supposed to look inside or not. I replace it on the table and step to the window. Across the back garden the living room is visible at the side of the house and light from the window illuminates the bank of leylandii bordering the garden. The moon is risen and the sky without cloud. I hear my mother in the kitchen. Hear the roar of the oven as she opens the oven door and the clangour of the roasting tin on the oven racks. I imagine Bea at the hearthside watching the embers of the fire and from here the corner where my father died is also visible and so I turn from the window and look once more at the pictures along the unit and then go back to the scattertube. I slide it across the tabletop towards me. Hesitate. My hand readied on the lidstring. Finally pull it off with a hollow pop. The aperture in the lid is narrower than the width of the tube and the ashes inside plunged in shadow. I take it and angle it towards the lamp and the light catches on the contents such that it dully glisters. I give it a little shake but nothing moves inside. With the tip of my finger I press lightly into it and rub some of the residue into the palm of my hand. It's damp and smears my skin and then with a little pressure is almost gone. I look up at my reflection in the windowpane wondering again whether my father's fetch might be there with me or whether some of his being might somehow have transmogrified to me but there's only absence. The scattertube merely a vessel and its ashes amorphous and without meaning. I replace it in the box and am about to leave when I see amongst the pictures on the unit one of my father in a dinner jacket with behind him an arched gothic window and I recall the night it was taken. An alumni reunion at his old college shortly before he fell ill. How I'd gone to pick them up at the station afterwards and they'd sat the both of them in the back for the journey home with the lights of passing cars sometimes drifting over them. Something almost childlike in their bearing.

After dinner around the fireside gifts are exchanged. Bea gives my mother the sweetmeats she brought and my mother in turn gives Bea a spring scarf neatly wrapped in crepe paper and tied with a bow. Bea tries on her scarf before the mirror and tells my mother how much she loves it and afterwards she and I sit on the settee and my mother in the armchair opposite and we drink coffee and later brandy with the pralines and talk long into the evening while embers glow in the grate and outside the wind picks up and the patio windows softly shudder. Sometimes I become conscious that we are sitting where my father died. Sometimes I look across at a photograph of him on the unit by the hearth. But it registers on only a superficial level as the fire quietly turns to cinders.

We leave early the following morning. My mother waves us off as we head down the drive and for much of the journey home Bea and I are silent. In the afternoon I go to buy groceries. The road is flanked on either side by restaurants and cafes and bars and grocers' stores. Beneath the awnings of the latter tiers of fruit crates are filled with papaya and honeymango and gourd and apricot and yam and plantain and scotchbonnet and the doors are without shutters for the stores never close and in the windows of the former stainless steel caterers' trays are oiled with bellpeppers and lahmacun and upon the griddles skewers of meat are turned over the coals to char. In patisseries royal icing warps on weddingdress cakes and quenelles of baklava dusted with pistachio bake on sunlit platters. Headscarved women thronging the glass counters within are handed ribboned boxes of cookies and sweetmeats. I buy eggs from a delicatessen on the corner in whose window display guineafowl and poussin and partridge are trussed and in a store just down the way I find flatbreads and smoked fish and yoghurt and dill. At home I soft boil the eggs and mix the yoghurt and fish with the dill and arrange them with the flatbreads on a platter and we eat at the table with the television on and afterwards take coffee to the settee and there remain for much of the afternoon watching films until the light starts to die outside. We order takeaway in the evening and I iron Bea's blouses for her against her protestations and prepare her a packed lunch of parcelled flatbreads with the fish paste for the following day when she will start her new role in the head office's human resources department. She starts to fret before bed. Checks and rechecks her bag. Ensures she has the documentation they told her to bring. Plans her route and leaving time and sets two alarms. I open wine but she drinks none and I take only a glass.

In the morning I get up with her before seven even though I have the day off. I make breakfast while she showers and we sit down at the table to it but she's distracted and eats little. I put my hand on hers but she pulls it away.

Are you okay?

Just a little stressed.

I'm sure there's no need to be.

I've never done this type of work.

You'll be okay.

J'espere.

And you know what's her name.

Lisa.

So you'll have a friendly face.

I guess.

I'll make us a nice dinner this evening.

Will you?

Of course.

What will you do today?

A bit of unpacking. There's still those boxes.

You don't want to wait for me to help you?

No. Most of it's my stuff.

After breakfast she goes to the bedroom to get ready while I clear the dishes away. She emerges a while later in her trousersuit and blouse with her hair up and makeup on and something stirs in me. Maybe pride. Maybe jealousy. Jealousy that she will be like this amongst unknown men. That I will be left behind on the shopfloor and she'll soon tire of me. I go to her and put my arms around her.

You look great.

You'll muss up my hair.

I kiss her. She recoils a little.

And my makeup.

She smiles back at me.

I'd better go.

I'll come and see you off.

You don't have to.

I want to.

She takes up her leather bag and slips on her heels and I follow her down the stairs and out onto the street and watch her until she is gone from view. I stay there a while after. Traffic goes by and the sun glazes the night's rain upon the roadways and pavements. Back upstairs I drink coffee at the table. The flat's quiet after the preceding commotion. I look at the boxes that need unpacking. I watch television. Clean the worktop. Look from the window at the street below. Eventually set to unpacking. My old folders I stack on the top shelf of the wardrobe. The same with my old artbooks and sketchpads. There are years' worth of bank statements and bills I've been meaning to go through but never manage to find the inclination. These I slide to the very back. In the kitchen I unpack boxes of pans and crockery and stack them haphazardly in the units and arrange upon a shelf some old ornaments. A set of sake cups. Some glassware of Bea's. An empty picture frame. Finally I come across a box marked home etc. A box I never unpacked even in my old place. Had it against the wall behind the clothes rail covered with shirts and jumpers. I brush the dust from it and peel off the packing tape. Inside old books. A photo album from my secondary school days. Some old scrapbooks and ticket stubs. These I pull out one by one until I find at the bottom my old shoebox. Taped and retaped these many years but for a long time left unopened. I bring it out and lay it on the tabletop. Get a knife from the drawer and sit there with it before me. My real purpose in going through the boxes today was to find it with Bea away. To open it and luxuriate over its contents. And yet I hesitate to do so. I look across at the unit on the far wall and see Bea's books intermingled with mine. See the framed photograph of us on the river that time. See on the settee her dressing gown and on the coffee table her last night's mug. Wonder then whether it represents some kind of transgression. Whether it might rouse in me feelings I had hitherto forgotten. And so I take it back to the bedroom. Place the chair by the wardrobe and stand upon it so that I can push the shoebox to the back. Back with those relics of a past remote and fabled.

*       *       *

I'm standing in the entranceway of the new store to which I've been promoted. It's warm out and across the carpark fumes rise from the petrol pumps of the adjoining garage. I'm already on my third coffee of the morning and the day ahead promises little occupation. It was Bea's idea for me to go for an assistant manager's position and I reluctantly interviewed for this one and despite my almost pathological indifference to the questions they asked me I was successful. It's a satellite store with its one main advantage being the general lack of custom. Hours can go by without patronage. Because of this it's not unusual to work alone as now. I'm about to go back inside when a car pulls in to the parking lot and a man climbs out and heads over. He's in his fifties with fair thinning hair but it's his clothing that really sends a jolt through me. A shirt and old college tie. Pleated trousers and brogues. The jacket especially. The same colour. Cut. Fabric. Everything. Right down to the brown buttons on the cuffs. He smiles as he steps past me and I'm transported to that gravel carpark on the outskirts of town not far from the industrial estate and refuse site. The building itself is unremarkable. A squat brick structure with casement windows and a small porch. At the entrance we are greeted by a receptionist who leads us into a waiting room and offers us tea. She's middle aged with her hair in a bob and glasses hung from a chain around her neck. My mother takes tea. I fill a plastic cup from the water cooler. The room is sombre. Manifestly uncluttered. Sconce lighting. Plain white wainscoting beneath lilac walls. Clusters of dark wood furniture arranged with almost geometric precision around the small space. The receptionist's long faux leather padded desk. Dutchback chairs with dark green trim. A coffee table with fleur de lis print coasters and a small pile of brochures. I flick through one. Biodegradable cardboard. Brightly coloured lids with cartoon prints for kids. Ornate oak. Dark mahogany with scrolled gold handles. The receptionist brings out my mother's tea on a tray. Cup and saucer. Tongs for sugar cubes. A biscuit in a wrapper. She sits with us and asks if we are both going in and whether at the same time or alone. My mother by way of question looks at me and I tell her I'd prefer to go in alone. I suppose this is the day before the funeral but it's all quite difficult to remember. The receptionist tells us there will just be a short wait. Asks us if we have everything we need. My mother says yes. Thanks her for her kindness.

131

After she takes leave of us I remember the days following his death. Sitting around with my mother with little occupation. Not knowing how to mourn. Not knowing what guise it would take. Not understanding why I wasn't already overcome. My mother crying intermittently though not often when she was around me. Seeing it instead in her eyes after she'd been absent. We watched television in the evenings and took turns to cook. She suggested I might like to go back for a couple of days. Back to my new life. See my friends. At first I resisted but she said it was fine. She would have to get used to being alone at some point and she was sure a break would do me good. And so I left. Driving out of the village that morning the sun was shining and glazing the damp road and the damply glistening verges and the dewdamp webs hung from the dead teaselheads amongst the grasses. The sun was low and the lanes soft and orange with a faint low mist rising from the coombes and in the sky dissipating contrails. At the end of the coombes where the field divides I pulled into the layby and turned off the engine. Dew upon the rusted ribs of the half hinged gate there. Upon the half rusted tangles of barbed wire strung from fenceposts sunk amongst the thickets. Silence of that lonely stretch of road. The faint birdsong through the open windows. In the rearview mirror the houses at the periphery of the village. The Bryce house. The meadow aft. Feeling then something akin to bliss. Feeling my father there with me. How long was I parked there? A few minutes. No more. The fenceposts leading to the upper banks of the coombes demarcating the route in days gone by we would walk on Christmas eves. My father and me. Along via the golf course and the old stables of the hamlet. Returning in the darkness to my mother. To the fireside. To mulled wine and homemade sausage rolls and mince pies warmed in the oven. Driving on again the feeling remained. His presence there with me. That newfound sense of rapture. Stayed with me as I arrived at the house an hour or so later. My flatmates making me tea. Tentatively asking after me. How I was feeling. Whether I needed anything. Saying no. Everything was fine. Really. Everything was fine. Alone in my room at the window looking out at the sun through the trees a sense of profound calm. That everything was as it should be. Going along later to hers. After her shift had finished. The street dark and some of the windows still aglow with Christmas lights but the pavements slung also with old trees from whose wet brown boughs needles fell and rotted amongst the hacked dead trunks. That look of surprise as she opened the door to me in her old frayed pyjama bottoms and frayed knitted jumper. The receptionist gives me the nod and then I'm led through. The corridor the same plain uncluttered lilac lit with dim sconces. At the next door the receptionist respectfully steps aside and tells me that I should take all the time I need and then she is gone and I am in there with him. It's the first time I've seen him since he was taken away that morning. The lighting in the room is diffuse. The walls pale magnolia. The carpet a deep burgundy. My father's casket is at the far end with chairs either side and a crucifix mounted on the wall above. There is a small frosted window off to the right framed by a net curtain. A vase of flowers. A table has been set out by the entrance with a carafe of water and glass and a box of tissues. As I close the door behind me the room falls silent. I stand there for a long time. Skin prickling. The casket is unadorned oak. The least remarkable in the catalogue. Plain handles and white velour trim. I pour a glass of water from the carafe and drink it unevenly. The sound as I replace it on the table echoes around the small enclosure. It crosses my mind simply to turn around and walk out again. To satisfy myself with the fact that I was there when he died and have no real compunction to see him again. But I'm walking towards him regardless. I know the details. The embalmment. What the procedure consists of and what to expect. Expect an effigy. A likeness. An approximation. Yet my skin continues to prickle as I approach and when he comes into view I remember my grandmother after they'd laid her out at the undertaker's. The same grotesque lustre to the skin. The same pinched lips. The same sneer. His cheekbones are sharp and his downturned mouth glued and yellowed at the corners. They've combed his hair. Trimmed and combed his eyebrows. Glued his eyes. Something unnatural about the lids. Wonder what's beneath them. Marbles. Ping pong balls. Or do they leave the eyes? Inject them with what have you? Chemicals. Formaldehyde. Remember my father's eyes. Though even now don't know were they green or blue? Grey maybe. Almost expect some kind of movement behind them. A flicker. Look at them a long time waiting. Look at his lips a long time waiting. To part. Part and draw breath. He's wearing a coarse tweed sports jacket and striped college tie with shields. His hands are resting lightly on his stomach and his lower half is covered by the coffin's foot panel. Seems smaller. Miniaturised. Will myself to touch him. Touch his hand. Touch his face. Reach out. Draw back. Wonder how long I have in here. Will they come to get me? I continue to stare. Waiting. The silence cryptal. I reach out again and this time touch him. Touch his face. Touch his cheek. Stupidly surprised at how cold he is. How unyielding his skin. I touch his hair and his hands. Everything abstract. Denuded of all feeling. This surreal form beneath me. For a long time unable to look away. Look at his nails. His neck where it meets the collar of his shirt. Wonder what's beneath. Whether they only polish up the bits that are visible. The rest all falling away. Wonder whether they sawed off the extrinsic tumours or left them there dryly suppurated. Remember when our first dog died. My mother telling me that for a few weeks I would not be able to see beyond her suffering but would soon recall her in her prime. Never did.

Always pictured instead the melanomas festering beneath her gums and around her eyes. Her putrefied breath. Said the same about my father. Recall nothing of him now but that one moment of his standing naked on buckled knees over the commode with the purulent scabs on his navel and beneath his armpits blackly weeping. Continue to stare. Still willing myself to feel. A few years later when I see my mother in much the same pose in a chapel of rest I will fall to my knees weeping before her lifeless body. But here there is simply numbness and unreality. I glance up at the crucifix hanging over him. The heavy curtains draped below. Remember the giving of communion. The mumbled words. The writhing. The vicar's hand on my shoulder. Wonder whether in those final hours my father became pacified. If he still believed even then. I'm there I know not how long. And then seemingly without forethought I'm by the door pouring myself another glass of water from the carafe. I drink it with my eyes closed before exiting. In the reception area my mother asks me if I'm okay. I can't look at her. I tell her I'm fine. That I'll be outside. I wait until she's gone through and then head out to the gravel carpark. It's drizzling and grey and...

I turn from the doorway to find the man standing there with the pricelist asking me a question about one of the reds on offer. I look down at it. Look at the cuffs of his tweed sports jacket. The buttons. The shields on his tie. Take him over to the counter and key the product code into the system. Yes we have it I tell him. Over in the old world. He wonders whether I might be able to find it for him because he's looked and looked. And so we go over. And of course it's the most prominent of all the wines on the stack. He says blow me that I didn't see it there and thanks me for my time. Back in the doorway I look out across the carpark. Beyond the petrol pumps the drizzle continues to fall and I remember the falling drizzle the morning of his funeral. Remember it falling over the cavalcade of hearses that pulled up at the bottom of the drive. Remember being out on the yard and looking down at the black suited undertakers blurred through the rainsplashed hearse windows with exhaust fumes tapering in the cold air. The length of rope hanging dripping from the rainslick sycamore bough reaching over the driveway. Slung there one summer for a swing with a log seat tied in the loop of its noose. Remember being pulled back almost to the yard then inversion. Remember riding plastic tractors to the gate at the bottom. Remember the smell down the drive of the dead deadnettles. My mother comes out. Looks spent. Mauve dress. No black she said. The first tears of the day are shed there beneath the sycamore. I give her a tissue. She tells me I look nice. Handsome. Touches my shoulder. I'm wearing a fawn suit and my shoes are new. I reach inside my jacket to check the sheet of paper folded in my pocket. Down the driveway the passenger side door of one of the hearses opens and the undertaker we met yesterday or whenever steps out. Grey pinstripe trousers. Black blazer with tails. Starched white shirt. Black tie. Gaunt with cropped white hair. A top hat tucked beneath his arm. My mother blows her nose. I look across the wintry garden. Wisteria and rosebriars are tangled dead on the trellises around the patio windows. Beneath the eaves against the magnolia pebbledash are shat the remnants of a swift's nest. Remember watching one summer from the picnic bench as it beaked mud pebbles into the crevice and fed mewing mouths. That year the cat sat below and had the chicks that fell out. Another it climbed the trellises and took the flycatcher's fledglings from the plyboard birdbox nailed to the cornerstone and ate them one by one on the yard. Crackle of their hollow bones popping beneath the contused veinblue tissue of their skin. Their gum afterwards smeared across the concrete. Smeared across the cat. Remember at the end of that summer the birds all gathered on the wire with their cries darkening the dusk.

The same that summer before I went away. On a deckchair beneath the apple tree with the spine of a book resting on my knee. Flicking pages without reading. My father bringing out gin in the gloaming clinking cubes against a tumbler. How he would take a seat on the patio picnic bench and face out across the garden with his hands resting on his knees and I would sometimes see him in silhouette and sometimes gilded yellow by the lounge lights behind him watching the last of the day fade from the sky and fall to darkness. I'd see bats skimming the roof eaves and in the patches of light on the patio what seemed scores of moths convulsing in the throes of their deaths. Barefoot you could feel the dew forming on the lawn. And then a few days later after we'd seen the horses grazing down by the water meadow and my mother had cried at the airport the cherry trees along the river would be alive with cicadas and in the dust of the school playing fields I would watch cheerleading practice or baseball and homeward the stirless green ricefields would simmer in the summer's heat until the first of the autumn winds blew down from winter mountain heralding the coming of the colder months when griddle smoke would drift from beneath the awnings of izakaya and on weekend trips to ancient towns and cities pagoda roofs would rise into the cold snowhung skies and in bars along the old narrow streets hot sake would be served in sake pots and the seasons would turn thus year upon year until in the drizzle continents later I would see through the train windows those familiar skylines of home regressing in layers of dank grey haze and I try to see echoes of this now across the lawn but the morning is bare of all life and colour and the only echoes are of passing and as the man keys his numbers into the cardmachine's keypad I look at the cuffs of his jacket and at the liver spots on his hand and at the thinned sweep of hair across his head and afterwards as he drives away along the wet street I watch until he is disappeared from view and watch as we start to disappear also. Down the driveway and into the soundless morning. My mother gripping my arm. The hearse parked at the driveway's end with spherules of silvered rain upon its waxed black sheen and my father's plain oak coffin bedecked with flowers within. My mother cries. The undertaker puts on his top hat and opens the door of the lead car. We climb in. I watch through the rainy windows as he walks around and climbs into the front seat by the driver and then we are pulling away. The cavalcade proceeds slowly through the village past the meadow where horses once grazed and the old farm building on the corner thrown up with mud from the road and finally past the row of houses on the Bourne and sloping away behind the lattermost the grassy meadow wet with the day's rain.

Once we have left the village the cavalcade speeds up and we are on the old route I used to take to school. Sometimes I glance across at my mother. In the hand resting limp on her lap is a crinkled tissue which she will periodically use to wipe her eyes. On occasion I look to my father's coffin in the hearse but generally just stare at the upholstery. The funeral procession turns and heads north. A part of me remembers this as the route we used to take to swimming club when I was a child but everything by now feels unfamiliar and surreal and after having grown up in this landscape and spent so long in its compass it's odd not knowing what to expect around the next corner or over the knap of the next hill and by the time we are pulling into the gated crematorium grounds a half hour or so later I'm utterly lost. My father's wishes were for his body to be burned and his ashes interred in the parish churchyard. At one time the notion of cremation was anathema to me yet now it seems apposite to burn all of it away such are the memories of his final days. Through the gates the cavalcade slows again and travels along a paved driveway overlooking an ornamental garden with shrubs scuttling the borders of a rolled lawn and the osiers of a willow brushing the drizzle stippled surface of a pond.

The main building is modern and redbrick. Turreted with squat spires. We draw in beneath a porte cochere and for a while idle there as the rest of the cavalcade falls in behind. I don't know who's in them. I didn't take the time to look and neither do I care. Probably the uncle and aunt and cousins I haven't seen or heard from in years and a few close friends from the village. From beneath the dripping roof eaves I stare for a long time at the trees while my mother cries quietly beside me. At length the undertaker turns to face us. Gives a curt nod and it is understood by this that it is time. He comes around and opens the door for us and helps my mother from the car and I follow after her. As pallbearer I am guided to the hearse where I linger unspeaking by the other undertakers. It's quiet and chill and the air given to a fine mist of cold rain. Presently I am joined by my cousin. He shakes my hand. He's dressed in pinstripe trousers and a dark jacket. Remember going round to his as a child when we were staying with my grandfather and playing in the backyard of his house or in later years sitting in his room looking at his porn mags. Apparently he's engaged now or his girlfriend's pregnant. Something like that. My other cousin is nearby with a baby I didn't know she had. Then our neighbour from down the drive comes over and finally a man from the village I vaguely recognise and it is the four of us together who will act as pallbearers.

We wait without speaking while others file into the crematorium building. After a time the undertaker comes and arranges us into two columns so that the coffin can be slid out onto our shoulders and the next thing I become conscious of is following him through the double doors with baroque music playing over the speakers and rows of mourners in the pews either side of the aisle. The coffin is heavier than I thought it would be and the weight of it cuts into my shoulder and my knees are near gone besides. Men from the undertaker's are there in support but we make it to the bier unaided and place it thereupon before the curtained backdrop with to its flank a plain wooden lectern. Afterwards I take a seat off to the side in the corner and throughout the service cannot bring myself to look at anybody and instead stare at the memorial plaques beside me and outside once it's over and I've hugged my mother on the threshold I wander up one of the pathways amongst the headstones and stare unseeingly at grit gravel blades of grass epitaphs the sky and sometimes back at the dark knots of shapes huddled by the entranceway and the turrets of the crematorium building cut against the drizzled cloud or at the long driveway leading to some quiet oblivion then later still when we arrive at the village church for the service the drizzle has eased and before going in I am alone at a fencepost along a grass verge with the view of the village below me. A low ceiling of cloud hangs over the rooftops and rain streaks are still visible in the distance. Cars line the verges along the lane by the church and the gates of the school. A few latecomers make their way up the hill. For a while I was with my mother at the entrance to the church but the arriving mourners began to grate with their hangdog eyes and recycled sentiments and questions after our general wellbeing. I suppose also I was looking for her. Wondering whether she might be amongst them. From a distance I saw her parents. The Bryces. David tall and pale. Her mother Jill with her hair shorter. Something of her daughter there. In her eyes and mannerisms. Her smile. Difficult to pinpoint. It was in seeing them that I had to walk away. Memories resurfacing of their living room through different eras. Of sitting out on their lawn in the summertime. Of the field round back where we'd walk our dogs.

I pat the pocket of my jacket and lean against the fencepost. The fence wire wet and dripped with rain. Wet splinters from the planed fencepost stakes. Up at the entranceway I see that my mother is finally alone and make my way over to her across the lane and past the weathered headstones lining the pathway and at the pathway's end the gale hewn yew. She's crying. I ask her if she's okay. Hug her. She's shaking. Tells me she doesn't know if she can do this. Over her shoulder I can see the rearmost pews of people waiting for the freakshow to begin. See them leafing through the orders of service I made. My father on the front in a meadow of clover and on the back in an old school photo in the middle row in shorts and garters with a cow's lick. The hymns and bible readings picked out by my mother on account of my complete ambivalence. I tell her we can wait if she needs another minute. She says no. She'll be okay. And then I'm leading her into the church down the aisle past the files of varnish worn pews with the metal grating sounding beneath our feet and ahead by the choirstalls one of our old neighbours straddling a cello playing a piece of classical music my father liked and that I will never be able to listen to again. The vicar is at the pulpit. He smiles at my mother and me and as we reach the front I step aside and let her in before me. Throughout the service I sit slumped at the front following proceedings in the order of service mouthing hymns but never singing and bowing my head but never praying. Another old neighbour does a bible reading. Then one of my father's old university friends a poem. When it's my turn I take from my pocket the eulogy I've written and traipse up to the front with it. I slowly unfold it onto the lectern and use the wooden surface to steady myself. Clearing my throat I scan the congregation before finding my gaze settling on Jill. There's a long pause before I begin for in looking upon her I feel myself taken back to those afternoons on her lawn

141

and later to the fields that summer when the emulsifying sun cast long shadows over the stubbles of corn and caught in its wake the long strands of her daughter's hair. Finally my eyes fall to the page. Fall to the scrawlings on the tissue sheaves by the till. Fall somewhere beyond the windows where rain dulls street corners and churchyards. Dulls the sheep fields and the conifers by some distant balcony in the wake of a storm greying textures of woodgrain and tile and leather and myriad eyes staring back from intangible eras and later still at a lectern in a different time recounting my mother's timeless life and sad demise in the same frayed suit and scuffed shoes I will watch a butterfly descend from the roof of the nave and settle on the floor by the pulpit. Thinking it means something. Thinking it's a sign. When really there are no signs. No meaning. I read my father's eulogy. It's short and cold and emotionless. I pause sometimes and stare out and there's no register in the eyes that stare back. The eyes of those who sent cards but never called. Called but never came. Those in whose church we now stand but in whose conduct there was little trace of its supposed virtues.

Outside we are a sad mimesis of those Christmases of old when after the service we would assemble snowclad before the entranceway with others from the village and in anticipation of the coming festivities of soot sweepings from the chimney flue and presents by the fireside I would tug at my mother's sleeve to hurry her along. She is engulfed by them now. I watch them filing by so that they can get to the cheap wine and finger buffet laid out in the village hall before making their carefully phrased excuses for departure. Before finally alone my mother and I return to the room where my father died and my mother asks me whether I believe in anything like the permanence of the soul and I shake my head no and after she's gone to bed I sit up long into the night drinking brandy from the cabinet until sometime in the small hours I fall asleep on the settee with his old wristwatch cradled in my palm. And now my mother comes and asks me whether I shouldn't like a lift down to the hall with her in the undertaker's car but I tell her I'll walk for I need to clear my head and I watch her through the window of the car staring blankly out as she disappears from view.

Much of the baulk has turned to a thin slippery mud and a couple of times I nearly fall. A few sheep bleat in the field and a chimneystack smokes below but the village is otherwise lifeless. Halfway down I pause to look back at the school. At the yellow brick hall. The football pitch. The church spire behind. To the side in the woods where we used to piss on pitfires and build bivouacs in the rootcaves of fallen trees. Crows can be heard from its depths and the faint reek of woodsmoke is in the air. Remember when the field was barley and the ears of it would sway in windwaves with poppies weeding through it in early summer and the mud would bake and grass and weeds would grow unkempt along its flanks and dust up kicked pollen in plumes. At the foot of the baulk through the kissing gate and along by the high walled alleyway I am out on the deserted street. Left to the hall. Right for home. Ostensibly to clean the mud from my shoes I choose the latter and skirt down past the village shop and the willow on the corner and the old red phone box and bench where teenagers congregate to smoke cigarettes and drink cider and then past the forge and adjoining cottage I am on our driveway. At the top on the yard I look for a long time at the windows. The kitchen. Living room. Up to my parents' bedroom. I suppose seeking some kind of apparition. A twitching of a curtain. His shadow. The light shifts. It is a winter's afternoon. A couple of hours off dark and overcast. In those windows and across the wet garden and in the shiftless sky nothing lives. Remember being in the living room before the hearth's cindered coals and the carpet strewn about with torn gift wrap. Of the day drawn to evening and the parlour games we'd play when the darkness came on. How we'd take coldcuts from the leftovers on the table and my father would open a dust encrusted port from the cupboard beneath the stairs and drink it from a port glass with crusted stilton. Smell of pinecones and smouldered ashes. Smell of the sootblack flue.

In the garage I sponge the mud from my shoes and buff them with the old brush and rag from the box on the washing machine and I'm about to head back down to the hall but find myself unlocking the front door instead and journeying through the halflit hallway to the living room with the couch now rolled back into the corner where my father died and everything silent and unearthly in its ordinariness. As if nothing had ever transpired there. I sit in my father's armchair and then on the settee. Now smoothing down the fabric. Now staring at my reflection in the pictureglass on the unit. Again searching for some kind of apparition. Seated beside me dark and spectral. An arm around my shoulder. Whispers in my ear. But the reflected image simply falls away. Disintegrates into chasms. And then I am upstairs in my parents' bedroom seated on my father's side of the bed going through the drawer of his bedside table. Finding his old spectacles. A magnifying glass. Superglue. Tweezers. Fountain pen. Down by its side his medical boxes. Pulp bowls. Plasters and gauzes. Antiseptic wipes. Moisturising lotions. Can't seem to shake those images of him. Of the cancer weeping beneath his armpit after I took him there so roughly. Of shaving him towards the end. His eyes half there and half someplace else. I lie back and stare up at the ceiling and try to see him in other guises but nothing comes and still I cannot find it in myself to grieve. To cry for him. I listen to water trickling in the pipes and the immersion in the airing cupboard. But nothing comes.

Later in the village hall I am walking amongst the display boards I devised of my father's photographic work either blown up from colour transparencies or his original darkroom prints in monochrome mounted on pieces of card. The sections organised thematically. Landscapes of my father's travels. Mountain passes. Sunsets over lagoons. Abbeys cleft into the rockfaces of vertiginous gorges. Cityscapes from business trips. Hordes of salarymen streaming over intersections pillared with neon. Ancient rickshaws. Monks in kasa collect alms by a tori. A section closer to home. Autumnal woodlands. Snowbound lanes out of the village. These I pass one after another. Pass the attendant mourners and studiously avoid eye contact with any of them. The hall filled with shuffled footsteps and murmured chatter and from the rear the serving of food and drink from the finger buffet my mother organised with her friends from the village. Standard fare of gouda on cocktail sticks cocktail wieners sausage rolls coronation chicken julienned cucumbers carrots dips crisps cakes fondant fancies. Standard fare of vin de pays and chenin blanc on promotion from the supermarket. I come to the portraiture section. A girl in the fashion of the era on a royal parks deckchair. Another leant against the ornamented reservoir of a fountain. A pair of schoolgirls seated on a bench outside a busy railway station eating doughnuts and immersed in conversation with the one of them covering her mouth as she giggles. My father took it when they came to see me out east. The girls were from my school but he hadn't known. Had taken it one afternoon when he and my mother went for a walk through the city. At the hall's end a series of family shots. My grandfather's pipesmoked profile. Grandmother beneath the apple tree in her garden with her hair set in a bouffant. Me in an old straw hat leaning over the backrest of a car seat. Mother on a picnic blanket with a hamper before her. Finally one of me next to a girl. We are sitting on the garden bench by the pond. I'm maybe five or six and wearing shorts and wellies with a plastic bucket by my feet. The girl is the same age as me. Wearing dungarees and a sunhat and sandals. I am looking at the camera and pulling a face. She is looking at me and laughing. I study it for a long time and though I remember much of her and of the childhood we spent together I can never recall the day this photograph was taken.

We have the same on our mantelpiece.

I turn to find Jill there beside me. She has in her hand a cup of wine and is looking at the photograph with a wistful expression in her eyes. Upon seeing her I'm instantly removed from the murmured hall. To a past remote yet omnipresent. The lawn and sloping meadow. The view across the adjacent fields. Her daughter in the desklight.

Do you remember your dad taking it?

I shake my head. She tells me it was the summer after they'd moved here. Tells me how kind my parents were. The first people in the village to speak to them. To have them round for dinner. The photograph was taken one afternoon when they'd come for a barbeque.

You two were inseparable that afternoon.

Yeah?

As you became most of the time.

I remember then those afternoons when after school her daughter and I would come home or she would come to mine and we would sit together and play or draw or watch cartoons. How we were both only children and how in spite of my having other friends in the village there never seemed to be anybody else but her. I look across at Jill. There are tears in her eyes.

I really am so very sorry about your dad.

Thanks.

He was such a lovely man. We really miss him.

She speaks of the meals they used to have together. They and others in the village. The themes. Tramps and whores.

Lords and paupers. One in which my father dressed as a fisherman in yellow waterproofs and wellington boots and carried through the village en route to the meal a fishing rod with a hooked trout swaying from its line. My mother has a photograph of that night on her dresser. Says it was one of the last times my father was ever really happy. Just before they found out about his cancer. Jill wipes her eyes. Smiles. Looks again at the photograph.

I'm sorry Emily couldn't be here.

It's okay.

She wanted to be but she's away at the moment.

On holiday?

No. A work thing.

Okay.

But she sends her condolences.

Thank you.

She should've liked to have seen you.

Yeah. Likewise.

Jill makes her excuses and is about to move on.

Is she okay? Emily I mean.

Apparently she's doing well. Working for a charity. It transpires that she lives not too far from me in town. It seems as if Jill's about to make some suggestion or other but then decides otherwise. Instead smiles and gives my hand a squeeze. Says how nice it is to see me again in spite of the circumstances. Tells me how well I look. Hopes to see me in the near future on a happier occasion. And then she is gone and the man from the store in the tweed is gone and the store falls to silence once more.

*           *           *

I am carrying in a plastic bag my father's ashes. A trowel. Foam posy pads. In my other hand a small vase of flowers.

Sheep are huddled in a corner of the field and elevated above the hardened gutters of mud is my old school and beyond this the spire of the church in whose quiet sundappled grasses my father's ashes will soon be interred. Pushing on through the school gate my mother suggests that I might like to give Bea a tour while she goes on ahead. I watch her disappear around the corner beneath the woodsplintered roof eaves adjoining the hall and flintwork staff room with the headmistress's darkwindowed office throwing back the dark spring sun. I take Bea to the playground. Up to the pond. Around to the old football pitch. Farther below where once we had a pool there is an allotment of broken canes for beans and plastic tags attached to the tired shoots of peasnaps. The netball loops are still the same but rusted like the chainlink fence around the field. Hopscotch grids and maze rings fade in the gravelly asphalt. I take her to the classrooms. We peer in at the windows through visored hands. The sun catches on clusters of tables and miniature chairs. On tubes of paint. On the laminated wordchains bedecking the walls. There is a rubber matted play area in the corner piled with beanbags and building blocks. In another corner a selection of musical instruments. Tambourines. Maracas. A guitar. By the window sprouts of cress on wads of tissue in rows of plastic berry punnets. We go by the hall. The floor darkly lacquered. Gym ropes hanging from the ceiling tethered to a clip on the far wall. Echoes of us there. Echoes of assembly mornings in autumn with the sun slanting in through the windows across the whitewashed walls. The record player in the corner. How we all filed in. Royal blue sweaters. Gold shield crests.

We go back to the playground and take a seat on the little bench by the pond. It's warm and the view over the pitpocked grit is of the village mantled by sprays of saplings. On a distant elevation the white specks of gulls trail a tractor. Lunges of them track its slow geometric procession the length and breadth of its course. Trails of sunsilvered cloud shade the valley of the village as flurries of wind coursing through the school grounds move through the curls of sedge bordering the pond and the unmown grass around the playing field. Around this time in the reedy shallows of the pond the jellied bulbs of frogspawn would split the oily skin of water and we would watch each lunchtime the black specks of spunklike fry slowly elongate before splitting the greasy albumen of their sacs. At home I'd catch them with pond snails in buckets and plastic boxes and watch them swill through the tinctured water. Embryonic prods of stump legs aft and fore. Clustering and eating alive the pond snails. In later months I'd lift their slab in the corner and count them in the slithered mudcracks before they flopped into the grimy pondwater and in the borders of the lawn I'd find toads lollygagging slimily through the raindamp flora. A cloud blots the sun and casts across the school grounds a tumour of consumptive shadow.

We go to meet my mother. She's there in the corner beneath the shade of a horse chestnut stooped over a headstone. It's a quiet and lonely part of the churchyard just before the long brush of the borders. At our approach she rises to meet us. Places her hand on my shoulder. It's the first time I've seen his stone. In one corner a scroll of carved wisteria. Inscribed into its face his name and the black numerals of his life's lease. Beneath this a short eulogy. Devoted father loving husband loyal friend. Some such. Flatly throwing back the day. For a while we stare down at it before finally my mother asks me if I like it. It's nice I say. Really nice. Trying to feel. To connect. Just before the stone's polished plinth my mother's already started to dig the foetus of a hole for his ashes. I ask if I should take over and she nods and silently hands me the trowel. I start widening and deepening until it seems sufficient to womb the clagged wet faggots of ash in his tubed tomb. My mother has popped the lid and it sits off to one side wet and claggy in the sunshine.

Bea is stood back from us. Seems unsure of her role here. Ill at ease as she thumbs a strand of hair across her shoulder. I look at the rows of weathered headstones beyond her. Eastward facing for the coming of some long forgotten glory. Those along the outer fringes anonymous now. Footnotes in an unthumbed parish register. I motion for Bea to come in closer and she steps beside me. My mother takes her hand and asks me if I want to go first. I tell her that I think she should and then I watch as she reaches into the tube and brings out a handful of dark ash. Hunkers down and lets it slip from her fingers into the dirt below. I see my father's face. Not as he was in life nor even on the brink of death but dead. Cold and shrunken. His pinched mouth. Pinched skin. My mother takes another mound of ash and lets it funnel from her loosely clasped fist. She starts to cry. I feel too numb to go to her. Just stand there. Bea gives her a tissue and places her hand on her shoulder. When my turn comes I reach deep into the tube and delve through the wet burnt bones and gristle and hair and nails and skin and innards of any nameless number of the dead and let it suck wetly through my fingers and I look at it glistening in my cupped palm as it stains black and grey the knuckles and joists of my skin. I push through its gristle with my forefinger and mould it into a small mound then reach down and turn my hand palmwards and let it slowly slide down onto my mother's palmed ash where it glistens in the wet dirt amongst the mucous tangles of roots and worms. I repeat this. Once. Twice. Then upon finishing I stay crouched by his tombstone tracing its unweathered edges and the notches of its black lettering. Bea takes a turn at my mother's insistence. Pinches up a niggard share and sprinkles it into the hole before stepping back. With the ceremony concluded the tube is still near full so we end up just tipping the rest of it in with drifts of it ghosting through the sun and ghosting the nearby brush and goosegrass and afterwards my mother bends to the ashpile and places two fingers upon it and solemnly and inaudibly says her final goodbyes and then I start to trowel the dirt back in and pat it down before finally replacing the little square of turf over the top and then it is done and I am wiping upon my trousers bits of mud and ash and staining with streaks of calcified fatherbone the light fabric until Bea reaches forward and takes my hand. My mother asks me if I'm okay and I nod and try to look sad but it means nothing to me. Not now. Not until much later.

Afterwards we go into the church and take a pew at the front and sit there for a long time in the stark silence. My mother leans forward with her hands clasped before her and mutters a short prayer and sometimes in shifting the pews will creak. In the churchyard through a latticed window pigeons are aflight. I slide restlessly away. Wander down the aisle to the back of the nave. An old parish flag hangs from a pillared wall. In the corner is a kind of creche with biblical figurines scattered on a threadbare carpet. Shepherds with crooks and their chipnosed flock. Little thatched huts. There is a small stand at the back of the pews with church lithograph postcards for sale. On an adjoining table I thumb through the visitors' book and touch in the light from the transept its old quills of faded ink. Looking back at the altar I see that my mother is crying again. Bea's hand is on her shoulder and she is comforting her. I watch the two of them and they are little more than apparitions.

We go to lunch at what was once a rambling pick your own strawberry plot but has since been converted into a cafe restaurant come farm shop. Before the meal my mother takes Bea through the latter and I trail behind watching as they pore over mason jars of piccalilli and chutney and royal jelly with ribbon tied lids and bottles of flavoured oils with lightning closures and handwritten labels. Watching as they sample crusts of ryebread dipped in balsamic vinegar and cubes of cheese on watercrackers. As they compare items of chinaware earthenware stoneware. Bea calls me over. Asks which of two butter dishes I prefer. I shrug and point at the one closest to me and when she asks why I say that it will go with the tablecloth. She looks uncertain and says maybe this one is nicer. Says she can picture it on the worktop next to the coffee jar. I tell her that of course she's right. She goes off to buy it but then comes back and exchanges it after further inspection for another. Goes off again and returns smiling. Pleased. Happy. Clutching the thing in its tissue wrapping and little boutique paper bag and it is scenes such as this that will haunt me much later on.

We go through to the dining room for lunch and are led to a table by the window overlooking some pastureland. The waitress brings us menus and a pitcher of water and we silently peruse the mains but I'm without appetite. Bea and my mother talk of the beef and halibut. My mother has had both here in the past and really can't decide which to go for now. She recommends the halibut to Bea. When the waitress returns I order a salad with a bottle of beer and my mother seems concerned by this. Worries that I won't have enough to eat. Wonders whether I wouldn't perhaps prefer the steak with gratin dauphinoise because I might be hungry later. But I tell her I can't really think of food right now and she gives me a look and touches my hand and I wonder if this is what mourning feels like. This emptiness. This feeling of disengagement from everything and everyone. Throughout the meal my mother asks me repeatedly if I've had enough and whether I shouldn't like some more bread or half of her beef or maybe another beer but I continue to refuse and in the end can't even finish the salad. She and Bea talk of French markets and how wonderful the peppers and aubergines and tomatoes are and how in this country they must do something funny to them to make them so round and perfect but so tasteless and I sit there largely in silence. For a while I watch an elderly couple on the table opposite and then I am looking across at my mother. At the sweep of her hair and the pendant around her neck that my father gave her on her fiftieth birthday and even in the throes of his death when the cancer had gone to his brain and he was barely even human I had found this moment of her loneliness difficult to imagine. The idea that he would no longer be in the house. Would no longer be there in his chair. Shortly after he died when I spoke to her on the phone she told me how she could still feel him there. How in the mornings when she woke she would see the depression of his having slept in the bed beside her or how in the evenings she would hear him moving around upstairs and would even call up to him expectant of a reply. How one time as she sat in the garden she could feel his presence so strongly that she was compelled to turn around and look up at the house and she'd seen him at the window.

In the car on the way home I am in the back and Bea is talking to my mother. I watch the scenery fall by. The yellowed buds of rape. The buds of trees along the lanes. The high banks coming into flower. The car still smells of those picnic trips and of longer journeys ages past through the massif central and there is cluttered on the dashboard and in the footwells the paraphernalia of those excursions. Wire spiral mapbooks. Tinned bonbons. Currency coins. My mother has since asked me whether I might like to go back with her at some point to the house by the sea but the thought of what would be a mourning makes me uneasy. I think sometimes of the dormant house shuttered to the hot Mediterranean days and airlessly layering with dust and of the times we spent there. But even this is tempered by a vague disquiet. The arguments. The faint revulsion at being this age or that and finding myself still holidaying with my parents. My father wearing socks with sandals beneath a parasol. Board games when it rained. The kinds of simmering tensions that revisit you later on.

Late afternoon with Bea and my mother baking a cake in the kitchen I say I need some air. That I want to be alone for a while. On the doorstep I pull on my walking shoes and in the shoebox I take them from are my father's old hiking boots cracked at the toes and his old sandals crushed and broken. I wonder whether there will be an eventual purge or whether shrinelike his spaces will remain unchanged until my mother's time comes and it is left to me to skip their old keepsakes. At first deliberating over this piece of porcelain or those old spectacles until wearied with grief it is all skipped or pawned off without remonstrance. Later after terminal cancer has attacked my mother's lymph nodes and inflated her neck and arm in elephantine grotesquery I discover the latter to be the case and will find in the bottom of her wardrobe buried beneath the shoes and scarves and old neckties my first woollen tunic and my first knitted booties and a lock of hair from my first haircut and in a small envelope a clinking of rotted milkteeth. But for now it is left to wonder and in subsequent visits to find some solace in his undisturbed corners and quiet spaces. To sit one afternoon in his old armchair and look out through the patio windows across the garden at the tits in my grandmother's old birdbath all mossed over and weathered.

Out through the village the water in the Bourne is low and streaked brown with reedy algae rilling over the shinglebed. The bristled heads of teasels climbing the banks to the road are here and there bent beneath the balustrade and on the far side the dense scuttling of undergrowth is curtained by swarms of gnats. I go by the disused bus stop. The walls and roof are sheathed in tangled meshes of ivy. Remember it clustered with knots of teenagers. Remember the tips of their tabs through the gloom and on the paintwork behind them the drips of their tagged initials split by arrowed hearts. I suppose all of them are gone now. Gone and to what end. Mothers or fathers. Tradesmen or clerks. Gone to a life with the past all but faded. In the meadow across the way the horse chestnut blanketing the gravel carpark is coned with white blossom and the field is empty. The village itself is lazily quiet. Faint voices can be heard in a garden someplace distant and maybe the low hum of a car meandering its way hither but the lane is deserted. I pass the row of cottages on the outskirts and see the slopes of cropfields ranging beyond and an hour or so later after I have rounded these and thrown stones in the chalk quarry and kicked the fissured lip of a green streaked chalk cliff into the gravelly dirt rubble below I am descending the old football field with the low dusk sun burning blackly behind the woods and the distant horizon hung with cocoons of duskblack cloud. In this dying light the grass writhes in silverdark tendrils and I look back at the silvered imprints of my steps and at the dim folding of my shadow and then ahead at the lighted windows of the cottages fringing the village. A wrangled coppice. The grey husk of a trough. A lone oak. I continue to wend by them and by knotted hedgerows of hawthorn and rosehip and bramble while the sky continues to darken and burn and greyblack streaks of cloud mull on the horizon. Askew through the serpentine gloom of the evening the darkened forms of the garden below begin dimly to manifest themselves. The palings of a hedgetwined fence. A grey steppingstone pathway. The dark spread of an apple tree. Perhaps only some distant memory that makes them so for really there is little to behold in that dusk until almost upon the path that leads back down to the lane around the garden some flurry of movement beneath the apple tree catches my eye. Some darkened form there. I am almost

155

beyond it when I hear a voice call my name. I stop and turn to see a figure approaching.

I thought that was you.

Not so much the darkness as some failure of recognition at first. And yet it is also unmistakably her. Emily Bryce. Jill and David's daughter. She comes from beneath the apple tree to the fence where I am standing and in the light from the living room window I am able to make out those features I have known so well. Where once she had hair to her shoulders it is now cropped and almost boyish and yet little has changed. The faint band of freckles across her nose. The smile that always seemed to play on her lips. That quality in her eyes from which I could never rid myself. As if time has suddenly fallen away. She is wearing an old linen shirt with faded jeans and sandals. For a while I'm silent. We stand over the overgrown rakes of paintflaked palings perhaps sharing in some kind of mutual recognition of all that has passed and when she smiles I see the same faint wrinkling at the bridge of her nose she always had.

What are you doing here?

I was just out for a walk.

Do you have time for a cup of tea?

Sure. Okay.

She leads me along the fence and at its end opens the little gateway where we embrace rather awkwardly and she kisses me on the cheek. I follow her to the back door and treading off my shoes on the threshold I'm suddenly conscious of my old trousers smeared with mud and ash and my unkempt hair and beard. We go through to the kitchen and she sits me down at the table and fills the kettle. The place is a time warp. The same fittings and furnishings. The same decorative plates hanging on the wall above the range. She comes over while waiting for the kettle to boil and leans against the worktop. I look at her. Look away. Down at the tabletop.

I was so sorry to hear about your dad.

Thanks.

And that I couldn't make it to the funeral.

That's okay.

I was away at the time.

I heard. I met your parents.

I wanted to be there.

I know. It's fine.

How was it?

Listening to the rasping of the kettle I suddenly wonder why she's here. Wonder where her parents are. Why she's alone.

It was okay. As funerals go.

My parents spoke about you after.

Yeah?

They told me what a nice eulogy you gave.

Really?

They said it was really heartfelt.

It was difficult to know what to say.

What do you mean?

To sum everything up.

Well they said it was lovely.

Good. I'm glad.

They told me how nice you looked.

I glance up at her. She's smiling and I feel myself start to redden.

I don't know about that.

You haven't changed.

How so?

You never could take a compliment.

The kettle clicks off. I watch her while she fixes the tea. Something almost cold about the precision of her movements. She brings it over on a tray with the teabags still steeping in the mugs and a bottle of milk and sugar bowl. I continue to watch her as she sets it down and sits across from me and presses with the back of a teaspoon the teabags against the sides of the mugs before dropping them on the tray and topping up the mugs with milk.

One sugar?

Old habits.

I smile inwardly at this little detail of remembrance. She stirs sugar into each mug then sets mine down in front of me. We settle into a momentary silence. I look around the room.

It hasn't changed.

What hasn't?

This place. Even the mugs are the same.

I know.

How come you're back?

Mum and dad are away. I'm minding the dog.

Where is he?

Asleep in his box.

Not much of a guard dog.

No. He's getting on a bit now.

Do you find it funny? Being back.

I don't mind it that much.

Are you still in touch with anyone?

No. Nobody. You?

Same.

How come you're back?

We came to do dad's ashes.

You and your mum?

Yeah.

I'm sorry.

Thanks.

He's up at the churchyard?

Yeah. Mum picked out the spot.

Where is it?

Round back. By the big horse chestnut.

How was it? Doing the ashes I mean.

Difficult to feel that much about it.

How so?

I don't know. It didn't mean anything.

She takes a sip of her tea. How these meetings after so many years and with so many questions can be punctuated by such silences.

You must miss him.

I don't really.

She looks up. Surprised a little. I glance at her then look away.

Not yet.

You don't have to talk about it.

It's okay. I don't mind.

She waits for me to go on. I take a sip of tea.

I was glad when he died.

I replace the cup. Look down at the coaster on which it rests.

It got pretty bad towards the end.

I'm sorry to hear that.

Yeah.

I saw him you know.

I shake my head.

When I was back one weekend.

Yeah?

Asked me about everything. What I was doing.

He always liked you. Mum too.

We talked about you too.

Hopefully it wasn't all bad.

He told me how proud he was of you.

I chew on a fingernail.

You know that. Don't you?

Yeah. I guess.

So's your mum.

We fall to silence. I drink my tea. She changes the subject. Asks me where I'm living now. Turns out she's not far from me. A few stops away. I tell her after a pause that I never meant for us to drift apart. That I wanted to look her up but after a while it didn't seem reasonable. I tell her I always wondered about her. About what happened to her. She says the same. On the doorstep a while later she hugs me. Whispers in my ear that it was good to see me again. The moon is up as I head home. The pale hue of it on the roads. A slip of paper in my hand. A number. An address. Promise of a future union. My mother in the kitchen when I get home.

You were a long time.

I went up round the fields.

Did you see anyone while you were out?

No. No one.

Do you feel a bit better for having a walk?

A bit.

Would you like tea and a piece of cake?

Sure. Why not.

We've just been putting the finishing touches on it.

On the table coffeecake with icing forked to wisps and walnut halves. The kettle is filled. Rasps to a boil. Steeped teabags. Sugared mugs. Pressing with the back of a teaspoon the teabags against the sides of the mugs before dropping them on the tray and topping up the mugs with milk.

\*　　　　　\*　　　　　\*

At the table after she has gone to work I have from the wardrobe shelf my old shoebox. Have spread from it the sheaves of photographs. All these past lives. Stratum of school. University. Beyond. Of far flung temples and beaches bleached with age and ageless. Of robe clad men sawing through the necks of sacrificial goats by a desolate river from whose banks crematorial smoke rises. Of jellyfish along a forgotten shoreline drying in the sun. Of hides drying on whitewashed walls. Of cowled pilgrims on a dirt track through the mountains. Of the rape along the lanes and a tori in the sea and karst cliffs on a glue gloss dawn river forged by raftsmen. A folly silhouetted against a northern sky and lenticular cloudscapes over the black silhouettes of palms. Glass waters. A pine cabin's log fire. A trek through highland woodland. Mountain clouds on grey scree slopes. That one of us together as teenagers at the villa. Sun bleached veranda. Deep jagged shadows from the oleander by the gatepost just where the roof eaves end. An awning. Dark varnished shutters. Wrought window grilles. The both of us on the wall. Tanned in shorts and flipflops.

Remember going to the beach with her that first afternoon. A blue and windless July. My parents had not long had the place. Had flown down once to finalise the property deeds with the notaire and then for the first real trip had waited until my exams were at an end and invited the Bryces down with us for a long weekend. The riverbank is grown high with reeds and bulrushes and the earth along the pathway petrified with gorged mud in whose treads the fossil remains of bugs are given reliquary. A path I will come to know so well but then uncharted. Out beyond the horse pastures across the river the slopes of the hills rise upon the arid horizon and light aircraft towing banner advertisements for supermarkets and hardware stores and local eateries will traverse the sky. At first we walk abreast but as the way narrows I let her on ahead and watch her passage through the coarse bent grown across the path. She is wearing a white shirt and a porkpie hat and around her waist is knotted a sarong that trails after her in the panicles of the brushed grassheads and the slapped sand of her flipflops. Beneath her shirt she's wearing a bikini top and the toggles of it tied at her neck overlay her collar and sash across her back. I watch her without respite until we reach the end of the river path and head side by side towards the dunes between whose tussocks the sea is visible in a thin strip. We come to the beach and here a breeze blows along its expanse and at intervals striped parasols planted slanted in the sand are agitated by its passage. Her sarong curls unfettered about her thigh as she kicks off her flipflops and then she is breaking into a run suddenly and without warning with fine patinas of sand flicking around her and even now there is a timelessness as she turns to beckon me to follow her with the crests of the waves beyond glistening in the sun. At the shoreline she turns to beckon me once more and then I am beside her in the surf. We are there in the tidelands looking out to sea and I can feel her breaths rising and falling beside me before we see the first of them. A man bronzed and shaved walks by us. His little dick and balls bobbling with his strides. Presently others come into view. In the sea to her knees the folds of a middle aged woman with rippled cellulite and a grey stubbled fanny. On a beach towel a potbellied man wearing nothing but a sunhat and stroking his navel. All the way along the shoreline to the far breakwater. In the surf with a dog. Playing bat and ball. Playing boules. Desiccating into the bones of walnuts. For a while we are silent. Silently watching these still lifes frothing in the shaggy surf. These scuttled splashes of hides and carapaces. And then she looks at me and I at her and she collapses into me laughing. Perhaps it's the first time I fall also. Easy to get lost here with everything somehow encapsulated and distilled into that moment. The vibrations of her body. The hand she places on my shoulder. The strands of her hair beneath her sunhat. The dim registering of a future real or imagined. Watching her feet making little furrows in the lathering surf. Watching years from now that couple in the sea and wondering how they were mapped out and to what triumphs and miseries. And then she is threading her arm through mine and I'm walking with her along the shoreline and then following her molten footprints as they are consumed by the receding waves. About us the pruned and sprawled forms of beachgoers lap their bare fannies in the sea or sun themselves out on sandbanks or pose by striped windbreakers on the dunes until we round a sandy bluff and the bathers and baskers are suddenly younger and clothed in little shorts and animal print bikinis chasing one another down to the surf and paddling rubber rings and dinghies along the yellow bobbed lines of buoys. As I continue to follow I watch her tasselled sarong hem trailing through the waves. Watch it drift around her as it's pulled by the eddying currents of water.

Another light aircraft in the sky. The sound of its propeller amplified in the heat. Out to sea the masts of yachts. The sand here is thronged. Beach towels shaded by parasols. Little dome tents. Sunloungers. A vendor hawking ribboned bags of candied peanuts. Wakeboards. Jetskis. Shouts and laughter. Music someplace. We go on by until we find a vacant patch of sand and after I've laid out the straw beachmats and arranged the bags at their head I watch as she tugs off her sarong in one deft movement and lets it slip down by her feet. Her legs are long and already tanned. She's wearing striped bikini bottoms knotted at each side with the toggles at her thighs. Skimpy but not quite tight. In another deft movement she trails her finger around the hem at the rear and then still facing away from me she is unbuttoning her shirt. I watch as she billows it out then lets this too fall beside her. I look at the smooth curve of her back tanned as her legs. At the loop of her bikini top bow. At her hair beneath her hat falling here and there from beneath its brim.

Still she is facing out to sea. I wonder at us being there together. At the preceding months. Of meeting her beneath the willow tree after so long an absence. How for many years

I did not see her but always yearned after her somewhere deep inside. Those intervening years in a private school. Removed amongst its cloisters from my own reality. Removed from what I had come to know as fate. I think of our being together in town. How we would look at each other across the tabletops of quiet bars but always there was a shyness within me that would prevent my reaching out as now. This girl in whom everything is laid bare and in whom everything is invested remains yet intangible. The sun contours her skin. Shows the swell of her thigh. Her softly shaded lumbar. The curve of her neck. In turning the swell of her breast paler at the side and couched in the loose cups of her top. How everything can become concentrated in such moments. I see in her everything I've wanted till now and will wish for hence. And yet inaction. To now and hence. She looks down at me smiling archly.

Well?

Well what?

Are you staying like that all afternoon?

I look down at my shorts and shirt. At the hints of pale skin beneath. She kneels down facing me on the beachmat and I glance at her lithe sun warmed body and feel my pulse quicken. She reaches up and takes off her hat and her hair falls about her shoulders. I glance again at her body and then look up at her and she's smiling back at me. I slowly unbutton my shirt. Stupidly didn't wear my swimming shorts down here. Still in pants for christ's sake. I tie a towel around myself and start to struggle out of my clothes beneath it. She continues to watch me. This amused look in her eyes. The closeness of her body to mine only exacerbating the problem of movement. Finally breaking into a laugh at my discomfort she tells me she's going for a dip and suggests I meet her down there and I watch as she walks amongst the other beachgoers down to the shoreline turning back once to wave before wading in to her knees then diving under.

While I fuss with my shorts I watch her languid strokes out to sea as she now and then submerges before surfacing a distance away smoothing back her wet black hair. The sun is upon the water and the wind along the beach brings finely gilt combs to the crests of the waves around her and as I close my eyes the impression of her is written indelibly in the blackness. Presently I arrive at the water's edge and after I've refastened the drawstring of my shorts I wade in and then I am beneath the waves skimming over the seabed's flickers of pebbly sand and plankton. I make it all the way out to her and in surfacing at her legs seem to glide the length of her body and in coming up beside her she puts her arms around me and kisses me once on each cheek before rising up out of the sea with her feet upon my thighs as her mount and projecting herself back with the water laving over her and shimmering in the haloed sun and this too leaves an indelible impression of her in the ethereal light of the afternoon.

Another day there's a thunderstorm. We wake to it. To the sound of rain. It lasts all through the day and only breaks towards evening. During the worst of it lightning illuminates the heavy air and thunder rumbles overhead. The two families congregate downstairs around the little table there to play boardgames as we wait for it to pass. Beyond the terrace the gravel roadway fills with water and across the way a shutter flaps against a wall and the palms beyond its tiled roof rouse in the thunderlight. We rifle bags of lettered tiles and scribble pictograms and mime the titles of books and films and plays. On the table are plates of cheese and sausage and a dish of nuts and another of pitted black olives and the smell is of coffee grounds in the cafetiere and hot rain permeating through the open patio doors. There is much laughter. Sometimes I glance over at Emily and she will look back with a flicker of cynical amusement in her eyes for we are of that age where we know all and nothing.

Late in the sodden afternoon our parents go off on some errand and she and I retire upstairs to the mezzanine. Rain is slanting in dirty canted streaks down the windowpane and rippling noisily on the skylight and we sit on one of the sofa beds surrounded by cushions and a cotton throw to read. She has her feet curled beneath her and I have mine upon the coffee table I have pulled over. For my book I've little concentration. I'll turn a page to simulate progress and will hear her do the same and I will glance down from the corner of my book to her bare thighs. She is wearing denim shorts and a vest and our legs are soon touching and her arm is draped across the backrest and perhaps this also brushes against me. I'm unable to move. Unable even to turn the pages of my book. This girl I've known for so long and about whom I now know so little. This girl with whom my childhood was somehow whole. I shift position. Make like I'm looking past her and out of the window. Use the ploy to glance at her. Impassive eyes downcast. Unmoving. Fingers poised over page. Alone together in this stormy light. The glow of the lamp over her. Breeze through the open window. See it like it's a movie. Gently reaching over. My hand caressing her hair. Her willing capitulation. Kissing first my palm then holding it against her cheek. Coming closer. Allowing me to kiss her neck. Kiss her shoulder. Kiss her chest. Peeling off her vest. Her bikini top. Peeling it back from her breasts with the ghost of it still imprinted on her bare skin. Kissing her torso. Unfastening her shorts and with the rain peeling down the window and the lightning seeming to recede the world is rainhazed and spectral. She turns a page. Moments fleeting. Until time having slipped by and given instead to cans of beer and small talk footfalls can be heard on the gravel beyond the window. The recognition years later at the coffee table with the wickerwork of aerials in the mews across the way that so much can seem lost in an afternoon. That opportunities which so seldom come can seem spurned.

Photograph of us around a restaurant table sometime towards the end. My father and hers. My mother and hers. The two of us. Husks of prawns and mussel shells in bowls. A breadbasket. Candlelight. Bottle of wine in an ice bucket. All of us intertwined and sharing in some privately acknowledged joke. I slide it back into the shoebox and bury it with the others. Bury them beneath pagodas and raked gravel gardens and steppelands.

By five that afternoon I'm heading out. The hour of my departure gives me enough cushion both to avoid Bea coming back from work and arrive first at our arranged meeting place. The reunion I've justified to myself for I've told no lie. I told Bea I was meeting an old friend for a drink. Somebody I'd not seen in years who had got back in touch recently due to a chance encounter. No other information given. By six I'm seated at a table in a pub in town not far from the lawcourts. Bankers and city types at the bar in pinstripe suits. The place suggested by her because of its proximity to her place of work.

The table I've chosen is around a corner in a recess from the rest of the bar but with a view out across it to the doorway. I sit there nervously toying with a coaster. Searching the crowds for the first glimpse of her. I check my phone but no messages come and as the time draws on I wonder whether perhaps she isn't coming. Wonder whether I even saw her at all for already our meeting seems almost fantastical. The bar starts to fill and I look at the suits of the drinkers and at the skin of my palms worn raw from the corners of boxes in the store and I'm troubled by a growing sense of degradation. Troubled by what she might think of me surrounded by so much that is unfamiliar to me. I think of Bea returning home from work and am gnawed by guilt at this infidelity. In Bea I have everything that for many years I craved and in Emily only a hazy idea of fate. And yet.

I scan the men at the bar again. The tables. The alcoves. And then at the doorway I see her. At first I'm not sure it's her for I've never seen her dressed this way. A starched white shirt. Pencil skirt with matching jacket. Heels. I watch her. Watch her scanning the bar. Watch the men there cast their eyes over her. An otherworldliness to her amongst them. She starts to cut through the crowd and risen in a crouch from the table I wave. At first she doesn't see me. Reaches into her leather briefcase to check her phone. Replaces it and looks around. I wave again more persistently and as I step nearer she sees me. She makes her way over and kisses me on each cheek and embraces me warmly. When I draw back I stare at her. At the faint cow's lick in her black hair. The faint ridge of freckles across her nose. Her black eyes beneath her mascara. Her parted lips. She looks back at my lips and then into my eyes and I feel myself disappeared there. Without substance.

I motion for her to sit. She places her case on an adjoining chair and smooths down her skirt and crosses her legs. I am stood there momentarily lost. Looking down at her. Trying to gather myself. She looks back up at me and smiles. I ask her what she'll have to drink and she thanks me and gives her order and then I am heading to the bar surrounded by echoes of her. Echoes I tried so long and hard to bury. Echoes that span junctures of time leading back interminably. At the bar I look at her and she is immobile and erect and staring impassively ahead and I know then that something has yielded in me irrevocably. Echoes there of so many different guises. Of distant beginnings with landscapes and buildings and people now blanched by some impregnable light. Of being with her at the window looking down across the meadow. Of the village beyond and above its rooftops a tumour of rain. Of days dense and languorous. Of the long ago in which a little girl is made to stand up in assembly one morning. She's wearing bright red buckled shoes and has dark hair in pigtails banded with ties the same shade of red. The headmistress is beside her with one hand resting on her shoulder and she tells us that she hopes we will all make the girl feel welcome because it's difficult starting at a new school and she's sure we must all remember how we felt on our first day here. After we've all filed out of the hall and into our classrooms the girl is put onto the table I share with four others and I'm asked by the teacher to show her where the sticky labels are so that she can write her name on one for her plastic tray. In watching her spell it out in blue felt tip I mouth each of the syllables and when we are back at the table again I am sitting next to her and at the teacher's behest showing her where we got up to the previous lesson. She creases down the first page of her new exercise book and copies down the last of my two sums. Feeling drawn to her even then. Seeing in her something other. An indefinable quality. The teacher writes some new sums on the blackboard and scaffolds the first so that we can do the next ten ourselves. Emily is quicker at them than anyone else on the table and when she's finished she lays down her pencil and sits there quietly neatening her little rows of numbers with a rubber. At playtime she goes off with some of the girls and at play with the boys I will now and then look across at her for she seems alone even in company. After the bell is rung by the dinner lady we line up in rows and I am behind her for we are in alphabetical order and I look at the curls of her dark hair behind her ear.

In the afternoon we are taken by the teacher to the quiet corner where we are allowed to sit on bean bags and she reads to us and we follow the story in our picture books with our reading fingers and sometimes we will repeat phrases after her or she will stop on a word and ask one of us to read it aloud. I get my word right and so does Emily and the teacher says well done to her and gives her a gold star for her exercise book. When school has finished Emily's mother comes to pick her up at the gate. She has dark hair and wears a summer dress and she hugs her daughter and takes her little leather satchel from her and helps her into the front seat and as I'm walking down the lane with some of the other boys I watch them drive by and Emily looks at me and waves from the car window and I go to wave back but it's too late and the car is soon disappeared from view.

I head back with the drinks and we fall into conversation and there is within our dialogue a quality almost perversely commonplace and mundane amongst so much shared history. I ask her whether she works nearby and she describes in some detail her offices and the charity for which she's employed and the wells they dig in remote desert backwaters. She describes the trips she's taken to villages moulded from mud huts with emaciated cattle hitched to stakes or lain dead in the dusty dirt tracks. Describes the holes from which the villagers have hitherto drawn water and the children she's seen wracked with disease and malnutrition. Describes baobab trees in arid savannahs and truck rides to market towns in caroming flatbeds. I stare at her. That she could have gone so far and to such distant continents. This girl from down the lane whose mother baked cookies for us after school and with whom I would watch cartoons on the floor of her living room. She asks then of my work and I give the vaguest of outlines. Tell her how what I'm doing is just a kind of stopgap. That after I returned home I just needed to find something to bring me back into the world. Of the broader questions she asks of my life I am evasive and do not mention Bea. She enquires after my mother and I describe something of the previous few months and Emily apologises once again for not having been at the funeral.

We lapse into silence. I look across at her. Our eyes meet. There is much I'd like to say to her. Much I'd like to ask her.

And yet a part of me is afraid to know. I look at her fingers on the tabletop. The little watchband around her wrist. The way her shirt is rolled at the cuff. It seems now like there was never a time she wasn't in my life in some way. She takes another sip of wine and then excuses herself and then I am watching as she pushes out her chair and rises and walks through the bar. The way her fitted white shirt clings to her waist and hips. The zip at the back of her pencil skirt. Her shingled hair sitting just above her collar. Beyond the open doorway the light is almost faded now and the yellow glow of streetlamps begins to mist the windows and in another guise towards the end of our time at primary school the afternoon light catches upon the various items scattered across the tabletop. It is nearing the year's end and warm. The smell of baked tarmac and pool chlorine drifts in through the open windows. The walls are collaged with a term's worth of blitz descriptions overlaying peeling artwork mosaics and a checkerwork of illustrated short stories and a reading leader board upon which Emily's name is uppermost. A corkboard in the corner is pinned with photographs of swimming gala podia and sports day sack races. The teacher is at the front in a sleeveless blouse and summer skirt. Her chalk dust pitches slowly through the air as she tells us boy girl pairings. Then the scraping of chairs. Pencil cases and exercise books sliding across tables. Frenzied migrations. Not wishing to be lumbered with one of the slow ones. The others at our table deliberate and eventually draw lots. But with Emily it is unspoken.

We are told that our final project of the year is to build a kite. First we are to research kites and then we are to design our own and finally we are to construct it using lengths of square dowels and stiff cardboard and glue and paper. There will be a prize for the most efficient and another for the most artistic. Books and photocopies are distributed amongst each of the tables and soon we are working methodically through them. Scanning the content. Copying in our own words the most relevant passages. Drawing reproductions of designs we like. Emily with her faster reading and neater handwriting concentrates on the former while I work on the drawing. It is the next stage of evolution in any number of projects we have worked on together. On the first just after she started I was asked to pair with her because she was new and we won a prize for our final piece. A slew of others followed. Presented in celebration assemblies at the end of each term I would follow her to the front waiting to receive a certificate and a book token or a set of colouring pencils and before long there were rumours that she was my girlfriend and people would sing songs about us sitting up a tree k.i.s.s.i.n.g. but that was all long ago and now our pairing is taken as a given. The teacher circulates with tracing paper and boxes of pencils and felt tips. She stoops and chivvies. When she passes us she gives us each a gold star in our exercise books. We work on it at school and then in the afternoons sitting out in her garden with our material spread out on her picnic table. Her mother brings us plates of biscuits and mugs of tea and supplies us with additional books she found in the local library. She buys us a ring binder with plastic sleeves to present our work in and we are soon starting to fill it with everything neat and ordered.

For our own design we decide on a box kite. We are there at hers beside each other at the picnic table when I start to draw it. First a rough version and then the final draft using a ruler and fineliner. Everything is three dimensional with each join represented and labelled. From time to time she will chip in and tell me what to annotate but for the most part she simply watches with her shoulder against mine.

Another afternoon there's a storm. We have little work left to do beside construction so we go up to her room and watch the sheets of rain falling over the cows in the adjoining field with their lowing mournful beneath the distant rolls of thunder and at some point as I glance across at her her profile is illuminated by a flare of sheet lightning. We watch the garden consumed by rain. Rippling across the picnic table. Dripping from the parasol. The lawn a slurry of writhing grass. The boughs of the apple tree black with it. After the storm has passed a relentless drizzle sets in and forbidding waves of it macerate the landscape. We sit on her bed and talk and I look around her room. The wrought bedstead. The little vanity unit. Everything a shade of blue. Her stuffed animals on top of the wardrobe. Ornithological posters on the walls. A framed print of her with her parents on holiday. Surf foaming at their feet. A blood sunset. Her collection of books ramshackle on a shelf the only unordered chaos. A long and almost endless afternoon with her. Some subtle change evident. Something to do with being older and alone with her like this. Walking home later my progress is slow. Rain crawls down the back of my neck and the verges are boggy. The Bourne is almost full and rushing in torrents beneath the low slung bridges and deadpooling along its banks. The memory of her at the door waving me off. Hazed by the rain.

The following day at school we start to measure out lengths of doweling and cut them to size with hacksaws. Sand down the edges. Number them in pencil. With a knurl handled craft knife cut to size the card triangles to mask the joists. All carefully counted out. The frame first. Each side laid flat on the workbench. Glued over sheets of newspaper. Time to dry the joists before masking with the card. Then lifting each of the sides to form the shape of the box. Doweling between glued down. At the end of the afternoon the finished frame measures a metre long by fifty centimetres across. At her house we finalise the design for the paper casing. Her idea. The four seasons. One on each side. For winter a stretch of snowbound woodland. Summer that thunderstorm over the cow pasture behind her house. Spring blossom and autumn harvest. The idea I guess to signify the passing of another year. And so too our passing from the school into the coming beyond.

The next day I draw out the designs on brown packing paper and then with poster paints we take two seasons each and block out the colours. Emily spring and summer. A fork of lightning beneath a raft of cloud. Black and white blobs of cows below. Brushstrokes of grassland. Brushstrokes of a pathway vanishing in the distance. Mine a snow scene. A lonely woods. Everything in monochrome. Another day the apple tree blossoming in her garden and my fruit thatch for harvest. A deadness of leaves in the background. Hints of them drifting from the trees. We trim the panels and glue them to the frame. The spool we fashion from two thicker lengths of doweling glued between two lollipop sticks. To the frame we screw an eyelet picture hook and from this we string a cord to the spool. Finally ribbons in pink and blue and orange and white are tied sequentially to the cord.

Having finished first we gain permission from the teacher to test it out on the playing field. In the depths of that warm blue June she walks away trailing a lengthening cord between us. Me rooted there. Clutching the turning spool. Watching the cord wound around it gradually falling away. Watching her gradually lose definition on the field. Calling out to me indistinguishably. Then a deft movement as she raises the kite above her head and releases it. The cord snapping taut. Ribbons in the sun. How it dips and rolls in that cloudless sky from the long white seam of its string leash. The hours we've spent working on it. Poring over it from its earliest inception. See her in that distance with her neck craned watching it roll and dip and dip and roll. But then the wind dies and it starts to drop from the sky. Skittering down. Sometimes finding some stasis before jittering earthward once more. Emily bearing beneath it. The spool now slack now taut. Dipping through another current. Finally falling on its corner. Hollow thud of the earth. We convene and assess the damage. The torn panel of a painted season. A rip through her summer pastureland. A length of splintered dowel wafting threads of glue. This loss of symmetry. We take it back to class and for the remainder of the afternoon try to patch things up. Tape over the torn paper. Glue new joists. Some delicate sanding. Retied ribbons on the cord. Later repainting the scarred pasture.

Another summer's day sometime in that eternal past our year takes to the field towing in their royal blue shirts and shorts their kites. Diamond. Sled. Delta. Box. A light wind blows the treetops as we disperse across the field. The teacher has a camera and stopwatch. We take our paired positions. One with kite aloft and the other teasing the pair's spool. Emily and I have swapped. Far off at the end of that ribboned cord the box above my head is already starting to fret in the breeze. And though we have done our best to repair it it still seems fragile. And so it goes. On the teacher's whistle I release it. Almost immediately it starts to jar in rising. One of the struts cracks. It twitches violently at its zenith and starts to spiral these long loops. Starts to fall. Crumpling in a heap on the grass. Emily rushing over to it trailing the spooled string. I stand there watching her. The first of all to fall.

Later we are down by the river on one of the bridges overlooking its blackly gelid waters with the broken reflections of the city's skyline cresting the fans of waves rippling its stygian surface. Windless amongst the buildings here it gusts around the bridges and along the walkways and the sound is of the waves eddying after watertaxis. Gulls are in the sky with the whites of their plumes against the black and strips of cloud illuminated by the moon beyond. A plane cranes earthward dry brushed by the moon. Theatregoers down

175

below mill in shawls with their shadows stretching across the promenade and the festooning of lights above them along the facades and soffits of the halls straining out into the night. We lean over the smoothworn balustrade. The buttressed piers and abutments below are streaked with gull shit and tongued by the darkly breaking waves. We too are soon on the promenade with the wind curling briny off the river and the curls of charcoal smoke from food trucks tapering off into the pupae of darkness webbing the treetops. Lights line the black balustrade and brick bridges. Beneath the sweep of their arches the black streaked brickwork drips into the river below. One such arch we sit beneath on a damp slatted bench and watch people browsing a bookstall. She leans back on the bench and I look across at her dark eyes and palely cold skin. Difficult I suppose to know anybody. An avoidance this evening over asking after her private life. Whether someplace a partner waits. A fiance or a husband. A baby. Lamp burning. Not wanting its sad confirmation. Thoughts too of Bea home on the sofa with her trousersuit hanging from the doorjamb. I watch the slow passing of another watertaxi trailed by the wraith of its lights. People at the windows. Slaps of waves against its hull. Wind gusts in off the river and lifts the strands of her hair. How years from now these destinations will be imbued with such quiet wraiths of passing.

We go to where the shawled patrons gathered. Their flutes and canape platters litter tabletops by a bar counter on the walkway. Serviettes furl. The building beyond is haunted by slowly moving forms. At cafe tables. On the stairs. By an empty stage. The men in suits and their wives gloving clutchbags. We walk on and later are sitting at the window table of a cafe looking out through the darkened glass at another black stretch of river with the lights of distant blocks swilling across the water's surface and Emily stirring with a wood stick a glass of foamy coffee. We have for a long while been silent and the cafe is quiet with the barista staring out across the lengths of tabletops beneath the soft striplights. I stir sugar into my coffee and roll and reroll the empty sugarstick looking at Emily's pellucid reflection in the dark glass. She stares away also. Into some unknown distance. She is there at the table with me long ago when my mother comes crying to the school to tell me the news. That I passed the entrance test. That I've been accepted. Is there at the table when I return nonplussed and another girl asks me why my mother was here. Emily catching my eye and smiling because she's already guessed. Emerging sense of my already starting to slip away. From them. From her. Remember earlier still a group of us meeting behind the sheds one lunchtime. Six of us. Three boys and three girls who had paired off. Who called each other boyfriend and girlfriend. The gathering arranged so that we could exchange our first kiss. The others went first. We watched them screw shut their eyes and press their lips together. Emily and me the same. Pursed lips. Neither breathing nor moving. Little knowing. Little realising. Just wanting it to be over. To disengage. Until in the village hall that final year when everybody threw discos for their birthdays and the first real feelings were awakened. Paper cups of coke and lemonade. The worn wood smell of the place. The damp kitchen. The old foldaway tables on rickety legs with soda sodden paper cloths. Mobile disc jockeys with walls of laser light and dry ice with the wisps of it at our feet and around the tangleweb rafters of the ceiling. Remember dancing with her. Our bodies pressing together. Her hair in a milkmaid braid entwined with daisies. Her white gown shimmering. The hall empty it seemed. Only then beginning to realise what it meant. Just the two of us in its unending dark. And now my own reflection with her also. Layered immutable in the dark glass.

My last view of her that evening is on the upper deck

of a bus drawing away into the night. She looks down at me once to wave and then I am walking lost amongst the streets with little will to return home. The night is cool and the sky a tainted orange beset with vapours of ebbing light. I see Emily in each face going by and on the bus much later I watch the unfolding dark beyond the window and I see her in its blackness and through its endless shadow plays. Bea is asleep when I arrive home. I sit for a while in the living room drinking whiskey with no compulsion to move. Later when I get into bed Bea stirs but says nothing and the next day we argue and she rails against me for returning home late without telling her but that night all seems well. I dream of a sea beneath a gunmetal sky with rotted groynes along the shoreline and somewhere amongst them the dark shape of a girl known though unknown seated on a beach towel. I am out at sea wading waist deep and underfoot there are knotted tree roots and the shore and the girl seem to be receding such that I continually lose them from view and soon the sea and the shore are as one and the light is almost gone.

\*            \*            \*

A railed park just off to the side of the road slopes away through the serried black fenceposts. I leave the van parked at the kerb and climb out. Music still radios from the cab and its warning lights strip the pavement. Why now? On this morning? Everything commonplace. Ordinary. A place I pass each day and barely notice. Flashes of joggers and dogwalkers or jogging dogwalkers. Everything blurred in passing blurred now with the sudden wakening of passing. How in his final hours there came a quiet acceptance of the passing of all things. How in the morning he was taken away and how dimly I had seen him sheeted then wheeled across the yard in whose gritted gullies puddles had formed from the night's sheathing rain. Puddles mirrored grey by the grey sky but watching it all as through muslin such that the details of whether it was by medics or undertakers into ambulance or hearse remain murky yet still somehow vividly formed with the minutiae of incidentals like the low dull creaking of the gurney wheels across the floor or the faint powdering of soot on the floor from the flue. In the afterdays and afternights trying to make sense of it all but finding that nothing fit into place. Instead sitting up long into the night with the embers of the fire fading in the hearth and the ash falling through the grate into the ashgrey ashpan. How one night it started to sleet and the smat of it could be heard against the windowpanes and the room grew cold and dark with the fading of the fire but of the dark and the cold I was little conscious. That time in their room with the sleet slush outside and in the sky a darkness of birds and the landscape cowed below and the neighbour in her garden hoeing a bed of mud and raking dead weeds into wet piles hunched in rubber boots and a wax jacket. Then withdrawing to the edge of his side of the bed with the impregnation of silence heavy in the air and still the moaning of the wind someplace and my father's things dusty on the bedside table and the watch he wore to work unwound. Unmoving. These remnants of a life. The wardrobe's musty hanger rail. Click of hangers. Faded workshirts. Dated neckties. Corduroy walking trousers. And below in a foldaway crate at the back strewn with shoes and old moccasins his leather camera cases and lens extensions and plastic cases of filters. This melancholy searching through jacket pockets for old coins and pens and slips of cards he'd written on.

Cuds of grass. Passing joggers dogwalkers cyclists. The first tears shed since. Since that night of falling rain. I am a long time there remembering. How once he had passed and we had both drunk brandy at the kitchen table we lay

179

there unspeaking in the lounge on mattresses with him dead beside us in that abyssal darkness. Could have gone to bedrooms now it was over. Could have slept in my old room surrounded by the paraphernalia of childhood. Decided to stay instead at the place of our vigil with the paraphernalia of his death on the shelves and ledges and in the moonlight beneath the sheet we'd draped over him the peaks of his toes and nose and of the rest of him nothing much remaining. All sunken and dead and without form. Had watched for a while the rain as it continued relentlessly to fall in the darkness upon the sagging leylandii bordering the back garden. Even then nothing much remained to be felt. How many times in the aftermath would I revisit that night trying to dredge forth the will to feel? Countless times I'd gone through his things and sat with old holiday albums and seen him through all those different eras trying to force myself into some kind of catharsis but there was little in the hue of his holiday tans and sock sandals to reconcile with what he became. Just this numbness. Had got drunk in the shrine of his armchair on whiskey when my mother was away. Trying to commune. Yet finding in the reflections in the blank screen of the television nothing but an empty solipsism. And back in the city had only periodically paused when walking on warm days to even try to remember what had happened. Something about the tedium of everything that made it all so unremarkable. Yet now it comes. Intangibly. Collapsed there at the railing. Hanging from its wrought black finials. The cold black touch of them. Then slumped on the pavement choking it back. Ignored by those going by. The hazard lights of the van still stripping over the pavement. Remembering too those people. Wellwishers or naysayers. Those who actually seemed to believe that survival was merely a matter of will. That the strong would pull through. Those at the funeral who I had not seen in years. Who shook my hand or touched my shoulder with such earnestness. Had heard of others dying also. A friend of my mother's who had it on the breast and was gone within weeks after it spread to her brain. An old neighbour who had it in the bowels and shat blood and collapsed someplace abroad and died in a hospice there. All of them wretched and without meaning. Had one night written a letter to the locum whose misdiagnosis had killed my father. Drunk by the end. Just pawing at the keyboard. The next day finding vitriol. Cocksucker. Arsehole. Cunt. But all that really remained was the yearning for this catharsis. This ending to numbness. Through the railings in the scrub and dust of dead leaves these desiccated fossils of litter. My throat starting to ache. In the cab of the van I hear my phone ring and I stare down at the ground as everything starts to bleed away. Bleed away into the raw nothingness of morning.

Not long after other such raw mornings bereft of recourse I hand in my notice. Feel my father there stooped over me as I type. Unfulfilled. Dissatisfied. Feel I can no longer contribute meaningfully. Have other ambitions I wish to pursue. Have enjoyed working here. Given me a range of invaluable skills. Thank you for the opportunity.

All the time watching my fingers over the keyboard. Disconnected from them. From the words fanning out across the page. Write that in the aftermath of my father's death I have a renewed sense of my own mortality. The intention to take it out after but in the end just leave it there. The whole thing in the end a treatise on how worthless life is specifically when tasked with menial labour. The intention to edit never realised. A long time just staring at it on the page then staring from the window at the buildings and people and sky then staring out across the empty store and before sending it go to the doorway lean against the doorjamb watch the mannequins at office windows the windows of passing cars of passing buses. A familiarity as if all has been seen before and all has been before. This selfsame procession of things. The petrol station opposite. Diesel fumes and slicks of spilt petrol. After it is sent I make tea and drink it in a nest of boxes. Each time I move bottles move above and the wood pallet creaks below. I pick splinters from it. Scuff beneath my shoe a dustshard of glass and from an old winefoil habillage I twist a filigree. I read a printout of the notice letter. A strangeness to it. Imagine them receiving it at head office and trying to make sense of it.

It causes us to have this massive argument. The thing is I'd forgotten or maybe ignored the fact she worked there at the head office in human resources. Probably was the first one to read the thing and when she got home and found me there on the settee she was holding it creased up in her hand. Her hair dishevelled. Shirt partly unbuttoned. The straps of her shoes loose around her ankles.

Shouldn't we make decisions like this together?

I don't know...

Because they affect both of us.

Yeah...

Why didn't you talk to me first?

It just happened.

What do you mean it just happened?

I was just...I was driving to work and...

And what?

I don't know. I just felt I had to.

Quit your job?

Yeah. Quit my job. I can't stand it anymore.

You still should have talked to me first.

Like I say it just happened.

And what kind of letter is this anyway?

What do you mean?

All this stuff about your dad?

It's true.

But why would you write it in a resignation letter?
Why not?
It's just not the done thing?
I don't really care what the done thing is.
But...
It goes on like this for some time. Recriminations and rebuttals and disengagement. For the next few days she hardly talks to me at all and I am not really there at all. Little more than a shell. Discomposed. Detached. At night while she sleeps I lie there staring up at the ceiling. One evening on my way home I pull the van over at the same kerb and climb over the railings into the park and there are people on the grass because it's a Saturday and warm and they are there with picnics or plastic bags of beer and I lie on the grass until it gets dark and stare at that sky with its layers of polluted light.

\*              \*              \*

It dies down. I guess maybe she thinks I'm going to change my mind and I start to wonder whether she's actioned my letter or merely taken it as some kind of lapse of reason on my part and expects me to continue at work as before. Eventually she starts talking to me again. At first tentatively. A few terse words about what to buy for dinner. The dripping tap that needs fixing. A letter that arrived from the landlady. In bed a couple of nights later she touches me for the first time in days and we lie there for a while staring at each other and I think about how little I really know her. How little I really know anybody. She drifts off to sleep with her hand in mine and for a long while I lie awake staring at her. I rise with the dawn and brew some coffee. Take it downstairs and sit on the doorstep watching pigeons in the mews opposite. I'm there maybe an hour before she comes down. Her gown around her.

Puts her hand on my shoulder and asks me if I'm okay. I nod. She asks whether it's about my dad and I tell her I don't even know anymore. It's about so much more than that. About so much less. She apologises for her mood and we're there a time together before going back inside. She makes eggs. We eat at the table with the television on in the background. I tell her I'm still going to do it. That I'm still going to quit. She nods like she knows this then says she's already set things in motion at head office. To her question of my intentions I tell her I don't know. I tell her I'll start looking. Maybe find work as a runner. As a production assistant. A junior researcher. She nods and tells me to do what I need to do. That she'll be there to support me. She kisses me and goes to shower and afterwards I watch her through a doorcrack towelling down in the steam and then in the bedroom pulling on her knickers and clipping at the back her bra then buttoning her shirt. I go to the window and watch her disappear down the street and I stay there a long while afterwards before finally withdrawing to the newfound silence of the flat. To its drab rental furniture and the few knickknacks we have accumulated together pewtered by the dull light coming in through the slatblinds. I go to work. At work nothing happens. At lunch I tell the trainee to mind the store and I go to the train station where I use my travel card to pass through the turnstiles and sit on a bench at the far end of the platform watching the trains. See them draw in and leave. The sun dull along the tracks. Dull along the overhead cables. My phone goes. I ignore it. I buy coffee. Take it back to the bench. Drink it slowly.

A month later a party is organised for my departure. The pub over the road from the old store then on to a club. People from what now seems a distant past. At the club reverberations through the floorboards. Pestling strains of music and strained conversation. We leave around three. Head out onto the roundabout to flag cabs. On the ride home beside Bea I stare from the window at the routes I've walked to work. The corner where I first heard of my father's cancer. The backstreets I walked to Bea's. The dark line of trees at the edge of the park. These we pass. Pass the rows of shops before the railway bridge beneath which drips seep from stains spread across the great slabs of concrete overhead and torn bills peel from the guttered brickwork. We slip soon after onto our street. Drifts of litter and dark windows and in the lawns of the council blocks a fox.

In the days and weeks that follow I sit around while Bea is at work and pretend to myself that I'm looking for jobs. Pretend to her the same when she gets home of an evening. Mostly I watch television. Drink tea. Now and then take a walk up the main street. One time stay in a cafe at the window seat the better part of two hours watching the traffic go by. I live out the remainder of my final month's wages then eat through what little savings I have. Nights when Bea is in bed I sit up drinking cooking brandy. Watching movies on television. Toying with my phone. By the time I wake in the morning she's long gone with the only signs of her the cold milkwebbed mug of tea I find left for me on the bedside and her plate and mug stacked neatly in the sink. In the evenings I cook. Eat without appetite. Sometimes Bea will call to tell me she'll be delayed or that she's going out with friends after work or at the weekends with her girlfriends into town. But rather than mourn these lost hours with her or wonder after ulterior motives I will quietly celebrate such is the increasing distance I feel from the world we have created for ourselves in the confines of the flat. Mooted projects like shelves and repaints are soon abandoned. Some nights we have sex and I will stare down at her and she back at me and in our eyes I will see little connection. Or I'll watch across the moonlit contours of her spine the waxing moon beyond the window and the pallor of her skin grazing in its ether and afterwards

185

when we lie there I will watch it veiled by banks of hoary cloud or will watch how the stars die. Or staring down at her see Emily or see her later in the depths of night when Bea lies inert beside me. Yet other evenings in spite of the apparent disintegration of things I will look on her as of old. As of those long afternoons in the store when I watched her at work amidst the pallets. When her shirt would ride up above her jeans and she would wipe the sweat from her brow. I will watch her while she washes up and through her shirt I will be able to make out the curve of her spine or through her jogging bottoms the shape of her hips. These times I will go to her. Stand behind her and push my hands beneath her shirt or into her waistband. She will lean back into me and I will kiss her neck. One time still in her marigolds she takes me in her hands. Ejaculate down her front after. Sliding down the cupboard doors behind her.

Finally I start trawling through the jobs pages on the internet. One evening I find a runner's position advertised. Temporary. A month to six weeks. Somebody who can drive a van. I apply for it and my phone goes a couple of hours later and the person on the other end introduces herself as Imogen and asks me if I can start the following night at eight o'clock south of the river. I tell Bea when she gets home from town and she kisses me on the cheek and puts her arms around me.

That's great.

It's not much. Just a runner's job.

At least it's something.

The pay's pitiful.

It's a start.

Yeah. I've always wanted to work in film.

That evening I cook spaghetti and we drink wine and afterwards we sit up long into the night. Music in the background. Spirits after the wine is gone. The job's for a month and I ask Bea whether when it's over she wouldn't like to come down to the house with me on the Mediterranean for a week or so. September time when the season is over and everywhere is quiet again. By way of answer she sits astride me and pulls off her shirt.

The following day we get up late. Hungover. I go out to buy coffee and muffins and we have these on the settee and spend most of the morning and afternoon watching films. Around six I shower and pull on some old jeans and a shirt and stuff a sweater and a bottle of water into a bag and head out. It's still warm and people are sitting out on the common by the station. I descend into the underground and board a train and stand by the open window between two carriages and I think of Bea and how she was last night with the moonlight across her pale white skin. I watch in the dark glass of the carriage the reflections of other passengers and on the floor of the carriage between their feet the cellophane wrap of a straw caught in a vortex of wind. Watch it slowly rise and fall and fall and rise and watch the expressions of the other passengers hued blue with intermittent white electric flare illuminating the piceous black piped tunnel behind them.

The street above the station at which I disembark is lined with the dun smears of tower blocks and the pavement strewn with debris from a torn bin sack. The roadways converge upon the guttered carousel of a vast roundabout leading into unknown warrens fronted by all night convenience stores and grocers' and letting agents'. The address I have written on a scrap of paper and I use the map outside the station to navigate past some kind of mall around which are clustered at the base below street level market stalls hooded by sheets of blue tarpaulin. The smell is of jerked meat and diesel fumes and music bleeds from a radio slung by a bungee cord from one of the stall frames and this is overlayered by an argument across the street and by the blared horns of traffic and far off a siren. A slender tower block beyond rises from the roadway with the lower husks of it blackened by fire soot and the upper extremities quilted by flapping laundry and pocketed by the light mooned discs of satellite dishes on the balconies.

Locating the estate to which I've been directed I find myself on a raised walkway overlooking tunnelled alleys and rows of disused shops and warrens of stairwells. Below me is a fenced off lawn with spring mounted animal rides and a seesaw and through the doorway of the building behind it a rack of clothes and a tea caddy and wheeled road trunks. I call out but no one hears. I follow the walkway to one of the stairwells and as I descend it the wind ticks the fan through the louvered vent flap grille and the floor is littered with bits of old roach and spent lighters and the walls tapestried with the dripped black tags of graffiti. I come to the lawn and call out once more and this time someone hears and I'm let in and introduced to a location scout and the other drivers. Instructions are given to drive the vans and equipment and generator to tomorrow's location across town and a while later after everything's loaded we leave in a convoy through the dark empty streets. I drive with the windows open. The van's old and rusted with various lights showing on the dashboard and the petrol gauge fucked and a rattling from somewhere beneath me. Rounding corners the load slides in the back and past outlying suburbs greyed by the moon and stretches of carriageway empty in the night we pull in at a wirefenced lockup and park the vans alongside one another and unhook the generator. There follows some discussion about how to get home or whether it might be more sensible simply to sleep in the cabs of the vans or in the hulks amidst the lighting rigs. After some deliberation we head for the nearest bus stop with the route flanked by dark windowed council blocks and on the bus into town we speak little. We alight someplace I've been to before and after we separate I wander around trying to work out where I am and then see a bus that will take me partway home and by the time I'm finally back it's already three and there is a lightness in the sky heralding the coming dawn. I open the door and remove my shoes and pad quietly up the stairs and then to the bathroom and finally the bedroom where Bea stirs. I kiss her on the cheek and climb in beside her and she asks me in her semiconsciousness something unintelligible before falling to sleep again and I beside her stare through the window at the moon until sleep takes me also.

I'm woken at five by my alarm and I make coffee and drink it coming to watching the signlanguaged news and then I am gone through the dawn towards the station and once we are at the lockup and rudimentary directions have been given we convoy to a network of caves south of the city for the day's shoot. Before the cast arrives we cart rigs along dark and labyrinthine rabbit holes and afterwards I'm stationed in a dank orifice abutting the set with the walkie talkie hanging from my back pocket now and then pitching static into the blackness. I stare through its depths and listen to the sometime rise and dip of voices from the adjoining cavern. The first assistant. The screams of the lead. Finally silence. I use my phone screen to illuminate the face of the rock beside me all scarred and waxen looking but the light reaches no farther. Merely webs through the mantle of darkness and diminishes into nothing. Throughout the morning I hear from the catacombs of the caves flurries of movement but no one comes by and I'm alone there until the call for lunch sounds. In the narcoleptic daylight we take from the caterers' table our fare of broiled chicken and salad and flatbread and eat it at picnic benches beneath the sap green canopy of the trees from which parakeets wrangling in the upper boughs shit through the thick bower berry red guano. It's barely eleven and warm out. Alone at the end of one of the benches I fork through my food and watch the crew. A strange hollowness to the light. In the sky beyond the trees an etiolated pallor. The clouds such as they are thin and wan. This enervated day sketched in the drawn faces of crew along the benches. Entering the caves afterwards the red blind patterning of the sun plays out across the darkness and after filming has resumed I am back in the cavern in the depths of its black crouched in the grit or slumped against the smoothworn walls with the remnant embers of light flaring up out of the nothingness and dying. See in their aftermath stars. See those stars in the night sky and the light from below faint and torpid in the dark. Music distant and strained. The grass still and damp and moonlit. A scene of long remembrance. An unshakeable sense of ending. Of all roads leading to this moment and after seeming without meaning or direction. See the forms of people down below at the windowed sidewalls or upon the lawn figures small and moonlit. Wondering which of any is she. Wondering which is he. The bleeding of their black shadows across the grasses. A wrenching mood of all things having passed. The moon's orb above timeless and cold and alien. See her as she'd been on the corner where streaks of beaded light from the streetlamp cascade down the osiers of the willow she walks beneath and fall across her. It is there where we meet with the long filaments of its boughs around us. Light glistering crystalline and lazy through the pinnate braids and plaits of its wickered leaves. Walking home drunk after a shut in at the pub oblivious to all but my own footsteps and the quietness of the night. And then seeing her. Years have passed and at first I almost go on by for it seems almost unreal and unnatural that it could be her. And yet the familiarity of not only her appearance but also the odd notion that this scene beneath the tree in the starlit night has already happened before and is happening eternally and has been etched into a history of time immemorial brings me inexorably to her. Feelings inceptive and ageless. I suppose it is sometime at the start of that final winter term of secondary school but really it's difficult to know. Difficult to remember. For all this is long ago as are all things. My father. These black caves. My mother's tumour. Years gone by since and to what end. To be here unshriven. To be so long unseeing. And yet here again I find myself beside her beneath the tree in the dark hinterlands of home. Why there alone? I never know. Never ask. Why there in the night by the bench? We talk first of the interceding years and try to remember when it was that last we met and it is agreed upon that it was at a village gathering in the field by the school with bunting bedecking the trees and ribbons festooning the wire fence surrounding it. We try to recall the occasion. All I can see of it if even we talk of the same day is the memory of her in the distance on the baulk as she walked home. Perhaps I was twelve. Already a year into seclusion from normality at a private all boys' school. Awkward around girls. Women. People in general. In a quiet corner of the field drinking pop from a plastic cup. On the baulk home seeing her recede and seeing beyond her the squat valleyed houses and nude green terrain and how the wind through the barley seemed to pool and purl and how the cloudshadow seemed forgathered around her such that she was bathed in the light of the sun. And seeing her on the baulk in the forgathered light how memories issued forth as from some past where light reigned omniscient. Of those primary school days. Of being alone with her after the others had dispersed and I would see her home and stop most days for the tea and biscuits her mother had prepared on a tea tray. Now in the summer on the lawn. Now in the winter at the window with the waning sun low and mooned across the fields and the starched trees stiff with cold. The ornaments on the sill. A smooth stone painted as a leveret. Another as a doe. A painted wood clog. A stacking doll. A gnarled fist of bogwood hung with necklaces. We knocked down dominoes. Watched cartoons or drew. For a month made models from matchsticks. Home time her mother would see me off at the door and I'd wave back at the bottom of the path and Emily would be on the step there and this is often how I remember her. On the step in her blue uniform by her mother's side. Waving back or watching. Weekends sometimes when our parents met we'd walk with them and the dogs out across the fields and when they took tea afterwards we'd go to her room and she'd a fishbowl with shubunkin and a fantail and in a cage with a wheel a chinchilla. The bedspread thrown with an old coarse hair blanket and pillows against the headboard. Bird posters on the wall. The dogs sometimes with us in a heap on the floor or curled on the beanbag by the dresser. Smell of their mudcaked fur. Sickled whites of their eyes eyeing us in the penumbra. Summer evenings we'd watch the spitsmoke of barbeques rising softly in the dark. At mine when we were younger we'd poke through the pondsludge with sticks and swill through the spawn and duckweed. We dug a pit in the back lot and spade ledges for seats in the hard flint dirt and ate dinners there from plastic picnic plates. Older we'd be on the picnic bench and oftentimes she'd read and I'd just sit alongside of her without onus to speak or be spoken to. Watching her. Watching the quiet concentration as she turned a page or paused to look out across the garden in quiet reverie. Perhaps this is what I liked most about her. That quietly transcendent intelligence. On the baulk that day as she walked away I'd seen what I'd come to know in the last few months of our time together as children. Had seen it once more on the village corner beneath the willow tree. At the party after I came home. Across the tabletop as we looked out over the river and our reflections in the glass merged without definition.

And now some call from the blackness. Radio static. Argent white spots that burn stark and phosphorescent through the tunnels illuminating the nude handsmoothed walls and ancient pick marks and eroded pocks and dust. Illuminating the stark faces of the crew huddled around monitors or spearing booms or trailing lengths of cables from gennies. Then the resumption of darkness. Of silence. Beneath the willow she asks me about school and I ask her the same. What subjects she's taking. What she wants to do. Not knowing where to look. Looking away. Looking down. Looking glancingly at her. See her smile. See her frown. See her look away also. The hallowed cloisters and gowned masters and chapel services just a slow whittling of time to now. Walking away the feeling of a lingering disquiet. A dread that our parting may once again span weeks months years. That in the intervening distance of time I may lose her anew. Back home I join my parents in the dim screenlit murk of the living room. Wineglasses ringing the coffee table. Black bead of claret down the wine bottle. Remnants of dinner congealed on dinnerplates. The television an opaque procession of images through which they sleep. My mother stirs and looks at me through heavy eyes. It's fine I tell her. Go back to sleep. And in that placid dark seeing beneath the willow her dark form and the dark details of her being but finding after a time these reconfigurations disintegrating and losing meaning. Losing definition. A sensation that intensifies over the coming days until I can no longer piece together her image. Sometimes after school I'll go by hers but once in the vicinity I will neither knock nor seek her out. Will merely skirt the long way around the back fields until I am standing aslope in the twilight looking down at the lights from the house spreading across the lawn and perhaps catching a glimpse of her grained against the window. Changing. Real. Imagined. Sitting there for what seems like hours oblivious to the warm cool winds of the cooling summer's eves and later the cooling summers' eves in the dewing twilight until sometime into autumn the meeting beneath the willow seems phantasmagorical. Drunk again one time I'm there on her doorstep. I suppose it's midnight or later. Dark and rainy. With my parents away for a weekend with friends I have been in the village pub and then on a bench in a field with a hipflask of rum watching the clouds descend on the village below and then draining the flask with the drizzle coming on apace and trudging to hers through the dark streets beneath the pale lowhung mothballs of lamplight I am looking up at its cornered dripblack facade and its wet grey roofslats slick in faded night. I am awhile on the doorstep beneath the tiled porch canopy with runoff from the fascia sliding cold and tremulous down my neck and my shadow faint against the woodpanel arch door. A long time staring at the weathered brass lion knocker. Swaying. Trying to focus. Listening for movement. Hearing only the rain in the undergrowth. Crawling through its rainsucked leaves. Reaching out and seeing my hand as if magnified. Poised in a stupor with the knocker to gavel it against the door then simply succumbing. Surrendering to the tattered wonder of the wet night. I go home to the empty darkness of the house or to the undergrowth to watch from the shadows the light play at the windows of her room and imagining her silhouette framed in ringent iridescence. Remembering the gauzy light play across her breasts beneath the willow and the darkness of her hair in the otherworldliness of the willow's arachnid limbs. The stifling rankness of undergrowth around me.

Intervening days weeks months stretching out as foretold. Oftentimes there of an evening with the cold growing through autumn until the trees are bereft and the nights are black and filled with cold stars. Oftentimes in the town on Saturday nights seeing replications of her in bars and clubs and seeing replications in the haemorrhaging of people onto the square past closing. Wondering after the other starlets gathered there whether they know her or have sat in the same classes or shared birthdays. My own weak form reflected in the dark shopfronts. Husks of my unhallowed eyes. Riding home in the night seeing the selfsame darkness against the car windows in cambered strips over the black heathen fields. Those long Sundays lost at my desk in piles of stacked workbooks. Tea rings. Breaks at the window looking out over the neighbours' masticated borders. Quietly asking penitence of her. Those long Sunday evenings lost at the dining table with the peeling of slow autumn rain against the windows and later of cold sleet. My father in his check shirt pouring decanted wine. The slow stark ceremony of it all. Steam still rising from the roasting tin on the kitchen worktop. Carcass of beef rib. Carcass of pork shoulder gristled in a tallow of yellowed fat butchered upon the blood soaked chopping board and the marbled gristles upon the dinnerplates. My mother still takes the dripping. Some forgotten past from when she was a girl. Spoons it into ramekins to crust in the fridge. The rinds and softened crackle gristled and larded in twine and hung from apple tree boughs for the birds. See them aflutter about it. Quiet conversation at the table. About this villager or that. The bank where my father works. The workplace in town of my mother. Sometimes school. The progression of things. The hope of some bright future. All the time drifting and seeing manifestations of that imagined future. Theirs. Mine. Weekdays a rut of revision and essays and annotations. Taking solace in those lonely vistas by hers where from spinneyed bluffs above the chalkpit I will look down upon her house and see a future for us skewed from couples I have observed walking down the street. Her arm through mine head on shoulder a skip to keep in time. Hear the wind about me. See cars along the lane and down below the rude stubble fields. Ploughed mud. Flinted blades of it. Moon through the bare trees. Moon on the dew. In the sky pooled in its own thrown hue.

Sleeping and waking there. Days in this manner. In a womb of cold dewed darkness. A monolith of cryptal damp and airless gouged stone such that day goes unheeded. Home when the houses along the street are couched in darkness. Stand in the living room with a faint web of blue shadow across the floor. A stillness. Pad to the worktop and fix some tea. In the stillness the steam through the hung motes of dust licking against the hob hood. Take it to the table by the window with the spider plant falling down through the gloom and the picked discs of candlewax on the sill. Tealight cups bent and stuck upon it. Too tired I suppose to sleep. Too tired for much at all. This blank and unseeing stare through the darkened windowpane. An ache in my back. Footsore. Too tired to retrieve the remote. Maybe I sleep there a while. On the wood chair at the table with the ceaselessness of traffic below and in the sky through the night's spent rain and near spent dark the moon. Then the slow dawning of light. At some point in these small hours conscious or somnambulant finding my way to the bathroom. Depleted and raw reflection there. Thence to the bedroom where in creased and mooncast sheets she sleeps and I beside her lie and sleep little awoken by my alarm upon closing my eyes and in the dawn drink coffee by the worktop and coffee on the way to the station from a flask I've packed and coffee from a vendor I pass.

One day we drive out to an abandoned hospital. We are there just after eight. A few of the crew are at the gates with croissants in greaseproof packets and thermos flasks. The old brick structure rises behind them from the graffiti daubed boundary boards and smartweld fencing surrounding the perimeter. Maws of old glassless windows puncture the facade. Wires of ivy and bindweed work through the mortar.

Before it an old potholed concourse lies bitten and cracked and grown through with grass and clover. Hailed by two shave headed men stood amongst the crew with a pair of bullneck mastiffs on chain leashes we take the vans round back with the broken down edifice rising through the pale morning. Here and there the window holes are patched up with old rotted chipboard. Above the rear loading bay strews of brown foliage jungle through the fissured brickwork. A rusted skip in the backlot undergrowth is filled with nameless debris. Coils of wire. A gurney. Twisted rags. After the rest of the crew have arrived and the gaffers join us we start to unload from the vans the lightrigs and lamps and filters and cableramps. The rear entranceway leads to a long and gutted corridor bled by dim ashen light from the adjoining rooms. Wires dangle from the fucked ceiling tiles. To one side a mattress blackened with dried blood and a wireframe gurney with buckled wheels lies bevelled at the walls as of some apocalypse wherein all are fled. Picture the raw white bones of them. The raw and pallid death masks. The rooms we pass wheeling sack barrows and trolleys along the snaggletooth flooring are gutted also. In one from a great bionic arm jutting from the ceiling a defunct operating lamp hangs above a padded chair and the floor about it is littered with the tinsel of the lamp's smashed lampbulbs. The room's white tiles have here and there been torn asunder exposing the rotted brickwork beneath. In another onetime private ward with windows overlooking the nondescript garden a bedframe is surrounded by the frayed rags of bed screen curtains hanging to the floor and half translucent with spatters and rings of old fluids and grease and a little wheeled surgery tray trolley by its side still loaded with scalpels and pliers and forceps and callipers and bits of old black swab and gauze and in the corner lengths of cable coil from an unknown machine whose knobs and dials bear lifeless testimony to catheter

197

tubes protruding from the raw urethra of cancered dicks or to surgical tubing piped down cancered oesophagi or to saline drips in the black puckered veins of withered arms or to anaesthetised cadavers raw and unsanctified. These we pass one after another with their bled grey light falling aslant the littered corridor floor and the walls echoic with the strangled rattle of sack barrow trucks and the muffled voices of the crew and the silences of the decaying rooms. When all is unloaded we meet in an old refectory with pale green walls and a gaping serving hatch through which the stained stainless steel worktops and spattered ranges of the kitchen fall away into the layered gloom. We take coffee and I drink mine black and there are platters of bacon rolls and danishes and fruit and during the talk from the first assistant director in which the day's plans are laid bare and instructions are given regarding timetabling I stare through the serving hatch and across the dusty kitchen's hanging pans and ladles and slotted spoons to a small patch of grass in the sunlight and a great horse chestnut on the nearby common. Remember one night in the aftermath of my father's death my mother telling me how much she missed him. Her eyes aglow. Telling me how she felt him looking over her while she went about the house. How he always knew so much and now knew the answer to that question above all others. How she wished to know also. She wouldn't have long to wait. A few years after all this. Elephantine in her hospital bed with the life gone out of her. Wheezing out her final incomprehensible words with the pneumonia mucus on her chest slowly strangling her. Her cards on the little unit. Get well soon. Thinking of you. Hope you're back on your feet again in no time. Ha ha. That day as the previous on the set. Wheeling lights and props down the corridors.

In the evening when all is done and the equipment stowed and the call sheets given for the Monday I head for the bus stop and then into town. It's a Saturday night and there are people abroad in their finery heading for bars and clubs. Girls arm in arm drunk and gelled men hither and yon. Fashionistas at pavement tables with jars of grog. Another part of town watching the queue for a club it starts to rain. A thin and greasy drizzle on the parched streets. Taxis and buses on the intersection. Eructations from the underground tunnels through the wet murk streets. Rickshaws lit with glowsticks and angel lights with their tyre treads listing along the rainblack gutters. My bus comes. People disembark. I look at the driver. He looks back at me. Waits for me to board but something holds me back. The doors cantilever closed and he pulls away. I watch the suggested shapes of passengers through the beaded rear windows before heading aimlessly up the road away from the main thoroughfare and into some side streets. Pass a row of terraced houses with hanging baskets in the porches and little plaques on the brickwork and wrought black railings rainpearled. Pass a gated mews with a picnic bench within and a child's toy tractor by the wall. Unaware such places existed here. A cafe with salamis and hams hanging in the window and on the shelf behind the counter chianti bottles in wicker baskets. A mural of vines below. Around the next corner come to a pub. It's not yet near closing so I go in and order a pint and take it to a table by the window where I settle back and look out over the empty street and listen to the quiet hum of conversation and the sometime muffled jukebox from the corner and the tapping of darts and scrawled chalk and the beer pumps swilling and popping. See in the dark glass the reflections of the other patrons. See echoed in those reflections an old town square from long ago where the pubs dispelled us. Around the old hart statue after closing. See picnic benches in the sun with chickens loose from the coop clucking back their dimpled pink wattles and a peacock warbling asunder yonder. Another

199

such lawn elsewhere with the rollered grasses of the common swept out below and teenagers drinking cider beneath the sweep of old oak trees and maples. She was first to reconnect. After those night time perambulations to view her at her window through the undergrowth or drunk on her doorstep in the small hours. One weeknight in her dressdown jeans and jumper at the door. My mother answers and shows her through to the kitchen where I am sat drinking tea not yet changed in my school tie and jumper. Come to. Stand. Stammer a greeting. My father rising to greet her also with a glance my way. And then we are the four of us seated around the table and she is fielding a volley of questions from my parents about where she's been and what she's doing now and how school is and what she's planning to do after she's finished and my mother fussing and asking her whether she wouldn't like to stay for dinner or perhaps some tea and a piece of flapjack and with the latter agreed upon it is duly brought over with some ceremony. She stays an hour or so but the conversation is almost entirely monopolised by my parents and it is only afterwards as I show her to the door that we have a brief window of time together. On the doorstep she asks me whether I'd like to go into town with her and a group of friends that Saturday and I try to maintain my composure as I say yes of course that would be lovely and she says great and tells me her parents will give us a lift and why don't I get to hers around seven thirty and then she is gone and I am left on the doorstep long after she has disappeared from view. When I go back through my parents are beside themselves saying well that was a surprise and wasn't it super to see her again and isn't she so pretty and so grown up now and such a lovely young person and I nod before retiring to my room where for the next few nights I am unable to sleep nor anywhere concentrate on much at all beyond what I will wear and where we'll go and what her friends will be like. The night itself I shut myself in my room to get ready. I iron my shirt and jeans. Fix my hair in the mirror. Drink vodka from the bottle beneath the bed. Brush my teeth. Repeat. At the front door my mother slips me a twenty pound note and tells me to have a good time. Tells me to call if I'm going to be late. This look in her eye. At Emily's I'm invited in by her parents as she is still getting ready upstairs. David hands me a beer and takes me through to the living room where I take a seat on the edge of the settee with him in the armchair opposite. He asks me how I've been. What I'm doing now. What I'm planning to do after school. I'm distracted. My responses vague. I look at the photographs on the mantelpiece. Time lapse of Emily these years gone by. Childhood through adolescence. On a ski slope. A beach. Aloft on the stile of a drystone wall with a panorama of heathered moorland behind her. I look at the window and the apple tree and privet fence and fishpond and the grass of the sloping meadow past the garden is imbued with a wild and melancholy blackness. Jill comes in. Brings peanuts. We exchange a few words. She leaves. The peanuts untouched while I nervously drink my beer. At length Emily comes down. Dressed in a fitted white shirt. Slim ankle jeans and heels. Has on a perfume that I will sometimes encounter over the coming years to be borne back to this night. I rise to greet her. Not really knowing what to do. Whether to shake her hand or embrace her. I do nothing. She puts on a brown tweed riding jacket from the banister and comes over and kisses me on the cheek. She's wearing lipstick that sticks to my skin and her hair falls about my neck. Her perfume again. Drawing back she asks me if I'm ready and I nod and then David grabs his keys from the coffee table and we follow him out. Going into town I'm in the back seat and I watch her the whole time along the pitch narrow lanes. We're dropped in the square and after the car's gone she leads me supplicant along the narrow pavements through town to a bar just beyond the old castle on the other side of the high road. There's a bouncer on the door in a long black overcoat and he greets us as we enter. I follow her through the dark panelled doors into a room of red faux velvet couches and gilt frame mirrors along the walls. At the bar countertop people wait three deep and around the room groups sit at tables centrepieced with flickering tealights in cutglass hurricane lanterns illuming the metal pearled condensate of cooler stands crushed with ice and the dark slunk necks of champagne bottles. She tries and fails to locate the friends we're here to meet. Afterwards shrugs and takes me to the bar and asks me what I'm drinking. I try to protest. Tell her I'll get them. But she puts her hand on mine as I reach for my wallet and her eyes are fulgid and her shirt bluewhite in the ultraviolet. She buys me a bottle of beer and for herself in a short glass with ice a gimlet and these we take to a table in the corner just made vacant and when we sit she sloughs off her jacket and crosses her legs and our knees touch. She clinks her glass against my bottle and drinks and having had so much on my mind that I wanted to ask her these past few days I'm suddenly voiceless. I try not to stare at her long legs crossed by mine. At her part open shirt. Instead look at her hand on the tabletop. The wall behind her. Ask finally if she comes here often. This seems to amuse her. She wonders if I use this line on all the women and I blushingly shake my head and my discomfort seems to amuse her yet further for she laughs again and touches my hand. She tells me then of the friends we're meeting. Lana and Claire. The classes they share. How they met. Because of the music we lean in closer to one another and I can feel her breath upon me. Visions of her with the kite upon the playing fields and at the picnic table in the summer on her lawn or beneath the willow tree or framed in the doorway this evening past. Rucking her lips now as she sips at her drink. Eyes then scanning the ruck of the bar over my shoulder. Alighting someplace. Touching my hand. That's them. They're here. Then standing with her to greet two girls. Introductions are made. Claire and Lana. Claire tall and blonde and Lana petite with auburn hair and hornrimmed glasses and a peplum top. I shake their hands and they kiss me each on the cheek. I ask them what they're drinking and head to the bar with their orders. The crowd seems sparser now and I am conveyed unharried to the countertop and in the mirror behind the spirits shelf I see the reflections of the girls around the table and from each of them sequential glances in my direction. When I take the drinks back over the light seems dimmer and the stand of candleflame in the midst of them flickers in the airless dark and casts through the cutglass lanterns straight and serrulate veins of yellow across the polished metal tabletop. I take a seat on a padded stool with the three of them lined along the couch as if for interview. Lana watches me closely. She's quiet and says little. The other girl Claire asks me about school and I'm obliged to tell them all where I go which they seem to know anyway. Claire asks me what it's like. What I study. What the other students are like. I play it all down because I find the stigma of private schools uncomfortable but the girls seem to cast little judgement. Lana is wearing a gold chain and she toys with this while I speak. I wonder at their perceptions of me. There's something almost motherly in the way they behave around me. They giggle at the jokes I didn't think I'd made and when I do try to make a joke it's lost on them. I blush every other word. Am ill at ease. They seem impressed when I tell them of my plans to go away travelling. They ask me where I'm going and I tell them how I will work for six months and then take a round the world trip. I ask them of their plans. Emily is going off to university. Lana will go to college. Claire is going straight into work at her father's firm. They each buy a round of drinks and at the end of the night Emily a round of shots. Later after we have seen Lana and Claire off Emily and I are on the main square awaiting David. It's approaching midnight and cold out. Emily hugs her jacket around herself and I wonder what's expected of me now. Whether to put my arms around her. Kiss her. Whether we are simply here as friends. She's looking away and in the keen autumn nightwinds her hair is abluster in fine dark strands about her brow and beneath her brow her fine dark eyes shine in the cold. I look at her lips and think what it would be to kiss her here in the chill and lonely square through which the wind riffles fallen leaves along the pavements and rouses the awnings over the shuttered restaurants and bars. I move a step closer. Her arm brushes against mine. I look again at her lips. At the paleness of her skin. The sublimity of her movements. A sense of indomitability grows in me. Even of possessiveness. Of our shared history growing up that transcends everything and everyone. Yet rather than hold her I continue to stand apart. I wonder why this passivity. Wonder what it is that holds me back. I tell myself that this is not the moment. That there will be others to come. A crowning ceremony. I'm lost in these thoughts when she suddenly speaks.

Lana liked you.

What?

She was quite taken with you.

I'm about to ask her what she means when David's car appears across the square. Emily looks at me and I'm lost for words. Can't figure out why she would tell me this. There's a moment's inaction before I'm abstractedly following her to the car and then responding numbly to her father's questions regarding our evening. On the ride home we are largely silent and from the backseat I look at Emily in front. The curve of her shoulder. The strands of her hair against the headrest. Her hand resting on her lap. Nearing the village I tell David that he can drop me at their place and I will walk the rest of the way. He tells me it's not a problem to drop me home but I say I'd like to walk. That I need to clear my head a little. He nods okay. Eyes in the rearview. Leaves us on his yard and disappears into the house. I am alone with Emily with the great panoply of stars in the cold sky above. She again takes my hand. I tell her how nice an evening I've had. How nice it was to catch up with her again. Nice this and nice that. Still with an air of bemused abstraction. She kisses me fleetingly on the lips and then is gone. I watch the lights go out. Hear the click of the doorlatch. Am there a long time on the yard with the feel of her cold lips on mine and a faint wonderment that she might be watching from a dark and gabled window. In the sacrament of moonlight my own faint shadow falls across the yard and the dark and brooding fields beyond are ploughed raw and cold and angular. I walk home then through the black and starlit night. Watch my shadow on the cold dark road illuminated by the sometime porchlights of houses. All silent save my footfalls resounding against the raw brickwork of the farmhouse on the corner and from the walls of the old bus stop and out across the meadow. I come to my driveway and the house is dark save the living room light through the curtain. I go to the pond and stare down into its choked pondsludge and broken reeds and then I am at the picnic table leaning back with my arms outstretched upon its weathered peeling slats and looking a long time up at the trough of the sky through the stripped and nightblack boughs of the apple tree. See Emily as she descended the staircase. In the bar before the others arrived. On the square after they'd gone. When finally I go inside my parents are asleep in the living room with the television on. They neither wake nor stir. I pour myself a brandy from the liquor cabinet and sit back in the armchair and only at the crawl of the film's close does my mother come to and look at me through heavy lidded eyes and ask me how my evening was but when I start to answer she falls back to sleep. Days to come I start to drift at school finding something immature in my relations with friends and an emptiness in the analysis of playscripts or the long brushstrokes of paint on canvas. At night I sit up late and drink from the vodka bottle beneath my bed oftentimes at the window overlooking the dark garden below. Replaying that night. The fragments of detail. What I said and didn't say. What perhaps I might have done. Searching around for photographs of when we were children just to rekindle her likeness. Eventually I go round to hers one evening. Jill answers and leads me through to the hallway. Calls up to her. Offers me tea. Emily comes down in a pair of old pyjama bottoms and slippers and an oversize knitwear top with red weft stripes across the chest and her hair up and a pencil through it at the back. She looks glad to see me. Smiles. Asks me up to her room. I follow as she ascends the stairs. Looking at her the while. The shape of her through her thin tattersall pyjamas. I come to the threshold of her room at the top of the stairs as she sits on a swivel chair at her desk with the light of the desklamp behind her gilding her hair. She gestures to the unmade bed and I go over to it. The duvet is heaped to one side and the undersheet baubled and lined with creases and there remains screwed through her pillow the imprint of her head and I glance at her and she gestures for me to sit. At the foot of the mattress there lies a balled white sock and beyond this her laundry hamper on the top of which is a tiny pair of stripy knickers and a polkadot bra skewed through a shirtsleeve. She kicks off her slippers and crosses her long legs and I look at the bedside table. A jewellery box with bangles and bracelets spilt from its crowded drawers. A row of finger puppets. Ceramic animals. A pig a sheep a cow. Her old posters on the walls and on a corkboard photographs of her with her friends. One of her with a guy. Their arms around each other. Books are piled on her desk and there's an open spiral notebook at its centre. I tell her I hope I'm not disturbing her and she tells me not to be silly. That she's glad of the break because her head's spinning.

Yeah. Mine too.

Revision?

Yeah.

Is this just a social visit?

I guess.

Great.

How's your work going?

It's okay. Standard.

What are you studying?

English.

Same.

We talk of our texts. She suggests that perhaps sometime we could study together. Her mother brings us tea and lingers in the doorway looking in on us. She has a plate of biscuits and after she's gone I take one and Emily too and I cup my palm beneath my mouth to catch the crumbs and she allows hers to fall across her lap and then brushes them onto the carpet. I look at the shape of her beneath her jumper. The shape of her breasts. Her thigh through the elasticised waistband of her pyjamas. She blows on her tea. And so it is that we begin these study dates. Always at hers. I will bring my books around and sometimes we'll work together and other times alone. I'll be on her bed or on the floor with my back against the mattress and she at her desk with her hair trussed up and sometimes with a crepe band tied through it and other times with it down and brushed behind her ear and she'll be in her pyjama bottoms or tracksuit and one of her old frayed jumpers and sometimes she will remove this and rather than study I will sit there and watch her in her thin cotton shirt. Her neck. The shape of her back. Her hips.

And when we take breaks and she turns to me and leans forwards to talk I will try desperately not to look at her cleavage through the scoopneck top of her shirt but will find this impossible. Not long after we start these meetings I am at her corkboard and I ask her of the people in the photographs and she tells me of her friends and where the pictures were taken. I ask her of the boy with his arms around her and she tells me he's just somebody she's been sort of seeing. I brood on this news for many days. Brood on the substance of our relationship. On why she keeps having me round to hers when she's sort of seeing someone. I brood on the phrasing. Sort of. Whether it means anything. Whether it's meant as a challenge. A provocation. I wonder why she wears those thin cotton shirts without bras. Wonder whether this too is a provocation or merely a signal that she feels comfortable around me. That I pose no kind of threat. One Saturday not long afterwards I go out with her again in town. A different bar this time. We find her group over at a table in the corner. Lana and Claire. Claire asks me how I've been. We talk about school. What exams are coming up and when. How much work we're all doing. Lana's quiet. Watching me intently when I speak and looking away when I glance at her. She's dyed her hair since last we met. Blonde highlights. The colour of her hornrims has also changed. Tortoiseshell red now. She's wearing a creased shirt and a faded denim jacket and upon her fingers silver and runic rings. As the night progresses I look at her more frequently. The way she turns her cocktail straw. Looks across at me. The way when she plays with the top button of her shirt the lace of her bra is fleetingly visible. At some point Claire goes to the bar to get another round of drinks and Emily says she'll go with her to help carry them back. While they're gone Lana glances up at me and by this stage I've drunk too much and can't really think of anything to say. I look across to the bar and notice Emily watching me.

Something in her eyes I can't determine. This I also come to dwell on over the coming days. The idea in my mind that she and Claire might have been trying to set me up with Lana. Or this dim notion that the quality of Emily's stare may have been jealousy. Lana finally breaks the silence. Asks me something of my home life. I focus on her across the tabletop. Drink from my bottle and replace it at the centre of the coaster and slide my finger down the damp label. She watches me. When she looks away I glance down at the pendant around her neck against her pale skin. At the heavy mascara around her eyes. At the runic rings on her fingers. We are next to each other and our knees sometimes touch beneath the table. She tells me she lives up the hill going out of town. Just her and her mother after her dad left a few years back. Talks of the stress this caused. Then about how all her friends have started pairing off but she's looking to meet someone really special. When Emily and Claire return Claire passes round the drinks and Emily looks at me as she sits and later when we're waiting for my parents to arrive to take us home she asks me what Lana and I talked about and I'm vague in my reply and make no mention that Lana gave me her number on a slip of paper and told me to call her if I wanted to go out for a drink. This comes to pass a couple of weeks later and later still at a house party I'm invited to by Emily Lana and I kiss at the bottom of the garden in the gazebo. I don't know whose party it is but it's out in the suburbs and the living room and kitchen are filled with people drinking and smoking and heavy music is rolling out through the night. Lana in a tight white shirt and kilt. Laddered stockings and buckled shoes. Heavy mascara and oxblood lips. Cider on her breath. Quiet incantations as I slip my hand up her thigh and beneath her skirt. Her heels scrape softly on the gazebo decking and the bench and balusters creak. The feel of her nylon tights. Her lacy underwear. We continue to kiss and grope in the dark and though I'm aroused I know that with Emily in the house all of this will come to nothing. Lana asks me breathlessly do I want her and though I say yes I effectuate no further development beyond blindly groping and kissing her and when finally we withdraw she looks sad hurt confused. She gives her head a little shake and retreats into the house and I am a long while in that quiet gazebo. I lean back and look up at the underside of the shingled roof hung with cobwebs and though I wish I were anywhere but there I know equally that to be apart from Emily would be similar torture. For that is the way of things. Torture in separation. Torture in union. On subsequent meetings with Emily she's quiet and withdrawn and I look at her at her desk as she chews on the tip of her pen. I suppose she knows what happened with Lana and so I phone Lana one night when my parents are out and break things off with her and by way of answer she simply hangs up and I am left in the hallway at home with a silence foreshadowing many such silences to come and not long after this I am at Emily's and I am looking at the photos on her corkboard while she is downstairs making tea and I notice through the collage of friezes that the guy with his arm around her is gone and when she comes up I am still standing there and I look at her in the mirror and see just the vaguest flicker of a smile upon her lips. Afterwards things continue much as normal with outside the slow turning of the seasons. I never see Lana again and when Emily and I go out into town we do so just the two of us and haunt the quieter pubs and bars in the suburbs and talk long into the night. One evening she asks me of our years apart. Of my removal from old acquaintances in the village. For a time after primary school I still kept on with them but gradually this fell away until we all of us became strangers. I tell her something of the culture of the school. Of its gowned masters and quadrangle. Of the long day that does not finish until half six and the homework afterwards. Yet these are excuses that ring hollow for the truth of this abandonment on my part was not a sense of superiority as might have been perceived but rather a sense of shame. That in going there I had betrayed in some way the core of who I was and in doing so betrayed her also. And though after my excuses have been made I see in her eyes a degree of understanding there is something else whose import I will not comprehend until many years later. Another evening I am looking at the gimcrack ornaments on her bedside and she tells me how one holiday when she was little she had saved her pocket money for the little animal trinkets and gone down to the shop at the end of the lane where she and her family were camping and bought them and as I'm going home that night she takes my hand and presses into it the pig. I carry it around with me at school in the days that follow and I will take it out in the cubicle of the toilet and study the smoothly polished porcelain and the black bead eyes. In class I will have it in my pocket and when called upon to answer a question I will stare absently at the teacher until he goes to somebody else and here I am ostracised and there ostracised and at home my parents at the dinner table will ask me if I'm okay and they will tell me I'm looking tired and thin and I will just shrug and fork around my plate the food my mother has prepared and afterwards go up to my room to drink from beneath my bed the vodka and I will look out over the garden below. Sometimes at night I will think of Lana and how we kissed on the veranda of the gazebo in that desolate and forgotten garden and will wonder whether this was an opportunity missed but by then the obsession with Emily has become all encompassing and in much later days I will begin to consider more deeply whether my ever knowing Emily was a curse. See impressions of her homebound through the voidlike night. On her desk chair. Impressing into my palm the little animal trinket. Later on the bridge over the river that night or in the cafe after with the river stretched out beneath us black and viscid in the dark and the backwash of boats lathering against the stark black buttresses of bridges and later still with the living room light through the doorway and the raindense zephyr of the wet night tapering through the open window I am at my wardrobe reaching for the top shelf. Bea is asleep behind me with the covers pushed down and her bare leg pressed against the wall. She stirs as I shift boxes and piles of paper and lever arch files filled with old schoolwork. I find the shoebox. Wound with masking tape long since tackless and almost turned to dust. Lift it down and take it through to the living room quietly closing the bedroom door behind me and switching off the light here also so that the flat is all but dark. I place the shoebox on the kitchen table and pour myself a large glass of brandy and then I sit at the table and remove the lid of the shoebox and root through the old photographs until I find at the bottom the pig trinket she gave me so long ago wrapped in a piece of tissuepaper. It's late. After midnight. I take a drink of brandy and then with the trinket I go over to the window and hold it up against the glass and turn it between my thumb and forefinger. Blue. White. Opalescent. Black bead eyes. I am there a long time listening to the rain on the window. I go back to the table and I look at a photograph of Emily in her bikini that time down by the sea and then I drink back the rest of my brandy and after some deliberation I take out my phone and send her a text in spite of the late hour. Asking simply how she is. Of course I don't hear back that night. I pour some more brandy and I remain at the table a long time ruminating in the darkness until sometime after two I hear the bedroom door open and Bea emerges in only her knickers. She comes and stands over me and asks me what I'm doing and I tell her I was just going through some old things and because she's been asleep she's squinting and her hair is mussed and there is a kind of unrefined glory about her right now. I tell her I'm sorry for waking her and sorry more generally. Sorry for everything. She asks me what I mean and I pull her to me gently by the waistband of her knickers and I sit her on my lap with her legs astride me and I put my arms around her soft waist. She looks down at me. Her arms around my neck. We start to caress each other. Her breaths grow heavy in the dark. I lift her onto the table and she lies back and the shoebox falls to the floor and I look down at her and her eyes are closed and her hair is splayed about the table and I pull down her knickers and toss them to one side and then I glance down and I see amidst the spilled photographs innumerate replications of Emily. On the beach. In her room. The two of us in a bar. I manoeuvre myself between Bea's legs and pull off my clothes. Enter her. Light falls across the photographs and across Bea's pale skin and as her breathing becomes heavier chasms start to open and flare through the darkness.

The next morning we wake late. Around noon we have coffee at the table and she asks me what I want to do. Says she thought maybe we could into town or something. I tell her I'm pretty knackered and have spent all week around town and couldn't we just stay around here. Sit on the settee and watch films. She makes a face and says she's barely seen me all week and wants to do something a bit more fun. Tells me to think about it while she's in the shower. After she's gone I check my messages and there's a reply from Emily saying she's fine. Saying how nice it was to see me again the other day and that we should do it again sometime. By way of reply I tell her about my job and that I'm working all hours and then going on holiday after it wraps but could meet her just before I go. Maybe sometime towards the end of August or even one night late in town or on a Sunday or whenever she wants. And then when I'm awaiting her response Bea comes out of the shower and I have to switch my phone to silent and hide it away. I suggest to Bea we go into town. Down to the river.

Eventide we are on the terrace of an alfresco popup serving overpriced wine near where all the theatres and concert venues are and I look across the table at her and I try to smile but I am barely able to maintain eye contact and at some point she asks me if something's wrong and I shake my head and tell her I'm just tired and back at ours she makes us cocoa and we watch television without talking. I don't sleep much that night and around three I find myself looking down at her and crying.

*       *       *

The knell of a flagpole's halyard sounds across the carpark as the tramontane blows the length of the beach whipping up drifts of sand along the blasted dunes and agitating the great palm trees along the raised promenade. I stare out to sea at the bright low moon cresting the waves' white breakers and listen to them shattering all along the shoreline in a torrent of curdled spume and spewed spray. Despite the wind it's warm and the night air thick and briny. A cormorant flies low over the sea by a line of guano spattered buoys tugged by the dark currents below as another breaker slaps onto the wet lather of the shore and rakes back shingle in its restless ebb. At the far end of the beach down near the harbour a single light on the farthest breakwater weakly probes the sea.

I walk a way across the rutted sand and sit by one of the dunes with the stringent grasses around me tugged by the wind and my shirt collar rippling about my neck. I remove my sandals and push my feet into the cold wet grains beneath me and dig through it with my hands and lift it in dank palmfuls and watch it fall between my fingers to the ground below. In the dune grass behind me I find a knot of calcified driftwood and shuck from it long blanched splinters and toss these across the beach and watch them carried by the wind into the darkness and then I am for a time with my eyes closed listening to the sibilance of the sea.

Presently I find my way down along the promenade. The square there is a relic now of the passing season with fossilised spatters of ice cream in the glow of a lone globe streetlamp around which are crusted the desiccated scabs of moths and insects. Strings of coloured bulbs hang from the restaurant awnings and shopfronts but these are unlit and buffeted by the wind and at the far end of the square just before the archway is a forsaken stage with a dance band banner hanging crookedly behind it. A couple of the restaurants are open but with only the occasional table occupied and waiters and waitresses seated at the counters or bringing in the place settings. I sit on the steps overlooking the square and watch litter blow across it and through a window at one of the balconies the flickering of a television set. On another balcony a tied parasol is stacked with a set of covered sunloungers and an untethered shutter claps against the wall.

Day following I roam the beach in the sunshine for the wind has cleared the air. I walk along the shoreline skimming stones and picking up old shells of razorclams and tellins and wentletraps and tossing them back in the surf. I lie out in my trunks in the sun and later walk up to the far end of the beach where the nudists go and I take off my clothes and stand at the water's edge with the sea lathering around my feet. I go in up to my thighs and look out to the horizon before diving in and floating on my back looking up at the blue sky. When dusk falls I go to the lagoon behind the beach and sit on the sand where the reeds part and look out across the water with the westering sun behind the distant mountains colouring pink through crimson and flintlike blue its surface. Kingfishers come from the river and disappear somewhere amongst the bulrushes along the shore. A man goes by along the pathway on a bicycle and when I'm walking back I see him on one of the old pillboxes in the dunes nude with his hands on his hips in the near dark and when I'm along the river the slate sky is filled with bats and there are crickets in the grass banks and the distant drone of cicadas from the grove by the marsh. Night I'm again on the beach and afterwards in a bar on the promenade drinking beer and the days go by like this without much recourse. Sometimes when Bea calls to ask me how it's going I can barely even talk. Some nights I don't answer. Other times I'll ring her and tell her I love her and that I'm missing her. My mother calls and gives me instructions regarding the maintenance of the small garden. I duly and reluctantly weed the paving cracks and water the olive tree and aloe vera and prune the oleander and the next time she calls she seems pretty choked up and I ask her what's wrong and she tells me after a pause that she's missing my father.

That night I find an old photograph of the three of us when we were down here together a few years ago and because I'm drunk I start to cry and I hit the wall so hard that I graze my knuckles and the next morning I wake up with the sheets bloodied and the skin raw and peeling from my hand. I look at the photograph on the bed beside me. I'd come to see them during reading week and by that time they'd already been there a month or two. They were both of them tanned and had been spending their days drinking glasses of muscat at lunchtime and going for drives to markets in market towns and my father had done some varnishing. They came to get me from the airport and in the evenings we would go out for dinner or eat alfresco on the terrace at home and afterwards I would get drunk and go for walks along the beach and stay out until two or three in the morning watching the moon over the sea. The day the photograph was taken we'd gone swimming in one of the breakwater bays down near the harbour and afterwards my father had set the timer on the camera with the three of us posed by the rocks. It was the day before I went back and the last time we were all here together and my only real memory of the trip was the lingering frustration I felt at being with them on holiday. Of being embarrassed in front of waitresses when my father ordered for me or irritable when my mother suggested going swimming together. And now I go downstairs and one of Bea's hairbands is still on the table with a length of her hair wound through it and I take this out to the patio and toy with it while I drink my morning coffee.

It is the end of September when we come down together. Just beforehand after the film has wrapped I find out from my mother that a classmate from primary school has been killed in a motorcycle accident and because I'm not working at that time I drive up to the old churchyard to see his grave. The headstone is not yet in place and there is a simple wooden cross at its head with a brass plaque bearing his name. Great bouquets of flowers still wrapped in cellophane and covering the raw clay soil are beginning to rot in the sunshine with the sympathy cards drained of colour and the ink from them almost gone. It's warm out and the churchyard is still very green with only a hint of the turning season in the horse chestnuts and yews flanking the grass. Crows are in the upper canopies and I watch them a time before looking back down at the grave. This boy with whom we used to go camping. Who would cheat off me in tests at school. Whose birthday parties I would go to up in the hamlet where he lived. I didn't suppose that seeing his grave would affect me much. I look at the ground and I look at the heap of crumbled soil and the wrought black rail around it and I think of his proximity to me now in the ground below with the dank pall of his putrefaction rotting through him and his shawled and shrouded confinement in the dark uterus of his narrow wood sarcophagus as he putrefies green and bloated and stinking and how this slow rotting will continue for many days and weeks and months unheeded in the damp earth. Afterwards I go to my father's headstone and I clean it with a sponge and bucket filled from the outdoor tap by the transept entranceway and I clean out the old dead flowers from the rosetop vase recessed in the stone and I stand there for a long time looking at his epitaph. I don't go to see my mother on the way back. This is just before Bea and I leave.

She stays for two weeks. The first week we hire a car. I drive her up into the mountains and another day down to a seaside town south of where the house is and we swim in the sea there and wander around the narrow streets and sit out on the promontory where the boats are moored and eat ice cream cones. She drives us back afterwards and she's dressed in cotton shorts and a vest and her legs are already tanned with a tan line at her thigh and I watch her decompress the clutch and accelerate and brake and the radio is on and she's singing along to French pop songs I've never heard sometimes looking over at me and encouraging me to sing along and laughing aloud when I try to and fail. I put my hand on her neck and stroke her hair at the back and the windows are open and the air that blows in smells of the sea and the car of suntan lotion and hot vinyl.

Other days we go down to the beach to sunbathe. We take a parasol and shift our beach towels beneath its shade as it sifts through the hot afternoon. We read books and swim in the sea together and stand up to our waists in the tidelands kissing and seawater will glisten on her tanned skin. Late afternoon we play petanque then go to the promenade for iced coffee at one of the little cafes. When we get back we make love up on the mezzanine or in the little bedroom on the ground floor and she'll smell and taste of the sea and as she lies back and I unfasten her bikini top and pull down her shorts sand will tumble out and afterwards she'll lie there stroking the knots from my hair. Evenings after I've cooked a meal of griddled meat and ratatouille we'll walk along the promenade and sit on one of the benches in the moonlight and she'll rest her head on my lap and look up at the stars and in the mornings we'll wake late and sometimes make love before showering together. Another day we go into town and there's an arthouse cinema there where we go to watch a film but the girl in the film looks unnervingly like Emily and afterwards when we are sitting on a cafe terrace along the river bank I find it difficult to talk to Bea and she sits there stirring her coffee with a long spoon and looking past me into the sun.

Before we come out here I see Emily again. It's a Sunday after filming has wrapped and the meeting is for my part clandestine. We are again not far from the river sitting out on the terrace decking on a picnic bench beneath bulbs hanging limp and unlit in the windless air with the river writhing dark and livid beneath us and floriated thunderclouds amassed over the skyline of the opposite bank. Awaiting their accession the sun falls across the shambling veranda illuminating the age riven tabletops and weatherworn deck slats. A riverboat goes by. One of those low slung vessels with the chop of the river water slapping hollow against the hull. Tourists on the deck. One waves. A man smoking at the terrace edge waves back. Turns to the person by him and smiles as the tall spired tendrils of his smoke taper in the still air. On the riverboat deck the sometime flare of flashbulbs and then they are gone. Hear the faint slap of water from the wake of the boat against the concrete revetment of the riverbank. And then all as before. Still and viscous. Sky and river. Emily looks at me across the tabletop with the contusion of stormclouds behind her welling caliginous from beneath the cowering skyline and her dark hair aureate in the stark sunlight. A drink before her on the weathered tabletop. She rests her fingertips on its lip and slowly turns the glass on its coaster. A gimlet as of yore. A ramekin of olives in brine with pips spat on the dish it sits on. She skewers another with a cocktail stick. Turns it in its brine. I watch her closely. Watch with a sort of morbid fascination the ritual of it all. The stick to her lips. Pulling with her teeth the briny olive from its tip and turning the spent stick at the corner of her mouth. All the time the thunderclouds building behind her. First the sullied virga streaking black the narrow head of light above the skyline. Then the cloudshadow darkening the moil of river water below black and resinous across the miasma of its breakers. The violet tint in the sky an augur of the coming rain.

It starts to fall. Nascent across the river. See it fluctuant across the surface as it erodes the water's dark lustre. See on the opposite bank in the dark of the cloudcover the streaks of headlights glistering the roadways and in the tower blocks the rain and the gutter run streaking black and taupe the wet concrete and passing along the pavements a fluorescence of raincoats and the domes of brollies. The last of the sun across the decking falls to darkness now and with it a raw wind courses up off the river. See the deck begin to clear. A few still at the rail watch the waves of rain across the river and then they too are gone. Heeltap on tabletops. Bottles along the rail. With a squall one falls and rolls into a slat joist. I'm watching it when the rain comes sweeping across the decking and then I am looking across at her and at first she makes no attempt to move as around her the rain as static blurs all. Wreathes the skyline on the opposite bank. Wreathes the tabletops. Erodes the darkly threshing surface of the river. Falling about us it sluices the summer's dust from the woodwork out through the deck joists to the noggins below. She stares back at me devoid of much expression and I see her as through some dim remembrance. I watch the rain slake through her black hair and slake her black eyes and streak her pale skin and I watch how it slakes down her pale neck and sops into the collar of her shirt such that it impresses against her chest the wetly wrangled fabric in mottled blots and traces out the straps and lace cups of her bra and for a long time she watches me and I her until by some communion we go inside where a pall of dank hangs in the air. We go to the bar. I buy us drinks. Follow her through to a table in the corner. Look at her seated across from me as she peels from her chest her rainwrangled shirt and fans it to wick away the wet. She's sort of smiling and her eyes are smeared black and wet black strands of her hair are swabbed across her brow and the tips of it are swept wet and dripping behind her ear. Behind her at the window rainsqualls thrash against the stained glass windowpane. She leans back and the cockled fabric of her shirt presses once more against her chest and ice cubes purl in the beaded glass before her as water slides down her neck to her collarbone. I look at the spidered pools of water on the tabletop and I look back at her. At the curve of her shoulder. The shape of her breasts beneath her shirt. Remember the thunderstorm long ago in the pastureland behind her house with the hairs of lightning in the bruised and portentous clouds and how at the trough in the mire she had slunk down with the black of her hair dripping into her lap and the hem of her summer skirt spattered with mud. Remember that look in her eyes. Something there I'd not seen before. The rain then as now dark. Elemental. A groan of thunder sounds. Sometime after a sheet of light kaleidoscopes the stained glass. She sips her drink. See her in her summer dress with her hair up at the windowed sidewall with the late sun falling about her. A bottle of champagne on the table before her. On

221

the table before her lengths of coiled ribbon and silver stars and stars and silver ribbon in her hair and the turning glitter globe on the ceiling pitching fractals of coloured light across her. The long procession of it all. Of the waning light through the sidewall windows and the latterly loosened neckties and empty bottles of champagne and dinner wines and always the blue summer dress she wears. At the table. On the dancefloor through the turning kaleidoscopes of light. Later on the lawn beneath the moon. The way it showed her bare shoulders. The cut of it to her thigh. Red heels. Red aliceband. The pendant she wore. How years later it refuses to die. Rather consumes.

Later in the mizzled evening we are at the station with the gore of rainfall all along the wet street. Stink of the bowels of the place. Stink of its festered musk. Newsvendors in tumbledown woodshacks palm papers and magazines weighted with stones to patrons and on the walls the stained brickwork glistens dully with wept rain. Buses and bikes and vans go by and taxis idle kerbside at the rank and in the midst of all things she stares back at me. Waiting for what. For me to embrace her. For me to take her hand or to kiss her cheek. I glance down at her shirt. At her dark eyes staring darkly at my parted lips. Waiting for what. Journey home this plagues me. See her in every face. On the train. Walking back by the park with darkness gaining on the streets. My street I look up at the redbrick tympanum slewed green with shit from the gutter and black with streaks of the day's rain. I look at the lighted windows and walk on by. I go along to the pub on the corner and sit at the window with a beer staring down at the floor. Waiting for what.

Plagues me on the beachfront on those lonesome walks with the waves breaking along the shoreline and against the shit streaked black bowsprits of breakwaters at shore's end. This is after she's gone and all is quiet. The second week with her things start to deteriorate. After lying with her those mornings and afternoons with the taste of sea salt on her skin. After coffees along the promenade or in town at the river's edge with the peddle boats below and parasols shading from the noonday sun the seared walkways. After those trips up into the mountains and stopping lakeside with the sun setting across the water and seeing in another lagoon at another sunset flamingos with the mountains enveloped in a veil of heat and wind turbines slowly turning or still along their arid spines. The old skiff half sunk in the water at the lake's edge there and its bay surface rippled by the skimmed passages of swifts. One night sitting up to dawn on the terrace drinking muscat and smoking the cigars we bought in the town down near the border in whose liquor store carparks whores sprawled on the hot boles of jersey barriers with truckers idling along the roads' dusty verges. Other dawns waking and going alone to the terrace nude to watch the breaking of the light with swallows over the river yonder and in the eaves opposite starlings and through the parapet's pilasters lizards. Before the day's waking. One time along the river alone in the long grasses of the embankment watching coypus and beneath the surface of the brackish water the scaled argentate bellies of fish flashing and catching in the streaky dawn light and later on the empty beach swimming nude in the calm and stirless sea. Those long and lonesome walks with my shadow stretching across the dune sands or returning across the river pathway with the wind faint in the reeds and the sky pale blue and coming on cloudless with the cirrocumulus burning away and the gibbous moon burning away beyond. Melancholy with remembrance and with the slow burning away of time. How sometimes when I came back with the starlings acry in the eaves and children at play on the gravel I would go up and sit on one of the wicker chairs on the mezzanine and with the morning light through the open window I would watch her sleep and watch as she stirred and I would remember that mezzanine from long ago when all had seemed imbued with a light softer and more permanent. Her bare breast nude from the rimples of the sheets wrangled around her hips with the sheets clinging to her or slipping away with the turnings and stirrings of her sleep but with this a strange hollowness.

Returning from one such dawn walk I find her at the kitchen table with a coffee from the percolator and in a paper packet pastries from the bakery. Hair baled in a band with the fine down of it down her neck. I think at first she's reading a book but when I come near and kiss her on the cheek I see she's riffling through some old photographs. Some spread out on the tabletop. Others in a sheaf. Others in the sleeve. Pictures from different eras. My mother and father on the terrace here. Some of me when I was ten or so sunbleached at the coping of a villa's blue pool and later on a stile someplace with the slopes of blasted moors behind me hung with mist and yet later in my room at the edge of my bed with at my feet a battered canvas bag and my eyes dark and cold and joyless. Pictures of my father in the garden at the barbeque with a spatula and novelty apron and cork hat and beer and about him in the borders of the lawn sprayed arrays of flowers and the fence old and weathered in the background with wort in the fucked fence slats. On a windblown bluff looking out across a desolate sea and the bluff hung with the dark shapes of gulls. Or long hence slim at the door of a new car hand upon hip hand upon the dripmoulding. Remember being in it later on a roundabout waiting for the odometer to trip a milestone. See it later towed to a scrapheap with the fucked arse of it scraping down the driveway. So too my father. His last end on the driveway. Father at a do. With my mother at the juncture of some walk. Packs slung by them. Slung packs of picnic lunches. Slacks and hiking boots and macs. By them daffodils rising upon a slope. On the slope the warm and timeless sun. Later on the lawn with the ghosts of the sun eroding his silhouette as now and always. How it comes to such atrophy now and always. Photographs of the three of us. Ceremony of my graduation muggy with swarms of stormbugs and down the main street by the steps of the union the slow passing of buses ferrying to and fro the cohorts matriculated below. Those final days in the house we all shared with the posters on the walls slowly stripped away and the crockery and cutlery and pans packed into boxes labelled and taped and left in the hallway and books bundled and removed to packing crates and clothes folded on bedspreads. Returning at the end to collect the last of my belongings and finding my old room stripped bare with the fittings all torn up. Remember that day in the drizzle and sunshine seeing a rainbow with a rainbow aura in the nebula around it and realising that such motifs had ceased long ago to have any meaning. Among these dioramas another effigy. Effigy of that summer long removed when on the mezzanine we had sat together with the rainstorm set against the window and the weaving streaks of it shadowed across the floor and the pools of it smattering in the skylight. Shot of us on the beach with around us the apparatus of the afternoon. Around us roll mats and sandals and rolled towels for headrests and above flapping coloured in the sun a parasol and the shade of its canopied ribs across the hot sand and across her bikini and wayfarers and her old straw porkpie hat with the snapped frets ragged around the brim. Her tanned legs stretched before her. Timelessness in her fey smile. Timelessness of her hale and limber youth. How such days could bear so little import and yet so much.

Looking down at her looking down at her. This collision of worlds. On the beach that day beneath a coloured parasol flapping in the sun I watch her prone beside me with the shade of the ribbed canopy across her and upon her back in a strip across her tanned skin the imprint of the bikini string she has unknotted and allowed to fall about her with the wrinkled cups of it mustered around her couched breasts. Along the beach the wind whipping at the coarse grasses hails from the dunes drifts of sand. There are others along from us stretched out on beach towels or nestled in the shaded slacks and slipfaces of the dunes or at the water's edge lapping surf over their bare cunts. Beyond the shore I watch a raft of raincloud scud across the sea with the black tendrilled wake of it darkening the harried waves below and in the distance the jib and mainsail of a darkly tacking yacht. I watch petrels skirr the surface of the water. The rainclouds reach us anon and bring to the shore a great shawl of gloom and the clouds though tumid remain ominously pendent overhead. Two nude men with shrivelled scrota dress rapidly at the threat of rain and slap by in their sandals to the berm. Others follow. The woman from down by the shore towelling dry and pulling over her pendulous dugs a summer dress of gingham. Trudging back over the dunes beyond which the ranges of distant mountains are hazed grey windward and aurified leeward by the vanquished sun. Bea has rolled over and is propped on her elbows with her gaze out over the dark sea and wearing only her bikini briefs the sand dimples her bare breasts. The wind blows along the beach and down on the foreshore breakers peal in the surf. She brushes from her skin the grains of sand and I watch in the niggard light how her breasts respond erectly to her touch and I look down at her midriff at the way the shade falls across her navel. Then wordlessly she goes to the shore and stands with the sea foaming around her ankles and ebbing away before the next comber cleaves landward heaving in its wake a mire of sand and shingle. Her arms are loose by her sides and she flicks hair from her eyes as she stares out across the horizon near silhouetted in the gloom against the grey and undulant sea. She crouches in the surf and the seafoam continues to ebb about her and her reflection is dimly cast in the receding barm and then she is wading in to her waist and I watch as she unknots the tie at the side of her bikini briefs and slips them free and the combers continue to roll forth and break about her and she meets them side on and the spindrift is flung skyward and in a trough she dives and resurfaces beyond the next wave pushing back her hair before paddling languid strokes awhile on her back with the peaks of her breasts now and then rending the surface of the sea and the water arcing dripping from her arms and the briefs wound round her wrist and her feet kicking in her wake a thin froth. She's there awhile in the tidelands and presently the sun pulls through the cloud and shines upon her and upon the turbid sea rips through which she swims and her strokes continue languid and lithe with the arcs of drips now gilt by the newfound light and later she dives under and then resurfaces and floats on her back with just her head and feet clean of the meniscus and the shape of her submerged amid the swells of the sea with mirages forming where the yacht tacks and forming along the dunes where the nudists shelter and then she is swimming shoreward and wading hither nude with the seawater dripping from her breasts and from the tapered quills of her hair which she pushes back from her eyes as the sun catches upon the sinuating wet of her skin. She comes and sits down on her towel beside me and brushes at the sand encrusting her feet and I watch the water glistening across her shoulders sometimes glissade down her back and I watch it beading her tanned legs and thighs and sliding to the towel. Later walking back the sun sets over the opposite embankment and swallows skim the surface of the river and in the marshlands waders pluck ripples in the pewter skin of the standing water. She is ahead of me in the dying light flicking up sand from her flipflops with the tassels of her sash shagging through the coarse embankment grasses grown over the pathway and one hand trailing lazily after her through the seed heads. On the mezzanine bed after we've made love she asks about the photograph.

What photograph?

The one with the girl.

I don't know who you mean.

Down here. When you were younger.

Oh. She was just some family friend.

You must've been close.

What do you mean?

Coming away together.

It was just a family holiday.

There follows a long silence. Through the open window the first of the night's bats are aflight in the darkening sky and there is laughter and chatter from one of the adjoining houses and the smell of barbeque smoke upon the air. Bea is leant against me and we are enswathed in a bedsheet nude. She asks whether she was my girlfriend.

No. Just a friend.

What happened to her?

I don't know. We drifted apart.

You looked so close in the photo.

I guess we were back then.

Almost like a brother and sister.

Yeah. Maybe.

When did you see her last?

At a party. After I'd been away.

Didn't you ever try to contact her again?

No. Never.

How come?

I just didn't.

You never wondered about her?

We'd already gone our separate ways.

The wind has started to pick up again outside and the open window creaks now and then on its latch and the shutter on its dog. The mezzanine falls slowly to darkness with just the dimmest glimmer of light from across the way throwing pale streaks of shadow across the walls. We are like this a long time. The dark enshrouding us. A while later after she's drifted off to sleep I go down to the kitchen for some water and notice on the little cabinet in the corner the photographs she was looking at earlier. I take them quietly to the table and start to leaf through those unheeded earlier. For the most part they're landscapes my father took. Fishing villages. Mountain passes. Vineyards furrowed on hillsides. But amongst these also the aeon of that summer long ago. Shots I took after we'd finished school or when we came here together or congregated on the lawns and fields at home. The picnic table beneath her apple tree with a jug of punch. A barbeque at ours. Here on the beach or on a drive out to the mountains or on the terrace drinking wine. One of us that final afternoon before she left for university.

That final afternoon it's warm and humid and the sky brindled with stratiform cloud. I get to hers just after noon and she comes to the door in cotton shorts and a vest and invites me in and tells me to wait in the lounge while she gets ready. I take a seat in the armchair by the window with the view out over the reaped wheatfields. Bales of straw are stacked the length of them and the trees are just starting to turn. I hear from upstairs the intermittent creaking of the floorboards and when she comes down again she's wearing a red halter strap summer dress with espadrilles tied around her ankles. I comment on how nice she looks and she smiles and we make for the door.

The streambed of the Bourne has long since run dry and the banks are overgrown with sorrel and the dry seeded wicks of docks. Craneflies are amongst the grassheads and

229

the undergrowth chirrs with crickets. As we walk she tells me of the campus where she'll be living and of her anxiety over the start of the semester and of the preparations she still has to make before leaving. Textbooks to read and friends to visit and trunks to pack. She asks me in turn of my itinerary and the job I've found in town to raise funds for my travels and wonders whether we'll see each other again before I depart. I find it difficult to formulate meaningful responses because I'm caught up in this almost demented mythologising of her. Of all we've shared and all she represents. Of how our adolescence seems to have built towards this moment.

We come to the meadow where we roll out the picnic blanket and arrange upon it the fare I prepared earlier. Broiled chicken and cherry tomatoes. Crisps and rolls. A bottle of chilled white wine. After we've eaten she lies back on the blanket and I watch her breaths rise and fall and the hem of her skirt sometimes curling about her thigh in the breeze and through the broken cloud stippled light drifts across the fields and the dark maw of woodland behind us grinds and mewls and the canopies of leaves pulse and crepitate and windwaves push through the grasses to the wildflower meadow below where the downcast heads of dead helianthus twined with bindweed stare forlornly at the ground. I watch her for a long time and for a long time I feel a mounting departure from the present. I see her through the years. With her plaited hair and red dress that first day of school. Beneath the willow tree after so prolonged a separation. Seated at her desk with the light from the lamp upon her. Ranging through the stubble fields at summer's end. I look at her now and think it strange that we will be separated once more and that when next we meet we will both of us have left behind our childhoods. I watch the faint movement of her eyes behind her eyelids and the faint twitching of her fingertips upon the blanket. I drink the remainder of my wine and lie back beside her and close my eyes and when consciousness comes upon me again it's to find her on her side facing me. We hold each other's gaze. My hand is touching hers and she takes it and pulls me closer to her and lays her arm across my chest. Light moves across the fields and the silverdark grasses kindle in its slow thrall. Years from then the remorse of a moment's inaction passing inexorably. Of staring at her immobile with the summer's light waning and from the trees at the meadow's edge the first few leaves of autumn already drifting hither.

Homeward we walk largely in silence through the dying embers of the afternoon with the sun fled and the cloud darkened to a leaden grey with spits of rain in the air and on the lane leading back down into the village past the eviscerated husks of roadkill the reality of our imminent departure is made manifest as I watch the shape of her body beneath her summer dress and nearing the village with its rows of gabled cottages and the meadow on the corner I wonder at how far removed from it she is already become. On her doorstep I ask her when next I'll see her and she tells me she suspects she'll be back for reading week or failing this Christmas. For a while we're silent. I look at her in the leaden light and behind her the clouds gather and the fields grow dark. She takes my hand in hers.

I'll miss you.

I'll miss you too.

Will you send me postcards?

Of course.

One from every country you visit.

Yes.

We embrace. I close my eyes. Feel her body against mine. The weight of it. Its contours. The cadence of her breaths. Feel the rain in the sunwarmed air. A moment fleeting yet immutable and without end. Endless and immutable in its reliving. The feeling of the sunwarmed rain. Of her breaths with mine. We withdraw and in withdrawing I open my eyes. My hands find her lower back. Her arms come to rest upon my shoulders. She looks at my lips. A sheen of rain is upon her shoulders. In her hair its fine distillate. The fabric of her dress dampening. Another moment's inaction. Easy with her parents away for us to go inside. Up to her room with silence all about us. The village itself as if entombed. To stand in the leaden light with the curtains closed and dust shifting in its filmy wake. Her skin cool and damp. Afterwards lying in the gloom with the clouds gone to dusk and the room slowly darkening. Through the open window the rainy sward and across the fields the fife of swifts. Across the fields the lengthened shadows of the gloaming. From the tips of her hair rain drips. Drips silvered in the famished light. She looks at my lips. Up at my eyes. Again at my lips. Looks in her old way. Around her everything enshrined. The gravel yard. The pathway to the meadow out back. Glimpses of the garden I've come to know so well. Whether to act. Whether in acting all would become forfeit. I move my hands to her hips. Her hipbone. Glance down at the sheen of rain upon her chest and think of those years apart. Think of those years cloistered. Skirting the quadrangle. Nodding greetings to masters in gowns trailing coloured chevrons. The archways of the porter's lodge. Those years of removal leaving me impotent. Unable to act. Knowing now that our congress would deliver the surety of a shared future.

At work in the months that follow I will spend my lunchbreaks in town outside the bars we used to frequent or on the square where we waited for her father and I will see her in the faces of girls but always in these faces an emptiness. On my travels I will stand upon the cool stone steps of temples and in the shaded bowers of palm groves. I will take a footpath through the woods and look down upon a glacier crevassed in the moonlight. On the shores of a great lake I'll watch ospreys fall from the skies. One night in a shack by a beach I'll go down to the surf to watch the moon over the sea and another night will sit on an old jetty staring out across the dark expanse of water. Yet these images will ultimately feel devoid of meaning. Seeing always that lonely walk home along the Bourne with the rain pooling the lane.

Bea calls down. I replace the photographs on the little cabinet in the corner and in the darkness mount the stairs. She's on the bed waxed nude by the paling netherworld light beyond. I lie back beside her and for a long while we're silent. Wind stirred shadow moves across the walls. Silent until she asks me suddenly did I love her.

Who?

The girl in the photo.

Why do you ask?

Did you?

A long pause. I reach back and stroke her hair. She kisses my neck but I feel myself tensing. Eventually pull away and stare off into the darkness.

What's wrong?

Nothing.

It must be something.

Another long silence.

Is it because I asked about the photo?

No.

It is isn't it?

Bea…

Because I asked if you loved her.

No.

What? She was your girlfriend?

Jesus. Can we just drop it?

It comes out too forcefully. I glance back to find her staring at me. I go to put my hand on her knee but she pushes me away.

Bea...
What's got into you?
Nothing. I'm fine.
Nothing. That's all you keep saying.
I know. It's just...
I was only asking.
I know.

She pulls away. Pulls the sheet around her. Rolls over. I ask her what she's thinking but she doesn't respond. Later she's sleeping and in the dark with the wind blowing outside and the shutter clapping against the wall I begin to hear the distant boom of the sea. I go to the window and look out towards the river path and the palm fronds at the edge of the residence are stirring and clouds lucent in the glow of the moon are lumbering across the sky. I glance back at Bea and then I am pulling on my underwear and shorts and shirt and at the foot of the stairs my trainers and then I am quietly opening the patio doors and stepping out into the night. For a while I stand on the terrace looking up at the sky and feeling the wind upon me and then I am going through the gate and across the gravel and then to the river path with the wind pushing through the palms and thickets and on the opposite bank through the bamboo grove. The path is heavily rutted with the gouged treads of dried tyre tracks and with hoofprints from the trekking ponies that come this way through the summer. See them farther along in the field across the river and in the sky above them the slow convolutions of gulls moonlit against the night. See too the slow current and silvered eddying of the river and in the reedy undercuts the murine writhing of rodents. Come to the beach path and from there go along the track past the broke down pillboxes rear of the dunes with the river delta beyond hewn from the sea by the breakwater at the end of the beach. I turn up over the duneslacks and descend to the seafront past sculptures fashioned during the day from the petrified shapes of driftwood and larger boughs washed up white and bonelike in the moon. Afore the sea's edge the wrackline extends black and gnarled the length of the beach twisted with the shattered hulls of seashells and the snapped shards and tresses of old cane and the braided knots of cystic kelp and splintered wood and with fragments of glass and plastic blunted by the roiling of the ocean. I follow this almost to the breakwater against the dark rocks of which the waves toil and shatter and lisp with the delta of the river coiling black and colubrine into their cradle before disemboguing into the ocean. I sit by one of the bone white boughs of driftwood and face out to sea watching its dark rips and raking my hands through the damp sand and now and then closing my eyes and feeling the wind against me and listening to the beating of the waves along the shoreline. Finally I take from my pocket the photograph. Photograph of that night. The moon glosses its surface and a wraithlike light passes across us. Passes across her party dress. Passes across the backdrop of her old apple tree wound with fairy lights and around the garden the wicks of torch candles flickering in the wind and amidst all this the marquee with its lighted windows leaching out into the night.

I am just returned. Received word of it on the eastern seaboard at the end of my journey. Hurried up the coast home. Counting out the weeks and then the days and on the plane above the ocean the final hours. Journey's end by then unkempt and slim and tanned. Seen remote islands and jungle and one dawn climbed the steep stone steps of an ancient temple and watched robed monks pray in the globed easterly light. Trekked to a hill village in the midst of a religious pilgrimage and another dawn watched kneeling supplicants at the headwater of a sacred river. Other times drank in bars on the shores of beaches with the moon over the water before returning to tin roof shacks amongst the groves of coconut palms. Photographs on undeveloped film in my bag with all the other regalia of the trip. Brochures and leaflets and ticket stubs. Beer labels and coasters. My diary. Ornaments from the far east. Objects that in the wake of my parents' death I discard in a skip or incinerate in the back garden of my mother's new house watching the flames grow around the charred hulk cylinder of the bin. My parents at the gate awaiting my arrival. Mother in slacks sandals plain blouse. Father in shorts boating shoes polo shirt. Their faces when I come through arrivals. We go on down to the carpark. Some consternation over how the ticket machine works. The both of them trying to remember which bay they parked in. Trundle of the trolley wheels over the tarmac. The final leg home the sun glinting across the marshlands beneath the viaduct. Nearing the village the wheatfields. All those familiar landscapes somehow miniaturised. My parents in front talking about the garden. About the neighbours' fence. About maybe going into town over the weekend to have lunch together because a new place that does nice paninis has just opened on the corner. When we go by her house I look across and catch a glimpse of the marquee in the garden but of her no sign. At home I take a long shower and when I come back down again my mother has prepared tea and scones and these we take outside to the picnic table and are there a long time talking. The party I'm told is to celebrate David's fiftieth and belatedly Emily's nineteenth. Jill has organised everything and I am regaled with tales of how busy she has been. How my parents have been helping her out at the cash and carry. Helping at the local wine merchant where I worked before I went away. How it was decided to turn it into a potluck party. And my mother tells me of the troubles she's had trying to find her salmon poacher and of a terrine she made that just wouldn't set.

Night of the party I'm wearing the new white herringbone shirt my mother bought me in town and the tan suit I had tailored on my travels. In the welt of the jacket still in the torn and crumpled envelope I bought them in are the polished onyx earrings for Emily. I take them out and hold them to the light of my bedroom window before replacing them. It's still early. My parents are getting ready and I hear them softly from along the landing. My mother's hairdryer. Mother's straighteners. Father tunelessly whistling. My backpack is dumped against the corner of the room as yet unmolested and so to distract myself I take from the top pocket the letter she wrote me while I was away. Remember picking it up in a poste restante someplace. The heat searing. Webs of golden orbweavers from the telegraph wires. Dustdevils along the highway. I unfold it. The paper already starting to tear at the seams from repeated readings. About little really. University life. Parties. Her studies. The campus. Yet for me a totem those long months away. I trace my fingertips across the ballpoint script. Across the familiar little caricatures and doodles. A totem still.

Before heading out I make myself a gin and tonic and take it to the picnic table in the garden. Rotting apples crawled through with wasps are scattered across the lawn and gnats hover in the dying light. The garden seems tired. Weathered. See it in the borders of the lawn. In the broken fence slats. In the chipped paving of the path to the front door grown through with tussocks of moss. The housefront discoloured and streaked with discharge from the gutter and in the corner with the gritted remnants of a martin's nest. The wisteria over the patio windows moribund stumps. I go over to the pond and with a stick root through the putrescent duckweed. Wander round back and pick through the bits of old ornament I used to shoot from my window. Plastic figurines. Mangled aerosols gone to rust. The model planes I used to make with my father on weekends. A cockpit. A tailfin. Shattered in the weeds a fuselage. From here I can see my reflection in the dining room window beyond whose glass pane years later I will remove from my father's urn the cardboard lid and stare into the blackened grits of its depths. Can see from here also the corner of the living room where he'll die wracked with cancer. Yet for now all the way through the living room and onto the front lawn past the patio windows I see them materialise hazed by the dying streaks of light across the glass. My father in his sports jacket and buttondown shirt. My mother in a summer dress. I hear them call out for me and for a long time I don't answer. Just listen to their voices echoing out. Staring at them through the panes of glass with my reflection burning darkly there. Oblivion in the layers of light. Layers of time. My mother comes round to find me. Asks me didn't I hear them calling. I shake my head. Join them on the front lawn for some sparkling wine. Before we leave my father sets the timer on his camera and captures a likeness of the three of us beneath the apple tree. Stories of apple seeds popping in a fire and foretelling love. Portent we pose beneath. A likeness for the ages. Later curling and warping in the rusted bin in my dead mother's garden with the flames spitting about its blistered face.

When we arrive at her house there are a couple of people I don't recognise smoking cigarettes on the front yard. About my age. Both dressed in the same outfit of jeans boating shoes shirts. One wearing sunglasses and the other with them hanging from his cotton oxford open two buttons at the neck. We go on by. Around back to the little gate onto her lawn. The pathway demarcated by torch candles. Lights in the trees and rising barbeque smoke. See people in the marquee and scattered from it across the garden. Those I recognise and those I don't and as the waves continue to buttress against the breakwater and gulls or shags move across the sky I see them as mourners at a wake. Old neighbours removed to far flung villages while those who have remained are closeted and broken by the vagaries of the intervening years. Paying their respects. I'm so sorry. He was such a nice man. A kind man. A lovely man. There at the entrance to the transept shaking their withered hands or in the hall by the buffet tables pretending that any of it has any meaning. Thank you. Do come to the wake. We're having a finger buffet. See my father on the fields or in the woods and remember how things used to be. See me on the verges along the lanes behind the village in wellingtons and dungarees or with a stick aloft for the leaping dog. Streaks of a life long since fled. See me fled through wheatfields reaped or in spring by the glowed rape fields or in the woods with the trees bare and the pathways scythed through tracts of fibred snow. Remember the feel of his hand. See the shapes of kittiwakes and all along the shoreline the snags of ossified driftwood in the moon's cold ether and at the shore's edge the lines of the night's fishers. These knots of shapes across the lawn we walk by. The vicar at the barbeque with spatula and tongs and at the picnic table faces of old in the light of the marquee and in the darkest corner of the garden seated in a ring of plastic picnic chairs a circus with the slope of the meadow behind. On into the light. Clusters of tables around a wooden dancefloor above which hangs a glitterball haemorrhaging broken mosaics of light across the sidewalls. The buffet formed of discoloured platters of quiches and dressed hams and roulades and pavlovas and my mother's poached salmon with its cataract eyes and fucked skinflaps folded roughly back and covered with lemons and dill and this all strewn about with silver stars and ribbon. Disc jockey in the corner a throwback to village fetes and primary school discos and the weddings of neighbours. We go to the gifts table to place amongst other such fare our gift wrapped bottle spruced at the neck with scissor coiled ribbon and as we linger there we are met by Jill and David who embrace with kisses each of us before asking me of my travels and telling me how grown up I look and how handsome and perhaps noticing my distraction as I scan the marquee for Emily they tell me that she's just gone into the house and will be out presently. I stand with them a while. Listen to their talk of the village. Of so and so's dispute with so and so over the positioning of a fence. Of the state of the church roof and the ongoing efforts to raise money for its repair. Of a petition over the planned closure of the post office. Finally I make my excuses and head to the drinks table where I pour myself a glass of wine and drink it back then pour another. I head outside. In a quiet corner I listen to the strains of music and laughter from within and watch the mantel of dark woodland bordering the meadow. I look about me at the others on the lawn. Those on the picnic chairs are unmoved and with the light cast about them I see the pair from the yard amongst their number. I watch as they draw beer from the torn crate at their feet and tap from the tips of their cigarettes their ash upon the grass. Just along from them is a knot of girls and I wonder whether Emily isn't amongst them. I take a step closer and in the dim light see that none of them is she. Girls in silken dresses and shawls. One of them sees me. Braided blonde hair. Slingback heels and a strapless dress. Shaded softly with her legs crossed and her thigh softly defined from beneath her ruche smock. I retreat back into the shadows at the edge of the lawn and drink the rest of my wine. Am about to go in for another when I see Emily through the semi opaqueness of the windowed sidewall. Blue dress interfuse through the rippled layers of the screen. The dying away of sound also. See her move amongst the knots of people. Sit at tables. Small talk with those in line for the buffet. With an elderly group in the corner. Across the dancefloor through the turning light another joins the group on the lawn. Seats himself at a vacant plastic chair and opens a bottle of beer from the crate with the fob on his keychain. Thickset and tall. Black hair brushed back beneath coronet sunglasses. Frayed bands around his wrists. Shirt half open. Voice sounding across the fields. Across the fields his laughter. I look back through the window. See her with her parents and mine as they scan the marquee. I suppose trying to locate me. Gesturing vaguely to the lawn. I shrink further back into the dark privet. Reluctant for some reason to meet her. Along the lane a car's headlights scan the black fields. I edge farther around the marquee past the laddered guylines. In another reach of the garden I look up at the house. At her window. Happenstance of that night beneath the willow that brought us back together. Misjudged passiveness of those times in town or on the mezzanine of the villa or on study dates. Wonder vaguely how things will be now. Try to locate her inside the marquee but see only spectres from past lives slumped around tables. Parents of those in our year. The churchwarden and his wife. The shopkeeper with her husband. Elderly seamstress who used to turn up my school trousers. Elderly woman who used to sell curds at fetes. Can still see from this aspect the group on the lawn and so it is on looking their way that Emily comes out to join them. In her halter strap dress and aliceband beneath the apple tree wound with lights with the spitsmoke rising around her in the dark. Hair shorter than before and with her fringe across her brow. Taller and more slender. Fuller in the chest. She goes first to the girls and pours them some more champagne from the bottle she carries and they make a toast together and sip from their glasses and share a joke and then she goes amongst the males. The thickset boy with the brushed back hair stands and kisses her cheek and puts his arm around her waist. She leans into him and puts her palm on his chest. I slip farther back into the shadows.

Look on them mute and breathless. Disinherited. Everything falling away. Look upon them in that carnival atmosphere with all things past a mockery. The first time I saw her at school. Those summer holidays walking the fields together. The trips into town when we were older. Realise then and in the repercussions of that moment for days and weeks and months to come that everything has been for nothing. I try to gather myself. Realise that I'm trapped here with no way back through to the marquee. I wonder how long she will be out here with them. Whether there is any focal point to this party. Speeches. Toasts. Crowning ceremony. Wonder whether I couldn't just walk on by unnoticed. Or if she calls out feign ignorance. I reach up to the welt of my jacket and feel secreted inside it the little onyx earrings. Remember buying them in a market. Remember that sense of expectation. Of being with her again. Of picking up where we left off. I'm just wondering whether I could scale the fence when she catches sight of me. Calls out. Comes over. She steps to me and places her hands on my shoulders and kisses me on each cheek. Oddly excited. Asks me

What are you doing out here all alone?

Just getting some air.

I didn't see you.

No.

Tell me everything.

Huh?

About the trip.

Later.

I go by her and head into the marquee without looking back. I find a bottle of wine and drink two glasses in quick succession. My parents wave to me and I pretend not to see them. I take the rest of the bottle out front careful not to make eye contact with anyone and walk along the lane out of the village with my shadow mooncast and continue on the pathway up through the field past the water treatment hut. Across the Bourne I turn back and look at her house and from here across the still summer's night I can hear their baroque laughter. All now seems redundant. I sink down onto the pathway's hard ground beneath the ears of wheat and swig back from the bottle and try to compose myself. I stare up at the sky. At the thin cloud silver in the moon. At the stars. I try to formulate some kind of plan. Some way in which things will be okay. I think that maybe I'll go home but the idea of its darkness and all the memorabilia of my youth is too much to contemplate. But so too is anything right now. To go back and to see her with him. To be amongst the marquee's guests. To walk any farther along this pathway. There is nothing and nowhere. Yet when I think of her there's this growing notion in my mind that it mightn't be too late. That perhaps I can salvage something. Get her alone with me and lay it all out. The bond between us superseding all. And so it is that once I have finished the wine and flung the bottle into the pitch and listened to it shatter someplace in the field below I straighten my tie and brush the debris from my trousers and jacket and start to head back. I will sometimes veer into the brush and on the bridge over the Bourne I fall against a railing flaked with rust and on the lane back into the village fall into the embankment and at hers before approaching the marquee I go into the house to the toilets where a small queue has formed and one in line is from her group and the others kith from the village. The former recognises me and nods a greeting and there is a mirror hung on the far wall into which he then looks smoothing down his hair and adjusting his shirt collar and I exchange a few words with the woman next to me whose son much later will die in a motorcycle accident. In the toilet when my turn comes I splash cold water on my face and stare into the chasms forming in the mirror with the pulsing encroachment of the walls around me all muffled and all submerged and I slump on the pad cover seat of the toilet with a figurine from the plinth in my palm. Ceramic stag. Antlers. One broken. Remember it from long ago. And presently there is a knocking on the door and somebody is asking if I'm okay and I wonder how long I've been in there for the figurine is on the floor at my feet and my head against the wall. I unlatch the door and exit without paying heed to those queued. Faces vaguely recognised. Relics. Ghosts. Staggering into the marquee I find that the partygoers have dispersed into small groups either seated at tables or moving in the balled light across the dancefloor or standing outside in ligatures beneath the apple tree boughs around which the fairy lights glister torpidly in the night and the uneasy darkness is trowelled across land trowelled across sky. Of Emily no sign. Neither of her group. See my parents. See hers. I wander across the dancefloor looking without recognition into the dancers' faces as lambent streaks of light are cast in shifting kaleidoscopes about them. Faces young and old. In some wound through their hair lengths of ribbon and this too I see across the floor. Ribbon whorled with innardlike streamers of coloured tissue from party poppers. The music to which they dance is the kind to which set routines are known and performed and later there will be a conga line whose slow and tawdry procession I will watch from a table in the corner drunk. I wander beyond all this and the tables are littered with plates of half eaten buffet food and gnawed chicken bones and breadcrusts and cocktail sticks and empty bottles and empty glasses and the chairs with discarded cardigans and jackets and neckties and here and there on the floor women's heels discarded for their barefoot procession beneath the glitterball. I find a bottle of wine and a plastic cup and sit at one of the tables with it. I scan the marquee for traces of her and I throw my jacket over the back of my chair and roll up my shirtsleeves and lean back. Jill comes over. See her cut through the gnarling of bodies across the dancefloor. Sits beside me and asks me if I'm okay. I tell her I'm fine. Slur my words. She smiles and pours me a glass of water and has me drink it. I try to focus on her. She starts asking me about my travels and the places I visited and I tell her of a mountain I climbed predawn to watch the rising of the sun. I tell her how the light had cut across the harbour below and how even from that elevation the halyards of yachts could be heard against the mastheads and there were gulls circling the bluff on the far side of the inlet whose cries could be heard also. She asks me where this was and I tell her with tears in my eyes that I can't remember. I stare at the stars scattered across the tabletop turning one between my thumb and forefinger and she has me drink another glass of water and finally I look at her and smile and she lays her hand on my shoulder and then is gone in much the manner of her arrival. I head outside for some air and I am alone at the picnic table contemplating once more returning home when I see her and her friends coming back towards the lawn from the field. She is barefoot holding her heels in one hand with her partner holding the other and the girl with the braided blonde hair is barefoot also and drinking from a bottle of champagne as she leads the party hither. See them skirt around the privet then disappear someplace. House. Marquee. I resolve to leave and am just about to go inside for my jacket when Emily materialises from the darkness and hands me a cup of wine. She kisses me on the cheek and embraces me and I glance around for her partner but he's nowhere to be seen. She gestures to the chairs and we sit beside each other facing the pond beneath the apple tree and are silent for a long time. There's very little I can say to her right now. A part of me no longer even recognises her. A part of me wonders if I ever did. I look across the garden at the people in the marquee and I find I no longer recognise much of anything.

Finally I ask her how her year has been and as she answers I stare at her consumed by the elusive beauty to which I have been beholden so long. I barely listen to her sketched history of hall parties and trips to dales and seminars. She asks me about my trip and I'm about to give another sketched and potted history but find myself suddenly unable to. I stare down at the grass. She asks me if I'm okay.

I don't know.

What's wrong?

I look at her and she at me and it is as if staring into some great chasm. After a pause I ask her whether she wouldn't walk with me a while.

Where?

Just up into the field.

She nods acquiescence. Frowning. Tells me to wait while she goes inside to change her shoes. I say that I'll meet her at the gate. I drink back the wine she handed me and head for the marquee where I retrieve from my jacket the onyx earrings and place them in my trouser pocket. I am first at the gate and she comes out to meet me a short while later in a pair of old walking trainers and with a shawl wrapped around her shoulders. I let her through before me and as I follow her up the path alongside the privet I watch her as in some previous life inhabited by none but us. I watch the shape of her beneath the dress she wears and her shoulders beneath the shawl and as the pathway yields to open field I walk silently at her side since time immemorial. The night is still and warm and moonlit and the grass through which we walk long and cloven by a scythed track that runs to a copse demarcating the upper and lower slopes and it is here that we stop. Wordless to now Emily faces me in the darkness as I scuff through the husks of hazel in the dust at my feet. She asks me what's wrong and I wonder whether she knows. How could she not? I face her now and am met by the same depthless beauty as before. For a juncture so long in the making I'm suddenly without words. I remember all that has come before and search for some reference that might encapsulate all. The afternoon in the meadowlands before we parted. In town in the candlelit alcove of some bar. In her room with textbooks spread across her floor and with the curtains rising in the…

I love you.

It is said suddenly and without forethought. The words hang in the air. I am staring down at the ground. Unable to look at her. She doesn't say anything for a long while and then she takes my hand and with it brings me to her such that I can feel her soft breaths and the soft strands of her hair against my cheek. I slowly raise my eyes and look at her dress in the moonlight and her pale chest as alabaster in its hue. Beauty now imbued with a kind of melancholy. Feel my hand in hers. The touch of her skin. All now without hope and consequence.

Mean so much to me

Been friends for such a long time

Good looking

But

Find somebody

Out there for you

University

Hope we can still be

Fragments. Asks me finally if I want to come back down to the party with her. Have another drink. Maybe a dance. I shake my head. Tell her I want to stay here a while. She embraces me and then is gone. I try not to watch her as she heads back across the grass. Just down from the copse is an ancient trough rusted and filled with dark slag and all fucked with dents and the ground around it churned and black and fucked and I go to this and sit with my back against it and look down to the marquee with no trace of her in the darkness and it is thus that all comes to its end. Comes to its end now and always with all before and all after forfeit. And so into the night. To the fucked aftermath of the party. See the conga line from a corner table and my parents in its throng. Vision of their life. See one of her number throwing up into the fishpond. See the woman whose son dies requesting a song. See her parents in the midst of a slow dance towards the end.

I don't see her again. Some nameless hour of the night the girl with the braided hair takes me to the field and I lie in the long grasses as she unbuckles my belt and pulls about my knees my trousers and tries to fellate me. I play with her tits. Play with her beneath her knickers and smock. But all pales and all begins to die. I writhe in the grass and look up into the black night and then she is gone and I am alone with a deepening foreboding that this juncture heralds the end of days. And so it is.

When Bea leaves there's an untold rift between us. I travel with her by bus to the airport and at the gates we kiss but all is devoid of vigour. I wait until her plane is flown. Watch its ascent into the scorched haze. Watch a long time after the echoes of its passing. That night and nights after I take the photograph drunk to the beach and lie with it with the boom of the sea all along the coastline. Lying sometimes naked beneath the stars. Sometimes wading naked into the ocean and thinking how easy it would be to fall submerged and to drift with the plankton into the darkness beyond. Yet finding myself washed up on the shore with the firmament cast dreadlike above and afterwards on the mezzanine this loneliness that I've not felt since that night by the copse with the throes of the party playing out below and the throes of all things borne out in the black limbs of the trees.

\*             \*             \*

After my return I find work in a makeshift office behind a car mechanic's cold calling funds for a film. Sometimes I don't turn up at all. Instead wander the streets or sit out in parks with the leaves turning and the evenings drawing in and at home I'll tell her all is well and that I have raised such and such and that my coming commission will pay the rent this month and next and so on and so on. She is home of an evening in her trousersuit and we sit on the sofa watching television and nights I lie awake watching shadows play across the ceiling and in the mornings after she has gone I'll go back to bed and at the office when taking up the telephone I'll stare out of the window at the mechanics stripping down the chassis of cars as I am sworn at or abused if even given shrift. Sometimes with the phone cradled against my ear I think of my father and all of the elation and misery and anger and guilt are starting to erode. Are starting to transmogrify into something else. Maybe numbness. Sometimes at home after Bea has gone to work I take out his photograph. The one my mother sent me of the three of us on a beach someplace. Find I barely even recognise him. Find I barely recognise any of us. Phone calls with my mother I will fall largely silent and as of old reply monosyllabically to her enquiries after my health job relationship flat life plans. Sometimes I will take out the fountain pen bequeathed to me. The one my mother said to take as a memento. I will study the fine nib now gritted with dried ink and practise my own penmanship with the tip of it scraping dry across the notepad. Will study too the finger marks across the section and barrel and wonder are they his or mine.

A long time since I've been back home. Bea keeps castigating and my mother gently cajoling but the thought of being in the house again oppresses me too much. I postpone and forge excuses and one time cancel a couple of days before because I'm not feeling well or claim not to be and that weekend Bea talks to me little and soon enough my sense of guilt starts to paralyse me. Talks to me little over the course of the subsequent week and nights we lie in bed with the space between us literal and metaphorical and when I try to move closer to her she pushes me away. These nights too I lie awake with the continuation of my own paralysis and whether waking or sleeping or somnolent I am preoccupied by thoughts of Emily and plagued by this gradual awakening in me that when last we met on the terrace decking of the pub just before I went away she had on occasion used the pronoun we when talking of her home life and it is only in the witching hours that I wonder whether I wilfully ignored it. I tell Bea that I'm sorry for cancelling the trip. That I wanted to see my mother but just didn't feel up to it. I tell her that I've been thinking about my father a great deal recently. That I've been mulling over his death. Because it relates to what she envisages as a burgeoning manifestation of grief we reconcile and afterwards when we cosy up on the settee in our dressing gowns I will stare at the television or at the wall behind it.

At work the kitchen upstairs is rank with unwashed cups growing gouts of mould and the floor with spatterings of teabags flung binward. By the end of the third week I am the most senior employee beneath the producers and during lunch breaks I roam the backstreets and sit on the terrace walls of terraced houses eating sandwiches and drinking cartons of iced coffee. Sometimes I go back to the office after. Sometimes not. One time in lieu of returning I go to the railway station and ride a train to the terminal of a distant suburb where I disembark and sit on a bench on the platform inspecting the photograph Bea found. Inspecting the expressions beneath creases and fingerprints. Other times to give the impression that I'm working late I'll delay coming home until gone eight and will return to find Bea at the hob cooking supper and she'll sit me down and fuss over me and bring me tea and after dinner stroke my hair while straddling me on the settee. Towards the end of the month with things tight and the commission still not forthcoming she lends me money that I tell her I'll pay back and this I will spend on meagre lunches so that I can afford a drink in the evening and neither do I feel much guilt over this. Not until much later.

Eventually one night alone in the pub I send a message to Emily and afterwards I toy with my phone on the tabletop waiting for a reply but none comes and I check too the next morning and throughout the next day but still nothing. With Bea I'm careful to keep my phone on silent for fear that it will sound and she'll ask who it's from and because of this I start taking it with me to the toilet or waiting until she's in the shower to retrieve it from my bag or running mystery errands to the shops so that I can sit on the wall on the corner going through old communications. Checking and rechecking their substance. At the end of the week I send another message asking if she's okay and I've all but given up when I finally hear back. She says she's sorry she didn't reply sooner. She's been out of the country on business. Her phone wasn't working. Didn't have reception. Another string of messages follows and though nothing much is said I will comb through the threads trying to derive meaning from them. Eventually I ask her whether she has any time over the next few days to meet and she replies that she'll get back to me but as she fails to do so I ask again to which she informs me that her weekends are all booked up for the time being but perhaps next month she'll be able to.

Later that week or the next smokers are standing in the archway at the pub's entrance staring despondently into the evening with runoff from the fascia curtaining their view and the redbrick edifice rising above them into the night slung black with rain. They pay me little heed nor I them as I pass into the warm fug of the pub. People are seated around candlelit tables or on the rows of stools along the bar atop the spirit shelves of which are displayed in cases hung with dust taxidermists' mounts with their stitching asunder amidst rude sprouts of foliage and above these the fluted plasterwork of the compartmented ceiling. I walk around the bar looking for Rick with the chequered floor lustreless and the archways draped with heavy velour curtains and on the far side I find him in a girdle of chesterfields facing the fire. Later on after we have caught up and reminisced over our house share I am telling him of my situation with Bea and of my past life with Emily and we are at this point drinking whiskey and rain continues to fall outside streaking with its grit the windows and once concluded he asks me whether I love Bea and I shrug and think how desirous I was of her when first we met when I would watch her amidst the pallets with her shirt riding up over her waist and the little bracelet she wore on her ankle or how when walking home together our strides would marry but this notion of my ever having loved her remains obscure. I tell him this. Tell him that in seeing Emily again everything had collapsed. I drink back my whiskey and go to the bar to order two more and slumped there awaiting service I dwell on these things I have told him and when I return he describes the first girl he loved at university and tells me how one night in the throes of depression he had gone to an overpass near his halls and climbed over the railing and leant with one hand above the traffic below willing himself to let go. I wonder are all as he and I. He asks me then of Emily. Whether she's with anybody and whether I might have any chance with her. And I tell him that I don't know who she's with but that I had always considered myself fated to be with her and that we had shared too much not to end up together but it is not until much later that I learn what fate really is.

You seem to know what you need to do.

What do you mean?

You seemed to have made up your mind already.

You think so?

Otherwise you wouldn't be telling me all this.

Walking home that night I find a great emptiness in the streets and arriving at the flat I find it deserted also for Bea has gone out in town with friends and so I pour myself a whiskey and stand a long time at the window until sometime after midnight the rain finally eases. I text Bea asking where she is but receive no reply and I pass out on the settee and awake sometime in the small hours to find her seated beside me in her finery. A miniskirt and heels and taffeta top. Drunk. High. Tells me she's been clubbing and has had cocaine and asks me if I want some. We cut it up on the tabletop and do a couple of lines each through a straw and drink some more and then she takes me by the hand and leads me wordlessly into the bedroom where she sits me on the bed and stands between my legs and I put my hands about her and feel beneath her skirt and push it up over waist as she pulls off my shirt and slips out of hers and unclasps her bra and lets it fall and I reach up to her and then she...

Emily replies finally towards the end of November. Apologises for not getting back to me sooner but has had a lot going on. Asks me if I want to go around to hers for dinner at the end of that week. I leave it a day before confirming if only to suggest detachment and in the days preceding I am beleaguered and with Bea cold and distant and at work when I go lacking in all engagement. I will sit with the phone against my ear and sometimes I'll experience this rising panic and sometimes defeat and sometimes elation.

I make my lies to Bea. I phone Rick to ask his complicity in them. That we are going drinking in town and won't be back until late. Night of the dinner I'm ironing my shirt and Bea is on the settee with an open bottle of wine on the table before her and her face blue in the hue of the television screen and on the stovetop the remnants of the meal she cooked for us. Meal of which I ate little. Rather pushed at with my fork. She asked me what was wrong and I told her I had a stomach ache. She suggested I cancel with Rick and stay in but I played the martyr and told her I didn't want to let him down. That a night out was perhaps just what I needed. Then I am before the mirror in the bathroom with from the living room the sound of a gameshow playing out on the television and I moisturise beneath my eyes and fix my hair and apply some aftershave and as I stare at my reflection I continue to be dogged by this absolute failure of recognition. Perhaps it is the juncture in my life that has given way to such an ongoing feeling of being other. Perhaps it is simply the afterimage of my father's death. Sometimes when I'm looking back through old photographs of him I begin to see the span of my own life. Sometimes I am in these photographs as well. Gnawed by time. By the lost avenues that have led me here and hence. When I go back through to Bea to kiss her goodbye I stare into her eyes and fail to find any recognition there also. As if we are suddenly strangers.

I stop off to buy wine and out on the street afterwards it starts to sleet and the sky is black and desolate without definition. The people I pass are hunkered down against the cold with their faces huddled in the collars of their jackets or covered by the peaks of caps or umbrellas with only the occasional glimmer of their lost and vacant eyes. Sometimes the wind will blow and the sleet will swirl and at the roadsides a grey slush begins to form from the sputum of cars and buses. I descend into the tube station and puddles rank with grime pool the stairwells and the air is stale and cold and mustily pungent and so too the platform with its torn and ancient hoardings. Beneath the tracks mice black with culm scurry amongst shreds of newspapers and the people lined along its yellow lip are huddled in dark clothing with their eyes downcast. When the train draws in I sit at the far end of the last carriage in the corner and I read and reread the advertisements above the scratched pane opposite and I look at my disjointed reflection in the dark glass sometimes rift by flares of static.

I disembark at the specified station and ascend into the cold night with a crudely sketched map on a scrap of paper. It's a part of town I've been to a couple of times before but know little and I am soon lost in the backstreets with the street names not correlating with those I have written down and the rows of housing all identical stately terraces with heavy white lintels over narrow hung sash windows and transoms over painted doorways up sets of concrete steps. The sleet continues to fall and to form slurry at the roadsides and to hang in beads from the clipped hedges and to cling to the sullied rosaries of streetlamps disappearing into the hazed vanishing points of the city. The streets here are quiet and lonely and most of the houses' windows either dark or their lights muted through heavy curtains and the few people I pass are dressed in heavy overcoats and the cars parked kerbside are family estates or four by fours. A part of me wants to give up and go back to Bea for there is within me a foreboding that seems to mar my progress. Yet a greater part of me renders this notion unimaginable and the anticipation of seeing her again in whatever guise drives me onwards. After I've doubled backed on myself and found my way without purpose onto the main street whence I came I ask a couple for directions and they examine my scrap of ink blotted paper with its crude roadways and scrawled landmarks and advise a route which I follow via a couple of dead ends until I am on her street by now numbed with cold and warming myself by breathing into the upturned collar of my jacket.

I come to her door. I'm about to rap on the brass knocker when I see a panel of flat intercoms on the wall. Her name is there with the name of another whom I take to be her flatmate. I press the button and there's some static and then I give my name and presently a hall light comes on and the door is opened. Not by Emily but by a man around my age. Dressed in faded jeans and a ribbed sweater with his feet bare. He wears glasses and is taller than I and broader set and he shakes my hand and gives his name as Tom and it is not until he is standing beside Emily in their kitchen that I recognise him as her beau from the party with his hair somewhat thinned and a hint of grey in the jowls of his beard and the beginnings of a paunch cinctured by the tightness of his sweater.

The despair I feel at seeing him with her is compounded by her own appearance. Her hair is grown out some and fixed with clips at the sides and she has a heavy tan incongruous with the cold of November. She's wearing a shirt creased tightly across her chest and a pair of faded jeans low at the waist. A rush of disbelief. Of realisation and resignation. That those riverside drinks with her now seem so defiled. I watch them around the kitchen. She is busy at the stovetop and he is setting the table and there is a synchronicity to their movements. Sometimes he will put his hand upon her waist or she hers upon his shoulder and there are photographs of them on a corkboard on the wall. A savannah on the threshold of a mud hut surrounded by half naked tribespeople. The summit of a mountain strung with prayer flags. Family meals with her parents smiling conspirators. Seated at the picnic table of her garden back home ladling out punch from a punchbowl. There are signs of the life they share throughout the open plan kitchen living room. In the stuffed animals on the cabinet beside a collection of rugby trophies. In the intermingled spines of their books on a floating shelf. For a while I'm near speechless. Responding to their questions with a series of nods and strangled whispers. Continuing to watch their progress around the kitchen. The way he lays out the cutlery and plates and glasses. The way when she lifts the lid from a pan on the stovetop steam bellies around her. Their easy way with each other born of long association.

Tom seems sure that we have not met before and it is Emily not I who tells him of the party at hers. He has a way of looking at me that is at once condescending and ambivalent. As if perhaps he can't quite work out what I'm doing there but doesn't really care. I'm given a beer and invited to sit on their couch. I continue to look around at their shared cohabitation. Tom sits away from me and flicks through a magazine and I'll glance at him or at Emily in the kitchen. At dinner sometime later I'm forced to listen to his work stories as he bolts down his food and at some point Emily interjects to tell him that I'm in film but he pursues this no further. Rather leans back and wipes his mouth with a serviette. She asks me how it's going and I try to elaborate as little as possible. Just the barest of details. Emily tells me in turn that she has been out of the country again with her charity and she shows me some photographs after dinner and I look at them without interest. I'm about to make my excuses and leave when Tom rises from the table and goes off to get changed because he's meeting friends in town.

After he's gone Emily makes coffee and bids me join her on the settee. She places on the table in front of us a tray on which she's arranged a plate of biscotti beside a cafetiere and cups and a little jug of cream and a bowl with crystallised sugar cubes and while we wait for it to percolate it's difficult to know what to say. I continue to look around the room. At the abstract print on the opposite wall. At the fairy lights garlanded around a vase of ornamental twigs by the cabinet in the corner. At the coarse woven throw on the armchair. Wondering where it came from. Wondering whether she was alone or with him. Thinking the while how proper and dull it all seems. How without character. Emily sits with her feet curled under her and I am at the edge of the settee as far from her as I can be and over her shoulder through the window I sometimes glance at the sleet and the melted slathering of it across the glass and aside from the sleet's light tapping against the pane the only other sound in the room is the burble of the dishwasher from the utility room. She asks me whether I'd like some music on. I tell her okay and she goes over to the unit by the television and chooses a jazz album and in the warmth of the room with the lights low and the music the space between us on the settee starts to shrink. I've already had a couple of beers and some wine and there is an intensity to her that I still can't escape. She seems to be watching me intently and I continue to avoid her gaze. Trying to think of something to say. Anything. Finally I limply ask her where she's spending Christmas and when she tells me back home I say that I am also. That I'll be there for around a week. She asks me of my mother and it takes me a long time to formulate a reply that even then is vague and desultory. She says perhaps we could meet when we're home. Maybe go for a walk. I wonder why she's saying this now. Why after tonight's revelation. I tell her we'll have to see. That I'm not yet sure of my plans. She tells me that she's still not been to see my father's headstone. That we could perhaps go up there together. I think distantly of that lonely part of the churchyard where his ashes are spread. That corner beneath the horse chestnut where his recrement rots into the cold and ravaged earth. His headstone there small and unexceptional with the gentle lamentation of its inscription and at its rear the nude meshed rosebriar my mother planted. Think upon it possessively. Selfishly. That it is for mine and my mother's mourning and ours alone. Yet my presence there with Emily seems equally foretold. That we will stand together in the decaying day and offer our own slow lament. That we will talk of what he and all things meant to us and afterwards walk amongst the gravestones and stop now and then to remark on the weather bitten stones of the nameless dead and of the recently dead. To remark on the boy from our class whose putrefaction in his greyed shroud and narrow wood sarcophagus continues unabated. All those parishioners dead and without vindication or validation. And then to journey past the church and to look up at the belltower with its old fucked clocks and gnawed gargoyles and spire and the old school buildings below set against the mudblack fields. Vestiges of our life there all but spent. I tell her okay. After coffee she asks if I'd like a drink of something and I accept on the proviso that she'll have one with me. She goes to the liquor cabinet by the dining table and brings out a bottle of cognac and two tumblers pouring into each a measure that seems to invite a protracted continuance of the evening. A long while later after a second measure is poured I ask her about Tom. I tell her I didn't know she was with anyone. She sits there silently swirling her brandy around in her glass before glancing at me and smiling in a manner vague and unreadable.

I thought perhaps I'd mentioned it.

I shake my head. She looks down and starts brushing lint real or imaginary from the arm of the settee and I watch her quietly with the music having finished unnoticed and even the sleet now stopped. She asks me whether I'm with anyone. I take a sip of brandy.

There is kind of this girl but...

But what?

I don't know. It's complicated.

She doesn't ask why and I pursue the conversation no further. I don't tell her the details. That we moved in together and for a time I thought of little else but her. Instead I excuse myself to go to the bathroom and to get there I have to walk along a hallway hung with picture frames of the two of them with streaks of light from the living room falling across their surfaces and illuminating palely their suggested details. At the hallway's end I push open a door and find that I'm not in the bathroom but on the threshold of their bedroom and I stand there taking in the way the light from outside shades the bedsheets and the jaws of a laundry hamper strung with her knickers and on the shelving unit burnt out candle stubs and bottles and vials of unnamed lotions. Their bedside tables. The one with a magazine and empty mug. The other with a dogeared book and stuffed toy. Picture in the drawers the prophylactics. Picture her afterwards breathless while he wipes himself down. Picture its sad routine. Other fragments start to coalesce into this allusion of a misspent life. Not just here but spanning other encounters. The way at our first meeting she had looked out across the river and there was a great melancholy in her eyes. Or in leaving her how she'd seemed to disappear into the night with an expression of almost fathomless coldness on her lips. A coldness repeated here and there in the snapshots along the landing or in the way in which in the kitchen earlier their easy domesticity had seemed to mask some kind of gulf. An abyss over which she seemed to stand. There is a soundlessness in the flat that becomes increasingly oppressive and as I look back down the shadowy hallway I almost expect to find myself elsewhere and for all of this to be revealed as some half dreamed fiction. Her life with Tom. Our childhood. My father's death. To wake with her never having existed. With Bea figmental. For my fate to have been formed through a different tangent.

A parallel in which all is as it should be. As I continue to stare down the hallway I begin to see this very clearly. That all is skewed. See it clearly when I stare at myself in the bathroom mirror. And as I go back through to her I find that all has been displaced. That there is an otherness to her that makes her almost unrecognisable. I sit back on the settee beside her and she pours me another brandy and as I turn the glass in my hand I notice that all of the fingerprints previously there are now gone with no trace of their ever having existed. She asks me if I'm okay and her voice is hollow. I nod quietly. Tell her then for no particular reason of the boy in our year who died and whose grave I visited in the churchyard. How in seeing it I had felt myself close to his putrefying body and how after my father's death I had driven away and pulled over in a layby overcome by elation. A bliss I can neither explain nor reconcile in my mind. I tell her of its strange intensity. That I'd never experienced anything like it before or since. She listens silently staring across at me and preening the strands of her hair and I look not at her but into some unknown distance neither in the room nor anywhere tangible with all the details of the environs reduced to nothingness. Tell her in a monotone that seems to come from beyond me how the cawing of the crows in the trees when I saw the dead boy's grave had reminded me so much of autumnal days at school when the leaves were beginning to fall and the landscape took on a quality of permanence that would become the one of my memory. A landscape neither light nor dark nor defined by any sense of contour. Rather imbued with an easy bleakness that seemed germane. Tell her how these two sadnesses were inseparable. I begin to tell her also the raw details of my father's death. How he had wasted away over a number of months and how each time I had visited another part of him had seemed gone. The day I came home and found him punching holes in his belt with the eyelet pliers from the ironmonger's. How on trips in the car we would pull over for him to throw up into the grass. Those final days waiting for him to die. Just sitting around. In the evening the sad meals at the table with my mother. I tell her I'm sorry to lay all this on her but I've never really opened up like this before and for the first time I feel that I'm not just saying this for effect or to provoke some kind of reaction. She has her hand on my knee and she's telling me it's okay and as I'm saying all this the room slowly begins to reform around me and around us and I look across at her and experience this newfound realisation that the avenues that have led us thus can be undone. That for us it is not too late. And I resolve that the next time I see her I will tell her so. I see it vividly in my mind as before. Up at the churchyard by my father's headstone in the coldness of winter. A moment to be replayed until its inception. At the door she embraces me and withdrawing looks into my eyes with an expression of consternation. Asks me once more if I'm okay.

Why wouldn't I be?
I don't know. You just seem…
What?
Different.
How do you mean?
Just different.
I'm okay.
You're sure?

\*       \*       \*

I walk behind her. The surrounding fields are fallow and clawed of all life with rude tufts of fucked grass and wrangled weed interspersed through the thick plots of mud. The school buildings beyond are squat and drear and carrion birds loop the crenelated and gargoyled spire of the church. She is in jeans and shitspattered wellies and an old anorak with frayed cuffs and the down exuding from its fucked seams. Is wearing an old woollen hat and fingerless gloves and a long scarf wrapped twice around her neck. I watch her footfalls ooze and slide through the path's churned mud and follow in her wake sliding and oozing. I'm wearing my old wool scarf and gloves and my old waxed jacket from which the torn pockets dangle and flap with my jeans spattered also and the wind clawing the fields and in the sky crows buffeted by its currents.

Walking in file we talk little. She has in her hand a red string handled crepe bag from which the crowded heads of flowers jostle and in an old plastic bag I carry a sponge and water bottle tinted green with soapsuds in its ullage. On this path once more with her after so many years. See her plaited hair. The red lunchbox she bore. How after school we would walk home together across the same field and in the wintertime a layering of mist would lie above the flinty mud and how alone on winter mornings the prints underfoot would be frozen into scars the length of the pathway. Then as now a stillness to the landscape suggestive of prolonged sleep. In the bare trees little stirring and the cattle in the adjoining fields standing rigid around troughs in whose murky depths their water festered beneath thin floes of pigmented ice.

We approach the school gate. The rusted links of the wire fence are grown through with fibroid strands of bindweed. I let her through first and follow her into the grounds where she pauses and looks to the playing field with the trees bare and across the concrete the faded relics of mazes and chalked hopscotch courts from long ago.

This is where we used to line up after playtime.

Yeah.

When the dinner lady rang the bell.

Yeah.

It looks so small now.

I know.

I follow her then around the route we would take to get back to class and at the hall's entrance beneath the covered walkway she pauses to peer in through the window. Visoring her hand across her brow and pressing her face against the glass I watch vaguely her darkened reflection.

Look at their little handprints.

Yeah.

Just like the ones we used to do.

She continues to peer in and I step back and look about me at the rafters overhead and at the little set of concrete steps leading down to the building housing the head's office fashioned as the church from unknapped flint with mullioned windows and a miniature belfry atop its roof gable. I experience a sensation in looking at this belfry and through the window mullion to the office and glancing now and then at Emily beneath the rafters of having lived two lives. The one now and the other a tableau of barely connected images populated by a being other than me. I wonder how it could be that I was schooled here. That at lunchtimes I would run by with abandon. Play with my peers on the field. In class pore over the projects we'd been set with an enthusiasm long since beggared. Walk home with her neither plagued by yearning nor self doubt. Wonder that there could be such a disconnect between these images and the heavy veil of now. She draws back from the window and turns to me and smiles and it is a look etched so indelibly upon the landscapes I inhabit that I know I will never be free of its yoke.

I can't believe how little it's all changed.

I know.

It's like a time warp or something.

We skirt around the hall and stop to browse at the laminated menu in the window of the canteen and then at the corridor to the classroom of our final year still mounted with the same rows of numbered coat hooks and with the vinyl floor throwing off the dull reflections of the wintry afternoon. From the coat hooks a couple of coats still hang suspended in the eerie stillness as if suddenly abandoned and so too hang garlands of tinsel above the doorway and in the classroom itself a pine all dead with an undisturbed ring of dried brown needles about its base. She is as before with her hands above her brow and her face against the glass.

It's just as I remembered it.

Yeah.

Nothing about this place ever seems to change.

No.

We come to the churchyard and walk the narrow pathway past the rows of headstones new and old and around the belltower with the crows now come to rest in its crenels in the blustery wind. The sky mulls above and all is damp with the boughs of the yews moistly black and gusted leaves across the pathway ochre or gnawed and brown and the smell is of damp earth. Leaves are raked into damp piles at the edge of the graveyard and there left to rot and by one pile an old fucked wheelbarrow eaten through with rust drips damp from its rusted lungs. Rounding the belltower we pass the ancient yew gnarled to a stump after a lightning strike one winter with lice crawling through its pappy innards. We come to and stand without comment at the boy's grave upon which freshly placed flowers still in their cellophane have started to rot and the black kerb of its perimeter is clung to by pearls of moisture and the newly erected headstone bears an inscription given to his parents' misery. About its lunette are engraved images pertinent to the fleeting interests that occupied and symbolised his life and I glance only briefly at these sad miscellanea before casting my gaze past the graveyard and out across the valley with its gradated layers of brown and grey and in the fields its clusters of livestock fated for slaughter. Neither do I look at Emily for she has knelt wordlessly at the foot of the boy's grave and is without movement. At length she rises and stands by me and then I watch as she takes one of the flowers from her posy and places it amongst the detritus upon his grave.

Shall we go and see your dad?

Okay. It's just over here.

I lead her along the grasstrod pathway past the rows of bucked headstones to his place beneath the horse chestnut and for a while stand wordless as we look down upon it at the polish of its grey stone in the attenuated light of the afternoon and the serifs of its engraving already starting to dull. The sudden moment of my conjuring and deceit has come to bear. To be here alone with her thus comes after offers and counteroffers. Arguments and recriminations. Comes after Bea had asked whether I should like to go home with her for the holiday or whether she might come home with me. Finding me reticent had asked whether we might simply spend Christmas in our flat together. Yet knowing that I could be with Emily instead even if only for an hour or so I had told her that my mother was not holding up particularly well and it would be better if I were with her alone. And after everything was organised and we had decided to part for the holidays we had received a Christmas card from my mother in which she'd expressed her sadness that we couldn't both have gone to see her. And because I'd opened the card with Bea at my side she had read it in all its glory. Had risen then from the settee and stormed out. My mother had enclosed a cheque for us so that we could enjoy a meal together before Christmas and looking down at this I had felt a sudden wave of almost unbearable sadness. For here in Bea I had all that I had wished for and still I was not sated. I'd gone after her to the bedroom but she'd closed the door on me and when I went to open it she told me to leave her alone and in the run up to leaving we'd spoken little and just before she went off to the airport she told me ominously that when she came back we had a few things we needed to sort out. With Emily also there had been much negotiation for my conversations with her were conducted in secret and there were long delays between messages. And because she was coming with Tom we'd had to devise a time when it could be just the two of us.

And so it falls on the twenty fourth. The day of my childhood when I'd walked at nightfall through the village and seen stardust in the sky and when put to bed had heard outside the window the ringing of sleigh bells or a great sliding down the chimney. I would rise through the night and look out into the scars of darkness and before dawn would find at the foot of my bed a woollen stocking twined with ribbon and scattered with glitter. So today will see a few hours from now the midnight mass my mother will attend while I will drink brandy at home and eat mincepies with a fire smouldering in the hearth. Will be sitting in the corner where my father died a year ago trying in my stupor to communicate. Will be there staring into the darkness when she returns.

It's a lovely spot.

Mum picked it out.

I look across at her. The mizzled afternoon moisture clings to the scarf about her neck. The crows from the crenels of the belltower have taken flight and trace across the sky and settle cawing in the stripped black boughs of the horse chestnut.

The stone's nice.

Hm.

The wording.

Her skin is pale and moisture clings also to the cropped black strands of her hair needled beneath the woollen lip of her hat. The space between us is that of the headstone. In the rosetop vase on the granite plinth at its foot a sprig of dead flowers rots. She crouches and on her haunches removes these and lays them on the grass by the side of the stone. She removes also the vase and tips from the tin cup base a feculence of slimy water.

Have you got the sponge?

Here.

I hand it to her with the bottle and watch as she wipes down the perforated top and sides and guts of the tin cup splashing suds of water over it from the bottle. Watch as she wipes down the plinth and the receptacle for the vase and then in broad strokes the stone itself using the corner of the sponge to clean the serifs of the lettering and the petals of the wisteria across the lunette.

Would you fetch me some clean water in this?

She hands me the tin cup and I head with it to the transept entranceway at the side of which is an old spigot mounted on a rickety waterpipe over the gunged mesh of a drain with buckets in the long grasses at the foot of the flintwork edifice and by these old slabs and tiles grown over with lichens and moss. I fill the tin cup and as I do so watch her hunched over the headstone no longer cleaning it but moving her fingertips through the grooved inscriptions and then laying her hand to rest at its crown. She is like this a long time and above her the wind can be seen pushing through a yew at the edge of the graveyard and in the distance virga slews onto the ruddy fields. She glances back at me and water is slewing from the spigot over the rim of the tin cup and so I shut it off and carry it back over to her. She takes it from me and places it carefully in the plinth's hole and over this sets the perforated lid and then from her bag takes her flowers and from her coat pocket some secateurs and uses these to snip the stalks so that they will sit in the vase. Her concentration as she arranges them into a fan is such that she seems barely conscious of my presence as I stand nervously over her wondering whether now is the right time. Whether such a time even exists. Finally with the flowers set she remains on her haunches admiring them and it is not until she rises that I see she has tears in her eyes.

He was such a lovely man.

I nod and then she brings from her trouser pocket a wad of tissue and wipes her eyes. I put my arm around her waist and rest my hand on her hip and then she turns into me and I embrace her feeling the damp must of her woollen hat and scarf and the coldness of her skin against mine. She continues to cry and my eyes are closed and there is between us a great nexus. A shared history experienced in that moment in which we are utterly entwined. Our childhood in the school. In the church dressed as magi as we carried the gifts of nativity. With my father during those summer barbeques on my lawn. Walking with him across the fields during the autumn when he would tell us of the old man's beard in the hedgerows and the rings of toadstools bordering the woods. I feel all this between us at that moment and eternally and the doubts I felt are soon superseded by a sense that this is the way it should be for this is how it was written from the day of our first meeting. She cries upon my shoulder and I open my eyes and look down at the flowers on the plinth of my father's grave and feel finally that I am meditating with the fabric of his death. Feel his presence in the space between us and in the cawing of the crows in the trees and in the wind that courses over us from the fields. And so it is that when she starts to withdraw I hold her close to me. She looks into my eyes and I into hers and then there is darkness as our lips start to meet and I can feel her breath upon me…

What are you doing?

The landscape begins slowly to reconstitute itself around me. I feel the space between us opening out again with all eviscerated and all bereft. She is looking at me. In her eyes coldness and hurt. Confused anger. I look away. Back down at my father's headstone and at the grass between our feet strewn with the dead flowers she had taken from the vase.

I'm sorry...

Is that why you brought me here?

I shake my head. Not so much in negation as with the realisation that all I had hoped for and all that had occupied me these past days months years was futile. She is still looking at me but I cannot bear to look again into her eyes.

You know I'm with Tom now.

She steps back yet further and starts to gather herself. Bends and takes up her secateurs from beside the headstone. Adjusts her scarf and hat and wipes once more her eyes only now with more purpose. And then she turns to go.

Emily. Wait...

The words have their own echolalia in that dismal air. She reaches the pathway and then stops. Still with her back to me. I hurry to her.

I'm sorry. I didn't mean to. It's just...

There is a deepening silence around us filled with the resonances of what has gone between us with all hushed in that wintered landscape. She turns slowly to me as I step to her on the pathway.

Just what?

I'm about to tell her another lie. That I was simply caught up in the moment. That with my father gone everything has disintegrated. That I wasn't thinking straight. But then it dawns on me that really there is little point. That in lying I will simply perpetuate all that has gone before. That the best we could hope for would be staid conversations on the deckings of riverside pubs or suppers at hers while her boyfriend stares at me with dull contempt.

I never stopped.

Never stopped what?

Loving you.

Some of the fight goes from her eyes and her expression softens. It is only I suppose that she feels sorry for me.

It was always us.

What do you mean?

That's how it's always been in my mind.

But all this…

She gestures at the surroundings.

It was all so long ago.

Not for me.

She shakes her head.

I've got a different life now.

I just…just always thought we were meant to be together.

Maybe once.

I stare down at the ground. Think about those times with her in town. On the beachfront. In her room during study dates.

But it was all so long ago.

# PART III
## DISMEMBERMENT

They give me a sledgehammer and tools in a barrow and send me to the lot at the far end of the development. The lot's a tangle of wiry briar. Glass shards. Paves of rubble. Choked dirt grown through with knots of weed grass. The hammer's gnarled and the handle blistered with dried concrete and the barrow's hull grained with baked mud. The day is young but warm with shadows across the mudslaked road from the rooftops' scaffold spires. The barrow's wheel caroms and clatters against the hull the hammer and reverberates upon the husks of houses lining the roadway. Others are about. On the scaffold. Mulling around gaping doorways. At the windows of the upper floors. Stooped at the entrance of the foreman's cabin below. Somewhere distant a pneumatic drill starts to pitch through the stillness of the morning and then at the road's end I reach the lot where the part formed houses peter out to a gnarled and blistered wilderness. I set down the barrow and kick at the wires of briary scrub gasping through the turned clags of dirt. I walk around the lot and locate the mortar. Locate the hole strewn through with chipped bits of old china and glassy flint and dull splinters of green bottleglass. Locate the remnants of old brickwork amidst the foliage. To mid morning I use an old sickle to hack through the briar and turn the dirt at its root with a hoe and pull up the hacked rootfibres. I'm wearing heavy gloves and my hands sweat and thorns from the briar knots rend welts in my arms. I sweat through my shirt. Sweat through my heavy jeans. Sweat through my boots. The briar I heap in the barrow and wheel to a roadside skip. Drink water from a plastic bottle warmed by the sun. At break I go down to the cabin and sit with the others and drink tea alone from a chipped mug while they play cards at the far table and I am silently picking at the dried mud on my jeans and staring from the window at the desolation beyond. Road sunlain. Road hewn with mud. Road that in and of its purpose will play host to the sad ceremonies of families. To their comings and goings years from now. Their children at play in the paved yards and front lawns of the houses. Their children cycling by. Their children grown old and flown and the faces of their parents at the windows before themselves moving on to retirement. To bungalows in villages and slow death. To homes for the elderly. To hospices with all their lives spent and their only solace the infrequent visitations of their estranged children or the visitations at night of the faces of the people they have known emergent from their growing darknesses. To be shovelled into dirt or burnt and their headstones kept clean a time and ornamented with flowers but these too dwindling until their names are gone and their histories forgotten and meaningless and so too their children and their children and the houses along the road soon crumbling also with the fascias and soffits old and cracked and the gardens grown through with ragwort and bindweed and all around a silent festering as of a slow and relentless passing. I see this in the shiftless sky over the rooftops and in the ribs of scaffold about the houses and in the faces of those at the cards. The one with tattoos on his knuckles. The one with combed black hair and cold blue eyes. The one short and stooped at the shoulder from the hod. From the window I see the foreman's cabin and the foreman at his charts or papers. I watch him as

273

one would a statue for there is in his immobility a deepening lifelessness. There is a woman behind the counter of our cabin looking on. Lunchtimes she serves bread and bacon and with the others exchanges vulgarities. Sometimes as now I find her staring at me and I smile and turn from her and watch the cardplayers. Back at the lot I choose over the hammer the scaffolder's pole they gave me crimped at one end to spear through the mortar lain amidst the husks of mud and the pole gorged with dried mud also and sometimes in striking the mortar or the brickwork sparks will flare in the grey prenoon and later still in the hour to lunch I use the hammer to break the brickwork hefting it aloft and feeling its weight overhead and then letting it fall and watching below the grained brick disintegrate watching the grained brick fucked to dust fucked to a nameless powder fucked from its mortar fucked into the sunblack dirt fucked amidst the shards of old china I root through teacup blue and white and bits of an old saucer white and blue and a plate fragment and the old fucked handles of mugs and amidst all this an old fucked length of fabric and an old plastic doll's arm and I hew upon these the hammer until they too are fucked into the dirt and powdered nameless and I strike down upon the dirt and watch the flat fucked indentations of the hammer and recall long thereafter its dull thud in the gathering noon. I recall too the vagueness of their outlines on the scaffold or in their windows or jiggering at the drill and long and hard I strike down upon the dirt until all those remnants all those flowerings of an old life all those flowerings of yore are dead and pounded to nothing and almost in a frenzy I dig the hole deeper with the shovel digging at its cleft sides and hacked dirt and hammering the tines of the fork into its bowels turning through old roots hacking with the hoe at the sides and sometimes clawing with my hands and pulling free clods of dirt or root or china and I continue to dig for no purpose widening the hole and deepening the hole for no purpose at all for soon it will be filled and turfed and landscaped and the remnants of the old brickwork remnants of the old lives will be buried beneath its surface. How many years will it lie buried? I pull clods from the trough of the hole and hack through root and kick at the sides with the heels of my boots and the mounds at the sides of the hole sometimes slip and these slipfaces are eaten through with worms and there are halfworms from the blade of the hoe in the trough squirming and to these I take the hammer through spite or mercy breaking and pulping them into the dirt and there are lice scrambling at the sides of the hole and these too I crush with a peinhammer from the barrow or let live to be filled with dirt or scoop up with the hoeblade and toss into the scrub or ignore and I sever the leg of a toad and it spasms in the pit and in the dirt are the trails of its blood and gristle before upon it I place a brick and break it with the hammer. At lunch the man with the combed black hair asks me of the lot and I tell him I will soon be finished burying the debris and he nods and the men return to their cards and the smell in the cabin is of fried bacon and upon the cabin tables are heaped rinds and gristle and the smears of dried sauce and beans and the crusts of cheap bread and about these the dried yolk tines of their forks and so too upon the tables smears of mud and grime and debris from the site and mugs of tea and then their cards in the midst and in the midst of these their coins or bills or matchsticks and on the benches their hardhats with the floor scattered about with the mudprints of their bootsoles and the foil wrappers of their bars. Afterwards in the lot with the sun at its zenith I am heaping into the pit the mortar and brickwork and raking it in with my hands and around two I am sitting in the dirt with a newly rent welt upon my arm and the clouds masking the sun are high and vapid and grey and blue with the streaks of the sun's shadows nigh invisible and I would fain it would rain or have the wind abluster or the sun penetrative for in the inclemency of these clouds lie lethargy and soullessness and the quietness of desperation. Wish it would rain unabated weeks hence such that the lot were a mire wherein the olio of brickdust and debris and the cadavers of toads and worms and lice streamed to the cabins below and all was flooded. I rake the soil over the pit and time enough it is as if there were no pit. Time enough no briars or brickwork or mortar. Time enough no blood upon the upturned soil. The blackened blood upon my arm I swab with spittle and in the evening in bathing a great and foetid scum rises to the surface of the water and festers at its edges. I lie amongst this scum and stare up at the spores of mould festering upon the ceiling and at the strands of cobweb caught in a draft from the fucked grille in the wall with its defunct ventflaps black and gristled. At my feet the tap drips and I will plug its limescale orifice with my toe and watch it sluice while water on the tiles here and there cracked or rove with chips slides down. Smell of the damp. Festering in corners. In the grouting. In a thin spackling of spores upon the part closed blind. Rotting the splinters of the wood sill. Festering around the implements upon the bath plinth. Seeming to fester through my submerged body. I stare at the razor. Father's razor. Father's lather and brush stand. Memories of him now beginning to haze between stories told or photographs upon the mantelpiece at my mother's or censored images of him above the commode and the effluent inside. Or of him cold and alabaster in the chapel of rest. At the door the carafe of water and about his cold body the obsolete emblems of idolatry. About his cold body a weighted darkness in the dark velour and the dark light and the dark passages of shadow recessed behind. I rise and in rising see through the condensation upon the mirror my reflection coldly impressionistic. I pull the plug from the bath and listen to the water swill and watch the scum and soap lather gather around the stained plughole as of some vile foamy thickening in a stormdrain and I step from the bath and pull a towel around myself and clear a patch of the mirror with my hand seeing briefly the dark circles beneath my eyes and the rawness of my skin before the condensation once more erodes all. I think perhaps I might be sick. I'm tired and there's a dull pain in my stomach and I'm partway sunburnt around my neck. I see stars before me. I clutch the lip of the basin and allow the feeling to pass. I go to the kitchenette and take a can of beer from the fridge and drink some back and go through to the living space and switch on the television and recline on the bed and watch not the screen but its light upon the walls. The bed's fucked bedsprings creak. In this room too there is damp. Gnawing through the coving in the corners and around the doorjamb. The bedsheets smell of it. The carpet. I drink back some more beer and switch the television to mute and listen instead to the world outside. To the traffic on the streets below and distant birdsong. I start to doze. Wake in the dark with the fucked tap in the bathroom dripping and silence through the flat. The day following is a Friday and the hodteam and bricklayers take cocaine in one of the garages just after breakfast and as I'm going up the road with my barrow and tools I watch them on the ladders and along the jigsaw turrets of their walls. The shapes of them against the colourless sky. Upon arriving at the end of the development I see the lot I cleared yesterday demarcated for formworking with hitched rods and tape and the adjoining lots already skeletal with concrete shuttering. I take from the barrow the scythe and in a new lot scythe briars as of yesterday and with the crimped pole break mortar as of yesterday and at lunch on comedowns the cabin is quiet with the cardplayers at their table and about them plates of bacon rinds and grease and mugs of tea. The woman looks at me and I at her and in the afternoon a light drizzle falls and I use a pick to deepen the hole and the pole some more to break brick and as of yesterday upon finishing the ground is raked over and tilled and the rain is falling now more persistently with the others about on the road trudging to the cabins below shouldering tools and reflected dimly in the rain upon the tarmac. Depths of that night I wake and lie in the dark with the bed's fucked bedsprings creaking beneath me and against the walls the stacks of packing boxes as yet unopened and labelled with marker kitchen or papers or books or miscellany. When dawn finally comes I know not how much or how little I've slept. I watch the breaking light and sleep some more before waking with my alarm and I pull back the sheets and switch on the television and then go to the kitchenette to make coffee before showering and rooting through one of my cases for something to wear sitting there in my towel with the clothes from the case heaped about me and the show on the television an odyssey through floating markets with flowers and produce upon pontoons and a riverside stall upon which a chef in shirtsleeves fries in a wok a handful of okra. I watch these things and I stare through them and then I am pulling on shorts and a polo shirt and taking from the table my keys and wallet and phone and a few loose coins and driving along the guttered stretches of carriageway bottlenecked at lights the knot in my stomach tightens. Pass retail parks upon whose forecourts the roofs of cars glare in the grey sun and drivethru chains along whose funnelled channels cars queue and supermarkets thronged at the entranceways with hordes of wheeled trolleys. Pass into the city's outskirts. Old familiar route. Lane I got lost in when I first came. Rows of eateries. Delicatessens. Those shutterless grocers' stores. Those basketball courts and bus stands and everywhere people. I pull into our street and stop a few houses up from the flat. See her car parked beside it.

See at the window flowers in the windowboxes my mother gave us. See the slatblinds. See foliage around the old tympanum. Stains beneath the gutters. I'm there a while watching the windows and watching pigeons in the mews across the way and watching the slow turning of time along the main street beyond with its buses and cars and people and bikes. And then I pull the key from the ignition and turn it in the palm of my hand. Finally open the door and climb out and wander down to the front door hesitating a moment before ringing the bell. Hear first her footsteps on the stairs. Then the latch. Then the door pulled to. She's wearing a hooded sweater and small cotton shorts and her legs and feet are bare and tanned. I glance down at them and back up at her eyes and she's looking at me and there's an awkward pause before she eventually speaks.

Hey.

Hey.

Her hair is tied up roughly and strands of it are about her brow and then I am following her up the stairs looking at her legs shorts the imprints of her bare feet upon the wood listening to the sound of her hand on the banister squeaking her footfalls my own and at the top I slip off my shoes and she leads me to the living room where my boxes are stacked the last of them and I look down at them not knowing what to do whether to take them straight out or to try and make small talk but not knowing even remotely what there is left to say.

Would you like tea?

Okay.

Unless you have to be somewhere.

No. Nowhere.

She goes over to the worktop. Fills the kettle. Puts it on. Leans back. Looks at me.

Are you going to sit down?

Okay.

I sit on the settee and the flat is very quiet and the cushions sound beneath me and then the kettle begins to whine. I look down at my socks and at the grains in the floorboards and at the outlines of life upon them. I glance up. Her perfect figure. Her long legs. She's playing with a strand of hair. Winding it about her finger. She lights a cigarette. I've not seen her smoke before. She toys with the lighter and flicks ash into the sink as the fug rises about her. She holds the cigarette with her elbow resting in her opposite palm and her thumb pressed against her little finger. The kettle clicks off. She takes teabags from the cupboard and puts them into mugs and fills them and leaves them to draw.

I think that's all of it.

Thanks.

You might want to check around.

She motions to the boxes against the wall.

I divided shared stuff as best I could.

Fine.

I didn't know which of the cups you wanted.

It's okay. I've got some.

I put a few in anyway.

Okay.

And the smaller of the saucepans.

You won't need it?

No. You take it.

Thanks.

She presses the teabags against the sides of the mugs with the back of a spoon and tosses them into the sink. Pours milk into each. Forgets I take sugar.

Was there any mail for me?

She brings over my tea and places it in front of me on a coaster.

It's in one of the boxes. I can't remember which.

Thanks.

Stop keep thanking me.

She draws on her cigarette and exhales smoke. It clouds around her in wisps and vanishes. She flicks ash into the sink. I ask her how work is.

It's fine. It's just work.

Her suit jacket is still hanging from the doorjamb. Notice that the furniture in the flat has been moved around. Table closer in. Old photos taken from the wall and replaced. New cushions. A beanbag. Traces of me gone.

How's yours?

It's okay.

What are you doing now?

Working out on a building site.

She stares at me. I think perhaps she shakes her head but it's difficult to tell. I look at her legs again and she sees me looking and goes into the bedroom and comes back out a while later wearing tracksuit bottoms. She sits at the table and lights another cigarette and plays with the ashtray. That ever I lived here. That ever I was with her. In the bed. On the table. The settee. In the shower. Dreams of an existence. Days in the store when I would watch her. Dream of her. Dream of what would become. I keep glancing at her and the silence grows more oppressive. Eventually to break it

Are you up to much today?

I might go into town.

She taps ash into the ashtray and draws on her cigarette and exhales.

You?

Just sorting this lot out.

I motion towards the boxes but she's not looking at me. She's staring at the wall. At nothing. When she speaks it sounds forced.

How is it? The new place.

It's okay. Small. I don't mind it though.

I drink a mouthful of tea and warm my hands with the mug. She goes somewhere. Comes back. Stands at the window with her cigarette burning on the lip of the ashtray behind her. I hear her sigh. Perhaps she shakes her head again.

Do you want me to go?

There's a long silence. I wonder if she's crying.

Bea?

No. It's fine. Finish your tea.

I continue to watch her. She takes her cigarettes from the pocket of her sweater and flips open the lid. Half pulls out a cigarette. Pushes it back in. Taps the pack against the sill.

When did you start smoking?

She turns and looks at me and her eyes are red and then she turns back to the window.

Putain de merde.

Sorry.

She lets out some kind of laugh. Some kind of sigh. Shakes her head. I drink another mouthful of tea wanting to be anywhere but here yet knowing I will probably never see her again. Remember how when I went to see my father die I went for a walk and ate the lunch she had prepared me for work that day. Hummus and carrot sticks. How entwined she became with my father's death. How inseparable.

Mum found a buyer.

Yeah?

They're just sorting the paperwork.

She reaches up I think to wipe her eyes and then sits back down at the table and plays with the cigarette in the ashtray watching it burn watching the smoke rise drawing on it a final time before stubbing it out.

How do you feel about that?

I don't know. Mixed feelings.

You'll go up there to help?

Yeah. Probably take a couple of weekends.
Where's she moving to?
North east of here.
Have you seen the new place?
Just photographs.
And?
It's pretty nice. A newbuild.
Bea nods pensively.
You'll say hello to her from me?
Sure.

It takes a couple of trips to get the boxes loaded. Bea offers to help but I tell her I'm fine. Afterwards I make a final scan of the flat checking I haven't left anything and I go into the bedroom and the bed is messy with the duvet hanging off one end and the pillows crumpled against the bedstead and her clothes about the mattress and on the floor there's a pair of her knickers and a couple of socks and a bra and there are cups of cold tea and beakers of water on the bedside table and the slatblinds are hanging crookedly over the crowded windowsill upon which an ashtray sits filled with ash and beside it some rolling papers with roaches torn neatly from the packet. She is in the living room smoking another cigarette. I sit on the edge of the bed and take one of the pillows and hold it to me. The same with the shirt lying beside me. Remember being here with her weekend mornings. Remember looking at the moonlight across her back. Remember holding her as she slept. I rise and go back through to her. She is at the table holding her knees to her chest with a cigarette burning. She glances at me and then looks away again. Stares at the wall and picks at a thumbnail.

I think that's everything.

My voice is weak. Strained. I stand there not really knowing what to do. Whether to go over to her. To say something. Or simply to leave. There is much to say that will never be said and perhaps too much said already. A silence ensues.

I guess I'll see you then.

These my words hang in the air and seem to grow. Perhaps it is the hollowness in them for really I know I will never see her again. That this moment is in itself an ending and from it will come another rebirth much invested with sorrow. I feel desperately sad knowing this. Desperately sad looking at her. I think of my father. Think of how she looked after me when all was done. She continues to stare at the wall and pick more insistently at her thumbnail. The ash from her cigarette falls onto her sweater but she pays it no mind. I take my car keys from the worktop and make for the stairs.

I'll let you out.

She picks herself up off the chair and follows me down. I open the door and step out and turn to her. She leans against the doorjamb and despite the ash on her sweater and her shapeless clothing and the redness of her eyes she is yet without flaw. I ask if I might call her in a week or so. She sighs and looks beyond me at the broken day. I wonder whether I should kiss her goodbye but she makes no overtures.

Bye.

Yeah.

I walk down the pathway and hear the door closing behind me. At the gate I glance back saddened deeply by her absence there and as I'm driving away past the flat I look up to the window in the hope that I might see her one final time if only a glimpse but she's not there and in the evening after I've brought my boxes in I go to the off licence on the corner and buy some beer and whiskey and by eleven I'm so drunk I can barely stand. Hungover the following day I open up one of the boxes from the flat and find inside it one of the mugs we bought at the farm shop when we interred my father's ashes and this more than anything fills me with a deep and bitter sadness. I consider calling her up if only to hear her voice again but am quickly disabused of this notion through memories of her coldness. Of how she would barely look at me. Of how she sat upon the chair smoking and staring away. And now this life of mine to come. This suburbia. This rising at dawn to reach the site by eight. To hoe and pick holes and with a pole or hammer hew mortar. To bury it beneath the earth and rake it over. Think of the life past. Life bereft. Think of the way in which of an evening upon the settee she would rest her head against my shoulder and I would place my arm around her. Late into the morning I sit on my bed watching television and drinking tea. Flicking between channels. Afternoon I go for a walk through the town and find a cafe down one of the side streets and sit at its window with a coffee growing cold staring out into the nothingness beyond and another day sees me in one of the houses where the plasterers have been with everywhere a fine powder. I pull on my elasticised gauze mask and start to sweep towards the stairwell. The air is soon as ash settling as a fine layer upon my clothing and skin. There is no sound save broom against floor and nothing to be heard of the world beyond and nothing to be gleaned from its relentlessly sad procession and upon the landing after I have swept all from the bedrooms and sent it cascading down the stairs in a great plume of dust there is little to see save echoes of a life. I go into the nearest room and prop the broom against the wall and slump down on the floor. Hear my breaths amplified through the mask. Wipe at my eyes with the back of my hand. Brush dust from my jeans. The air is still and no breeze cuts through the powdered mist. No fluctuation or movement. No wake to be seen within it.

By the end we are simply living out the echoes of a life.

On the twenty fifth in the bleak afterglow of the churchyard with Emily I speak to Bea on the phone. All this so long ago now. She doesn't pick up at first. Finally relents after a few attempts and then she's frigidly laconic. Asks me if I'm okay. Says my voice sounds off. Says it doesn't even sound like me. I repeat the worn excuse to her about the circumstances. That I felt I needed to be alone with my mother. She listens silently. I am upstairs in the study looking out over the garden. Cloud lingers endlessly without rain. I hear my mother in the kitchen downstairs. Hear her preparing dinner. The clatter of pans and the sometime furnace of the oven upon its opening. She is playing carols and these too drift sadly up. Sad for the memories they bear of the old church. The cardboard rocket from which candied sugarcanes spilled. The procession homeward along the lane. About us a wonderment long since lost. It is just gone noon and I am drinking eggnog. Before this while my mother was at church brandy. Sitting alone with it in the lounge in the corner where my father died. Staring out through the patio windows and across the garden. The tree lights I left off and this brought a great cheerlessness to the room. The fire not lit. The sootblack fireplace in shadow with all about the brick hearth greetings cards and candlesticks and tinsel and affixed to the sides stockings filled with wrapped empty boxes. I kept staring out across the garden unable to move. Kept thinking about that drear scene up by my father's headstone. How Emily and I had parted. How I suspected I would not see her again. Yet this I could not quite bring myself to believe. Eve of that day a lingering sadness penetrated the house and I could not stir myself to try to alleviate in some way my mother's suffering and I took her frequent and melancholy glances at me as empathetic. The mistaken belief that the grief I felt was for my father. As we sat down to dinner she lit candles and poured us both wine and we pulled crackers and both of us put on our hats but this seemed only to amplify the melancholy resonating through the house that night. She asked me whether I was missing Bea. Whether my father. I answered yes to both. It seemed always easier to blame my moods on the latter. My mother had tried to comfort me. Had put her hand on my shoulder. Said she was missing him also. Yet something fixed inside me made such talk and such opening up of wounds for dissemination utterly impossible. Tiresome. Repellent. I had nodded quietly and drunk some wine and smiled. Mimes of a time gone by. Had stared resolutely at the centrepiece as I ate. Sprigs of holly and mistletoe sprayed with fake snow. Upon the table gold and silver stars. But at these especially I could not look for long. Sat up into the night drinking after my mother had gone to bed. Sat in my father's corner with the animal trinket and onyx earrings in my lap sometimes holding them up to the firelight. Sometimes staring at the framed photographs on the mantelpiece. The one of me as a child on the banks along the lanes behind the village. Timelessness of the curtain cloak flapping in the wind as I run. For all of the past and the lives led therein I became filled with an almost depthless antipathy. Antipathy for its innocence. For its walks through the snow. Its family holidays. Its show and tell at school. Its fetes and dos and treasure hunts and the deception of its safety and comfort. For this is what it becomes. This is how everything ends. I got up and went to the window and stared into the darkness. And now I cradle the phone against my ear and look out across the village. She asks me once more if I'm okay. Says I sound distant. Asks me to speak up for she cannot hear me. I ask her in turn how her holiday is going. How it is being home. She starts to tell me and I altogether stop listening. Everything about speaking to her now is difficult to comprehend. Not her voice or her accent or her diction but the very notion of our shared existence. The notion that I will see her again. That we will return to our home together and I will continue to live out a lie with her. I try to remember her face but see only Emily and this too is already beginning to lose its focus. To become distorted by so many other conceptions of her. I begin to wonder whether those study dates with her in her room ever happened. Or the picnic in the meadow or the nights out with her in town or the little girl in the red dress beside me at school. I begin to doubt very strongly whether all the lives I've led to now were real. Whether I could have lived so long away and travelled alone through such vast stretches of land. After I've hung up I'm there a long time in the study listening to the sounds from downstairs and to the heavy silence that has settled around me neither wishing to be here nor with my mother nor anywhere. Wishing rather for oblivion. I look out below at the dank garden and the old rusted oil tank with the paint peeling from its husk. There's a tremor in my hands I can't seem to control. I drink back the remainder of the eggnog and place the glass on the bureau behind me. Bureau from whose drawers papers protrude. Upon whose surface little is visible beneath the mounds of files and envelopes and photographs and old boxes of my father's medication. The protein shakes and pulp bowls and on the planners on the wall notes my mother has made pertaining to hospital visits and funeral arrangements. I wonder why she has kept it all. Kept piled on the floor box after box of files from old places of employment. His and hers. From the days when he worked from home as a recruitment consultant after his informal retirement or redundancy from his job at the bank. Call it a redundancy. Call it a meagre pay off for a life of drudgery in the city. For commuting those interminable distances day after day so that I might live in some comfort. Become something one day. Rise above the mundane. I wonder if in his final hours he saw the folly of it all. Saw me standing over him palely and meekly. Saw the ruin I was to become. I wonder if surrounded by us he died alone. I pick up one of the pulp bowl spittoons and turning it over in my hand I remember how we would stop at the side of the road on those outings while he retched in the bushes and spat out bloody phlegm and wiped his mouth upon a handkerchief with the remnants of spittle on the polo shirt my mother had prepared for his day out. Washed and ironed and chosen as a match for the new chinos she had bought for him. My hands start to shake so much that I can no longer hold onto it. Instead let it fall back down on the desk. I sit on the chair and try to cry but nothing comes. Instead just a dull ache at the back of my throat. I go down to the kitchen. My mother is busy basting the turkey. I know I should ask to help. If only to keep myself occupied. To alleviate some of her pain. Yet the thought of chitchat while I cut parsnips is too much to contemplate. I ask instead if she'd like a drink. She holds up a glass and smiles. Says she's fine. Asks me if I'm okay. I say I'm okay. I go into the garage and take from the box by the doorstep one of the celebration ales she bought for me in the supermarket and this I pour into the earthenware tankard my father bought me on a trip to a brewery in the country some years ago. The celebration ales are from a Christmas selection pack and it is kindnesses such as these that make me feel so sad. So unworthy. That I always seem to be foremost in her thoughts. I'm about to go into the lounge or maybe to my room when my mother speaks.

How was Bea?

Fine.

Is she having a nice Christmas?

Seems to be.

I wonder what they do differently over there.

I don't know.

We'll have to ask.

Do you want me to set the table or anything?

In a bit. Not right now.

She's still playing carols. A recording of a concert someplace. Voices in a cathedral.

Would you like a sausage roll?
No. Thanks.
Or some mince pies?
Not now.
You sure?
Maybe later.
She slides the turkey back into the oven.
I really like her you know.
Who?
Bea.
Hm.
Your dad would have liked her too.
I know.
I'm so pleased you

By the end we are simply living out the echoes of a life.

I listen to the dull shudder of a construction lorry outside.
I can taste the dust even through the mask I'm wearing. I haul
myself up and take a long drink of water. It's coming up to
lunchtime. I decide to finish at least the top floor before then
for by now having remained idle for the past few minutes
a dust has once again settled. I sweep it back towards the
stairwell and send it cascading downwards and then I sweep
it from each step as I descend. I go through to the living
room. Go to the window and look out over what will be the
back garden. Try to imagine how it will be. A paddling pool. A
climbing frame. Flowers. There are streaks across the glass.
Handprints. Upon the windowsill dust and screws and dead
insects. Bits of masking tape. A tin of something like paint
or varnish. Stubs of cigarettes. In the corner of the room an
old stereo with a broken antenna and stains across it. With
my hand I brush dust from the windowsill and watch it fall
to the floor. I start to sweep it all towards the doorway but

quickly lose interest. Head down to the cabin for lunch. Take my usual seat in the corner and bring out from my bag the simple lunch I've prepared.

Do you want a game?

The man with the tattoos across his knuckles is looking at me as he riffles a deck of cards. The others around him glance up at me. One of them nudges up. I go over and sit at the vacant place.

Shithead.

What?

Shithead. Do you know how to play?

No.

They go through the rules with me and we play a dummy hand. Part of me wishes I'd declined. Had remained in my corner eschewing human contact with the serving woman's eyes upon me. Yet another part of me feels gratified by this newfound acceptance. The cards are pristine and entirely free of dirt or fingerprints and I wonder that this could be so amongst so much grime. Presently the woman appears and gives the man with the black combed hair a plate of fried food. Two eggs two sausages beans mushrooms bacon fried tomatoes two slices of toast. The man with the tattooed knuckles wears thick glasses near opaque with dust and dirt. The third man drinks from a mug that has massive cunt written across it in faded black letters. His fingernails are black with dirt. The man with the knuckle tattoos speaks to him.

Did you see that bird again over the weekend?

Yeah.

What was her name?

Carla.

And?

And what?

How was it?

291

A gentleman never tells.

You're not a fucking gentleman though are you?

More than you are.

Give us the details then.

Put it this way.

Yeah? Come on.

They shared a wonderful evening together.

They? What do you mean they?

Her finger and my arsehole.

Laughter.

Wonderful evening. You cunt.

The one with the tattoos turns to me.

What about you then?

What?

Got yourself a bird somewhere?

No. Not at the moment.

Play the field do you?

Not exactly.

Not queer are you?

No. I just broke up with my girlfriend.

Why did you dump her?

She dumped me.

Why was that then?

I guess we just sort of drifted apart.

You're better off without them if you ask me.

Maybe so.

Yeah. More trouble than they're worth.

Afternoon I'm back sweeping out another house and then another and from its upper floor windows I watch the men at work on the scaffolding across the way and when I walk by later on they call out to me and I wave back up at them. Drunk that night I am very close to sending a message to Bea suggesting that perhaps we might see each other in the next week or so and I compose the message and for a long time sit with my finger hovering over the send button but eventually in spite of my drunkenness I see the futility of it all and for not the first time that week I reread many messages from her and from Emily and I pass out on the settee sometime later with fractured images of the two of them coalescing in the gloom.

At the airport after that Christmas separation I'm there at arrivals with a sign I've written ironically on cardboard and the letters askew and I stand by the rails amidst the others with signs or without signs expectant of their loved ones and I watch waves of travellers come disoriented through the gate and scan the crowds at the rails and I watch and wait idly for her little knowing what the next few weeks might bring and now and then I will lean back and check the board and try to determine who has come from where and whether anyone looks as she and I will try to look at the labels taped to their cases and the coffee I hold goes cold and before long my hands are shaking and when she finally comes through I again experience utterly a failure of recognition. See instead this stranger upon the concourse and neither does she at first see me and almost goes by and there is inside me this almost overwhelming desire to let her. To stand by the rails the rest of the day and watch these faceless travellers and I feel too in my heart a kind of revulsion like a sickness born of circumstance and simply being. Being here amidst these spectres. See a child aloft his father's shoulders and think how without worth it seems and when Bea is almost gone by I raise my hand and call out to her and she comes over and there's an awkwardness as I kiss her and then I am taking her bag and leading her from the concourse to the ramp down to the buses and the air is cold and the sky through the walkway roof spat through with drizzles of rain or a dirty restless sleet and going by are other such refugees and her hand in mine feels incongruous and there is something almost repellent in its exploratory purchase as she grips and regrips. As if once again trying to find me. To rediscover our lost nexus. As if all that has gone might have dissipated through a fortnight's separation. All my brooding. All those petty arguments. Night when she's asleep I'm locked in the bathroom staring into the mirror staring at a kind of hollow ruin in my eyes but this is just one night and in the afterdays when the world begins anew from its slumber it is easy to settle into a familiar detachment born of workaday routine born of purposeful lapses in communication on the sofa at night or waking in the morning and passing one another numbed as we set about our preparations for another day. Easy too to continue a time with this fable of a career in film. A future. Christmas trees begin to appear on street corners to rot left at lampposts and splashed about with the nights' piss of night animals and the piss of drunks and pappy half chewed tortillas and smashed prosecco bottles and in one some ribbons of old tinsel still in another a candycane and these days following Christmas are grey and sodden and it seems as if always there is drizzle and in the evenings a mired drizzle upon the panes of the windows and always a bonecold wind. Find work in a company in a film studio out in the suburbs. Long high street flanked by charity shops and bookmakers' and workmen's cafes and dark windowed pubs. Sometimes spend lunch in my car in the underground carpark staring at the walls and the coppered pools of stagnating water on the ground sometimes wander along the high street sometimes a small park but most days in charity shops amongst the motheaten piss smelling clothes of old dead women. Sometimes take lunch to the railway station and stare along the tracks from the bridge at the trains sometimes a bench behind the casino surrounded by pigeons with gnarled legs and mangled plumage. The work itself monotonous. Strategic toilet breaks or elongated routes when sent off on deliveries. Some days when there is little to do tasked with filing or other such menial contrivances. Office formed of three rooms. In the middle room the typists and the adjoining room the manager and his wife and their dog and the other room two script supervisors stooped with dictaphones over the cranks of small handturned projector screens. Typists there some twenty years. Everyone bitching all the time about everyone else. In the studio grounds I will occasionally see an actor or an actress or somebody who used to be famous for something like ice skating or weather forecasting being ferried around in a golfcart with their faces stretched and starched and their chauffeurs fawning over them. Mornings I'll take coffee in the upstairs cafe of the town's supermarket and before long the woman behind the counter starts to recognise me and will prepare my order without my having to ask for it and I will sit at the same table in the corner and the smell will be of fried toast and beans and grilled tomatoes and I will barely be able to hold down my coffee but will instead sit there cradling it between my hands and staring at the people around me. One morning after coffee I watch a teenager in a hatchback pull doughnuts in the icy carpark before finally crashing into a lamppost. One morning get to the roundabout and simply drive on. Stop out in the country and walk along an old overgrown bridleway. Come to a meadow and sit upon a stile and look into the distance with my work shoes barkled with black furrows of mud and moisture from the mist upon my beard and it is with looking out thus that I begin to recall that final conversation with Emily up in the churchyard. How in walking away she had receded into the nothingness and I had looked down at my father's headstone and felt nothing but numbness. Blankness. Had stood there a long time with neither the faculty nor the desire to move. Afterwards during my own trek down the baulk had felt as if weightless. Sedated. Semiconscious. Had wondered whether I might have seen Emily farther along shrouded in the winter haze but she was gone. Had wondered how long I had stood in the churchyard for time in the cold afternoon had seemed to cease. Become moot. That view of the ages stretched out on the scuttled horizon. Chimneysmoke. The cold weathered foliage. The dead trees. The dead and ploughblack slopes. On through the village with the streets empty. No one at the windows. And upon the stile all seems to have happened long ago. Indelibly and eternally. In the evenings talk with Bea of matters trivial and inconsequential. Take turns to make dinner. Never together.

Are you sure you're feeling okay?

Why?

You just seem...

What?

Distant.

I'm okay.

Sure?

Curled on the sofa with a cup of cocoa and her trousersuit hanging from the doorjamb and her slippers on the floor by the coffee table and sometimes those weeks I'll really try will go out to buy her flowers on the weekend or prepare breakfasts sourced from grocers' along the main street take her on trips out to the country into town to the theatre settle I suppose into an easy kind of charade one in which others might seem fooled in which sometimes even I am. That the dogging loneliness is dormant or imagined and that all that has come before has been relegated to a dimly remembered history. A life led by someone other. Our intimacy somewhere close to how it was before. Familiar contours. Patterns. Familiar behaviours. Talk sometimes of the future though in vagaries. Generalities. Always noncommittal. Seeing that future from within a diving bell. See it led by someone other.

See my own future as a blankness. Lacking in any kind of promise. Any substance. Wonder sometimes how long we can go on in this way. Sometimes when she goes out in the evening or if I happen to be home before her I will find little solace in distraction. Will sit on the sofa with the remote in my hand but with the television off. At my laptop on the homescreen wondering why I opened it. Searching vainly for music to suit my mood. No longer any kind of agency. Lie awake of a night. In my mind the notion that my life and all that becomes me is little more than white noise. These problems so trivial. And yet in living these trivialities a sense of utter hopelessness such that all seems vain. A mockery. As little more than treading water. As if the life for which I was destined had already been led.

The first of it after she has had an offer accepted is the loft. I go there straight from work one Friday in my filthy work clothes with the evening warm and over the viaduct the caramelised sun across the marshlands below and fishermen and houseboats along the river and ripened heads of corn rising upon the slopes in the distance. Along the river a cyclist and a heron in flight and by its bank a commuter train. I turn off onto the sliproad and am soon along the lanes with sparrows amongst the grain ears of corn and in the sky swifts and martins. I go by hers. Glance up at the gravel yard and the porch of her house and the sun sliding across the windows. A sense of its being empty and abandoned. But then the village too is as if deserted. The meadow's goalposts are rusted and the crossbeams sagging. The bus shelter whitewashed with mosses grown over its rooftop and ivy along the rotted wood frame of its glassless opening. Potholes along the road. The Bourne dry and the tall evergreens without movement in the balmy air. Momentary disbelief at the sold signboard at the foot of the driveway. I turn up into it and watch the house's facade materialise from beyond the sycamore. See the patio doors open and the roses and wisteria along the trellises and the lawn neatly mown and flowers in the borders. Lick of paint on the garage door. A skip on the yard. Weeded pathway to the front door. My mother out on a garden chair in the sun. I think asleep. Looks older. Greyer. Something irresolute about her. A sort of tired resignation. She doesn't hear the car and neither does she hear when I climb out and close the door. Does not stir until I am almost upon her. Then still half asleep looks up at me.

I didn't hear you.

You okay?

I must've fallen asleep.

Looks like it.

I was just having a cup of tea.

Mug tipped over on the grass by her side. Feet resting on a pouf. I lean down and kiss her on the cheek. She starts to get up.

I'll make you some tea.

It's fine. You stay there.

It's no bother.

Really. I'll do it.

If you're sure.

I'm sure. Would you like another?

Yes okay. There's cake too.

Would you like a slice?

Why not.

I grab my stuff from the car and head inside. Something immediately different within. As if perhaps the process of removal and of becoming unfamiliar is already underway. A newfound sterility. The sense of its having become an impersonal shell. The net curtains over the window are whiter and arranged beneath them in a vase are flowers that look almost too perfect. The surfaces are less cluttered.

The table clothless with a fruit bowl centrepiece. The units polished with their ornaments artfully arranged. The smell of something like bleach. I run my finger along the worktop. The stovetop. All as if never used. As if here there lives no history. The kettle new. I look for the teabags but nothing's in its rightful place. Eventually locate them in an art nouveau tin next to a spaghetti jar I've never seen before. Locate the mugs on a mug tree. The light in the fridge working. The mouldering foodstuffs frozen to the back panel absent. As I fill the kettle I look out across the lawn at my mother. Wonder whether there was ever any point to it all. She's wearing a sunhat and her shadow lies stretched across the grass. The cake is on a plate in the corner. Coffee and walnut. Icing crisscrossed with a fork. Walnut halves patterned across it. Glance down at my work clothes. Crusts of dust and dirt on my shirt. Jeans. Holes in the toes of my socks. Wonder whether we were ever meant for more than this. I cut two slices of cake and put them on plates with a fork each. Fill two mugs from the mug tree and steep the bags and push them against the sides of the mugs and fling them in the plughole and stir in sugar. The same old tired routine of being. Take all out on a tray barefoot. My mother stirs. Sits up. Makes space on the pouf for the tray. I pull up a chair and sit beside her and for a long time we are silent. She takes up her tea and sips at it. I take up my plate and am awhile with the fork in my hand poised to eat.

The garden looks nice.

Doesn't it?

. Very.

I've been busy getting it all ready.

I put the plate back down on the pouf and drink a mouthful of tea shielding my eyes from the lowcast sun. There are butterflies in the borders. Think of times past here. Summer evenings after school was done. Reading weeks. Those evenings when I was first home. Coming out for air as my father lay dying. How he'd just withered away into nothing. His death still redolent everywhere. Can see why my mother chose to leave. Imagine living with that strangulation day after day. Believing that some part of him still remained. For me those memories beginning to recede now. His cold suffering some kind of abhorred imagining.

I've already made a start on things.

Okay.

The main thing's the loft.

Right.

There's a lot of stuff up there.

I know.

I don't need you to do it all this weekend.

Okay.

Maybe just break the back of it.

That's fine. I'll get it done.

It's a bit of a mess up there.

I know.

It's just that I don't really like going up in the loft.

Okay.

That was your dad's thing.

It's fine.

You might have some stuff up there as well.

Okay.

Some old school stuff.

Yes.

Some stuff from your bedroom.

She's looking out across the lawn at the butterflies or suchlike. Not long now until she too will be dead. Leaning in to catch her dying words. Not making any sense out of them. First thing I find in the loft is a binbag of old clothes. My father's. Woollen hats. Gloves. Some old flannel shirts. Corduroys. A burl jumper. His old walking jacket. I pull them out one by one. Recognise the burl either from real life or photos. Difficult to say which. Unimportant. Start to toss it all down through the hatch and watch it disassemble on the landing. Everything beginning to disassemble. Old walking jacket landing crucified on the top. A kind of crippled effigy. The loft dark and dank. Gnarled fists of dead arachnids caught in black catscradle webs upon the hiprafters and fucked black sheathing. Balancing on the beams before unearthing old planks of ply from beneath the stacks of boxes to squat upon. Years of accumulated junk. In one corner shredded newspaper and the black pellet grains of mice shit. My mother below sorting the clothing into piles and beginning to bag it. Watch her a while. Surprised to find her largely emotionless. Guess she's done enough of this by now to be desensitised. She glances up at me.

Is it bad up there?

No. It's okay.

Is there lots of junk?

Yeah. A fair bit.

I'll leave you to it if that's okay.

Yes. Fine.

I need to make a start on dinner.

She heads downstairs and I pull a box from the corner. My name on the side in black marker. The tape near disintegrates as I pull it free. Inside old toys. Plastic figurines. Robot dinosaurs. Building blocks. A fortress. A farmyard. The paper it's all wrapped in curled and yellowed. Some dim but valueless kindling of memory there. I suppose it's all worth something to someone but it's as much as I can do to look at it. I tape it back up using a fresh roll and write charity shop on the side in marker and climb down with it and stand it at the top of the stairs ready to be carted away to town. Pause by the landing window to look out over the village rooftops. View familiar and somehow estranged. See on the street corner the old willow. Remember her words in the meadow with the marquee afire below. Mean so much to me. Friends for such a long time. Good looking. Find somebody. Transmogrified to her desolate stare in that desolate churchyard with the cloudhung sky churning above. Looking out across the village it's difficult to know what day it is. What month. What season. No sound from downstairs of my mother. As if all has come to its end. I look about me at the bagged clothing and the boxes stacked by the chest and am there a long time without spur. Somewhere beneath me my father's quiet tomb. His soulless entity at the window. The encroaching sense of guilt that I could have done more. Could have visited whenever I had the time yet chose not to. Inventing excuses. Given thenceforth to the dawning of regret. Yet even now being amongst these boxes and heirlooms and keepsakes and even knowing that the drear flat to which I will go once this is over is filled with so much sadness and loneliness and bitterness the feeling of being back here with all its bitterly sad memories and the despair in my mother's stare has me willing away the hours until I can leave. I hear her now downstairs in the hallway. Hear the kettle. Hear cupboards being opened and closed. I look back out over the village and see beneath the willow tree a girl of seventeen or so waiting beneath its sunlit osiers. I shift a couple of boxes clear of the stairs and when I look back again she's gone. My mother calls up asking if I'd like tea. At first I don't respond. Unable to summon the energy or the will. She calls up again. I call down okay. And then forcing myself to move I climb back into the loft and it seems in looking into its recesses as if little has been achieved. Boxes are still stacked almost to the rafters in places and barely a patch of the floor is visible. I crouch by one of the slanting crossbeams trying to figure out what to tackle next. Presently I hear the ladder rungs creaking below me and then my mother peers through the hatch.

Gosh.

What?
You've made a big dent in it.
You think?
Yeah. A big dent.
There's still loads of stuff.
We've got time. It's still early.
Hm.
And you've broken the back of it.
Yeah.
Are you feeling okay?
What do you mean?
Going through it all. It's not making you upset?
No. Why would it?
There's a lot of old family stuff here.
So?
Lots of your dad's things.
It's fine.
I can always get someone else to help.
Mum…
If it gets too much for you.
Really. I'm okay.
As long as you're sure.
I'm sure.
Okay. Well. There's tea here for you.
Thanks.

She smiles. Withdraws. The ladder rungs creak and then I hear her at the top of the stairs rustling through the boxes and then she's gone. A flurry of wind moans through the roof eaves. I rise and move to another pile of boxes. Open the top one. Recognise some more of my belongings. Begin to pull them out. Find some old notebooks underneath. A photo album from my year out after school. I start to leaf through it. Colour prints with typewritten captions. Static as I turn the pages. Leaf back to the beginning. To the first shot of me at the airport. Sense of hope. Expectation. Optimism on my face as I head out unbridled into the world. How many forgotten landscapes? How many shorelines in the moonlight? How many stark and arid panoramas? I peel back the plastic sheathing and start to pull the photographs free from the stickyback pages. They curl and tear. The intention what? To keep the photographs and throw away the album to cut down on space? Or to start to dismember? As I pull them out I make a vain attempt to press them flat but they curl back again and before long I am tearing them into pieces. Tearing at these images of a distant youth. See myself torn bodily. Torn limbless. Torn headless. Until all that remains are the typewritten captions. See the shreds of these images in a mound with their backdrops all disconnected. I throw them into a binbag with the album. Throw in the notebooks. Some old exercise books from school. Throw these in without even opening them. Then simply take the box whence they came and upend the rest of the contents into the binbag. Beneath is another such box. This one filled with old school folders. Old projects. I leaf through the first folder and then none more. Simply drop them headlong into the binbag. That first folder art history. Remember the speech day prizes I won before I left. Find photographs from my sorry university graduation. Remember putting on a gown and mortarboard for the ceremony. My mother and father so proud. Father smiling broadly. Mother's hand upon my arm. Sending me off into the wide world. To the wide emptiness of it. I tear up these photographs and drop them into the binbag and now it's filled with such precious cargo I take it down to the outside bins immediately. Out in the daylight my mother is on the lawn weeding the borders. I don't know why. She doesn't see me and I watch her. Then I go back inside.

One Saturday in springtime after that Christmas we go

to my mother's and she takes us out for a walk wanting to show Bea the woodland floor bestrewn with bluebells. And so it is. Sunlight about them. Dappling them through the broken cloud. Bestrewn beneath the trees. Trees in bud or bloom difficult to remember. A stillness unbroken. In the evening at the table a growing separation. Wonder whether Bea sees it also. Unable to meet much her eyes. Mother across from me. Food on platters. Sounds of spoons in platters. Sounds of oven cooling in kitchen. Sounds of their murmured conversation. In my old room lying back on the single bed as Bea stands at the sink in her underwear brushing her teeth pulling the hairband from her hair so that it falls across her shoulders and with her back to me unclips her bra. She tosses it over the chair at the desk and goes to the window and stands there looking out and I see her reflection dimly registered in the glass see the shapes of her breasts and her eyes wondering whether she looks out or in at me at my reflection until finally she turns to me walks over and looks down at me and I back up at her trying to find some kind of shared truth some shared agency and we are like that a while looking back at one another and the light above her softly shades the contours of her midriff and she's wearing only her black briefs and the peaks of her round bare breasts are contoured in the shade and above the bow of her black briefs the skin runs pale and delicate.

Are you getting undressed?

Hm.

Are you or aren't you?

Yeah.

You don't have to.

I will.

What's wrong?

Nothing.

You're quiet.

305

I'm just…

What?

I don't know.

She lies down beside me and I can feel her breaths grazing my skin.

What are you thinking about?

Nothing.

It must be something.

I don't know.

Your dad?

Does it have to be something?

No. I guess not.

She pulls the duvet over us. Pulls off my t shirt. Trousers. Slips her hand down my pants. And thus it continues. In the midst of it staring up at the ceiling and watching it defocus focus defocus. In the aftermath of it lying there in the dark with her beside me and moonlight across the ceiling.

I didn't mean to snap before.

It's okay.

Sorry.

I just wish you'd talk to me.

It's nothing. Really.

It seems like we don't talk much anymore.

I know.

Not like we used to.

I know.

I feel like there's something on your mind.

Maybe.

Something you're not telling me.

I lie there silently and rigidly feeling her fingers upon my chest before they slowly withdraw. She sighs and turns and pulls the duvet around her and perhaps sleeps perhaps not. Untold shadow the next morning at the breakfast table. As before unable much to meet her eye. Don't know why. The conversation strained. Feeling myself on the edge of things. The normalcy of it all. Cups of tea. Pastries. My mother fussing. Then later as we're pulling away down the drive I look at her on the yard in the rearview and there is something unnerving about seeing her like this and I have this sense for a long time afterwards that she had appeared already as dead. A ghost conjoined with the house. With my father's corner there.

How do you feel about the house?

What about it?

About your mum selling it.

Okay I guess.

You don't mind?

I still need time to process it.

And then once more we are silent and we pass by Emily's house and I glance across at it and perhaps I see some suggested forms there of Emily or Emily's parents and on the lawn the marquee of lore.

Later that afternoon nearing dusk I find in the corner wrapped in a damp and festering pillowcase a series of photographs of my father from his younger days. The first is of a small group of judoka with my father front centre. His arms folded. A full head of hair across his brow. At his feet a collection of trophies. I brush dust from its glass casing. An inscription beneath. The date. Some kanji. Everything in its monochrome faded with fossilised flies and mould spores in the corner where the frame has come free. Only dimly knew that he practised judo at university. Wonder at his position front centre. Whether he was captain or was simply able to manoeuvre himself thus. His expression one of confidence bordering on arrogance. My father and not my father. Another of him in the garden of my grandmother's house with a girl not my mother. Late in his teens or early twenties. Remember my mother bringing up his previous girlfriends. How she would name them each with a certain disdain. Realise how little I knew him. Knew only his paternal essence but of his history and his life prior virtually nothing. I guess because a son is all consuming. At the bottom of the pillowcase I retrieve two more photographs. One of my father with his father leaning against a car in a mountainous layby. Another of him with my mother shortly after they first met. Of my paternal grandfather I had oft heard mention. I look for a long time at this forgotten ghost of a man dead many years before I was born. A sense of kinship in how he and my father stand together. A picnic blanket spread upon the small patch of grass behind them. A flask on the bonnet. Alpine backdrop. Imagine their progress through gorges and across mountain passes. Stopping in bistros and cafes and in guesthouses by the sea. In the latter my mother and father on a similar mountain pass. My mother in a floral dress and a wide brim sunhat. My father in flares and a polo shirt. Their arms around each other. Smiling. Wonder at the depths of their feeling that they could be together so long. Through love? Forbearance? The yoke of a son? I remove the picture of my father with his old girlfriend in the garden and replace the rest in the pillowcase. This odd thought that I might bury them beneath the loft's fibreglass insulation for another eternity. Another lifetime. Instead take them down and lay them on my mother's bed. Near to where I found the pillowcase I unearth another series of photographs. Large blowups taken by my father and developed with his darkroom equipment. A series of them in black plastic sheaths. I pull out the first of these. Village scenery. A leafless tree along a snowy lane. A sunset over the Bourne. Stretches of autumnal woodland. These pique little interest. Some sense that I've seen them all or their likeness before. I slide them back into the sheath. Open another. Family portraiture.

Mother wrapped in a bath towel on the stairs of the first house they bought together. Mother in a bikini by a villa's blue pool. Grandmother in a luncheon hat. Grandmother beneath the tree in her garden. These I replace also. I'm about to move on when I decide to open one more sheath and find inside a set of black and white portraits. A girl on a beach in a string leotard crouching amongst the pebbles or with her legs splayed over the lounger on which she reclines and her hand shielding from the sun her brow. Another of a girl on a pathway jumping aloft. Stockings and suspenders showing beneath her miniskirt. Finally a series of shots of a girl with dark hair and dark sultry eyes. The photographs seem to have all been taken in the same room with the girl in various stages of undress. In the first she has her leg over the arm of the chair in which she sits. There's a plant on the table beside her and light shining upon her from an unknown source. In this she's wearing a light cotton dress and her breasts are outlined beneath it. Shoeless. Stockings. An amethyst ring on her finger. The dress slid up towards her thigh. Another is a close up. Those dark eyes. The lobes of the plant shadowed on the wall behind her. The next finds her standing in her underwear by the chair with her arm draped over its backrest and one hand on her hip. The final shot she's in the chair with both legs over the arm and her head over the opposite arm with her hair falling into the darkness there. She's nude. One hand on her knee and the other resting on her midriff. Her nipples are dark against the whiteness of her breasts and so too her black pubic hair against her thighs. Her eyes are closed. A stocking dangles from one of her toes. The other is draped across the backrest of the chair. I turn the photograph in the light wondering who she was. A girlfriend perhaps. Perhaps a model he'd hired for the day. Something about her eyes in the headshot suggests the former. A familiarity in her gaze. Wonder what came to pass with her. Whether my father ever lay with her. Whether there was once a future for them and wherefore it all went awry. That sense again of never really having known him. That there was a history to him I neither know of nor took the time to ask about. All buried now. I replace the photographs in the sheath and consider throwing them away so that my mother won't ever have to see them. Instead decide to take them back with me to keep as artistic mementos of my father's life. Really because of their timelessness. That these women now have their own lives and their own cancers and their own mourning sons or daughters. Or perhaps grew old bitterly regretful of the world. Lonely and lost. Never knowing that something of their image remains indelible in a loft or hanging upon the wall of a flat. Images capturing their youths and their fashions. A certain quality of their youthful bodies in certain lights. I take them down to my car and carefully place them on the back sill.

One night that spring when Bea is out I am on the sofa drunk on whiskey and my phone is beside me and I'm wearing my dressing gown and the tumbler of whiskey is on the arm of the sofa and the whiskey bottle is beside the sofa and there are empty cans of beer along the worktop with one on the floor where it fell. Bea is out someplace with friends as is her wont these past weeks and I don't know whether they are work colleagues or old acquaintances or new. She did not say what time she would be coming back nor where she was going and nor with whom and there had seemed before she left something that she wanted to say but I was in a mood and I watched her get ready and watched her in her underwear holding dresses against herself in the full length mirror and watched her along the landing applying her makeup before the mirror on the dresser and watched her pour herself a vodka and sit with it at the table by the living room window and sip at it and then finally she left.

Had been arguing with her about something during the week. Something I was supposed to have done but didn't or something I did but wasn't supposed to have done. When we rowed and I had looked at her I had experienced this sensation that she had come quite genuinely to hate me and that we no longer knew each other in any real sense but we had made up and had sat on the sofa and talked and as she talked she smoothed her hair and played with its knotted ends and the television was on and the light from it played in her eyes. The light in her eyes was bluish and there was a sadness in them I couldn't abide and we hugged and as we hugged I looked over her shoulder at the wall and there was nothing on the wall to behold no shadow no contour no texture just its blankness and I had considered how attracted I was to her even now and how much she meant to me and why I couldn't find it in myself to simply let go. Perhaps she was crying. After a while we lay back on the sofa and I continued to hold her and the light drew in before finally coming to darkness. I stared up at the ceiling. At its blankness. At its paucity of texture. Contour. Definition. Stared up at the dust about the lampshade and the light cast by an occasional car thinking how alien everything felt. Thinking how sterile. And now I get as far as dialling Emily's number and even let it ring awhile before hanging up. It's late and the call is a long time coming. A long time holding the phone and turning it over and over on the arm of the sofa. Turning it on and off and on and seeing old messages and old threads and pouring myself more whiskey and stalking to the window and back. I let it ring. Hang up. Look at the screen before it cuts black and after at its light etched upon the darkness. Turn it to silent. Turn it over on the arm of the sofa and leave it face down to delay the inevitable. That if I can neither see nor hear it I won't know whether she has called back or not. That she either has or hasn't but for a time it could be that she has.

To say what? I changed my mind. I enjoyed having you make a pass at me over your father's headstone. It was the perfect time and place. Later I turn over the phone and check the screen and it's blank. Wonder whether or not she saw she had a missed call. Consider the possibility she might have deleted me or blocked my number. By now drunk enough that I send her a message.

hi

it's me

i miss you

Nothing more or less. Barely even registers that I've sent it. Pour another whiskey with the nausea rising and my vision beginning to split. The room losing focus. Walking to the window once more then propping myself against the table and then lifting the sash beneath the slatblind and looking out down below. Am there who knows how long looking down. I go to the worktop and drink a glass of water and then another. Go to the bathroom and wash my face in cold water. Consciously avoid looking at my reflection in the mirror. Sense that it will be beyond all palatability. Or that I will see my father. Sit on the edge of the bath staring down at the floor. Floor shifting. Staring down into the darkened stairwell. Think of Bea. Think whether I want to see her again tonight or to go to bed and sleep. Decide on the latter. Think about brushing my teeth. Lose focus. Close my eyes. Sensation of pitching and turning. Listing. Finally succumbing.

The rest as dust. I find my father's old darkroom equipment. The enlarger mounted on a piece of old plyboard with about its stem a gnarled coil of exposed electrical cable and the unit itself dented beyond repair. Find in a box his stained developing trays and frayed changing bag mouldering at the sleeves and flasks of fixer and some old reels of film and film spools and his developing tank and reel. I take these down to my mother now busy in the kitchen.

What do you want done with this?

What is it?

Dad's old darkroom stuff.

Might you use them some day?

No.

You're sure?

Yeah.

Maybe a charity shop?

Or just bin them.

It seems such a waste.

They most likely don't even work anymore.

She's rolling out pastry on the worktop. I ask her what she's making. She tells me a pie for dinner and asks if I want more tea. It's coming up on five so I fetch a beer from the fridge instead and take it up into the loft having deposited the darkroom equipment in the skip on the yard. I sit on an old plyboard plank and survey the raftered gloom. Patches of exposed insulation emerge through gaps in the floorboards. A few piles of clothing and old picture frames and broken bits of old box still litter the hatch's entranceway. In the farthest corner there are more boxes and a nest of tables and some other pieces of furniture dotted around. Chairs and dressers from the looting of my grandparents' houses. A rolled carpet sagging with damp. Something draped in a large soiled bedsheet. I drink back a few mouthfuls of beer and press the bottle against my neck. The residue of fibreglass irritates my skin. I drink back the rest and root around a while. Pick at various boxes. Peel back their taped orifices. Peer inside. Inside old ornaments and antiques. Inside a collection of old ledgers and spiralbound notebooks and another box containing my mother's diaries. The box with the notebooks and ledgers I drag to the light and leaf through some of the pages. My father's script. Pages of pencilled kanji hiragana katakana. Notes from lectures. Old journals from school. Beneath these old school reports from his masters. Tucked in the back of one a photograph of my father when he was maybe six or seven. Dressed in shorts and a school blazer with some of his classmates. At the end of the line a master in a gown. An inscription on the back in pen gives the date and location. I turn this against the light and look closely at each of the faces coming finally to my father's with a deepening silence descending upon this dusty cavity of the house as I continue to stare at the photograph and then at his reports and his journals with the pages brittle and in the folds spores of mould and the notes when written in ink showing through to the underside and when in pencil faded but legible and my father's hand recognisable yet unrefined. His school reports detailing in some subjects an average student and in some a bemoaning of indolence. A lack of grasp on chemical formulae. On the balancing of equations. On trigonometry. In others a celebration of his learning. In the humanities and languages and art. His notebooks immaculately kept. What to do with these records? These memento mori? These traces of a life? What of his photographs and his magazines of slides chronicling the unfolded years? The sense here of an ending. That after my mother has passed on my father will live through me in whatever guise I see fit. Remember in the aftermath of his death feeling as though he were living through me and guiding subconsciously my decisions. Thereafter replaced by this creeping notion that there was nothing left of him. No beyond. I flick through my mother's diaries also. Not reading them but scanning all the different scripts. The changing writing. The sometime illustrations. The doodles. The pages left blank. The diaries themselves are of all shapes and sizes and in no discernible order. And with my father's notebooks and mother's diaries side by side at the hatch of the loft and the landing below fallen to silence and the world beyond seemingly fallen to silence there seems a living connection between the two of them such that they are bound both in life and death.

It's Saturday morning. Didn't hear her come in last night. She's in the living room when I wake.

Who is she?

Who?

You know who.

What are you talking about?

You don't know?

No.

Guess she slept there. Eyes bloodshot. Hair a matted mess. Wearing pyjama bottoms and an oversize cardigan. Her clothes from last night on the table by the window. Piled there. Heels at the head of the stairs. Notice my phone on the arm of the sofa. Suppose left there after I passed out last night. I'm hungover. I put the kettle on. Her eyes on me.

Do you want tea or coffee?

Do I what?

Want tea or coffee.

No I don't want any fucking tea or coffee.

What's going on?

She snatches up the phone from the arm of the sofa and holds it out to me at arm's length. Her hands are shaking. I sit at the table by the window and push her clothes to one side. It's starting to get warm out already. The sky cloudless. Late spring weather. The kettle comes to a boil and clicks off. Then silence. I guess she's waiting for an explanation. I sigh. Massage my temples. Try to figure out what to tell her. Hatch out some lie perhaps. She's an old school friend. Somebody from work.

Who is she?

Bea...

You're what? Missing her?

Truth is I'm sick of it. Sick of mistruths. Of leading this double life. Sick of us tiptoeing around each other. Sick of her moods and mine. Sick of the guilt and the lies and the silences. Sick of knowing it's not right between us.

Are you going to tell me?

Can I make some coffee first?

She doesn't reply. I go over to the worktop. Heap coffee into a mug. A couple of sugars. Pour it black. Watch the scum pool on the surface. Toss the teaspoon into the sink. Sound amplified. Take it to the table. Pigeons in the mews opposite. A rising drone of traffic from outside.

Emily.

Emily?

Emily.

Who is she?

It's only now that I'm able to look at her for everything is become forfeit. She's crosslegged on the sofa hugging her knees and staring at me. Meaningless platitudes run through my head. Cliches. That I'm sorry. That I didn't mean for it to happen. That nothing passed between us. That I was drunk last night and didn't even realise I'd sent the message. That the last thing I want to do is hurt her. That I was...

It's the girl from the photographs. Do you remember that time in France and you were asking me about her? About whether I loved her? Well that's Emily. I knew her from when we were children. We had a pretty intense relationship. Friends from the start really. But as I grew older I began to develop feelings for her. She was so much a part of me. Part of what I became. She was like a part of the landscape of my childhood. It was like she represented more than just a person. More than just a friend. She represented everything. She was of that time and place. A part of it. A summation. Anyway. We eventually went our separate ways and what I

had thought of as fated turned out to be a misguided fantasy.
I don't know. Maybe I was too reticent. That there were these
missed opportunities. Maybe if I'd taken them things might
have turned out differently. But I was just that. Reticent. I
never knew if she felt the same about me or if everything was
born of my imagination. Maybe I misread all the signals. We'd
have these study dates when we were teenagers. I'd spend
hours with her in her room. But maybe they were study dates
and nothing more. I'd invent these little tests for myself. Like
if I managed to throw a piece of paper into the bin from a
distance then fate would be on my side. Silly little things
like that. And the funny thing was the paper always missed.
Maybe even a part of me knew that it would never happen.
And when it didn't and when I found out she'd met somebody
else it completely derailed me. It might seem farfetched to
say it but I'm not sure I ever recovered. You see there was
never anybody else but her. I'd never even look at another
girl. Then when she was out of the picture it was like this
huge hole had opened up in my life. I went to university. Went
away after. But couldn't get what had happened out of my
head. Couldn't form any new relationships. It's only recently
that I think I've finally moved on. I'd not really thought too
much about her these past few years. Just looked curiously
whenever I went by her house. Wondering what became of
her. And then I met you and I was finally able to bury it all.

I take a sip of coffee and stare down at the table.

But then I saw her again. It was just after dad died. I was
coming down the field when she called me from her garden.
She has that house at the end of the village and I'd taken a
walk. She took me through into her kitchen and made me
tea and we chatted about this and that. And afterwards
we started to see each other. I met her in town a few times
and I lied to you whenever I met her. Like I'd tell you that
I was meeting a friend or colleagues from work. But it was

to meet her. We quickly settled back into our old friendship. After a while she invited me round to hers for dinner and it was only then that I discovered she was with somebody. That she'd been with the same guy for years. But by then I think it was already too late for me. I'd regressed so much in that short space of time. All the distance I'd put between us had suddenly been bridged. Effortlessly so. I know it will come as little solace but I would have been so happy with you if I'd never seen her again. But you must understand it was something more than just fancying her. It was like I'd been made whole again and I realised how much a part of me had been missing all these years.

It comes out as a breathless confession. When I'm done there's a long silence. Finally Bea goes out of the room and into the bedroom and quietly closes the door behind her. I shower and dress and take a walk. End up in small park near where I used to live. It's bright out and there are families on the grass and groups of young people seated in clusters drinking and on the street below there's an ice cream van from whose antiquated speakers strained music plays. From the tennis courts comes the periodic sound of scuffed gravel and the whump of tennis balls or net cords. The palace and its parklands are visible and upon the slopes there are a great many people sprawled in the spring sun. I think how deeply I have hurt Bea and of how misguided I have been in my endeavours. I think of my father and for the first time I find it difficult to care. Difficult to care about any of it. Difficult to care about my mother's suffering or Bea's or my own. I look at the grass beneath me and then at the sky and everything seems unreal. Colourless. Without substance. There are practical considerations also. The certainty that I will soon be required to find a place to live. That all will have to be disassembled. Dismembered. I will dismember all. Dismember us. Dismember my ties with her.

With her dismember the substance of my being. Will start to dismember all familial. Will be alone again.

Alone and without recourse.

Her reply moot anyway.

Please stop contacting me.

There's really nothing left to say.

Another weekend dulled with alcohol and my mother asleep upstairs I take a walk up to the churchyard. It's dark out and the sky hung with cloud and a fat drizzle in the balmy July air. I suppose it might be two or three in the morning but I've little sense of time. On the baulk I turn and look out over the village. Drizzle slickens the dark rooftops. The cloudhung sky is indistinguishable from the dark landscape rising from the opposite side of the valley. I continue on and come to the school and go through the rusted gateway and on across the schoolyard chalked with faint games marks and at the hall I pause as of old and look in through the windowed doorway. A heavy curtain is pulled across it but through a gap and with a faintness of light shining in from an opposite window it's possible to make out the climbing ropes hanging down in the gloom. But here too a sense of transition. I suspect some workers are in over the holidays. The walls have been stripped down and the displays are all piled torn on their corkboards and there are tools on a workbench in the corner. I cup my hands over my brow to better see but really there is nothing to see. Only this faint and godless aura as of sudden desertion. I continue on past the kitchens to the corridor of my old classroom and unlike previously the coat hooks are bare and here too there are signs of upheaval. Sawdust across the floor. The electrical sockets pulled yawing from their orifices. Wires hanging down from the ceiling. I walk around the school and end up on the playing fields with the air dank about me and the grass of the fields bristling in its dank thrall. Beads of damp cling to the goalpost's crossbars. Cling to the wire fence. To the boughs of the birches at the field's edge. Over to my left the church spire builds remorselessly and desolately into the foetid sky. A football has been left out and I kick this into the darkness and it skids across the gravel yard and rolls away into the trellised hedgerows where once the pool stood. Time passes on the field. My clothing clings in the drizzle to my skin. Water will sometimes drip from my hair and crawl down my neck. I try to remember myself here. During school afternoons. On fete days. With the kites aloft in the blue sky. But now there is little more than blankness. Little more than a composite that in its melee yields nothing. I try to summon in my mind a picture of Emily. As she was then. Or then. Or then. Yet here too is blankness. I continue on around the rear of the school buildings where they meet the periphery of the churchyard with between them a narrow pathway hung with dripping hazels and saplings of birch and above these rising into the darkness a horse chestnut from whose boughs conkers cluster amidst the knots of leaves. I come to the gate that leads to the churchyard and it groans upon its rusted hinges as I push it to and close it behind me. In the dark the headstones are lined row upon row angular and jagged with those closest to me the newer and some bedecked with flowers or with plastic figurines glistering damp and their plain wood crosses or blanched tablets and tilled soil glistering damp. These I pass and pass too the lichenous headstones closer to the church building upon which as children we would frottage epitaphs with sheets of paper and crayons and glue into exercise books as a kind of testimony I suppose to the long dead. I round the spire and glance up at the water drooling from the gargoyles' mouths and at the flintwork slimy with rain and the weathervane hailing yonder. Come finally to my father's headstone beneath the horse chestnut and as of another age I fill from the spigot a bucket I find at the transept entranceway and the bucket has within it an old sponge and I take this to my father's headstone and wipe down mechanically its face and the face has already been expunged by the rain and by my mother's frequent visitations besides but there is something cathartic in the process that has me continue and in this continuance I read not the inscription but find instead some solace in the touch of its cold grooves and serifs and the flourishes of engraved wisteria. I lose much sense of time. Struggle even to remember the season or what has brought me thus. I see vague impressions in the darkness of Emily and of Bea. Think for a time that the latter is waiting for me back at my mother's. In my bed there with the bedsheets about her. Or perhaps that there never was any Bea. That Emily and I consummated our love that time on the picnic blanket by the woods and then fell into marriage and children and a detached house someplace quiet. That perhaps now hunched over my father's cold headstone all is fictive. That the past never was and never could have been for all was fated differently. Wonder how it could be thus. That I could be living in a flat in some anonymous suburbia and labouring on a building site. That this my homeland will soon become a place foreign and alien with my mother's desertion and all those from the past deserting also or falling ill or dying and populating as ghosts their houses of old and as ghosts staring out of darkened windows as they await their children's return. This notion of a fictiveness grows yet stronger. That all that has come to pass could never have. That in the intermingling of past and present and future and of so skewed a present as this nothing could have come to pass in this manner. That I could find myself alone drunk in the witching hours at the foot of a headstone upon which my father's name glistens damply with the slime of a summer night's ponderous rain. So too in that darkness beneath the dark spread of the horse chestnut's meshed boughs and by the swollen collapsing sky a burgeoning sense as of old of the dawning of my own consciousness. Of becoming self aware such that my movements and my senses and my very thoughts draw inwards and I look out at a world from the depths of an inner void dreamlike and phantasmagorical. See in the procession of images a kind of hysteria. See in the infinite needles of rain or in the numberless leaves above or the clouds of vapour or flints upon the church's edifice or deeper the soil sucked through with worms and slime and the decayed particles of bones an overriding sense of the impossible. That this could not be so. That there is no way I could be here and bear witness in this manner to the infinitely textured landscape before me. And all the time drawing gradually more inward and seeing in the glistening damp of the night my hand stretched before me darkly glistening with damp and aural and the veins distended and disjointed as of some husklike shell of another. I wonder at my father's consciousness beneath me. Wonder at his ashes. Wonder whether there is anything left of him in the ether beyond his own husk or whether burned there is but nothingness. Nothing but nothingness. It seems as if he has never existed and really of his essence I begin to doubt any comprehension then or now. How could it be that I knew him when it is so difficult to conjure in my mind anything of this essence? And of this when my mother has died and when one day childless and alone I will follow there will be nothing left of any of us. A headstone clawed through with lichen and with the names erased through the passage of the years only drawing breath through the sometime crayoned rubbings of a child. Slowly I rise and swill in the bucket the sponge and watch in the dark water the clouds of mulchy grit float from its fibres. For a long time I look down at the headstone. At the beads of wiped water slowly succumbing to the falling rain. And coming back slowly to the world and slowly from inside of myself I see imprinted in the sopping grass at my feet the imprinted footsteps of old. Of Emily beside me and of the pitiful congregation of mourners after my father's funeral or at the ceremony of his ashes the group of us. My mother. Bea. Me. Pushing into the ground the dust of his being. A way off I see the grave of the boy I knew from school and upon its soil clusters of dead shapes all sodden and all dead. I touch once more my father's headstone and then I turn and am gone.

I don't understand.
You're not supposed to.
What's that supposed to mean?
Nothing. Nothing.
You'd take her over me?
What?
This girl? You'd take her instead?
I thought I explained it to you.
But she's just an idea.
A what?
An idea. Or an ideal. She's not real.
Bea...
She isn't.
I don't know what you mean.
You're throwing away what we have.
Bea...
Over an idea you have.
An idea of what?
Of childhood.
What?
Of something you imagine but which isn't there.
What do you mean isn't there?
She tells me that she's here. Here in reality. Tells me in

a low flat whisper that we said we loved each other. That we shared a bed. A flat. That she gave herself to me. Asks me if I remember those days in the store. Those evenings when we'd walk home together after work. The time we first held hands. Became intimate. She talks of Emily. Tells me that it's just a notion in my head. A fantasy from my childhood. That I barely even know Emily anymore. That I'm just misconstruing all these little events from the past. Misremembering them. Inventing a narrative for myself that simply isn't true. Elevating. Suppressing. She asks me can't I see that? Can't I see what I'm doing? Can't I see what I'm prepared to throw away?

Another weekend with the loft done and various other rooms in the house in the final stages of clearance I start on my own room. I poke around in some drawers and throw a few inconsequential things into the binbag I've hung from the doorhandle. I leaf through some old books. Stuff from school and university. I look at the photographs tacked to the walls of the tallboy and in its wardrobe some old clothes. Jackets I wore on walks when I was younger and would track deer through the woods. Jeans worn at the cuffs. Old plaid shirts. In the drawer beneath my bed I find catapults from when I was a boy. The slings all perished. I find old tins of airgun pellets and in a box some rolling papers with squares torn from their sleeves and a pouch of old tobacco wiry with age. At first I'm reluctant to let anything go. Lined along the top of the tallboy are old soda bottles I used to collect on the continent and from a later phase of kleptomania glasses stolen from pubs and then a collection of empty miniatures of origins unknown. All coated in layers of dust. These I bring down almost reverentially and I start to brush the dust from them one by one and clean them over the sink with a sponge. But then I lose impetus and soon enough I am placing them in a binbag with the catapults and the pellets and lugging them downstairs and out onto the yard for the skip. My mother is out in town on some errand and so I have the run of the house. On the return trip I walk through its dismembered spaces and bristle at the silence. I go into the living room which with its guts removed is now little more than a sofa and a television and a nest of tables with the rest stacked in the corner or already carted in boxes to the garage awaiting removal. I stand in my father's corner but feel nothing and then I move on. Back in my room I empty from my drawers and wardrobes my old clothing and I start to sort through it all but before long I decide instead to stuff it into binbags and cart it all out to the skip. I go through old toys and souvenirs from holidays and books from school. These I start to sort also before again losing impetus and simply stuffing into binbags and jettisoning into the skip. When my mother arrives home I have partly dismantled the tallboy and dragged it in pieces outside onto the yard and am systematically breaking it into pieces with various blunt instruments. She goes inside and watches me from the window. I break apart the wardrobe section and this is where my various photographs are still tacked but rather than remove them for posterity I simply hammer through them. It's a cheap unit made of chipboard that breaks easily but I progress to a sledgehammer nonetheless and in going through the desktop I manage to tear through my leg with one of its splinters and I watch as blood trickles across my skin and soaks into the fabric of my socks but rather than attend to it I leave it to scab over and break into pieces the rest of the tallboy. Once done my mother emerges from the kitchen with a cup of tea.

Didn't you want to keep that?

It's in splinters on the floor and in the skip. Fucked.

No.

She places the tea on the lip of the step of the yard and withdraws inside. I lug down a chest of drawers and go about this with the sledgehammer also. From time to time I will glance up and see my mother peering at me from this window or that and in seeing me she will recede back into the shadows. The sun burns the back of my neck but I continue regardless until each of the matching pieces of furniture from my room are all in an indistinguishable jumble in the skip spattered with little droplets of blood from the open wound on my leg. My room becomes a shell. My fish tank sits empty on the floor and for a while I deliberate over what to do with this before taking it out onto the yard and going at it with the hammer. My mother briefly raises an objection to this but it is by then too late. I heave it into the skip and gravel spills from it and ricochets upon the metal surfaces before coming to rest and seeing its shattered hull is perhaps the only moment that day I feel some sense of regret for I remember receiving it one Christmas morning many years ago. Later when I am up on my bed taking a break my mother comes in.

Can we chat for a while?

I get this sinking feeling. She comes and sits beside me on the bed and it's a while before she speaks.

Are you okay?

Yes fine.

About moving and everything.

What of it?

You grew up here.

I moved out a long time ago.

I know. But still.

Really. I'm fine.

She shifts on the bed. I stare down at the floor. At the bits and pieces still scattered across the carpet.

The house is too big for me on my own.

I know.

Your dad and I had talked about moving anyway.

Yes. You mentioned it.

I'm sure you'll like the new house.

It looks nice from the photos.

I hope you'll come and visit me there.

Of course I will. You know I will.

I meet her eye and she smiles and I look away at the pale hot sky beyond the window.

Are you okay?

What do you mean?

With your new place and everything.

Yeah it's fine. I mean it's not much but...

And there's no chance of...

Of what?

Of you and Bea getting back together?

No. Not now.

I liked her a great deal you know.

Things just got complicated. That's all.

Sometimes things like that can be fixed.

This one can't.

I don't want you to end up alone.

It's just for the moment.

With each utterance my mother seems to be carefully framing her words. Before each there's a pause during which she will shift uneasily on the bed. I continue to stare at the sky.

You were alone a long time before you met Bea.

It's just the way things turned out.

Did something happen with her?

No. Nothing.

You seemed so happy together before.

Nothing happened. We just drifted apart.

And work. Is it okay?

It's a building site. How good can it be?

You're not going to work there forever are you?
I let out a short bitter laugh by way of answer.
Not with your education. Your degree.
I'll find something else.
I thought you had your heart set on film.
It wasn't for me.
In what way?
The people.
You didn't like them?
No. They were arseholes.
Not all of them?
You'd be surprised.
I want you to be happy.
Don't worry.
But I do worry.
This work's just temporary. While I find my feet.
I thought as much. I don't mean to pry or anything.
It's fine.
It's just that we haven't talked much recently.
I know.

My mother is so melancholy and sombre and yet there is nothing in me that can make any attempt to comfort her. I wonder at how difficult this move must be for her. A move she was supposed to have made with my father. Not long after she will die also. Will tell me on her bed in the hospital room that she will fight it. That she will not let it take her as it did my father for she cannot bear the thought of my being alone. Cannot bear the thought of my grief. And yet die she will. Die with barely breath to speak. Die with pneumonia filling her lungs. Die in that anonymous room with her cardigan hanging from the hook on the door. I look across at her unable to speak. And thus we fall to silence.

That week after the arrangements have been made

Bea and I barely acknowledge each other as we pass in the hallway or on the stairs or by the bathroom. Notes are left on the fridge. What little efforts we made towards reconciliation are quickly shelved. I am exiled permanently to the sofa where in the night I will lie awake a long time before drifting into an uneasy sleep in the small hours then waking abruptly and wondering where I am and wondering why I'm there. Mornings I will wait until she has showered and left the flat before rising. Work I left the week before. Was sitting one morning in my car in the underground carpark staring out at the fucked walls and the fucked lighting and the spills of oil and the fucked girders and had simply driven home again ignoring my phone the rest of the day. Had not told Bea and she had not asked. Afterwards had gone about our respective business. Mornings I spend gathering boxes and going through belongings and sometimes in the afternoon I will take a walk to the pub or to a cafe or to the park. Evenings she will go out or I will. Should we both be there together we will retire to our separate spaces. She to her room. Me to the sofa. It comes to packing my belongings. First I go through my wardrobe and fill my old travel bag with my clothing. With my underwear I find a pair of Bea's knickers. They are lace and black and meagre and I sit with them on the edge of the bed and ball them up in my hands feeling the texture of them. I feel the texture of the lacy waistband between my thumb and forefinger. I remember dimly slipping them from her those nights. Remember slipping my hand in them as I caressed her. Finally I fold them and place them in her wardrobe in the drawer where she keeps the rest of her underwear and there is amongst it a pair of knickers I've not seen before and it crosses my mind that perhaps she has already found someone. I quickly load my travel bag and the rest of my clothing I stuff unceremoniously into binbags. Packing comes in fits and starts. Were I to put my energies into it I would be done in the space of a couple of hours. But there are aside from these individual storage spaces shared areas. A third wardrobe and an entire closet at the top of the stairs narrow and packed to the ceiling with our belongings. Items we never sorted through after the move. Items we bought together. I try to go through the pans in the kitchen and the mugs and cutlery and crockery but I know not which is mine and which hers and feel besides too miserly divvying up such sundries. And so I leave them be. Take only what is strictly necessary. Two of each of most items. A small milk pan. The oldest of the frying pans. There are our shared books on the bookshelves and I leave these also. The same with films and music. I pull the bed out for there are boxes stored beneath it and in these I rummage and find souvenirs we bought on holidays together or little tokens we have picked up along the way on trips to my mother's in town or in the farm shop where we lunched that afternoon. Little ornaments. Pieces of porcelain. These I leave. Merely prod pensively amongst them and find little comfort in their existence and little comfort in the history we shared for it is become this way through my own volition. Through my own allegiance to the past. I pack into boxes jumbles of papers and the books that I own. These bags and boxes I stack against the wall of the living room ready to be carted away in my car the following weekend. I deliberate for some time over what I should do with my old shoebox. I even get as far as taking it to the bins outside. Get as far as opening one and lowering the box inside. But then I hesitate and with the moment gone I am left standing there bearing it as if some talisman. A curse. I leave a note on the fridge towards the end of the week asking Bea if she wants to have dinner with me but she leaves a reply flatly stating no. She does not. And that weekend she goes away I know not where and it is left to me to depart in silence and with no ceremony. Taking what I can in my car. I suppose I deliberately leave some of my items. Wanting for some masochistic reason to go back there. To see her again. If only for one last time. And so it is. Leaving the city the sky is impregnated with cloud and yet the rain never comes. It looms thick and thunderous and blackly smeared across the rooftops rising into the beyond showing slivers of light and yet just as the rain never comes the same is true of the light for that day the city is a formless grey and so too its people.

That final day of the move there is little to do. My mother has organised removal men and they come in the early morning in a lorry that they manage to back up the drive and while they load it with the boxes we have taped and written upon in marker and stacked in easily accessible locations these past few weekends she and I sit out in the garden on the picnic bench in the sunshine for the day is fine with barely a cloud in the sky. The lawn has been freshly cut and bees go amongst the borders and there is from the hedges the drone of insects. Sunlight falls warmly upon the grass. The picnic bench. Falls dappled through the apple trees.

We watch the removal men come and go with the boxes. Sometimes one or other of them will ask my mother a question about this or that and she will answer in some detail as I stare blankly at them. She makes them tea and gives them slices of a cake she has baked and these they consume around the tailgate of their lorry looking in at the boxes or down at the gravel on the yard while exchanging small talk with one another. After so much work these past few weekends the morning is oddly uneventful. The men are organised and they are done quicker than I had imagined or thought possible. In the forenoon arrangements are made for the journey. My mother gives them keys to the new house so that they can unload all into specified locations while we follow on in the car.

And then they are gone. The lorry disappears down the drive and everything falls silent but for the ambience of the garden. The bees and the insects in the undergrowth and the engine of a microlight somewhere overhead. We pack the last of the belongings into my mother's car. I have driven mine here and will follow her to the new house. She washes the men's plates and mugs in the sink while I take a walk around the house. Ostensibly this is to check for anything we might have missed and to ensure all windows are closed but really it's to have a final look at the place. I go up first to my room. There are patterned indentations in the carpet from the old furniture. On the walls evidence of pictures hung. The light fittings are bare. I go to the window and look out over the garden. Already this seems to be receding in my memory even as I look down upon it. I go next to the empty study and then to my parents' room and finally down to the living room. I stand in my father's corner trying to feel some of his essence even as it fades in my imagination. A gutted shell now with all that gave it meaning stripped away. Eventually my mother calls through from the kitchen. I don't answer her at first and then go to join her. She asks me to close off the stopcock and then we take meter readings together. I think that's it she says. I think we're done. I go out onto the yard while she locks up. I hear her close the door. Hear the key in the lock. And then she is out there with me. I think she might be crying. I embrace her and as I do so she breaks down into fits of sobbing. This moment comes and goes. She draws back and wipes her eyes.

I'm sorry.

It's okay mum.

I didn't mean to get like that.

It's okay.

We look up at the house. Sunlight shines on its facade. On the trellises of roses. Of wisteria. I ask my mother if she's going to be okay to drive. She tells me yes. She'll be okay. I tell her not to wait for me. That I have directions and know how to get there. I see her into her car and she kisses me on the cheek and thanks me for everything and tells me that she'll see me later. I watch her down the drive. After she's gone I stay awhile on the yard trying to think. Trying to feel. But everything becomes blank and meaningless. I take a last look at the house and then climb into my car.

As I'd intended I stop at the edge of the village and walk back the short distance to Emily's house. I'm careful to avoid being seen should anyone be there but it looks empty anyway. I skirt around the hedgerow until I am in the meadow sloping away from her house and I follow it up to the trough and copse. I have in my hand a trowel and finding the rough location where she had rejected me all those years ago I dig a small hole. I take then from my pocket the items I have brought with me. The animal trinket. The black onyx earrings. And then I am a long time standing over the hole willing myself to drop them in.

Driving away my last impression of the village is of her house in the rearview mirror as it slowly recedes into nothingness. Into little more than echoes of a life.

# ACKNOWLEDGEMENTS

My heartfelt thanks to Sean Campbell and the team at époque press, whose faith in a complete unknown has saved this novel from languishing in obscurity.

My thanks, also, to Robert Alderson, who for many years has read and critiqued my work, providing invaluable insights.

Finally to Sophie Lebrun-Grandié, for putting up with me.

London, 2012

Ste Marie la Mer, 2021